'It's good to see you up.' Stefano hooked an arm around Anna's waist, dropped a kiss on the nape of her neck and inhaled her delicious soft floral scent.

Turning his back on her in the early hours of the night had been hard, but necessary. He'd sensed her desire simmering beneath her rigid surface and known that with only a little persuasion on his part she would be his for the taking. But it was too soon. When he seduced her anew he wanted his wife to be a tinderbox of desire for him. He wanted her to beg for his possession. He wanted her helpless to do anything but melt in his arms. He wanted her fully fit and knowing exactly what she was doing.

The more heightened her emotions and her desire for him, the greater the low that would follow when he exacted his revenge.

Michelle Smart's love affair with books started when she was a baby, when she would cuddle them in her cot. A voracious reader of all genres, she found her love of romance established when she stumbled across her first Mills & Boon book at the age of twelve. She's been reading—and writing them—ever since. Michelle lives in Northamptonshire with her husband, and two young Smarties.

Books by Michelle Smart

Mills & Boon Modern Romance

The Perfect Cazorla Wife
The Russian's Ultimatum
The Rings that Bind

Brides for Billionaires

Married for the Greek's Convenience

One Night With Consequences

Claiming His Christmas Consequence

Wedlocked!

Wedded, Bedded, Betrayed

The Kalliakis Crown

Talos Claims His Virgin
Theseus Discovers His Heir
Helios Crowns His Mistress

The Irresistible Sicilians

What a Sicilian Husband Wants
The Sicilian's Unexpected Duty
Taming the Notorious Sicilian

Visit the Author Profile page at millsandboon.co.uk for more titles.

ONCE A MORETTI WIFE

BY
MICHELLE SMART

This is a work of fiction. Names, characters, places, locations and
incidents are purely fictional and bear no relationship to any real
life individuals, living or dead, or to any actual places, business
establishments, locations, events or incidents. Any resemblance is
entirely coincidental.

First Published in Great Britain 2017
By Mills & Boon, an imprint of HarperCollins*Publishers*
1 London Bridge Street, London, SE1 9GF

© 2017 Michelle Smart

ISBN: 978-0-263-92516-6

Our policy is to use papers that are natural, renewable and recyclable
products and made from wood grown in sustainable forests. The logging
and manufacturing processes conform to the legal environmental
regulations of the country of origin.

Printed and bound in Spain
by CPI, Barcelona

ONCE A
MORETTI WIFE

This book is for Jennifer Hayward,
writer extraordinaire and a wonderful friend. xxx

CHAPTER ONE

How much had she *drunk*?

Anna Robson clutched her head, which pounded as if the force of a hundred hammers were battering it.

There was a lump there. She prodded it cautiously and winced. Had she hit her head?

She racked her aching, confused brain, trying hard to remember. She'd gone out for a drink with Melissa, hadn't she? *Hadn't* she?

Yes. She had. She'd gone for a drink with her sister after their Spinning class, as they did every Thursday evening.

She peered at her bedside clock and gave a start—her phone's alarm should have gone off an hour ago. Where had she put it?

Still holding her head, she looked around but saw no sight of it, then forgot all about it as her stomach rebelled. She only just made it to the bathroom in time to vomit.

Done, she sat loose-limbed like a puppet on the floor, desperately trying to remember what she'd drunk. She wasn't a heavy drinker at the best of times and on a work night she would stick to a small glass of white wine. But right then, she felt as if she'd drunk a dozen bottles.

There was no way she could go into the office… But

then she remembered she and Stefano had a meeting with a young tech company he was interested in buying. Stefano had tasked Anna, as he always did, with going through the company's accounts, reports and claims and producing her own summary. He trusted her judgement. If it concurred with his then he would invest in the company. If her judgement differed he would rethink his strategy. Stefano wanted her report first thing so he could digest it before the meeting.

She'd have to email it and beg illness.

But, after staggering cautiously around the flat she shared with Melissa, holding onto the walls for support, she realised she must have left her laptop at the office. She'd have to phone Stefano. He could open it himself. She'd give him the password, although she was ninety-nine per cent certain he'd hacked it at least once already.

All she had to do was find her phone. Walking carefully to the kitchen, she found a pretty handbag on the counter. Next to it was an envelope addressed with her name.

She blinked hard to keep her eyes focused and pulled the letter out. She attempted to read it a couple of times but none of it made any sense. It was from Melissa asking for Anna's forgiveness for her trip to Australia and promising to call when she got there.

Australia? Melissa must be having a joke at her expense, although her sister saying she was going to visit the mother who'd abandoned them a decade ago wasn't the slightest bit funny to Anna's mind. The letter's postscript did explain one thing though—Melissa said she'd gritted the outside step of the front door so Anna wouldn't slip on it again, and asked her to see a doctor if her head hurt where she'd banged it.

Anna put her hand to the lump on the side of her head. She had no recollection whatsoever of slipping. And no recollection of any ice. The early November weather had been mild but now, as she looked through the kitchen window, she saw a thick layer of frost.

Her head hurting too much for her to make sense of anything, she put the letter to one side and had a look in the handbag. The purse she'd used for a decade, threadbare but clinging to life, was in it. It had been the last gift from her father before he'd died. Had she swapped handbags with Melissa? That wouldn't be unusual; Anna and Melissa were always lending each other things. What *was* unusual was that Anna didn't remember. But they must have swapped because in the bottom of the pretty bag also sat Anna's phone. That was another mystery solved.

She pulled it out and saw she had five missed calls. Struggling to focus, she tapped in the pin code to unlock it.

Wrong pin. She tried again. *Wrong pin.*

Sighing, she shoved it back in the bag. It took enough effort to stay on her feet, never mind remembering a code with a head that felt like fog. It was times like this that she cursed their decision to disconnect the landline.

Fine. She'd flag a cab and go to the office, explain that she was dying and then come home again.

Before getting dressed, she took some headache tablets and prayed her tender belly could keep them down.

She always put the next day's clothes on her bedroom chair and now she hugged them to her chest and gingerly sat back on her bed. Where had *this* dress come from? Melissa must have muddled their clothes up again. Not having the energy to hunt for something else, Anna decided to wear it. It was a black long-sleeved, knee-length jersey dress with a nice amount of swish at the hem but it took her an age to get it on, her limbs feeling as if they'd had lead injected into them.

Damn, her *head*.

She didn't have the energy to put on any make-up either, so she made do with running a brush gently through her hair and then she staggered to the front door.

On the rack in the entrance porch was a pair of funky black boots with thick soles she hadn't seen before. Surely Melissa wouldn't mind her borrowing them. That was the best thing about living with her sister; they were the same dress and shoe size.

She locked the front door and treaded carefully down the steps. Finally luck was on her side—a vacant black cab drove up her street within a minute.

She got the driver to drop her off across the road from the futuristic skyscraper near Tower Bridge from where Stefano ran his European operations. As Anna waited at the pedestrian crossing next to the road heaving with traffic, a shiny stretched black Mercedes pulled up outside the front of the building. A doorman opened the back door, and out came Stefano.

The green light flashed and, working on autopilot, she crossed the road, her eyes focused on Stefano rather than where she was walking.

A tall blonde woman got out of the car behind him. Anna didn't recognise her but there was something familiar about her face that made it feel as if nails clawed into Anna's already tender stomach.

A briefcase whacked her in the back and, startled, Anna realised she'd come to a stop in the middle of the road, dozens of other pedestrians jostling around her, some swearing.

Clutching a hand to her stomach to stem the surging rise of nausea, she forced her leaden legs to work and managed to make it to the pavement without being knocked over.

She went through the revolving doors of the building itself, put her bag on the scanner, waited for it to be cleared, then went straight to the bathroom, into the first empty cubicle, and vomited.

Cold perspiration breaking out all over, she knew she was an idiot to have come in. Her hangover—was it a hangover? She'd never felt anything like this—was, if that was possible, getting worse.

Out of the cubicle, after she'd washed her hands and swirled cold water in her mouth, she caught sight of her reflection in the mirror.

She looked awful. Her face was white as a sheet, her dark hair lank around her shoulders...

She did a double take. Had her *hair* grown?

After popping a mint in her mouth, she inched her way around the walls to the elevator. Two men and a woman she vaguely recognised were getting into it, chatting amiably. She slid in with them before the doors closed.

She punched the button for the thirtieth floor and held onto the railing as it began the smooth ride up.

All talk had stopped. She could feel their eyes on her. Did she really look so bad that she'd become a conversation stopper? It was a relief when they got out on the floor below her.

A gaggle of secretaries and administrators worked in the open space in front of the office Anna shared with Stefano. They all turned their heads to stare at her. A couple were open-mouthed.

Did they have to make it so obvious that she looked

this awful? All the same, she managed to get her mouth working enough to smile a greeting. Not one of them responded.

She looked around for Chloe, her newly appointed fresh-faced PA who cowered in terror every time Stefano made an appearance. Poor Chloe would not be happy to know she'd have to take on Anna's duties for the day.

Anna hadn't wanted a PA of her own. *She* was a PA! But Stefano had thrown so many responsibilities her way in the year and a half since he'd poached her from Levon Brothers that when he'd caught her working at nine in the evening, he'd put his foot down and insisted on hiring someone for her.

'Do I get a new job title?' she'd cheekily asked, and been rewarded with a promotion to Executive PA and a hefty pay rise.

Maybe Chloe was cowering in the stationery cupboard, waiting for her arrival so she could hide behind her. The girl would get used to Stefano soon enough. Anna had seen it with most other employees. It was that mixture of awe and fear he inspired that curdled the stomach, but eventually the curdling settled and one could hold a coherent conversation with him.

Anna had skipped all these stages herself but had seen the effect Stefano had on others too many times not to sympathise with it. He inspired terror and hero-worship in equal measure.

She let the office door shut behind her and came to an abrupt halt. For a moment she forgot all about her pounding head and nauseous stomach.

When Stefano had offered her the job and she'd learned it entailed sharing an office with him, she'd said on a whim that she would only do it if he decorated her side in shades of plum. Her memories of her first day working for him were ones of laughter, when she'd walked into the sprawling office and found one half painted a functional cream, the other varying shades of plum.

Today the whole office was cream.

She'd just reached her desk when the door flew open, and Stefano stood there, as dark and menacing as she'd ever seen him.

Before she could ask if he'd had an army of decorators in overnight, he slammed the door shut and folded his arms across his broad chest.

'What are you doing here?'

'Not you too,' she groaned, half in exasperation and half in pain. 'I think I had a fall. I know I look awful but can't you pretend I look like my usual supermodel self?'

It had become one of those long-running jokes between them. Every time Stefano tried to cajole her into coming on a date with him, Anna would make some cutting remark, usually followed by a reminder that his preferred dates were the gorgeous supermodel type, whereas she barely topped five foot.

'You'll get neck-ache if you try to kiss me,' she'd once flippantly told him.

To which he'd immediately replied, *'Shall we find out now?'*

She'd never dared mention kissing to him again. Imagining it was more than enough, and wasn't something she allowed herself to do, not since the one time she'd succumbed to the daydream and then had spent a good week pretending not to have palpitations whenever she got close to him.

There was no denying it, her boss was utterly gorgeous, even when her eyes were struggling to focus as they were now. There was not a single physical aspect of him that didn't make her want to swoon. Well over a foot taller than her, he had hair so dark it looked black, a strong roman nose, generous lips and a chiselled jaw covered in just the right amount of black stubble. He also had eyes capable of arresting a person with one glance; a green colour that could turn from light to dark in a heartbeat. She'd learned to read his eyes well—they corresponded exactly with his mood. Today, they were as dark as they could be.

She wasn't in the right frame of mind to dissect what that meant. The paracetamol she'd taken hadn't made a dent in her headache, which was continuing to get worse by the second. She grabbed the edge of her desk and sat down. Straight away she saw something else that was wrong, even with her double vision. She strained to peer more closely at the clutter on her desk. She never left clutter. It drove her crazy. Everything needed to be in its correct place. And…

'Why are there photos of *cats* on my desk?' She was a dog person, not a cat person. Dogs were loyal. Dogs didn't leave you.

'*Chloe's* desk,' he said in a voice as hard as steel.

Anna tilted her head to look at him and blinked a number of times to focus. Her vision had blurred terribly. 'Don't tease me,' she begged. 'I'm only twenty minutes late. My head feels…'

'I can't believe you would be so brazen to turn up here like this,' he cut in.

Used to Stefano's own brand of English, she assumed his 'brazen' meant 'stupid' or something along those lines. She had to admit, he had a point. Leaving the flat feeling as rotten as she did really did rank as stupid.

'I know I'm not well.' It was an effort to get the words out. 'I feel like death warmed up, but I left my laptop behind and needed to get that report to you. You'll have to get Chloe to sit in on the meeting.'

His jaw clenched and his lips twisted into something that could be either a snarl or a smirk. 'Is this a new tactic?'

Was her hearing now playing up along with the rest of her? One of the things she liked about working for Stefano was that he was a straight talker, regularly taking his more earnest employees to task for their corporate speak. 'I taught myself English,' he would say to them with disdain, 'but if I'd tried learning it from you I would be speaking self-indulgent codswallop.'

She always hid a grin when he said that. 'Self-indulgent codswallop' was a term she'd taught him in her first week working for him. His thick Italian accent made it sound even funnier. She'd taught him a whole heap of insults since; most of which she'd initially directed at him.

Which made his riddle all the more confusing.

'What are you talking about?'

He stepped away from the closed door, nearer to her. 'Have you been taking acting lessons, Mrs Moretti?'

'Mrs...?' She closed her eyes and gave her head a gentle shake, but even that made the hammers trapped in it pound harder. 'Have I woken in the twilight zone?' It didn't sound completely mad when she said it. Quite credible in fact. She'd felt disjointed from the moment she'd woken, Melissa's letter stating that she was flying to Australia only adding to the incoherence.

When she opened her eyes again, she found Stefano by her desk, his large frame swimming before her eyes.

'You're playing an excellent game. Tell me the rules so I know what my next move should be.' His tone was gentle but the menace behind it was unmistakable, his smooth voice decreasing in volume but increasing in danger.

Anna's pretty hazel eyes widened. She had clearly been practising her innocent face in the month since he'd last seen her, Stefano thought scathingly.

It had been a whole month since she'd humiliated him in his own boardroom and walked out of his life.

He placed his hands palm down on her desk and gazed at her, taking in the beautiful face that had captivated him from the start.

'I honestly don't know what you're talking about.' Anna got slowly to her feet. 'I'm going home. One of us is confused about something and I don't know which of us I hope it is.'

He laughed. Oh, she was something else.

'You should go home too,' she said, eying him in much the same manner as a person cornered by a dangerous dog. 'If I didn't know better I'd think you were drunk.'

For a moment he wondered if *she'd* been drinking. Her words had a slurred edge and she seemed unsteady.

But those luscious lips were taunting him. *She* was taunting him, playing a game he hadn't been given the rules to, trying to catch him on the back foot. Well, he wouldn't fall for her games any more. He wrote the rules, not this witch who had spellbound him with lust.

She'd planned it all from the start. She'd deliberately held off his advances for eighteen months so he'd become so desperate to possess her he would agree to marry her just so he could sleep with her.

He'd admit it had been a bit more involved than

that but that had been the crux of it. He'd thought he'd known her. He'd thought he could trust her—*him*, Stefano Moretti, the man who had learned at a young age not to trust anyone.

She'd set him up to marry her so she could divorce him for adultery, humiliating him in front of his staff for good measure, and gain herself a hefty slice of his fortune.

He couldn't believe he'd been stupid enough to fall for it.

When he'd received the call from his lawyer telling him his estranged wife was going to sue him for a fortune, he'd quelled his instinct to race to her home and confront her. He'd forced himself to sit tight.

Sitting tight did not come easily to him. He was not a man to wait for a problem to be solved; he was a man to take a problem by the scruff of the neck and sort it. He reacted. He always had. It was what had got him into so much trouble when he'd been a kid, never knowing when to keep his mouth shut or his fists to himself.

He'd spent nearly two weeks biding his time, refusing to acknowledge her lawyer's letter. In ten days they would have been married for a year and legally able to divorce. Then, and only then, would Anna learn what he was prepared to give her, which was nothing. And he was prepared to make her jump through hoops to reach that knowledge.

He would make her pay for all her lies and deceit. He would only stop when she experienced the equivalent humiliation that he'd been through at her hands.

One hundred million pounds and various assets for barely a year of marriage? Her nerve was beyond incredible.

But despite everything she'd done, seeing her now, his

desire for her remained undiminished. Anna was still the sexiest woman in the world. Classically beautiful, she had shoulder-length silky dark chestnut hair that framed high cheekbones, bee-stung lips that could sting of their own accord and skin as creamy to the touch as to the eye. She should be as narcissistic as an old-fashioned film star but she was disdainful of her looks. That wasn't to say she didn't make an effort with her appearance—she loved clothes, for example—but rarely did anything to enhance what she'd already been blessed with.

Anna Moretti née Robson, the woman with the face and body of a goddess and the tongue of a viper. Clever and conniving, sweet and lovable; an enigma wrapped in a layer of mystery.

He despised her.

He missed having her in his bed.

Since his release from prison all those long years ago he'd become an expert at masking the worst of his temper and channelling it into other areas, but Anna could tap into him like no one else and make him want to punch walls while also making him ache with need to touch her.

She wasn't a meek woman. He'd understood that at their very first meeting. All the same, he'd never have believed she would have the audacity to walk back into this building after the stunt she'd pulled.

'I'm not drunk.' He leaned closer and inhaled. There it was, that scent that had lingered on his bed sheets even after copious washes, enough so that he'd thrown out all his linen and bought new sets. 'But if you're having memory problems, I know something that will help refresh it.'

Alarm flashed in her widened eyes. He didn't give her the chance to reply, sliding an arm around her waist and pulling her to him so he could crush her mouth with his own.

He felt her go rigid with shock and smiled as he moulded his lips to hers. If Anna wanted to play games she had to understand that *he* was the rule maker, not her. He could make them and break them, just as he intended to eventually break her.

The feel of her lips against his, her breasts pressed against his chest, her scent... Heat coiled in his veins, punishment turning into desire as quickly as the flick of a switch...

All at once, she jerked her face to the side, breaking the kiss, and at the same moment her open hand smacked him across the cheek.

'What do you think you're doing?' She wiped her mouth with the back of her hand, her tone half shocked, half furious. 'You're...' Her voice tailed off.

'I'm what?' he drawled, fighting to control his own tone. The potency of the chemistry between them had become diluted in his memories. He'd forgotten how a single kiss could drive him as wild as an inexperienced teenager.

She blinked and when she looked at him again the fury had gone. Fear now resonated from her gaze. The little colour she'd had in her cheeks had gone too. 'Stef...'

She swayed, her fingers extending as if reaching for him.

'Anna?'

Then, right before his eyes, she crumpled. He only just caught her before she fell onto the floor.

CHAPTER TWO

WHEN ANNA AWOKE in the sterile hospital room, her head felt clearer than it had all day. The heavy pounding had abated but now came something far worse. Fear.

She didn't need to open her eyes to know she was alone.

Had Stefano finally left?

The memory of their kiss flashed into her mind. In a day that had passed as surreally as if she'd been underwater, his kiss was the only memory with any real substance.

He'd *kissed* her. It had been almost brutal. A taunt. A mockery. The blood thumping through her at the feel of it had been the final straw for her poor, depleted body. She'd collapsed. And he'd caught her.

He seemed to think they were married. The hospital staff were under the same impression.

Swallowing back the panic clawing at her throat, Anna forced herself to think.

Her memory of the day might be blurry but she remembered snapshots of it. Stefano had carried her to his office sofa while shouting for someone to call for an ambulance. He'd travelled to the hospital with her. He'd been with her through all the prodding, probing and question-

MICHELLE SMART

21

ing she'd endured when she'd been awake and coherent enough to answer. He'd even come to the scan with her. If it weren't for the dark tension radiating from him she would have been grateful for his presence, especially since Melissa hadn't shown up.

Where on earth was she? It wasn't possible that she could be on a flight to Australia. She wouldn't have done that without telling her. No way. Besides, they lived together. Anna would have known!

Just what the hell was going on?

Never mind all the so-called marriage nonsense, which had to be some kind of elaborate hoax, but since when had Stefano hated her? They'd always sniped at each other and communicated through sarcasm but it had always been playful, with no sting intended. Today, despite his seemingly genuine concern for her health, it had been like having a Rottweiler guarding her with its teeth bared in her direction.

The door opened and the consultant from earlier stepped into the room, clipboard in hand. She was followed closely by Stefano.

Anna's heart rate accelerated and she eyed them warily. They had the look of a pair of conspirators. Had they been talking about her privately?

'What's wrong with me?' she asked.

The consultant perched herself on the edge of Anna's bed and smiled reassuringly. 'You have a concussion from your fall last night.'

'I don't remember the fall,' Anna said. 'My sister wrote it in a letter…have you got in touch with her yet?'

'Her flight hasn't landed.'

'She can't be on a flight.'

'She is,' Stefano chipped in. He was seated on the

visitor's chair just a foot from her bed, his stance that of a man who had every right to be there. Even if she were to ask for his removal, no one would dare touch him.

His break away from her bedside seemed to have done him good though as he'd lost the Rottweiler look he'd been carrying all day. He looked more…not relaxed, not happy exactly, but…pleased with himself.

'Melissa's taken a month's leave to go to Australia and celebrate your mother's fiftieth birthday,' he finished.

'That's not possible.' The stab of betrayal pierced her hard. 'She couldn't have done that. I'd know.'

'The chances are you *did* know,' the consultant said. 'Your scan has come back clear…'

'What does that mean?'

'That there's no bleeding on the brain or anything we need worry about in that regard, but all the evidence is pointing to you having retrograde amnesia.'

'Amnesia?' Anna clarified. 'So I'm not going mad?'

The consultant's smile was more like a grimace. 'No. But it appears you have lost approximately a year of your memories.'

Anna exhaled in relief. Amnesia she could cope with. There had been moments during the day when she'd thought for certain she was losing her mind. And then she remembered Stefano's insistence that they were married…

'Don't tell me I'm actually married to him?'

Now the consultant looked uncomfortable. 'You're on our records as Anna Louise Moretti.'

There was silence as the meaning of this sank into Anna's fragile head.

She didn't know what was worse. Being told Melissa

had gone to Australia to see their mother or being told she was married to Stefano. Discovering that there was life on Jupiter would be easier to comprehend.

She turned her head to look at the man who claimed to be her husband. His long legs were stretched out before him, his tie removed and top button undone. He was studying her with an intensity that sent little warning tingles through her veins. It was the look he always gave when he was thinking hard, usually when he was debating to himself whether he wanted to risk his money and reputation on a particular venture.

When Stefano chose to back a business he didn't hold back. He gave it everything. He thrived on the gamble but liked the odds to be in his favour. He liked to be certain that he wasn't going to be throwing away his time, resources and money. It didn't matter how many reports she produced, he would play it all out in his mind, working through it on his own mental spreadsheet.

And now that gaze was directed at her, as if she were a business venture that needed to be analysed. He was mentally dissecting *something* and that something had to do with her.

'We're really married?' she asked him.

A slow smile spread across his face as if she'd said something amusing but the focus in his eyes sharpened. '*Sì.*'

None of this made sense. 'Why would I have married you?'

He shifted his chair forward and leaned over to speak directly into her ear. His warm breath stirred the strands of her hair, making her pulses stir with them. 'Because you wanted my body.'

His nearness meant she had to concentrate hard

to form a response. 'This is no time for your jokes. I wouldn't marry you. I have self-respect.'

He sat back and spread out his hands. 'No joke. We're married.'

'I don't believe you.' The very idea was preposterous.

'I can give you proof.'

'We can't be.'

There was no way she would have married Stefano. He was gorgeous, funny when he wasn't being brooding and impatient, and rich, but he also had a revolving door of girlfriends. She had always maintained that she wouldn't touch him with a ten-foot bargepole and had told him so on numerous occasions.

Always he'd responded with a dazzling grin and, 'You can't resist me for ever, *bambolina*.'

To which she'd always replied with her own grin turned up to full wattage, 'Watch me.'

This time there was no comeback. He pulled out his phone and started tapping away. After a few moments he leaned over to show her the screen. Her pulse made another strange leap at his closeness and the familiar scent of his tangy cologne that had always filled their workspace. She blinked and focused her attention on what he was showing her.

It was a photograph of them standing together on a beach. Stefano was dressed in charcoal trousers and a short-sleeved open-necked white shirt. She wore a long white chiffon dress that had a distinct bridal look to it, and was clutching a posy of flowers. Oh, and they were kissing.

Anna stared at the screen for so long her eyes went dry. Her heart was pounding so hard its beats vibrated through her. When she dared look at him she found him watching her closely.

'Did you drug me?' She could hardly believe the evidence before her. It wasn't possible. It had to be fake.

'We married on the twentieth of November. Our first anniversary is in ten days.'

'That's impossible.' She did some mental maths. She remembered as far back as her Spinning class, which had been the day after bonfire night, November the fifth.

He expected her to believe she'd married him two weeks later? Did he take her for a complete idiot?

But then she looked again at the photo on his screen.

'We married in Santa Cruz,' he supplied. 'It was a very...I can't think of the word, but it was quick.'

'Spontaneous?'

'That's the word, *sì*.'

Despite the mounting evidence she still couldn't bring herself to believe him.

'If we're married, why did I wake up in my own bed in mine and Melissa's flat?'

There was only the barest flicker of his pupils. 'We'd had a row.'

'About what?'

'Nothing important. You often stay the night there.'

'Why were you so angry to see me in the office this morning? And why has Chloe taken my desk?'

'I told you, we'd had an argument.'

'Cheating on me already?' she asked, only half jesting.

There was a tiny clenching of his jaw before his handsome features relaxed into the smile that had always melted her stomach. 'I've never cheated on a woman in my life.'

'You've never stayed with a woman long enough *to* cheat.' Stefano had the attention span of a goldfish. He thrived on the chase, growing bored quickly and moving straight onto the next woman to catch his eye.

'We've been married for almost a year and I've never been unfaithful,' he stated steadily.

'Then what were we arguing about?'

'It was nothing. Teething problems like all newly-weds deal with. You weren't supposed to be in this week so Chloe's been working at your desk.'

The image of the blonde woman following him out of his car popped back into her mind. She had no memories of that woman but the way she'd reacted to her, the way her already tender stomach had twisted and coiled, made her think she *had* met her. 'Who was that woman in your car this morning?'

Before he could answer, the consultant coughed unsubtly. Anna had almost forgotten she was there.

'Anna, I appreciate this is hard for you. There are a lot of gaps in your memory to fill.'

She sucked in her lips and nodded. A whole year of memories needed to be filled. A *whole year* that she'd lost; a big black void during which she had married her boss and Lord knew what else had occurred. 'Will I get my memories back?'

'Brain injuries are complex. There are methods that will help retrieve the memories, things we call "joggers", which are aids to help with recall, but there are no guarantees. The country's top specialist in retrograde amnesia will be here in the morning to see you—he'll be able to give you more information.'

Anna closed her eyes. 'How long do I have to stay here for?'

'We want to keep you under observation for the night. Providing there's no further issues, there's no reason you can't be discharged tomorrow after you've seen the specialist.'

'And then I can go home?'

But where *was* her home? Was it the flat she'd shared with her big sister since she was fourteen? Or with Stefano?

The nausea that had eased with the help of medication rolled back into life.

She couldn't have married him. Not Stefano of all people.

'You'll need to take it easy for a few weeks to recover from the concussion but your husband's already assured me he'll be on hand to take care of you.'

'So Stefano knows all this? You've already discussed it with him?'

'I'm your next of kin,' he said, his thick accent pronouncing 'kin' as 'keen', something that under ordinary circumstances would make her laugh. Right then, Anna felt she would never find anything funny again.

'No, you're not. Melissa is.' Melissa had been her next of kin since her sister had agreed to take sole guardianship of her when she'd been only eighteen and Anna fourteen.

The uncomfortable look came back to the consultant's face. 'Anna, I understand this is difficult for you but I can't discharge you unless you have somewhere to go where you will be looked after, for the next few days at least. Your husband is your next of kin but you don't have to go with him. Is there anyone else we can call for you?'

Anna thought hard but it was hopeless and only made her head start hurting again. The only person she was close to was Melissa. They both had friends—lots of them—but it was only each other that they trusted. Their friends were kept on the fringes of their lives and there wasn't a single one she could impose herself on for however long it took to be deemed safe to care for herself.

But Melissa was on an aeroplane flying to the other side of the world to visit the woman who'd abandoned them for a new life in Australia with a man she barely knew.

The betrayal sliced through her again, tears burning in her eyes.

'Anna, your home is with me.'

She closed her eyes in an attempt to drown out Stefano's hypnotic voice. She wished she could fall into the deepest sleep in the world and wake to find the normal order of things restored.

The sad truth was there was no one else who could take her in or, if there was, she couldn't remember them.

Whatever was wrong with her head though, wishing for something different wouldn't change a thing. Her world might be all topsy-turvy but this was her reality now and she needed to deal with it. Bawling her eyes out and burying her head in the sand wouldn't change anything.

She looked directly at him. 'I don't remember it being our home. I don't remember a thing about us other than that you're my boss and the bane of my life, not my husband.'

Was it her imagination or was that satisfaction she saw glimmer in his eyes?

'I will help you retrieve the memories. I don't deny our marriage can be…what's the word? Like many storms?'

'Tempestuous?' she supplied, fighting the urge to smile.

'That's it. We are very tempestuous but we're happy together.' He straightened his long frame and rolled his shoulders before flashing his irresistible smile. 'I need to get back to work and get things arranged so I can care for you like a good husband should. I'll be back in the morning for when the specialist gets here.'

He handed a business card to the consultant. 'If you have any concerns, call me.' Then he leaned over and placed the briefest of kisses on Anna's lips. 'Try not to worry, *bellissima*. You're the most stubborn woman I know—your memories won't dare do anything but come back to you. Everything will feel better once you're home.'

The endearment, *bellissima*, sounded strange to her ears. The most endearing term Stefano had ever used towards her before had been *bambolina*, Italian for little doll, which he'd thought hilarious. He'd often said he would mistake her for a princess doll were it not for her blunt tongue.

Anna watched him stroll from the hospital room, the good, faithful husband leaving to sort out his affairs so he could dedicate his next few weeks to caring for his poor, incapacitated wife, and all she could think was that she didn't trust him at all.

Until her memories came back or until she spoke to Melissa, whichever came first, she would have to be on her guard. She didn't trust Stefano any further than she could see him.

Stefano strode through the hospital entrance with a spring in his step. It was at times like this, when he had something to celebrate, that he wished he still smoked. But smoking was a habit he'd kicked a decade ago.

He was going to bring his wife home. The woman who'd used, humiliated, left him and tried to blackmail him was going to be back under his roof. He had big plans for her.

Those plans would have to wait a few days while she recovered from the worst of her concussion but in the meantime he fully intended to enjoy her confinement. Anna hated being fussed over. She was incapable of switching off, always needing to be doing something. Having to rest for a minimum of a fortnight would be her worst nightmare.

It cheered him further to know he would be there to witness her live through this horror.

Stefano intended to keep his word and ensure she was well-looked-after while back under his roof. He might despise her all the way to her rotten core but he would never let her suffer physically. He could still taste the fear he'd experienced when she'd dropped in a faint at his feet and knew he never wanted to go through anything like that again. It amazed him that she'd been able to get into his offices without collapsing, something the consultant had been surprised by too. If he hadn't been so angry at her unexpected appearance and unprepared for seeing her for the first time in a month, he would have paid more attention to the fact she'd looked like death warmed up.

Fate had decided to work for him.

Anna didn't remember anything that had happened between them. The whole of the past year had gone, wiped clean away. He could tell her anything and with her confined to his sole care and her sister on the other side of the world, there was no one to disprove it. Judging from the way she'd blanched when she'd learned Melissa had gone to Australia, she would be too angry to make contact with her any time soon.

All he had to remember was to keep his bitterness that she'd fooled him into marrying her inside. Anna could read him too well.

He'd called Melissa as soon as they'd arrived at the hospital, knowing Anna would want her sister there. He'd been put through to her boss and told that Melissa was on leave and had been planning her trip for months. Considering Anna had never mentioned it—and she surely would have done—he guessed Melissa had put off telling her for as long as she could. Certainly, when the two sisters had gone away for their trip to Paris, which *he* had paid for as a treat for his wife and which Anna had returned from early, determined to catch him up to no good, she hadn't known anything about it.

He found Anna alone in her private room flicking through a magazine, dressed in the same black jersey dress from the day before. She greeted him with a wary smile.

'How are you feeling?' he asked.

'Better.'

He sat down in the visitor's chair. 'You look better.' Then he grinned and ran a finger down her soft cheeks, causing her eyes to widen. 'But still too pale.'

She jerked her face away and shrugged. 'I slept but it was patchy.'

'You can rest when we get home.' The consultant had told him in private that the best medicine for concussion was sleep.

'I just can't believe I've lost a whole year of my life.' She held the magazine up. 'Look at the date on this. To me, it's the wrong year. I don't remember turning twenty-four. There are stories in here about celebrities I've never even heard of.'

'Once we get you home I'm sure your memories will start to come back.' But not too soon, he hoped. He had plans for his wife. 'Do you not remember *anything* about our marriage?' He wanted to make double sure.

'Not a thing. The last I remember you were dating that Jasmin woman.'

Jasmin had been the date who'd got food poisoning an hour before his scheduled flight to California for the industry tech awards. It had been her illness that had given him the chance to coerce Anna into attending with him in her place. It was only because it was far too short notice for him to get another date that she'd agreed. That, and the designer dress he'd had couriered over from the designer personally had helped make her decision. The awards evening had ended with Anna insisting the only way she would have sex with him was if he married her.

He didn't doubt her memories of their time together would eventually return. If anyone could bring them back, it would be his wife, the most stubborn, determined woman he'd ever met in his life. But in the meantime…

'Our marriage is a shock for you.'

'That's one way to describe it,' she murmured. 'I'd promised myself I would rather date a baboon than go on a date with you, never mind marry you. Have you really never cheated on me?'

He forced his tone to remain light through the blood roaring in his veins. 'Not once. We've had a few issues but nothing serious. We've been working through them.'

A few months ago he'd been pictured dining with one of his new Swedish directors, a blonde statuesque beauty he hadn't felt even a flicker of attraction towards. Anna had shrugged the ensuing press melee off but he'd known it bothered her. A second photo a fortnight later, this time of him dining with one of his female employees in San Francisco, had only added fuel to the fire. He'd explained his innocence, proving the picture had cropped out the other half-dozen employees also dining with them, and she had outwardly accepted it. But her distrust had grown and she'd no longer bothered to hide it. Her attitude had infuriated him so much he hadn't cared to explain that he liked socialising when he travelled abroad without her because it made the time pass so much quicker.

He should have known from that point that she'd wanted to catch him out just as much as the media had. She had wanted proof of his supposed infidelity.

Her hazel eyes were filled with the suspicion he'd become too familiar with. 'What kind of issues?'

'You've found it hard to be my wife. You don't like the media.' That much at least was true. Anna loathed being under the media spotlight. 'There have been many stories about our marriage being in trouble. If we were to believe the press we've split up a hundred times since we married. It is all poppycock. We married quickly. It is natural for us to have the teething problems.'

Her nose wrinkled. 'When you found me in your office it was as if you'd found the Antichrist trespassing. What was the argument about that made me sleep at Melissa's? Was it that woman I saw you with?'

Dio, even with amnesia her mind ran to suspicion. He'd already told her there was no one else. There hadn't been anyone else since they'd flown to California and their relationship had irrevocably changed.

'That woman you saw me with is my sister.'

'Oh. Sorry.' She looked shamefaced. 'I saw her getting out of the car after you and…'

'And you assumed I was having an affair.' She'd made that exact same assumption when she'd found Christina in their apartment. Finally she'd found the proof she'd been waiting for from the very moment they'd made their vows. If she'd bothered to ask for the truth he would have given it, but she hadn't cared for the truth. All she'd wanted was evidence of infidelity so she could bleed him for as much of his hard-earned money as she could get her grasping hands on.

He'd planned to reveal his sister in court, in front of a judge, so the law could see Anna's accusation for the entrapment it was. He'd looked forward to her humiliation. Now he had a different kind of humiliation in mind, one that would be far more pleasurable. If she retrieved her memories before he could pull it off then so be it. He would enjoy it while it lasted.

'Sorry,' she repeated. 'I thought you were an only child.'

'So did I until recently. I'll tell you about it when you're not so exhausted.'

On cue, she covered her mouth and yawned widely, then blinked a number of times as if trying to keep her eyes open.

'Lie down and rest,' he said. 'The specialist will be here soon and then we'll be able to go home and you'll be able to sleep as much as you need.'

As much as he despised the very air she breathed, seeing her vulnerable and weak sat badly inside him, made him feel strangely protective. It made him want to hold her close and stroke her hair until she fell asleep. He much preferred it when her wits were sharp. It put them on equal footing. Her amnesia was a weapon in his own arsenal that he would use to his advantage but he wouldn't unleash its full force until he was satisfied she was over the worst of her concussion.

She nodded and lay down, curling up in the foetal position she always favoured when she slept. After a few minutes of silence when he thought she'd fallen asleep, she said, without opening her eyes, 'What did we argue about that was so bad I spent the night at my flat?'

'It wasn't anything serious. It's still your flat too and you often stay there. We've both been playing games. We're both stubborn, neither of us likes to admit to being wrong, but we always make it up.'

'If it wasn't serious, why were you so angry with me yesterday? You were grumpy for most of the time in the hospital too.'

Typical Anna. When she wanted an answer to something she was like a dog with a bone until she got it.

'I was hurt that you rejected me. I didn't understand you had amnesia. I was out of my mind with worry about you. Worry makes me grumpy. I'm sorry for behaving like that.'

Her eyes opened, an amusement he hadn't seen for a long time sparkling in them. 'An apology and an admission to hurt feelings? Have you damaged your brain too?'

He laughed and leaned over to press a kiss to her cheek. She scowled at the gesture, which made him laugh more.

It was as if this Anna beside him had been reset to factory settings before marriage had even been mentioned between them.

'I know you have no memories of us. I have to be hopeful they will return.' But not too soon. Too soon and he wouldn't be able to fulfil the plan that had formed almost the instant the consultant had informed him that his estranged wife had amnesia.

Their wedding anniversary was now only nine days away. To celebrate it, he had a surprise planned for her that no amount of amnesia would ever allow her to forget.

CHAPTER THREE

ANNA GAWKED AS the driver came to a stop along the Embankment. She'd always been curious about Stefano's home, situated in a high-rise residential complex overlooking the Thames, which, at the time of building, had been the most expensive development in the world. So naturally, Stefano owned the most expensive apartment within it: the entire top floor.

The driver opened Stefano's door. Before he could get out she touched his arm, only lightly but with an instinctive familiarity she'd never used before. 'You could be telling me anything about our relationship. I can't disprove any of it. How do I know I can trust you?'

'In all the time you worked for me did you ever know me to lie?' he answered steadily.

'I never caught you out in a lie,' she conceded. In the eighteen months she'd worked for him their relationship had been nothing less than honest, brutally so on occasion.

'So trust me.' He held her gaze with that same intense look that sent tendrils of something curling up her spine.

'It doesn't seem I have much choice.'

If she could remember her phone's pin code she could reach Melissa and ask her but even if she could, she knew she wouldn't make that call. Not yet. The thought of speaking to her sister made her feel sick. She wouldn't call her until she could trust she wouldn't scream down the line at her and say things she knew she would regret.

She must have known about Melissa's trip. Melissa's letter had said as much. She'd asked for her forgiveness.

How could she forgive that? After everything their mother had done and put them through? Their father had been six feet under for less than six months when their mother had started seeing an Australian man she met through a dating agency. Anna, who'd been desperately grieving the loss of the father she'd adored, had tried to understand her mother's loneliness. She really had. She'd resisted the urge to spit in the usurper's tea, had been as welcoming as she could be, believing Melissa's private assertion that it was nothing but a rebound fling by a lonely, heartbroken woman and that it would fizzle out before it really started. If only.

Three months after meeting him, nine months after she'd buried her husband, Anna's mother had announced she was emigrating to Australia with her new man.

Stefano pressed his thumb to her chin and gently stroked it. 'When your memories come back you will know the truth. I will help you find them.'

Her heart thudding, her skin alive with the sensation of his touch, Anna swallowed the moisture that had filled her mouth.

When had she given in to the chemistry that had always been there between them, always pulling her to him? She'd fought against it right from the beginning, having no intention of joining the throng of women Stefano enjoyed such a legendary sex life with. To be fair, she didn't have any evidence of what he actually got up to under the bed sheets; indeed it was something she'd been resolute in *not* thinking about, but the steady flow of glamorous, sexy women in and out of his life had been pretty damning.

One of her conditions for accepting the job as his PA was that he must never ask her to be a go-between between him and his lovers. No way would she be expected to leave her desk to buy a pretty trinket as a kiss-off to a dumped lover. When she'd told him this he had roared with laughter.

When had she gone from liking and hugely admiring him but with an absolute determination to never get into bed with him, to marrying him overnight? She'd heard of whirlwind marriages before but from employee to wife in twenty-four hours? Her head hurt just trying to wrap itself around it.

Had Stefano looked at her with the same glimmer in his green eyes then as he was now? Had he pressed his lips to hers or had she been the one...?

'How will you help me remember us?' she asked in a whisper.

His thumb moved to caress her cheek and his voice dropped to a murmur. 'I will help you find again the pleasure you had in my bed. I will teach you to become a woman again.'

Mortification suffused her, every part of her anatomy turning red.

I will teach you to be a woman again?

His meaning was clear. He knew she was a virgin.

Anna's virginity was not something she'd ever discussed with anyone. Why would she? Twenty-three-year-old virgins were rarer than the lesser-spotted unicorn. For Stefano to know that...

Dear God, it was *true*.

All the denial she'd been storing up fell away.

She really had married him.

And if she'd married him, she must have slept with him. Which meant all her self-control, not just around him but in her life itself, had been blown away.

She'd taken such pride in her self-control after her mum had left. Events might fall out of her power but her own behaviour was something she controlled with iron will. All those teenage parties she'd been to when alcohol, cigarettes and more illicit substances were passed around and couples found empty spaces in which to make out… She'd been the one sitting there sipping on nothing stronger than a cola and taking great pride in the fact that she was in control of all her faculties. Her self-control was the only thing she'd *had* control of in a life where she'd been powerless to stop her father dying or her mother moving to the other side of the world and leaving her behind.

A different heat from the mortification ravaging her now bloomed as her mind suddenly pictured Stefano lying on top of her…

His eyes still holding hers as if he would devour her in one gulp, Stefano trailed his fingers down her neck and squeezed her shoulder. 'Let's get you inside. You must rest. You're exhausted.'

Anna blew out a long breath and nodded. For once she was completely incapable of speech.

She'd shared a bed with him.

She'd shared more than a bed with him.

Trying desperately to affect nonchalance, she had no choice but to allow him to assist her through the grand atrium of his apartment building to his private elevator. It was either that or have her unsteady legs collapse beneath her again.

She'd always been physically aware of him before but with his arm slung protectively around her shoulders that awareness flew off the scale.

The dividing line she'd erected between them and worked so hard to maintain… Noting Stefano's easy familiarity with her; the way he was so comfortable touching her now along with the flirting she'd long been used to… Yes, that dividing line had been demolished.

She just wished her body didn't sing its delight at his new proprietorial manner with her.

It was such a relief to be led to a sofa to collapse onto that it took her a moment, catching her breath, to take stock of Stefano's home.

Her home.

It was like stepping into another world.

She was sitting in a living room so vast and wide she felt like a toddler who'd stumbled into a ballroom, the room complete with a gold-leafed crystal chandelier gleaming magnificently above her.

Floor-to-ceiling windows covered the entire perimeter and from one aspect gave the most amazing view of the Thames—was that Westminster Bridge she could see in the near distance?

Not a single memory was jogged by any of it. She'd lived here for almost a year but she was seeing it for the first time.

She looked around wondering where everyone was. 'No staff?'

'I don't have staff. The concierge service runs my housekeeping for me and I pay them a fortune for it.'

When Stefano had first made his fortune in his home town of Lazio, he'd employed live-in staff but had soon learned to dislike having other people in his space.

Housekeeper, cleaners, butler, chef, gardener...the list had been endless. Being waited on hand and foot sounded fantastic in theory but in practice it was a drag and he'd put the staff on day-only duties within weeks.

He was a fully grown man who'd been caring for himself since he was fifteen. He didn't need someone to dress him or run his baths. He saw his peers with their homes full of enough staff to fill a cinema and thought them fools for allowing themselves to revert to infancy.

It was all the fawning he couldn't abide. That was one of the reasons he'd been so keen to employ Anna as his PA. She'd been completely unaffected by meeting him, a reaction he hadn't received in years. In a business setting he was used to fear being the primary reaction; in his personal life he received desire from women and enthusiasm from men, both sexes looking at him with dollar signs flashing in their eyes. Anna had looked at him with disdain.

He'd strolled into the Levon Brothers offices when they'd been in early discussion about him buying the business from them and she'd been behind the desk in the office guarding theirs. He'd handed her his coat as he walked past for her to hang for him and heard a sarcastic 'You're welcome,' in his wake. He'd paused at the door he'd been about to open and looked at her, standing with his coat in her arms, challenge set in her eyes, jutting chin and pursed lips.

'What did you say?' he'd asked.

'I said that you're welcome. I meant to say it in my head just as I'm sure your thanks for me taking your coat off your hands was said in *your* head, but it slipped out.'

It had been a sharp salutary reminder of the importance of manners, something no one had dared to pull him up on for many years and it had taken a scrap of a woman to do just that.

He'd put a hand to his chest, made a mocking bow and said, 'Thank you.'

She'd nodded primly and crossed the room to hang his coat on the stand. Shorter than the women who usually caught his eye, she had the most exquisite figure, perfectly proportioned. He remembered exactly what she'd been wearing that day, a billowing checked skirt that had fallen below her knees, long tan boots with spiked heels, a tight black vest and a fitted khaki-coloured jacket, all pulled together with a thick belt with studs that looked sharp enough to have someone's eye out.

'Do I dare ask if you make coffee?' he'd asked, fascinated by her.

'You can ask but beware—refusal often offends.'

Roaring with laughter, he'd gone into his meeting. Within an hour, when the beautiful, sarcastic secretary had been brought in six times to explain the report she'd compiled for him but which the idiots running the company didn't understand, he'd known he was going to buy the company and poach her to be his PA. It turned out Anna was the real brains behind Levon Brothers. Without her by their side and covering their messes, it would never have taken off. With her by Stefano's side, Moretti's could only strengthen further.

It had been the best business decision he'd ever made. He'd learned to trust her judgement completely.

He'd believed her to be as straight as a line. He'd thought that with Anna what you saw was what you got, when all along she'd been nothing but a grasping gold-digger.

Now the bravado that always shone in her eyes was muted by alarm. 'It's just you and me here?'

'We like our privacy,' he said. 'We can walk around naked without having to worry that we'll frighten anyone.'

Her cheeks turned the most becoming crimson but she raised a tired brow and wanly retorted, 'I can assure you I won't be walking anywhere naked within a mile of you.'

Amused by her stubbornness even when she was so clearly ready to fall into a dead sleep, he whispered into her ear, 'And I can assure you that when you're feeling better you will never want to put your clothes on. Believe me, *bellissima*, we spend a lot of time together naked.'

'If I don't remember it then it didn't happen.'

Studying the firm set of her lips, he remembered what it had been like between them when they'd first married. He'd had no idea she was a virgin until she'd blurted it out when they'd walked into the bridal suite hours after exchanging their vows. She'd stood as defiant as she did now but there had been something in her eyes he'd never seen in her before: fear. That had been a bigger shock than her declaration of virginity.

He'd made love to her so slowly and tenderly that night that when he'd felt her first climax he'd been as triumphant and elated as if he'd been the first man to conquer Mount Everest. That night had been special. Precious. And it had only been the start.

Once Anna had discovered the joy of sex she'd been a woman reborn and unleashed.

She had no memories of any of it. When he next saw her naked, for Anna it would be the first time, and he remembered how painfully shy she'd been then.

He took one of her hands and razed a kiss across the knuckles. 'Can you walk to the bedroom or shall I carry you?'

Her eyes flashed and she managed to inflect dignity into her reply. 'I can walk.'

She allowed him to help her to her feet and held onto his arm as he led her to the bedroom he'd slept alone in for the past month.

The last twenty-four hours had brought such a change to his fortunes that Stefano was tempted to wonder whether it was *he* who had suffered a bump to his head.

His wife was back under his roof and shortly to be back in his bed.

He caught her unconcealed surprise when he opened the door to reveal a room cast in soft muted colours and dominated by an enormous emperor bed.

'We chose the decor together,' he told her. '*You* chose the bed.' It had been the first thing they'd bought as a married couple. He'd known she would hate sleeping in a bed he'd shared with other women.

And now they would share it again. Anna needed to know that this was *theirs*, a bedroom they'd created together, a room they'd made love in hundreds of times. He needed to consolidate in her mind that they were a properly married couple and that it was natural for them to sleep together.

He couldn't begin to dissect his own feelings about sleeping by the side of the woman who had played him for a fool so spectacularly.

'Seriously?' she asked in a voice that had gone husky.

'*Sì*. And when you're better I can promise you'll enjoy it as we always used to. But all that can wait. Consultant's orders are for you to do nothing but rest for the next few days. I promised I would take care of you and you know I am a man of my word.'

He always kept his word. To his way of thinking it was what separated humans from animals. He'd married Anna giving his word that he would be faithful. He'd given his word that if he ever felt the impulse to cheat he would tell her before acting on it and they would go their separate ways.

She'd given him her word too. She'd promised she would trust him. Her word had been a lie. Her intentions had been a lie. It had *all* been a lie. Their entire marriage had been built on lies and deception. No sooner had she left him than she'd hit him with her demands for a massive slice of the fortune he'd built from nothing.

Anna was a greedy liar who had made a fool of him, and for that she would pay the price.

But however greedy and conniving his wife was, right then she was too wiped out for any games.

She slumped onto the bed and sat there blinking to try and keep her eyes open. He sank to his knees and unlaced her boots before carefully removing them, then got her settled and comfortable under the bed sheets. She was asleep before the automatic curtains had finished shutting.

His guts twisted as he took in the sallowness of her complexion and the dark hollows under her eyes. He fought his primal reaction to lean over and smooth the hair from her face and place a kiss on her cheek.

He closed the door on the darkened room. There was no place in their relationship for sympathy. Anna's amnesia and her current vulnerability did not change what she'd done to him. Nothing could change that.

Soon her concussion would pass and she would be physically fit again.

Then the games could commence in earnest.

When Anna next opened her eyes, her first conscious thought was that someone lay beside her.

Not *someone*. Stefano.

When had he come to bed?

She hardly remembered getting into bed herself her exhaustion had been so sudden and so complete.

Stefano had brought her to the apartment early afternoon. Judging by the absolute darkness shrouding her it now had to be the early hours of morning. She must have slept for a good twelve hours straight and she felt better for it. The nausea had gone and her head felt thick and fuzzy rather than pounding. Her throat was parched but even if she knew where the kitchen was she didn't dare move from the bed. She hardly dared to breathe.

That was Stefano lying beside her, sharing this bed. If she moved her foot it would brush against his leg.

Did he have clothes on? Or was he lying there naked…?

The only sounds were his rhythmic breathing and the thundering of her heart.

It was the strangest feeling in the world to be in such an intimate environment with him, especially after eighteen months of doggedly keeping their relationship on a professional footing. She'd spent more time with him than anyone else when their working lives had bound them together. They'd travelled all over the world together, eaten together, had the occasional drink together, sniped at each other, laughed at each other, laughed with each other, sworn at each other, thrown things at each

other…yet she had never allowed him to cross the threshold into her private life and had steadfastly refused to
cross the threshold into his. They'd never been alone as
they were now.

And here she was. Married to him and wholly aware
that during their marriage they had done far more than
merely sleep in this bed.

Stefano awoke with an almost painfully obvious erection.
In their marriage's previous life he would have pulled
Anna into his arms and made love to her before either
of them had opened their eyes. Today he jumped out of
bed and took a shower before he could act on that urge.

While he'd told himself that it was no big deal sharing
a bed with his wife again, he'd had to psych himself up
to join her in it. That had been unexpected. He'd gazed
at her sleeping form in the dim light and experienced
the strangest combination of loathing and compassion
sweep over him.

He'd never known Anna to be ill before. He'd never
seen her vulnerable. He'd lain beside her unable to get
out of his mind that she was there, in his bed, the place
he had once believed she belonged. It had taken him an
age to fall asleep.

As he lathered himself with his expensive shower gel,
it occurred to him that this was the first time in a month
he'd woken up feeling this kind of desire.

Celibacy was not a healthy state to live by and he
could only assume it was his loathing for Anna consuming all his waking moments that had stopped him
seeking another woman in the month since she'd gone.
He hadn't even thought of another woman to warm his

bed; no wonder he reacted so viscerally just to have her back beside him.

But he wouldn't act on it yet. Seduction of his wife would have to wait for now.

Anna was awake and sitting up when he returned to the bedroom with only a towel around his waist. He noted the way her eyes widened at his bare torso and smirked.

'Feeling better?' he asked. She looked better. Her face had regained its colour, although that could be due to embarrassment at his semi-naked form. This was the first time in her memories that she had seen him anything but fully clothed. He worked hard to keep himself in shape and she had made no secret of her appreciation of his body.

She jerked a nod and pulled the covers tighter. That she was still wearing the jersey dress she'd collapsed in two days ago only made her embarrassment more amusing.

He strode over the thick carpet to his dressing room. 'Can I get you anything? A cup of tea?'

Anna was addicted to tea. He'd once counted her drink nine cups in one day.

'Tea would be good, thanks,' she muttered.

'Painkillers? Food?'

'Just painkillers, please.'

Deciding not to torment her further by dressing in front of her, he threw on a pair of jeans and a black T-shirt in his dressing room, then went to the kitchen where her teapot and teabags still lived.

He automatically reached for her favourite morning mug, a vessel so large it could reasonably be classed as a bucket, and a fresh burst of fury lashed through him.

He should have got rid of all her possessions instead

of keeping them here as a constant reminder. He'd given in to his anger only the once since she'd left him, in their San Francisco apartment, and had despised himself for his momentary weakness. Since then, his fury had been internal, simmering under his skin, crawling through him, festering.

Anna's amnesia had given him the perfect means to channel his rage into something far more satisfying than making a bonfire from her belongings.

His rage was back under his full control when he took her tea to her and placed it on her bedside table.

'I've ordered a light breakfast for you,' he said, handing her the painkillers.

'I'm not hungry.'

'You need to eat something.'

Anna took the pills from him and pulled a face, but her retort about not wanting to eat died on her lips when she noticed his bare wedding finger. She looked at her own bare hand and asked, 'Why don't we wear wedding rings?'

'You didn't want to. You said it would make you feel like a possession.'

'You didn't mind?'

'It was a compromise. You agreed to take my name on condition of no rings.'

'I would have thought it would be the other way round and that I'd refuse to take your name,' she mused.

His smile was fleeting. 'You wanted to be a Moretti so when we have children we can all have the same name.'

'We want children?' That shocked her almost as much as learning she was married to him had.

He shrugged then flashed his gorgeous smile. 'At some

point. When we're ready. Until then we've been enjoying practising making them.'

Something poked in her memories, squeezing her heart and making her stomach clench so hard his unsubtle innuendo barely registered. Desperately she tried to capture the feeling but whatever *it* was fluttered out of reach before she could put her finger on it.

'What is it?' he asked, staring at her with drawn brows.

'I don't know.' She shrugged and shook her head. 'Not a memory. A feeling.'

'Good or bad?'

'Painful.' That was the only word she could think of to describe it. She'd always wanted children but it had been something shoved to the back of her mind, a 'one day' want. She'd imagined she would one day reach the stage where her biological clock started ticking furiously and then be forced to make her decision. And that would have been hard as she'd always avoided relationships. If her own mother hadn't loved her enough to stay, how could she trust any man to?

When had she looked at Stefano and decided she could trust *him*?

She'd been attracted to him from the first moment she'd met him but which woman wouldn't be? The outrageously handsome, infamous boss of Moretti's had strolled into her office as if he already owned the building and had arrogantly placed his coat in her arms without a single word of greeting, never mind thanks. When she'd sarcastically responded with, 'You're welcome,' to his retreating back, she hadn't cared about offending him. Being a woman in a heavily male-dominated environment had caused her to grow skin as thick as leather and she'd adopted an unwillingness to tolerate sexism

in any form. She'd known her worth to Levon Brothers
as well as they had. She'd merely been given the title of
secretary because her two bosses there had been too un-
imaginative to think of a more appropriate title. They'd
only been a few years older than her, a couple of eggheads with more brains than an elephant and less common sense than a dormouse.

Stefano had paused and turned to face her and in that
moment she had experienced a flicker of nerves at crossing some invisible line with a man with such a ferocious
reputation; a billionaire who'd come from nothing and
served time in jail, but then their eyes had clashed and
something else had flickered inside her. Attraction.

So attractive had she found him that she'd thought long
and hard before accepting his job offer. He'd assumed
she was playing hardball for more money and increased
his offer, but money had been the least of her concerns.
Stefano had a magnetism about him, a power that clung
to his tailored suits and the dashing looks of a matinee
idol. All this and the element of danger that oozed from
him had proven a potent mixture and one she'd been wary
of committing her working life to.

In the end, the pluses of taking the job had outweighed
the minuses. She had never regretted her decision. She enjoyed working with him. Even on those days when they'd
be working towards some deadline that would see them
in the office late in the evening, bad-tempered and shouting at each other, she had never regretted it. That she'd
spent most days fighting her own responses to touch him
or act in any way inappropriately was something she had
learned to live with. That Stefano seemed to know exactly
how badly she desired him was something she had sworn
to never give him the satisfaction of confirming.

So how had he worn her defences down enough to persuade her to marry him and consider having children together?

A ring vibrated through the apartment, startling her.

'That will be our breakfast,' he said.

'That was quick.'

'That's why I pay such a high price for the service.' He reached the bedroom door. 'You need to build your strength up, *bellissima*. I need you fit to fly in a few days.'

'Why? Where are we going?'

'California.' The smile he gave was unlike any she'd seen on his lips before. 'It's the industry awards next week. And our first wedding anniversary. Where better to celebrate it than where it all started?'

Stefano waited until he heard the shower running, then dialled the contact on his phone.

Anna had spent her second day in the apartment sleeping on and off. After her small evening meal she'd declared she needed a shower. Her health was improving by the minute.

His call was answered within two rings.

'Miranda, it's Stefano,' he said. 'How would you like the celebrity scoop of the year?'

CHAPTER FOUR

FOR THE SECOND night in a row Anna woke to darkness and the regular deep breaths coming from her right. The covers she'd burrowed under had been pulled down and the chill of the winter night covered her skin.

Holding her breath, she turned her head to look at him. Stefano slept with his back to her, the covers twisted around his waist. As with the night before, he slept deeply. She couldn't keep her eyes off him. Her heart seemed to make a clenching motion and the urge to rest her hand against his warm skin grew almost overwhelming.

Cautiously, she tugged at the sheets, trying to dislodge them without waking him. She managed to free a couple of inches, and tried again.

She didn't want to wake him. There was something about the darkness of night that heightened the intimacy being alone in his apartment evoked in her senses.

She would never have believed he could be so attentive. Nothing was too much trouble for him, not the endless cups of tea, the regular small meals…he'd even had a pair of pyjamas couriered to her from Selfridges. She was certain that if she were to wake him up and ask him for something he would do it without complaint. It made her realise that she must mean something to him as a wife, that he had true feelings for her. If only she could remember what her own feelings towards *him* were.

Eventually she came to the conclusion that she would have to wake him. It was either that or freeze.

'Stefano,' she whispered. When there was no response, she repeated his name, louder. Still no response.

She would have to touch him...

She took a deep breath, then quickly poked him in the back. 'Wake up. You've stolen all the covers.'

It was like arguing with a corpse.

After trying to wake him a few more times with minimal contact, she sat up. Now holding her breath, she put a hand to his shoulder and gave it a quick shake before snatching her hand away.

That did the trick.

He rolled over. 'What's the matter? Are you feeling ill?'

'You're hogging the bed sheets.' She lay back down and fixed her gaze to the ceiling, making sure to keep a good distance between them.

'Sorry.' He yawned widely then untangled himself and breached the small distance she'd created to pull the covers up to her shoulders. Then he settled himself back down next to her, on his side, facing her. A centimetre closer and he would be pressed against her. 'We decided long ago that you're a refrigerator at night and I'm a radiator.'

Going by the heat coming off him now she could believe it.

She swallowed and croaked out a reply that was nowhere near as witty or nonchalant as she wanted. 'I normally sleep with bed socks on.'

Bed socks were as unsexy as they came and right then

she was prepared to grab at anything that didn't make her think of sex.

He chuckled lightly, as if he knew what she was thinking. He was so close his warm breath whispered against her skin. 'You don't need them any more. We both sleep naked. I keep you warm.'

She tried to breathe but suddenly it seemed as if all the air had been sucked from the room. As hard as she tried to resist, her head turned of its own accord to face him.

A flame flickered to life inside her, turning her core to liquid. If she rolled over she would be flush against him.

Help her, she wanted to be flush against him. Her lips tingled to feel his mouth on hers again but this time for her to be coherent enough to savour the moment.

As if he could sense her silent yearning, Stefano breached that last, tiny distance and brushed his lips to hers in the softest of caresses.

And then he pulled away and rolled over so his back was to her again. 'Go back to sleep, *bellissima.*'

Anna only just stopped herself from crying out. She clamped her lips together and lay there rigidly, waiting for her heartbeat to return to its normal rhythm and the flames still flickering inside her to subside.

If they weren't married she would be plotting her escape from this dangerous situation where the biggest peril was herself. Yet somewhere in her past, in the blank space that was her memories, Stefano had worn her defences down. She'd acted on the desire she felt for him.

And now, God help her, she wanted to act on it again.

Anna managed to fall back into a light sleep, a restless state where her body didn't know if it was awake or dreaming. Stefano seemingly had no such problems, sleeping deeply while she lay fidgeting, her mind a whirl, questioning everything: her marriage, her sister's betrayal... When six o'clock finally struck she decided to get up.

Physically, she felt a lot better. Almost normal. Her legs had lost the jelly-like feeling she'd been experiencing every time she stood and the ache in her head was now a dull thud rather than rivalling a pneumatic drill.

Tiptoeing over the thick carpet so as not to wake Stefano, she opened her dressing-room door and closed it quickly behind her so the light wouldn't disturb him. It was the first time she'd entered this room.

She experienced another in a long list of surreal moments. Floor-to-ceiling fitted white wardrobes lined the walls, while at the far end of the room sat a vanity desk, a full-length mirror and a squishy armchair. And it was all hers.

She opened the nearest door and found a row of trousers and jeans. The next door opened to display a row of tops. As she fingered the expensive material of a silk green and black checked shirt that caught her eye, a memory flickered, a sudden image of herself in this very room looking at herself in the mirror wearing this very top.

It was the first concrete memory of her missing year since she'd woken three days ago.

Stefano woke to a bed he knew was empty before he opened his eyes. Through the duration of their marriage he'd become accustomed to waking next to Anna, usually with their arms and legs entwined. He'd learned as a teenager to sleep anywhere he could rest his head but nowhere did he sleep as deeply or as sweetly as when Anna lay beside him. He hated that fact about himself.

He shrugged on his robe and went in search of her. He found her in the kitchen looking through a drawer, dressed in her favourite green and black checked shirt and a pair of slim-fitting dark grey canvas trousers. Her hair was brushed and pulled back in a loose ponytail and on her feet were the fluffy duck slippers he'd bought as one of her birthday presents. He'd chosen them as a joke but of all the things he'd bestowed her with on that day, which included a surprise holiday to the Seychelles, the slippers had been her favourite.

He'd spotted a pair of fluffy lamb ones only a week ago and his first thought had been to buy them for her as an early Christmas present. A split second later he'd remembered that Anna no longer lived with him and the only Christmas present she would receive from him would be his contempt.

'It's good to see you up.' He hooked an arm around her waist, dropped a kiss on the nape of her neck and inhaled her delicious soft floral scent.

Turning his back on her in the early hours of the night had been hard but necessary. He'd sensed her desire simmering beneath her rigid surface and known that with only a little persuasion on his part she would be his for the taking. But it was too soon for her. When he seduced her anew, he wanted his wife to be a tinderbox of desire for him. He wanted her to beg for his possession. He wanted her helpless to do anything but melt in his arms. He wanted her fully fit and knowing exactly what she was doing.

The more heightened her emotions and desire for him, the greater the low that would follow when he exacted his revenge.

She stiffened but didn't pull away or shrug him off.

He pressed one more kiss to her neck and stepped back.

'What are you looking for?'

She cleared her throat but kept her back to him. 'My phone charger. I can't find it anywhere and yours doesn't fit into my phone.'

'You probably left it at the flat.' There was no probably about it.

'Can we go and get it?'

'Sure. What do you need it for?'

She turned her head and cast him with a glance that contained a trace of amusement. 'To charge my phone, obviously.'

Oh, yes, she was definitely on the mend.

Then her amusement turned to a scowl and she flung the phone to one side. 'I guess it doesn't matter if I get the charger when I can't remember the pin code to get into it. Do you know what it is?'

'No.'

'Can I use your phone?'

'What for?' he asked cautiously.

'I want to call Melissa.' There was the slightest tremor in her voice. 'You must have her number.'

'I do,' he admitted. It was pointless to lie. If Anna was determined to speak to her sister she would find a way. His job at this point was to deter her. 'Are you sure it's wise to speak to her yet?'

'I want to know why she's gone to visit our mother… unless you can tell me?'

'Her decision to go was very sudden,' he said, thinking quickly. 'I shouldn't speculate what her reasons were.'

'I only want to know why she's gone. You say you're

my husband—this is the sort of thing a husband would know.'

'I *am* your husband, Anna, but Melissa's reasons are hers alone. I don't think you should contact her until your memories return. If they come back to you before she gets home from Australia then you will know the truth for yourself. If they haven't come back by then, the two of you can sit down and you can hear her reasons from her own mouth.'

Her eyes flashed with anger. 'Our mother abandoned us to live with another man when our dad wasn't even cold in his grave. I don't want to wait for a month to know why Melissa's suddenly decided to forgive her.'

Stefano strove to keep his features neutral. Anna must assume he already knew all this but he'd only known the basics about her mother's emigration to Australia. The way she'd always spoken about it was that staying in England to live with her sister was something they'd all been happy about and that the two sisters' estrangement from their mother had grown organically over time, a simple result of living on opposite sides of the world.

He didn't want to know any more. She'd had a year to confide her secrets to him but had chosen to keep them to herself.

Stefano held no truck with traumatic childhoods. His own was there for the world to see. He wasn't in the least ashamed of his past but could think of nothing worse than sitting down to dissect its effect on him. The only effect had been to act as fuel for his success.

He didn't want to know anything more about his wife than he already did. He didn't want to delve into her psyche and would not allow her to delve into his.

That chance had long gone.

He took her hands in his and brought them to his lips. 'I know you find Melissa's actions painful but all that matters is getting your memories back. Everything will fall into place when they return.'

She held his gaze, the ire slowly evaporating from them until she sighed. 'It's not just Melissa. Or you. I feel so out of the loop with everything. I was watching the news earlier and there's so much happening in the world I know nothing about.'

It was only eight o'clock. 'How long have you been awake?'

'A couple of hours. I've had so much sleep that I'm all rested out.'

'You should have woken me.'

'I knew you'd say that. And I did think about it but, other than my head aching a little, I feel normal. It would have been mean to wake you. Besides, you sleep like the dead.'

'Fed up of being fussed over?' he teased.

The wry smile broadened and she sniggered. 'Fed up and bored rigid. There's not even any housework for me to do. Everywhere is spotless.'

'I knew it wouldn't take long for you to get bored,' he said smugly. 'But I have a cure for your boredom. Let's fly to California tonight. The sun and change of scenery will do you good and being there might act as one of those joggers the specialist spoke about.'

California was where she'd reeled him in like a fish on a hook. It was only fitting he did the same in return.

Her face suddenly brightened. 'I did have a memory come to me when I was in my dressing room. Nothing significant, just a memory of wearing this shirt.'

A sharp stabbing struck at his brain. 'It's your favourite,' he confirmed, forcing his features to relax. 'And that memory must be a good sign.'

'I hope so,' she said reverently. 'It's a start in any case.'

'It is. So do I tell my crew they're taking us to California today?'

She thought for a moment then nodded. 'Do it. It can only help me.'

'I shall make the call now.'

'Aren't we going to San Francisco?' Anna asked when Stefano's driver took them down a different highway from the route she remembered. She'd travelled with him on business to San Francisco a number of times, stopping at a hotel while he would stay in his penthouse apartment.

He grinned. 'Your amnesia means I get to surprise you twice.'

'What do you mean?'

'You'll see.'

They'd landed on a sunny late afternoon. The Californian warmth felt wonderful on her skin, the majestic redwood trees lining the route as they wound through the mountains…

'Are we going to Santa Cruz?' she asked as they drove past a sign with the name of an approaching town she recognised. She'd gone for a hike in the summer through the Forest of Nisene Marks State Park on her day off during a week spent in the Moretti's San Francisco building.

'You'll see,' he repeated. He took hold of her hand and brought it to his lips to breathe a kiss across the knuckles.

She snatched it away. 'Can you stop playing games for two minutes and give me a straight answer?'

Although she'd slept for most of the flight, her body thought it was the early hours of the morning, not the early Californian evening they'd landed in. It was driving her crazy that he wouldn't give her a straight answer to anything, not even their destination.

He cast her with hurt eyes that didn't fool her for a second. 'I like to give you surprises.'

'Don't give me that. You're on one of your power trips. You're loving having me at your mercy.'

'I don't have the power trips.'

'But you don't deny that you love me being at your mercy.'

His voice dropped to a murmur as he leaned close to speak in her ear. 'I love nothing more than having you at my mercy, *bellissima*. And you love it too.'

'And you can stop with the innuendoes,' she snapped. 'You're supposed to be helping me get my memories back. All you're doing is alluding to sex. Is that all our marriage amounts to?'

'It's the best part of it.'

'Well, from now on you can take it as read that I know we have a fantastic sex life.' She could feel her cheeks burn as she spoke but refused to allow herself to be distracted. 'So I would appreciate it if you would remember that I know nothing of our life together and am relying on you to fill the holes—and if you make an innuendo out of that I shall get a flight straight back to London.'

His lips twitched and he settled back and folded his arms across his chest. 'What do you want to know?'

'Where we are going for a start!'

Right on cue, his driver took them over the border into the hip, arty city of Santa Cruz.

'We're going to our beach house,' he confirmed. 'We bought it a few months ago. This is the city we got married in.'

Slightly mollified, she said, 'Why did we marry here?'

'California allows quick marriages. I told you to name your city. You chose Santa Cruz.'

'*I* chose? You didn't frogmarch me to a register office?'

'Marriage was your idea.'

'I don't believe you.'

He shrugged. 'It's the truth. You flew to San Francisco with me as my guest for the awards ceremony. At the end of the evening I got my driver to drop you at your hotel first.' He spread his arms. 'We had our first kiss in this car. Things got a little…hot but you wouldn't let me come to your room. I asked what it would take to get you into my bed and you said marriage.'

'I must have been joking.' She *must* have been. Anna had never even thought of marriage, had assumed she would grow into a grey-haired spinster surrounded by dogs—not cats—and had been comfortable with that. Singledom was safe. It wasn't men specifically that she didn't trust, it was people. People were selfish. People put their own needs and wants first. They broke hearts and left others to pick up the shattered pieces.

'You said you were.' He shrugged again and in the movement she thought she glimpsed a darkening of his features that passed so quickly she guessed she'd imagined it. 'But the idea took hold with both of us. I came back to your hotel in the morning knowing I was going to marry you that day. It was what we both wanted.'

'But *why*?'

'We wanted each other and we'd both reached our limit of you keeping me at arm's length. Think about it, *bellissima*—what couple was better suited to marry? We'd worked closely together for eighteen months. We'd seen the worst of each other. We'd fought. We spent more time together than with anyone else but we never quit. If a man and a woman could truly be friends then that's what we were.'

'You're my boss. I'm paid to be nice to you.' But even as she made the jest she was wondering where love had come into it. That was why people married, wasn't it? Because they trusted someone enough to give them their heart as well as their body? It was why she'd never thought *she* would marry.

He snorted with laughter. 'When did that ever stop you saying what you think of me? We married knowing exactly what we were getting into. It made perfect sense.'

And as Stefano finally explained how he'd worn her defences down, a warm feeling spread through her.

For all their sniping at each other in the workplace, they'd forged a strong camaraderie. A bond. She would attend meetings with him, sit in on interviews for both staff and acquisitions, travel the world with him... She'd got to know him so well she would know his opinion on a person or situation before he'd opened his mouth to vocalise it.

She'd learned that though he was an exacting task-master, his word was his bond. She might even have learned to trust him.

Suddenly she could see exactly why she'd married him.

Not only was he the sexiest man to walk the planet, but by marrying her Stefano had proven he wanted her as more than just another notch on his endless bedpost.

Love must have been a gradual progression between them. It appeared Stefano was wisely avoiding talk of it knowing it was pointless to talk of love with someone who had no memory of it. His pride must be so hurt with it all, she thought, feeling a twinge of compassion for him, having to be the one to hold her steady until her memories of the life they'd forged together returned; having to trust that they *would* return and that she would remember all they'd meant to each other.

'I can see how it happened,' she said quietly, nodding slowly as she processed it all. 'But I must have asked for some kind of reassurance that you would be faithful. Your track record with women hardly inspires confidence.'

If he hadn't been such an unashamed womaniser he might have given in to her desire for him sooner. There had been nights when she would lay awake aching for him, filled with pent-up frustration that working so closely with him brought. Day after day of breathing in his scent, watching his throat move while he ate and drank, catching a glimpse of exposed torso when he'd rip his constricting tie off or a glimpse of his forearms when he'd roll up his sleeves… She had become obsessed with those arms. She would dream about them. She would dream about him.

'Your only request was that I tell you if I met another woman I wanted to bed so you could walk away with your dignity intact. It was a promise I was happy to make.'

'It's good to know I didn't completely lose my marbles.'

'You did,' he assured her solemnly but with a glint in his eye. 'I told you I would wear you down eventually and I was right.'

'You're always right.'

'*Sì.*'

'In your own head.'

Catching his eye again, Anna suddenly, inexplicably, found herself unable to stop laughing.

'What's so funny?' he demanded to know.

'Everything.' She covered her mouth with her hand, trying hopelessly to regain some composure. 'You must be an amazing kisser if one kiss in the back of a car was enough to make me marry you.'

The wolfish gleam in his eyes and the way he leaned closer made her suddenly certain that he was going to show her exactly what it had been like, right here and now.

She waited in breathless anticipation for his mouth to press on hers.

But then he grinned and the moment was lost. 'We're here.'

CHAPTER FIVE

ANNA SNAPPED HERSELF back to the present. They'd entered a private enclave lined with clean wide roads fringed with palm trees.

As they got out of the car, the salty air of the Pacific and its accompanying breeze filled her senses, along with a tremendous sense of déjà vu. She *knew* this place.

The house they'd stopped outside was stunning, a modern Spanish-style beach home that, from the outside and despite its grandness, looked surprisingly cosy.

Cosy was a word she'd never used in association with Stefano before.

She followed Stefano through the front entrance and into a home that made his London apartment seem like a shoebox.

'Take a look around. I'll get us a drink.' He disappeared through an arch and into the kitchen.

Intrigued by her surroundings, she trod her way through the ground floor, over marble floors, under high ceilings, soft furnishings and elegant decor. The only room accessed by a door was a cinema with a dozen plush leather seats.

Carrying on with her tour, she found an indoor swimming pool, a gym, a majestic dining room… She finally came to a stop at the rear of the house. The glass walls overlooked a palm-tree-lined patio area and another swimming pool, which in turn overlooked a glorious sandy beach and the deep blue Pacific. On the left of the room was the most enormous rounded sofa she'd ever seen, almost bed-like in its proportions.

'You said this is ours?' she asked in amazement when he joined her a short while later holding two tall glasses of fruit juice.

'Sì.' He handed a glass to her. 'I would have poured us champagne but it's not a good idea for you to drink alcohol until you're fully recovered from your concussion.'

She raised a brow. 'How do you know I'm not?'

'Because I know you, *bellissima*. I don't want to rush you. When you're fully better we can celebrate.'

'Celebrate what?'

'You being here.'

She couldn't know what a truth that was. Stefano wasn't about to tell her that they hadn't spent a night together under this roof, that the purchase had been finalised three days before she'd left him. Especially as part of the settlement she'd instructed her lawyer to hit him with had been a demand for this house. Now he would taint the memories of it for her as much as she had tainted them for him. Here, in this house that was supposed to have been their first real home, the one they'd chosen together, he would seduce her so thoroughly that all the pleasure they shared would haunt her for ever. Her humiliation would be twofold: public *and* private. Just as his had been.

Her cheeks coloured. She cleared her throat and took

a sip of her juice, then looked around again and said conversationally, 'You like your glass walls, don't you?'

'What do you mean?'

'Your apartment in London has external glass walls. Is there a theme?'

'I don't like to be...what's the word when things are too near to you?'

'Hemmed in? Cramped?'

He shrugged. 'Both could be it. I like space and light. I had enough of being cramped when I was a child.'

'You weren't put in a cupboard under the stairs, were you?' she asked teasingly.

'I spent a year living in a cellar.'

Anna eyed him warily, unsure if he was joking. Everyone knew of Stefano's torrid childhood—he wore it as a badge of honour: the teenage drug-addicted mother who died when he was a toddler, the teenage drug-addicted father who'd disappeared before he'd been born, the grandfather who'd raised him until his own death when Stefano had been only seven at which point he'd been sent to live with a succession of aunts and uncles. He'd always been fighting and causing trouble and being kicked out to live with the next family member until there had been no family members left willing to take him in. From that point on he'd been alone. At the age of fifteen.

He'd spent years begging and fighting to make a living, finding work wherever he could in the seedy underbelly of Lazio's streets. At the age of nineteen, to no one's surprise including his own, he'd been sent to prison but, within a year of his release, the adolescent who had been expected to spend his life as a career criminal had formed the technology company known to the world as Moretti's and the rest was history.

This was all public information. Stefano was happy to talk about his formative years with the media, proud of being the bad boy who'd made a success of himself.

As a PR strategy it had worked fantastically well, capturing the public's imagination and adding an edgy aura to the Moretti brand. It had the added advantage of actually being true, or so Anna had always assumed. Stefano's past crossed the divide from professional to personal so she'd never asked him anything about it other than in the most generic terms. Well, not in her memories in any case.

'Really? A cellar?'

'That was when I lived with my Uncle Vicente. My cousins there wouldn't let me share their rooms.'

'They made you sleep in a cellar because they didn't want to share?'

'They were scared of me—and for good reason. You do not keep kicking a dog and not expect it to bite. I was an angry teenager who liked to fight.'

Fighting was the only answer Stefano had had. A patchy education had left him severely behind at school, which, coupled with always wearing threadbare clothes either too big or too small, had made him a target for bullies. Once he'd realised he could silence the taunts from cousins and school friends alike by using his fists he'd never looked back. A volatile temper and a rapidly growing body had quickly turned him into the boy everyone crossed the road to avoid.

'Were all your family afraid of you?'

'They were when I hit puberty and became bigger

than all of them. I wasn't the skinny kid they could bully any more.'

'Why did they bully you?'

'My mother was the bad girl of the Moretti family and brought shame on them. I was guilty of being her son. They only took me in because it was my *nonno*—my grandfather—his dying wish. They hated me and made sure I knew it.'

'That's horrible,' she said with obvious outrage. 'How can anyone treat a child like that? It's inhuman.'

'It makes you angry?' he asked with interest.

'Of course it makes me angry! If Melissa had a child and anything should happen…' Her voice faltered and she blanched at the weight of her own dark thoughts. 'I would love that child as if it were my own.'

Yes, she probably would. If his wife was capable of loving anyone it was her sister.

She shook her dark hair and took a drink of her juice. 'Do you ever see them now?'

'You know I don't…' But then he remembered she knew nothing of the last year and how all their time not working had been spent in bed. When they'd been only boss and employee she had determinedly made a point of asking him little about his free time. 'The last time I spoke to any of them was when my Uncle Luigi turned up when I was still living in Italy asking for money. My answer would make a nun blush.'

Her face broke into a grin and she laughed. 'I can well imagine.'

'Do you know, I walked out of my Uncle Vicente's house—was kicked out for breaking my cousin David's arm in a fight—thinking of only one thing. Revenge. I would make such a success of myself that my family would have to see pictures of my face everywhere they went and read details of my wealth and know they would never get any of it. Whatever they did with their lives, I would do better. I would earn more money, eat better food, live in a better home, drive a better car. My success would be my revenge and it was. Everything I gained only drove me to get more.'

His revenge had fuelled him. The cousins who had begrudged him the clothes they'd outgrown, the aunts who'd begrudged feeding him, the uncles who'd treated their pets with more respect than they had their orphaned nephew... None of them would see any of his hard-earned gains.

'If the success you've had is any measure, your thirst for revenge must have been huge.'

Almost as great as his thirst for revenge on his wife.

He kept his voice steady as he replied, 'I am not a man to forgive. I forget nothing.'

Anna sat on the sofa, tucking her feet under her bottom and wishing she could put a finger on the danger she felt herself in. She kept her gaze on Stefano and was met with a sparkling gaze and the curve of his lips, yet there were undercurrents to this conversation that she was missing. She could feel it. A darkness, like a shadow that only showed itself intermittently.

'How did you do it?'

'I told people I was eighteen and found jobs on building sites and in clubs... Work was easy to find and working in the clubs meant it was easy to find a woman and a bed for the night.'

'When you were *fifteen*?'

'I didn't look fifteen. Women like a bad boy. I saved as

much as I could earn. I'd saved ten thousand euros when I was sent to prison and lost it all in legal fees.'

'What did you go to prison for? Fighting, wasn't it?'

'I saw a man in one of the clubs I worked at hitting a woman.' He raised his shoulders. 'I stopped him.'

'You beat him up?'

'He deserved it. He was two times her size. She couldn't defend herself. It was one of many fights I had in those years.' His smile was wry. 'The man I beat up that time was a policeman's son who made sure I went down for it.'

'Was prison really awful?' she asked tentatively.

He pulled a face. 'The worst thing was probably the food. Then the boredom. I had quite an easy time compared to many people but when I left I knew I would never go back. It gave me the focus to change. No more fighting.'

'What about the bedding of beautiful women?' she tried to say in a joking voice.

He pulled another face that quite clearly said she was pushing her luck.

If the thought of him bedding others didn't make her chest contract she would laugh.

'I had a little money left. I took it to a casino.'

'You gambled your savings?'

'A hundred euros. That's all I had left. If I lost it, I would have earned it back the next day and started again but I had a feeling… Like… Like…' His face scrunched as he tried to think of the word, and Anna was reminded that his English was entirely self-taught.

'Do you mean you had a gut instinct?'

'*Si*. That's it. I played it on the roulette table and I won. I won big. I went outside for a cigarette…'

'Since when do you smoke?'

'I haven't for years but I did then. There was another guy out there. He told me about this app he'd designed to track mobile telephone devices. Apps were babies then. Smartphones were babies compared to now. I didn't understand it but I understood that he did. It was a risk but I'd won that money and decided on one last gamble. I put one hundred euros in my pocket and handed the rest to him. We wrote an agreement on a napkin. Two months later he found me and gave me back my investment plus the interest we'd agreed on. For me, it was the start of everything. Smart technology was my future. I didn't know how to develop it for myself but I'd proved I could spot a winner. I backed the brains and reaped the rewards.'

'You've always seemed so confident and knowledgeable about the technologies you invest in,' she said with bemusement.

'That first deal made me one of the first people to see their full potential. I would say I got lucky but luck had nothing to do with it. Instinct and hard work were what got me where I am.' He grinned. 'The best deal I ever made was investing forty per cent in developing that social media site. I made seven billion dollars when it floated on the stock exchange.'

'I remember that.' It had happened before he'd bought Levon Brothers and she'd begun working for him. 'Have you gambled again since that night? In a casino?'

'Gambling is for morons.'

She laughed and drained her glass. 'Your revenge must taste very sweet.'

'It does. Like strawberries and cream at Wimbledon.'

Another burst of laughter escaped her but there was

anger underlying it. 'I'm glad. Your family don't deserve anything after the way they treated you.'

'If they had treated me better, do you think they would have deserved something then?' he asked.

'That's not what I meant,' she protested. 'Your money is yours. You earned it, you're the only one with a right to it. If you choose to share it with anyone then it's that—a choice, not an obligation.'

'You don't think you're entitled to a share of it as my wife?'

'Of course not.'

His eyes burned intensely. 'But say we were to go our separate ways, would you not be tempted to sue for a large share of it?'

'No. And if I know you at all I would gamble my own money that you made me sign a prenup.'

For a brief moment his lips pulled together and his jaw tightened but then his features relaxed. 'We married too quickly for that.'

'So I'm not the only one who lost their marbles, then?'

That made her stomach settle a bit, knowing whatever madness had caught them in its grip to compel them to marry had been mutual. She'd always known Stefano had worked like a lion to build his fortune and enjoyed the fruits of his spoils like a sultan. Until that moment she'd thought she'd understood it but she'd underestimated him. The fight and grit it must have taken for him to build what he had was mind-blowing and her respect for him only grew.

Stefano finished his drink and smiled tightly. 'I think we both went a little mad that day.'

It was an insanity he would never allow himself to fall into again.

Anna put her empty glass on the coffee table. 'Has getting your revenge helped?'

'*Naturalmente.*'

'But has it helped you emotionally? You had such a lot to deal with…'

'It's over,' he interrupted with a shrug. 'I dealt with it at the time and moved on.'

'That's a lot to deal with and you were so young.' Her pretty eyebrows rose disbelievingly. 'I thought I'd been dealt a crummy hand but at least I've always had Melissa.'

Stefano flexed his fingers. He didn't want her sympathy or attempts to delve into his mind.

Anna's actions had hit him in a place his family had never reached.

'We make our own luck and fortune, *bellissima*. The past stays where it is.'

'I'm not so stupid that I don't know my dad's death and my mum's desertion affected me,' she said stubbornly.

'Are you calling me stupid?'

'Of course not. I'm just saying that I don't see how your revenge could have been enough…'

'It was more than enough.' He could feel his ire rising. Anna was the only person who dared speak back to him. They could argue and shout at each other like a pair of wildcats.

Those arguments had always made him feel so alive even before the days when they'd settle cross words in bed.

'We've had a long flight and you're exhausted. Rest for a few hours and then I'll order some food.'

She got to her feet and folded her arms across her

chest. 'Do you always brush me off like this now I'm your wife?'

'I'm not brushing you off; it's just not a subject worth wasting my breath on.'

Seeing her face turn mutinous, he forced a more conciliatory tone of voice. 'Let's not have an argument when we've only just arrived. Come, I'll show you the rest of the house.'

Anna stepped into a bathroom on the second floor with an external wall made entirely of glass.

'I've been in here before,' she said, the words popping out of her mouth as that feeling of déjà vu hit her again, all residue of their almost-argument forgotten.

This memory was more than a feeling though. This one had substance.

She hurried to the glass wall and looked out.

Just as she'd known, the bathroom jutted out over the sunroom on the ground floor giving an immaculate view of the ocean and their strip of private beach.

Excited at this burst of memories, she faced him. 'I remember this! This glass…you can't see in from the outside, can you?' She pointed to the free-standing bath. 'I remember saying how brilliant it would be to have a bath in here and watch the ocean. I *remember.*'

'I didn't think a bath would act as a jogger,' he said drily but with a stiff undertone that made her look at him.

He'd come to stand beside her. His face was inscrutable as he gazed out. 'Are you remembering anything else?'

Her excitement diminished as more longed-for memories stayed stubbornly stuck in the void. 'No.'

'More will come. I don't think it will be long.'

'I hope so,' she said fervently. 'It's so frustrating. You're going to have to fill me in on everything about work if they don't come back soon.'

'Forget work.' He gathered a lock of hair that had fallen onto a shoulder and smoothed it off her neck. 'I don't want you thinking about it until we return to London.'

'I can decide for myself what I think, thank you.'

'Your beautiful mind is one of the many things I adore about you.' He placed his other hand on her neck and gazed down at her. 'But all I want is for you to get better. I'm thinking of you, *bellissima*.'

'I *am* better.'

'Almost.' He stepped closer and inhaled. 'You're almost there.'

CHAPTER SIX

'Do you miss Italy?' Anna asked some hours later. She'd had a three-hour nap in their four-poster bed, which even had muslin curtains, then a shower, and gone downstairs to find Stefano had ordered Italian takeaway for them.

Now they were sitting outside on the terrace, the roar of the Pacific their music.

'I miss the food.' He removed the lid of one large box to reveal a sharing platter of antipasti.

'What about everything else?'

He thought about it. 'I miss speaking my language.'

'Your English and Swedish are excellent and your Japanese is pretty good too.'

'Is not the same. When I speak my language I don't think about the words before I say them. Is natural for me.'

'Okay, so that's the food and the language. Anything else?'

'Our summers are better than in London.'

She gave him the stern look with one raised eyebrow that she'd often fixed him with when she'd worked for him.

'I am Italian. I will always be Italian. It is in my blood and when I retire I will move back there.'

'You? Retire?'

He laughed. 'When I get to fifty I will stop working and enjoy what I have built for myself.'

She smiled. The soft hue of the patio lights lent her face an extra glow that only enhanced her natural beauty. If Stefano didn't know of the poison that lay behind the beautiful façade, he would be entranced.

'I can live with retiring in Italy.'

He made his lips curve. 'You've said that before but I think you will find it hard not to have your sister on the doorstep.'

Her smile faded into a grimace, pain flashing in her eyes. 'I think so too. I want to stay angry with her but it's too hard. She's my sister and whatever's happened between us I still love her.' She blew a puff of air out and shook her head. 'I need to speak to her.'

'You'll be able to soon. She's only away for a month. You two will sort it out, you always do.' As close as the two sisters were, they often argued. Some days Anna would hear her phone ring, see Melissa's name on it and say, 'I'm not in the mood to talk to *her*,' with a scowl. Other times they were quite capable of spending two hours on the phone, their conversations only coming to a close when one of their phone batteries ran out.

It came to him that when he went ahead with his plan to humiliate her at the awards ceremony she wouldn't have her sister to turn to.

Before his conscience could start nagging at him about this, he opened the bottle of wine he'd placed on the table and poured himself a healthy glass.

Anna stared from him to her own glass and the jug of iced water he'd put beside it, her nose wrinkling.

With equal parts amusement and irritation, he watched her pour herself some wine.

'You shouldn't be drinking.'

She rolled her eyes. 'One glass isn't going to kill me.'

'You have to be the worst-behaved patient.'

'You've lived with me for a year. That shouldn't be news to you.' She took a chunk of focaccia and dipped it in the *pinzimonio* before popping it into her mouth whole and devouring it with relish.

It was the first time she'd eaten anything with enthusiasm since her injury.

Suddenly he remembered all the meals they'd shared together and her love of good food. Anna had an appetite that belied her petite figure. This wasn't the first sharing platter they'd had between them, and when she picked up a tooth pick to swipe the largest bite of Parmigiano Reggiano before he could take it, the boulder that had been lodged in his throat settled in his chest.

'I've never known you to be ill before,' he said.

'Melissa says it's like caring for an adolescent toddler.'

He laughed at the mental image this provoked.

'I haven't taken a painkiller all day,' she pointed out. 'And speaking of sisters, you never did tell me how yours found you. Her name's Christina?'

'*Sì.* Christina. She reached out to me when our father died.'

'So your father was alive all this time?'

He nodded with a grimace. 'All those years I thought he was dead he was living in Naples, not even a two-hour drive away. I even had his name wrong—I always believed he was called Marco but it was Mario.'

'How awful.' Her hazel eyes were dark with the same

empathy he'd seen in them earlier. 'He was so near to you all that time? Didn't he want to see you?'

'He wasn't allowed.' There was little point in evading the subject. Anna had that look about her that meant she would chip away until she had all the answers she desired. It was what made her so good at her job: that refusal to leave any stone unturned. 'My *nonno* paid him to leave Lazio before I was born. He blamed him for my mother's addiction. My father took the money and ran, then he grew up and got himself straight, got a job and a place to live. He tried to get in touch with my mother and learned she had died. Nonno didn't trust him and told him to stay away from me. Rightly or wrongly, he agreed. He didn't trust himself any more than Nonno did but he did stay clean, met another woman and had a child with her—Christina. His wife encouraged him to get in touch with me directly but by then Nonno had died and I'd been kicked out by the rest of my family and living on the streets. He couldn't find me.'

'But he looked?'

'He looked, *sì*, but at that time I often used different names and I never gave my real age. He was searching for someone that didn't exist.'

'What about when you started to make a success of yourself?' she asked with wide eyes. 'Did he not realise it was you, his son?'

'He knew,' Stefano confirmed grimly. 'But he thought I wouldn't want to see him; that I would think he only wanted to claim me as his son to get some of my fortune.'

All those years he'd blithely assumed his father was a no-good junkie who didn't want him. But he *had* wanted him. His father had wanted to put things right. And now it was too late and he would never know him and never be able to tell him that he forgave him. His parents had been little more than children when they'd conceived him, and immature, addicted children at that.

While they'd been talking, they'd cleared the antipasti so all that remained were the pickled vegetables neither of them particularly liked.

'My father left me this watch.' He rolled his sleeve up to show it to her.

She looked at it with a pained expression, taking in the shabbiness of the leather strap and the scratches on the glass, then looked back at him. Her smile was tender. 'At least he died knowing you'd made a success of yourself. That must have given him comfort.'

He nodded and took the lids off their main courses, biting back the sudden anger that rushed through him that she could act so supportive now, when her platitudes were worthless.

Christina had given him a letter written by their father. He'd said Stefano had made him proud.

He'd never made anyone proud before.

He served the *linguine con le vongole* onto Anna's plate. She beamed. 'That's my favourite.'

'I know.' He served his lemon sole onto his own plate and took a bite.

Anna, who was a real pasta lover, twisted some linguini onto her fork, stabbed a clam, and asked, 'When did you learn all this?' before popping it into her mouth.

'A month ago.'

He'd learned the truth about his father while Anna was away with Melissa in Paris, the night before she'd flown back early and stormed into his boardroom to accuse him of having an affair. And he'd thought treating

Anna and her sister to a few days away together would be a good thing!

She'd called and left a message but he'd spent most of the night with Christina, talking and steadily making their way through numerous bottles of wine. He hadn't seen Anna's message until he'd gone to bed at four in the morning; too late to call her back. Then, with hardly any sleep, he'd had to get his heavy head to the office, leaving his new-found sister in the apartment.

While he'd been reeling over the discovery of a grown-up sister and a father who *had* wanted him, Anna had flown home early with the sole intention of catching him with another. Why else would she have come back, armed with accusations, without leaving a message of warning?

He'd been fool enough to think she cared when all she'd ever wanted from him was his money.

They ate in silence for a while before she asked, 'What's Christina like?'

'Very young, not long turned twenty but young for her age and very sheltered.' He pushed his dark thoughts about his beautiful wife to one side and smiled wryly. 'Reading between the lines, our father was afraid to let her out of his sight in case he lost her as he lost me. But we're building a relationship.'

'Has she been staying with us?'

'No.' Anna, damn her, was the only person he'd ever been able to stomach living with. 'I've rented a flat for her in London and she's doing some work experience at the office.'

'She doesn't have a job?'

'She'd just started her second year at university when our father was diagnosed with cancer. They thought they had more time so she arranged with the university to take the year off and return next September. Until then, she's going to stay in London and work for me and improve her English.'

'What about her mother?'

'She's in Naples but will be coming to London at Christmas.' Seeing Anna open her mouth to ask another question, he said, 'How's your meal?'

As with the rest of his life he had no qualms about discussing it but Anna had this way of listening that made him want to talk about more than the facts, to lay bare everything living under his skin.

It was an unburdening he'd fought to escape from in their marriage and he was damned if he would do it now when their relationship was days away from being over for good. The only unburdening he wanted from her was her clothes.

Anna was ripe for seduction, just as he wanted.

If he took her into his arms there would be only the slightest resistance. He could see it in the eyes that undressed him with every hungry look.

But something still held him back from acting on it. Whether it was the hint of vulnerability that still lingered in her eyes or the wine she'd been drinking when she really shouldn't so soon after her concussion he couldn't say, but, either way, not even his deplorable conscience would allow him to act on his desire yet. When he made love to her again he wanted to be certain that it was the Anna he'd married he was making love to. The vulnerability was almost gone. Almost. And when he was certain she was as well as she could be then, and only then, would he seduce her into an ecstasy she would remember for the rest of her life.

'It's beautiful, thank you.'

He raised his glass. *'Salute.'*

'What are we drinking to?'

'To us. You and me, and a marriage you will remember for ever.'

Anna's belly was comfortably full. It was the only comfortable part of her anatomy.

They'd long finished their meal and the bottle of wine and now sat, Stefano's eyes burning into her while she waited almost breathlessly for him to suggest they go to bed.

Heat flowed through her veins as her imagination ran amok wondering what it would be like, what it would *feel* like, to be made love to by him. To have that hard, naked chest she pictured every time she closed her eyes pressed against hers…

'Earth to Anna,' he said, elbow on the table, cheek resting on his hand, a gleam in his eyes that made her wonder if during their marriage he'd developed the power to read her thoughts. 'What are you thinking that makes your eyes glaze over like that?'

He flirted with her, he was tactile, he left her in no doubt he couldn't wait to bed her again…but so far he'd made no real move on her.

Was he waiting for her assent?

When she'd woken up three mornings ago feeling as if she might die, she'd had no idea that she was married. No idea that she'd shared a bed and her body with someone, let alone him.

Stefano was the only man she'd ever fantasised about. The only man she'd ever wanted. Her brain might not remember what he did to her but her body did. It ached for him with an intensity that made her bones liquefy.

And she was married to him! At some point in her past she'd found the courage to confirm her desire for him, both in words and deed.

She took a breath and looked him right in the eye. 'I was thinking that it's time for bed.'

He returned her gaze then slowly nodded. 'Go ahead. I'll join you later.'

She wasn't quick enough to hide her dismay. 'Aren't you coming with me?'

His eyes flashed before he closed them and inhaled slowly. 'I'm not tired enough to sleep yet.'

But she didn't want to sleep and she was damned sure he knew that.

Stung at his rejection, Anna got quickly to her feet. 'I'll see you in the morning, then. Night.'

'Anna.'

She ignored him to dart away from the table, not wanting him to see the mortification she knew would be written all over her face.

After all his innuendoes and hungry looks, he was rejecting her?

She couldn't escape from the terrace quickly enough.

'Anna,' he repeated in a voice that demanded to be obeyed.

Almost at the door, she reluctantly turned to face him. 'What?'

Under the soft glowing light she saw a knowing tenderness on his handsome face that took a little of the sting away.

'You're beautiful.'

His words were so unexpected that she found herself gazing from the simple blue shift dress she'd chosen from her enormous dressing room, slipping it on with thoughts of Stefano in her mind, to him, the man she ached to make love to.

Then he smiled wryly, poured himself another glass of wine and raised it to her. 'Sleep well, *bellissima.*'

The house was eerily silent when Stefano headed down the stairs the next morning wearing only his robe.

He found Anna at his desk in his office, his laptop open in front of her.

'What are you doing?' he asked with an easiness that belied the impulse to slam the lid shut.

'Trying to hack into your laptop.' She didn't look at him, and nor did she look or sound the slightest bit penitent at what she was doing.

'You can't get into your own phone. What makes you think you can hack into this?'

'Because you're extremely predictable with what you use as your password.'

Stefano had always given her free access to his laptop when she worked for him and he'd trusted her with his often-changing passwords for it. Of course, he only used it for work purposes and it was for this reason he didn't want her getting into it now. It would take her all of a minute to discover that he'd sacked her and then all his plans would come tumbling down. Everything would come out and the revenge he was working so carefully towards would be ruined.

He ignored the nagging feeling in his guts that it might just be a good thing for his plans to be ruined. 'What do you want it for?'

'To get onto the Internet.'

'Why? To email Melissa?'

'I agree with you that I shouldn't speak to her yet but she must be worrying that she can't get in touch with me.'

'If she's worried she'll contact the office. They'll tell her where we are.' And then Melissa really would have something to worry about. She knew all about their vicious split.

All he had to do was stop Anna contacting her for four more days.

Her eyes lifted to meet his. She scowled but not before he read the hurt on her face.

He hid his satisfaction.

She was still smarting at his rejection of her the night before. Declining her open invitation had taken a huge amount of willpower and he'd had to keep himself rooted to the chair to resist following her inside and up to the bedroom. *Dio*, he had wanted her so badly it was a physical pain. Now, in the cold light of day, he could hardly believe he'd been so selfless. Being selfless was not on his list of attributes.

There was no hint of any vulnerability in those flashing hazel eyes now. And she was stone-cold sober.

'Is something troubling you, *bellissima*?'

'No.'

He sat on the edge of the desk beside her, taking in the tight shorts and the coral T-shirt that caressed her small, beautiful breasts.

Her jaw clenched and she stabbed at the keyboard and hit return.

Suddenly her face brightened and she cast him with a wicked grin. 'I'm in!'

The grin fell when she saw what was on the screen.

It was a letter of termination he'd got Chloe to write for one of the men who worked in his development lab.

He'd been reading through it before he'd remembered a meeting he was supposed to be at. Forgetting a meeting would never have happened when Anna was running the place alongside him. He'd left the laptop open and had just arrived at the meeting when a breathless member of staff had run up to inform him that his estranged wife had barged her way into his office.

He'd closed the laptop without shutting it down on his return from the hospital and hadn't opened it since.

'You're sacking Peter?' she said, reading it quickly.

'He's been selling patent application details to one of our rivals.'

'You have proof of this?'

'Enough for me not to give him the benefit of the doubt.'

'Have you confronted him?' she asked suspiciously.

'We had a little chat.'

'Did I sit in on it?'

'It was just me and him. I wanted to give him the chance to confess. His behaviour in that meeting was very…what's the word? When someone can't sit still or talk properly?'

'Nervous? Jittery?'

'Both of those. His body language made his guilt obvious.'

'For heaven's sake, Stefano,' she exploded, sliding the chair back to slam against the wall. '*Anyone* hauled in for a private chat with you is going to act nervous and jittery. You can be terrifying and Peter is a nervous soul as it is.'

'Someone is selling secrets from that department. Too many things are being leaked and he's the only person it can be.'

'Maybe the system's been hacked!'

'Maybe we have a traitor in our team.'

'Who in their right mind would turn traitor on you?' Now she was on her feet with her hands on her hips. 'You're a terrifying ogre but on the whole you're a good person to work for. You pay extremely well and you're generous with perks—you've one of the highest staff retention rates in the industry! I *know* Peter. You hired him as a graduate only a couple of months after you hired me. He's as timid as a mouse but one of the brightest brains you've got, and he's *loyal*. Are you really going to sack him without concrete proof?'

'I can't risk keeping him on!' He conveniently forgot to mention that neither Peter nor any of his other staff or even his business had crossed his mind since she'd collapsed at his feet.

'Have you even looked into the possibility that one of your rivals has infiltrated the system?'

'Our system is foolproof as you very well know!' he shouted back.

'Rubbish! If even the Pentagon can be broken into then your system can be too. Do you want to ruin a life with no proof? Do you want to be sued for unfair dismissal?'

'No one has grounds to sue me.'

'Of course they do, you moron, if you treat them like this.'

'Now you're calling me a *moron*?'

'If the boot fits then wear it!'

This was what he'd missed in his month without her; someone to call him out and make him see things from a different angle. Everyone else was too damn scared to speak up.

Everything had gone wrong since she'd left him. He

couldn't think straight, too consumed with his anger and humiliation at her hands to think clearly.

Anna would never have let him meet an employee without a witness to report the unbiased facts and protect both parties.

That he had the highest staff retention rates in the industry was down to her. Sure, all the wages and perks were his to be proud of but with Anna gone there was no one there to fight the staff's corner, no counterbalance, no one to make him listen to reason.

This was just as it had always been between them, Anna thought through the blood pounding in her brain.

Stefano was facing her with the same angry stance she knew she must have, both of them glaring and snarling at each other until one of them backed down and apologised.

Except this time she was wearing only a pair of skimpy shorts and a tiny T-shirt, and he...

He was wearing a loosely tied dark grey robe with nothing underneath.

And then, without her knowing how she got there, she was in his arms, his mouth devouring hers, he was kissing her, she was kissing him, in the way she'd yearned to for so, so long.

Sensation such as she'd never known existed skipped over her skin and down into her pores. His tongue swept into her mouth, their lips dancing to a tune she hadn't known she'd already learnt, and she swayed into him, closing her mind to everything but the feelings firing through her.

This was everything she'd been dreaming of and more. His taste, his scent, the feel of his lips, the roughness of his stubbly jaw, the strength of his arms and the hardness of his chest crushed against her… It was heat in its purest, most carnal form.

He rubbed his cheek into her neck and clasped her to him. His other hand gathered her hair together into a sheath and roughly, yet gently, he pulled her head back.

'Now do you understand why we married?' he asked coarsely. 'That night we both drank more champagne than was good for us and I took advantage of it to kiss you, just as I did now, and you kissed me back.'

His hand holding her ground her to him.

She gasped to feel him huge and hard against her abdomen.

No wonder they'd married so quickly. If she'd felt even a fraction of the desire in that car as was swirling through her now…it was the headiest feeling imaginable. No wonder she'd demanded marriage. It was the only thing that would have a hope in hell of putting him off the idea and leaving her safe.

Yes! It wasn't a memory that came to her then but a feeling, a certainty that this was how it had played out.

She'd had no idea the attraction she'd held so long for him would turn her into fondue at his touch. She would have had to scramble to hold on to her sanity. But Stefano's own sanity had been scrambled too and he'd agreed to her flippant remark.

She didn't need to hold on to her sanity now.

They had made love many times in their marriage, and now she would get to experience it for the very first time all over again…

Fresh sanity suddenly struck her.

She didn't know what to do.

Stefano felt her hesitation.

Cupping her cheeks in his hands, he gazed deep into

her eyes and saw nerves merging with the desire, just as he'd seen the first time they'd made love on their wedding night, and with it he remembered that she had no memories of their lovemaking. None at all.

Sex was the only aspect of their marriage he had no doubts about. Clever little liar that she was, no one could fake those reactions. It had never been a case of going through the motions for a quick release but a real, deep connection that had scorched them both. He knew he would never find that with anyone else and he hated her for it; hated her for destroying his faith in what they'd shared.

For a few more days he could enjoy it all again but this, their first time together in over a month, was the first time for Anna. He had to remember that. When she'd confessed her virginity, although shocked, he could not deny his primal reaction had been elation that he would be her one and only.

'I'm not making love to you in here,' he said hoarsely before sweeping her into his arms.

She hooked her arms around his neck but the trepidation was still there. 'Why did you reject me last night?'

'Because I was waiting for my Anna to come back. When you shouted at me so passionately...' he kissed the tip of her nose '...I knew it was you.'

CHAPTER SEVEN

STEFANO SHIFTED HIS HOLD so she was secure in his arms and carried her up the stairs.

His Anna, he thought with a possessiveness that caught him off guard.

Only his.

But only for a few more days.

He couldn't think of that right now. Right now it didn't matter that the whole reason they were here was so he could seduce her so thoroughly that when he publicly ended things between them she had the added humiliation of knowing she had willingly lost herself to his touch and screamed out the name of the man who was playing with her all along. All he wanted at that moment was to sink himself into Anna's tight heat and lose himself in her.

The bedroom door was open, the bed sheets still unmade from the frustrated, tortured sleep he knew they'd both shared.

Something *more* had made him wait until he'd been certain she would be asleep before joining her, and it wasn't just that he'd wanted to be sure she was truly recovered and sober. It was that nagging in his guts speaking to him, putting doubts in his mind.

Now, having shared those searing kisses and felt her taut and hungry against him…

He laid her on the bed and in a moment had shed his robe and climbed on top of her.

Anna waited for him to kiss her again. He'd placed his hands either side of her head, his legs long and lean between her thighs, and he was staring at her…

He was staring at her as if he could eat her whole.

She thought of all the women that had been before her, those faceless women she had been desperate to keep away from, desperate not to know, terrified that if any of them were to meet her they would recognise the secret feminine signs of a woman in love. She had feared their pity. She had feared she would hate them for it. Now she was the one to pity them.

It wasn't possible that Stefano had looked at another with the hunger with which he was looking at her.

Stefano was hers. All hers. She would never share him with anyone.

How beautiful he was, as if sculpted in marble by a master and then injected with life. To feel him against her inner thigh, hot and ready, his own desire wholly evident even to a novice such as her…

Flames licked her everywhere.

She reached out to touch him again, pressing her hand to his chest, feeling the heavy thuds of his heart. She sighed and closed her eyes.

Never had she imagined his skin would be so warm and smooth to her touch, or that the fine dark hair that covered his chest would feel so silky. Slowly she trailed her fingers down to the hard muscle beneath the damp skin of his abdomen and heard his sharp intake of breath.

Still gazing at her, he took hold of her top and, with only the smallest movement from her, pulled it off.

His devouring gaze took in every inch of her but she was far too gone to feel any embarrassment. Her only moment of shyness came when he tugged her shorts down and exposed her most private area. Even that shyness flew away at his deep groan.

'*Dio*, you have the sexiest body,' he said in a pained voice. Then he brought his mouth back down on hers and she wound her arms around him and responded with all the passion alive in her heart.

Fresh heat enflamed her body, desire uncurling inside her, the yearning for Stefano's possession growing.

And as she rejoiced in all these wonderful sensations, she was jolted from the moment with a thought that had her turn from his hot mouth to gasp, 'What do we use for contraception?'

'You've had those injections since we got back from our honeymoon,' he muttered raggedly, hardly pausing for breath before his lips found her neck and her heart accelerated at the thrill racing over her skin and the burning in her veins, all worries of contraception happily dispatched.

Everything was heightened, all her senses were converging together. She started as she felt his mouth on her breast, then shut out the last of her nerves and succumbed fully to the pleasure being evoked in her every last cell.

His mouth and hands were everywhere, kissing, nibbling, stroking every inch, bringing her desire to a boil that was on the cusp of spilling over. Every touch scorched, every kiss burned and soon she wanted so much more than this heavenly torture. When his lips found hers again, she parted her thighs at the same moment he put a hand to them.

He muttered something, shifted, then took hold of himself and suddenly she felt him there, right at the place she most wanted him to be, and just as suddenly her fears returned and she froze.

Stefano must have sensed something wrong for he stopped what he was about to do and, the tip of his erection still poised in the apex of her thighs, stared intently into her eyes.

'There is nothing to fear, *bellissima*,' he whispered. 'Nothing at all. I would never hurt you.'

His lips came back down on hers and she returned the heady pressure of his kiss. As his tongue swept into her mouth she wrapped her arms around him then cried into his mouth as she felt him push inside her, so slowly and with such care that she could have actually shed tears.

But then all thoughts of crying were swept away because *he was inside her*.

All her fears were unfounded. There was no pain. She'd known in her head that there couldn't be, that her virginity was only in her head, but that sensible voice hadn't been enough to quell her anxiety that somehow her body would have forgotten along with her mind.

There was only pleasure. Deep, radiating pleasure.

In their time together Stefano must have learned exactly what she liked because the thrusts he was making inside her felt heaven-sent.

His movements increased, the groans coming from his mouth in her ear making the pulsations inside her thicken. She put her lips to his neck and inhaled his tangy, musky scent, driving him deeper and deeper into her.

The world became a distant blur, shrinking down to

just them and this magical moment. The secret torch she'd carried for him for so, so long had been lit into a furnace and all she could do was let the heat from it burn until it reached its peak and she was crying out his name, over and over, pleasure rippling through her in long waves.

Stefano gave a hoarse groan and drove so deeply inside her at his own climax that she wrapped her legs even tighter around him, wanting to savour every last bit of this incredible moment.

When he collapsed on her with his face in the crook of her neck, she held him tightly. She dragged her hands up the length of his muscular back and up to his head, threading her fingers through the thick dark hair. She could feel his heartbeat hammering in time to hers and thrilled to know that he too had felt the joy she had experienced.

'Is it always like that?' she asked when she had finally caught her breath. Dull pulses still throbbed inside her.

He gave a sound like a laugh and lifted his head. A smile played on his lips. 'Always.'

The next morning Anna woke up in her second strange bed of the week—the third if one counted the hospital bed—and stretched before turning her head to the sleeping figure beside her.

The early morning light illuminated him perfectly and for the first time she allowed herself the pleasure of gazing at Stefano without interruption from the doubts in her own head.

Making love to him had been beyond anything her imagination could have conjured up.

She covered her mouth to stifle the laugh that wanted to explode from her. If she'd ever imagined it to be even half as good as it had been she would have resigned on the spot. There was no way she could have dealt with working by his side day by day with those rampant thoughts.

The second time had been even better. And by their third time the last of her inhibitions had been vanquished.

Having got so little sleep she should be shattered but she wasn't. She had never felt anything like this, as if there were a beehive in her chest, all the worker bees buzzing to make honey inside her.

Climbing out of the bed carefully so as not to wake him—although, as she'd already learned, an earthquake would have trouble disrupting Stefano's sleep—she tiptoed naked out of the bedroom and walked to the bathroom at the other end of the landing.

She shut the door behind her and headed straight to the window to look out at the cerulean sky.

It was going to be a glorious day, she could feel it in her bones.

She ran the bath and added liberal amounts of bubble bath to it, then climbed in.

Doing nothing more than lying there in the steamy suds, she gazed out at the beach. In the distance she could see someone walking a small dog, the first signs of life in Santa Cruz. She wondered if she and Stefano had ever spoken of getting a dog. She'd had one as a child, a soppy cocker spaniel that had been as daft as a brush and as useful a guard dog as a packet of pasta.

An image came into her mind, so vivid that she bolted upright.

Making love to Stefano in their London apartment.

She hugged her knees, the image forming, becoming more than just a picture in her head. This was a memory, pure bona fide remembrance of them being together.

Anna had no idea how long she sat in that bath, her attention wrenched away from the view, thinking as hard as she had ever done, so hard her brain hurt. It wasn't until there was a tap on the bathroom door that she realised the bathwater had turned cold and the bubbles gone.

'Come in,' she called, startled out of her reverie.

Stefano strode in wearing nothing but a pair of white cotton boxers slung low on his hips and a sexy lopsided grin. His sleep-tousled hair swayed as he walked to her and crouched down to rest his arms on the side of the bath.

'You should be in bed.'

She raised a brow at him, her senses jumping in so many directions just to see him so that it took a moment to find her tongue. 'I'm remembering things.'

Stefano's stomach lurched.

He'd woken to an empty bed and with only one thought in his mind, namely finding his wife and dragging her back to it. In the middle world of sleep and waking, and distracted by the ache in his groin, this time *he'd* been the one to forget everything.

He searched her face carefully. There didn't seem to be anything dark or suspicious lurking in her clear gaze, only animation.

He allowed himself a small breath of relief. 'What are you remembering?'

'Us. Patches of us. Our wedding.' Her cheeks flushed with colour and she lowered her voice. 'Making love for the first time.'

'What are your memories of that?'

She palmed his face with her hand, a look of bliss spreading across her beautiful face. 'It was wonderful. *You* were wonderful.'

His chest filled with emotion. 'What else?'

'Business meetings. Did you promote me?'

He nodded. 'Nick retired. I gave the job to you.'

Her eyes widened. 'You put me on the board of directors?'

'Who else would I trust to keep the place running when I had to travel? You're an exceptional businesswoman—the whole board was behind your appointment. And not just because they're scared of me,' he added, before she could quip that they would back anything he said out of fear.

In hindsight he recognised that promoting Anna had been when their troubles had begun. As his PA she had travelled everywhere with him. As Vice President of Moretti's UK, second only to the US in his burgeoning technology empire, she had needed to be on hand in the UK when he travelled to America. They'd gone from seeing each other all day every day and sleeping together every night to spending up to a week apart at a time. That was when those insecurities had set in.

But she'd been—acted—insecure from the beginning, he reminded himself. Her accelerated promotion had only given her the tools to up her campaign.

Yet the wonderment ringing out from her eyes at this moment put more doubts in his head.

Anna was clever and stubborn. She could by turn be sweet then sour. She was good cop to his bad cop but people were always aware that her being good cop did not make her a pushover. If she thought someone was being an idiot she had no qualms about telling them so, just as she had no qualms about telling him. Until she'd hit him with that ludicrous demand for a hundred million pounds of his fortune she would have been the last person he'd suspect of being a gold-digger. The last person he would have suspected of having an agenda. He'd trusted her as he hadn't trusted anyone since his *nonno* had died and to discover it had all been a lie had shattered him in ways he couldn't explain even to himself.

Her fingers gently massaged his cheek. It was such a simple sign of affection but one that made his heart expand.

'I don't remember everything,' she whispered, bringing her face to his so the sweetness of her breath sighed against his skin. 'All that I remember of us as a married couple is spending long days in the office and long nights making love. I don't remember falling in love with you but I know that I did. I *know* I did. I can feel it as clearly as I can feel the bristles on your jaw where you need to shave.'

And then her eyes closed and her lips pressed against his, not moving, just breathing him in.

Stefano gripped the back of her head and held her tightly to him to deepen the kiss, his mind and heart racing.

She spoke of love? *Love?* That was a word neither of them had ever said before.

That was *not* what their marriage was about.

Then what was it about?

It had been about desire. The primal need for a mate. A partner. Someone to have *bambinos* with.

He had long wanted children. To have a child would be to ice the delicious cake that was his life. His hated cousins had an abundance of them, and he'd beaten them in everything except in the *bambino* stakes. But to have children he needed to find a woman to have them with and he hadn't trusted any of the women in his life with a vase, never mind a child. Still, he'd looked forward to seeing miniature versions of himself running around and causing havoc one day; a bloodline to pass his wealth on to.

He'd be damned if he'd leave anything to the other members of his family.

When he'd started making waves in the world of technology, and journalists had learned of his rags-to-riches background, the shady acquaintances of his early years, the prison sentence…suddenly they had wanted to interview him and hear his story from his own lips. He'd been happy to oblige, especially if it involved having his photo taken in front of his yacht or his private plane. Stefano had become a poster boy for the kids of Lazio, an icon to look up to, the local bad boy who'd turned out good. He didn't doubt for a minute that his family, who all still lived in the same homes in the same close-knit area he'd been dragged up in, knew everything about him. And he didn't doubt that his success made them sick.

See? he would say to them through the lens of the camera. *This is what you threw away. If you'd treated me like the orphan boy of your blood that I was and not like some kind of wild animal, these riches would have been yours.* He was Italian after all! Life and its riches were for sharing with family. But he'd decided when he was fifteen that he had no family. Everything he earned, every penny of it, was his and his alone.

When Anna had so flippantly—but trembling after that first passionate kiss they'd shared—declared that if he wanted to bed her he'd have to marry her, he'd known by the next morning that she would be the mother of his children. There was no one better suited. They worked fantastically well together, shared a chemistry that was off the charts and they already knew each other's faults. Marriage and babies together? Well, why not? If not her then who? At least life with Anna would be fun, he'd thought. And she was straight down the line. As sexy as a nymph. He'd trusted her. But love? Love was for romantic fools who needed to put a name to their desire rather than just accepting it for what it was: chemistry.

The only person who had ever shown him love or affection was his *nonno*. When he'd died, Stefano had quickly learned he was not a person to inspire affection. As he'd grown older and started catching the eye of beautiful women, he'd discovered lust but had known their desire for him was based solely on his physical attributes. If they could see him without the outer shell, they would be repelled.

Anna was the only person since his *nonno* to see beneath that shell and still want him. He had never repelled her. He'd infuriated her—yes, he could admit to that— but seeing the real man hadn't made her run. She was level-headed enough not to want to try to change him.

In her own way, she was a misfit like him. They'd understood each other as no one else could.

But then she'd so spectacularly accused, humiliated and dumped him and he'd realised that it had all been an act. What Anna had seen beneath his shell *had* repelled her but she had bided her time until she'd been in a position to go for the kill and take him for everything she could get.

Had she planned her scheme right from the beginning as he'd thought since that torrid black moment in his boardroom? Or had it formed over time...?

Things were getting confused in his head. He had to focus. He mustn't let what was happening between them now and her words of love cloud his judgement any further.

The feelings she was now mistaking for love were its opposite: hate. Only the utmost loathing of him could have made Anna do what she had done. If she'd felt even a flicker of love for him she would never have gone through with her grand plan.

And now he loathed her. *His* grand plan was coming together better than he could have hoped.

Stefano pushed the disquiet in his guts aside with force and concentrated on the desire blazing in his loins. He lifted her out of the bath and carried her wrapped in an enormous towel to their bed.

They spent the day making love but, during the spent times when they dozed, he couldn't shake the voice in his head telling him that his plan was in danger of un-ravelling.

Anna's dressing room in their Santa Cruz beach house was even larger than the one she had in Stefano's London penthouse. It took for ever to rifle through the racks of clothes, all of which still had their tags on. She guessed they hadn't spent much time here since they'd bought the house.

After much internal debate she selected a pear-green silk sleeveless wraparound dress that was cinched at the waist and fell like soft leaves to the knees, held together by a thin belt studded with dainty diamonds. She also earmarked a gorgeous red dress to wear to tomorrow night's awards ceremony.

Delving further into the shelves uncovered a shoe-lov-er's paradise and, after much consideration that involved trying on half a dozen pairs, she settled on sky-high beige

diamond-encrusted mesh heels that she suspected she
would never have been able to afford even if she'd set
aside a whole month of her generous salary.

Stefano had never stinted on displaying his wealth.
It seemed that same generosity extended to his wife, a
thought that sent a pang through her chest. Four whole
days in Santa Cruz, just the two of them, had revealed a
side to her husband she had only suspected before. Not
only was Stefano an amazingly considerate lover but he
was considerate of *her*. It was the little things, like holding her hand to keep her steady when she got out of the
swimming pool; taking her beach towel a long distance
from her to shake the sand from it…all the little things that
made her heart swell and made her rethink her original
assumption that she'd lost her marbles by marrying him.

Marrying Stefano had clearly been the sanest thing
she'd ever done. Their first anniversary was only days
away, proof that they must have been happy together
and that Stefano had kept his promise of fidelity. She
just wished she remembered more than snapshots of it.

She must find an anniversary present for him. They
were going to San Francisco tomorrow morning ahead
of the awards ceremony. She'd see if she could sneak out
and get him something there.

She checked her reflection one last time and left her
dressing room.

She found Stefano hunched over the end of the bed
reading something on his phone. He looked up as she
entered.

His eyes gleamed and a slow smile spread over his
handsome face. '*Bellissima*, you look beautiful.' Then
his eyes drifted down to her feet. 'Should you be wearing shoes that high in your condition?'

'What condition?'

'You've had severe concussion,' he reminded her.

She waved his concern away. 'I feel fine…' But as she said the words something tapped at her, another of those sensations of déjà vu she kept experiencing.

Condition…

The image of an oblong stick with a small window flashed through her mind. 'Have I been pregnant?'

His brows drew together. 'No. What makes you think that?'

'I don't know.' She blinked and shook her head in an attempt to clear the image.

He got to his feet and stepped over to her. He put a hand on her shoulder, peering at her intently. 'Anna? Are you feeling okay?'

She nodded then shook her head again. This was awful. There was something in her memories screaming to escape but she was helpless to find it. All she knew with any certainty was that this memory was bad and the only thing soothing her heightening fears was the sensation of Stefano's hand against her bare skin.

She took a shaky breath. 'Are you *sure* I've not been pregnant?' She didn't see how she could have been if she had used the injectable contraceptive.

'Very sure. I told you we said we would try for a baby one day in the future. Are you getting memories of that?'

'I don't know what I'm getting memories of.' She sighed, loosening the panic that had been trying to crawl up her throat. 'Nothing's clear.'

'It will come. Give it time.'

'You keep saying that. What if they never come back?'

'They will.' His fingers slipped lightly over the shoulders of her dress and rested in the arch of her neck. His gaze didn't leave hers.

Her chest filled with a feeling that was tight yet also fluid, moving through her veins and into her limbs; she was intensely aware of his closeness and the sensations shimmering through her at his touch.

One touch and she was a slave for more.

She looped her arms around his neck. 'What time have you booked the table for?'

The best way to shake off the dark uncertainty that kept trying to cloud her was by making love. Stefano's touch drove all her fears away.

He laughed huskily into her ear. 'We're already late.'

CHAPTER EIGHT

THE RESTAURANT STEFANO had booked them into was a short walk from their home in the Westside of Santa Cruz. Anna adored the clean, affluent neighbourhood. This was a district to soak up culture, enjoy the amusements and raise children.

Why did she keep thinking of children? And why did it feel like a blade in the chest whenever she did?

She pushed the thoughts aside. This was their last night in Santa Cruz and she wanted to enjoy every last minute of it, not have her unreliable mind take her in directions she couldn't understand.

The Thai Emerald was, as the name suggested, a Thai restaurant, located on the bustling beachfront.

She glimpsed a small room with a handful of tables before they were whisked up narrow stairs to a bright, spacious room with an open front overlooking the beach.

They were shown to a small square table near the front and menus were laid before them. Their drink order was taken and then they were alone.

Anna read her menu with a contentment in her heart she couldn't remember feeling since childhood.

'You look happy,' Stefano observed with a smile.

She beamed at him. 'Thai food is another favourite.'

'I know.'

'Do we ever cook?'

'No.'

He answered so firmly that she laughed. 'Melissa always did the cooking and I did the cleaning...' Her voice tailed off as she thought of her sister.

'You are most particular about tidiness,' he said with a grin.

'Melissa says I'm a control freak.'

'You like order. There's nothing wrong with that. I'm the same.'

The waiter came to their table with their wine and poured them each a glass.

'I've been thinking,' Anna said once their food order had been taken. 'I'm going to get in touch with Melissa when we get back to London.'

'I thought you were going to wait until she got home?'

'I'll drive myself crazy if I wait that long.' She sighed. 'I miss her. I can't wait another three weeks to speak to her. I'll borrow your phone if that's okay and call her.'

He nodded thoughtfully. 'If you're sure.'

'I am. I just feel...' She shook her head. 'Betrayed. I know it's selfish of me but I want to know why. After everything Mum did to us, to up and leave to celebrate a birthday with her? I mean, she left us. She left me in Melissa's care when I was fourteen years old and scarpered to the other side of the world to live with a man she'd known for only a few months. What kind of woman does that? What kind of *mother* does that?'

How many times had he heard all this? she wondered when he didn't answer.

Her mother wasn't a topic Anna liked to discuss. It was the judgement call she could read in people's eyes when they learned about it, as if they were wondering what kind of daughter she must have been if her own mother abandoned her so soon after her father had died.

It was something that ate at her. What kind of hateful child must she have been to elicit that desertion?

But Stefano was her husband so it was only natural that in the course of their marriage she had opened up to him. And all he was doing right then was listening to a story she must have shared however many times but couldn't stop relaying again now.

'I often wonder what would have happened if I hadn't put my foot down and refused to go with her. I don't see how our relationship would be any different other than the fact I would have been on the other side of the world to my sister. Melissa couldn't have gone. She'd just started university and was starting her adult life. I didn't want to leave her or my friends. I didn't want to leave my father.'

'Your father was dead,' he pointed out quietly. 'Didn't you want your mother to be happy?'

'Of *course* I did but it was so soon; his death was so sudden.' Her father had been killed when a wall had collapsed on him at the building site he was a manager of. 'All my life it had been the four of us, a tight family unit... How could she have loved Dad if she started seeing Mick so quickly after burying him? How can you visit a grave when you're on the other side of the world?' She rubbed her eyes, only slightly aware that they were wet. Where had those tears come from? She hadn't wasted tears on her mother in years. 'And how can you leave your fourteen-year-old daughter behind?'

'She knew Melissa would look after you.'

'Melissa was only eighteen. She shouldn't have been

put in that position.' She inhaled deeply, trying to keep her composure, but the tears leaking from her eyes seemed to have a life of their own. 'She was as devastated as I was at what Mum was doing. She didn't want either of us to go. I can't remember whose idea it was for me to stay with her, whether it was hers or mine…'

Anna took a large drink of her wine and carefully wiped more tears away. She didn't want Stefano seeing her with smudged mascara, not tonight. 'I didn't want to go and I didn't want my mum to go either. I wanted her to stay and be my mum. I really thought if I refused to go that she would stay. Even when she bought me and Melissa the flat with Dad's insurance money and set up a monthly allowance for us I thought she'd stay. Right up until the moment her plane took off, I thought she would stay.'

The pain she'd experienced when she'd realised her mum had gone—had really gone—had been indescribable. It had been like having her heart stabbed with a thousand knives.

There was a long period of silence before a warm hand covered hers and sympathetic green eyes held her gaze.

'When did you last see her?' he asked.

'She came to England for my sixteenth birthday. That was her first and last visit. All she could talk about was how brilliant Australia was and how good Mick was to her. We had a massive argument. She called me and Melissa selfish bitches and said she was glad to be rid of us.' The words almost stuck in her throat. 'She flew back early.'

From the shock resonating in Stefano's eyes, it appeared this wasn't a part of the story she had shared before.

'Have you had any contact with her since then?'

She shook her head. 'She sends us cards and gifts for birthdays and Christmas, and she's written a couple of letters, but that's it.'

'What did the letters say?'

'I don't know. We burned them without reading them.'

The waiter returned to their table with their starters. Anna sniffed her *kung sadung nga*, deep-fried prawns in sesame batter and glazed in honey, and felt guilty for lowering the mood.

After all her good intentions she was in danger of ruining their last night here.

Before she could apologise, Stefano said thoughtfully, 'You've been coping with this for a long time. Do you think it's time for you to deal with it and talk to your mother and see if things can be mended?'

'You don't want to mend things with *your* family,' she said, stung.

'That's different. I will never forgive them for how they treated me. I will never forget. I don't want reconciliation. All I want is for them to see me rich and successful; everything that they are not. But my family is not yours. They never cared for me but your mother cared for you.'

'She left me,' Anna said, coldness creeping through her. 'How could she have cared for me?'

'You said yourself you were a proper family before your father died. She loved you then. I would guess she told herself she was doing the right thing.'

'I was a minor. I'd lost my dad, puberty had just struck…my head and emotions were all over the place. I needed her. Mel should have spent her uni years living it up and behaving atrociously, not having to be guardian to her bratty younger sister without any support from the woman whose job it was to care for us. How can you make excuses for that?'

'I'm not,' he said steadily, 'But Melissa clearly thinks it's worth trying and you trust her.'

'But that's what I don't understand. What made Mel change her mind? She hates Mum as much as I do. We've always sworn we were better off without her.'

'You can't tell me you don't miss her.'

Suddenly terrified she would do more than leak tears, Anna bit into one of her prawns and concentrated on not crying.

Only when she was confident she could talk without choking did she say, 'I'm sorry. I didn't want to ruin the evening.'

'You haven't.' But his eyes had lost their sparkle.

'You're right that I've only been coping with it and not dealing with it,' she admitted. 'You're the first person I've trusted since she got on that plane. Other than Melissa.' Then, aware she was sinking the mood even lower, forced a bright smile on her face. 'Don't let me ruin the rest of the evening.'

'Anna…'

'No.' She put her hand on his and squeezed it. 'We can talk about this when we get back to London and reality, but our time here has been very special to me. We're making good memories and I don't want my mum spoiling them.'

A flicker of darkness crossed his features before he gave the dazzling smile she loved so much and leaned closer to her. 'We have a whole night to make even better memories.'

* * *

Night had fallen when they left the restaurant, lamps illuminating the streets, the sound of the Pacific clearer.

The longer the meal had gone on, the smaller the restaurant had seemed until it had shrunk to just the two of them. She hadn't seen anyone else. Her eyes had been only for Stefano. The restaurant had been busy but she couldn't describe a single diner or even remember the colour of their waiter's hair.

And Stefano's eyes had only ever been on her, seducing her, making her heart race so that she forgot she was eating possibly the best pad thai she'd ever tasted.

After the discussion about her mother he'd regaled her with gossip about the industry and his rivals, making her laugh aloud more than once.

But now, with the cool night air on her skin, her thoughts drifted back to her mother.

Her abandonment was a ten-year open wound.

Had her mum made a big deal during her one visit to England about how amazing Australia was in the hope her daughters would join her there? *Had* she missed them as much as they'd missed her?

She left you without a parent when you were only fourteen years old, Anna reminded herself.

It didn't change how much she missed her, even now. Stefano was right about *that*.

She'd been a loving mum, she remembered. Always busy, but always with a smile on her face. Quick to scold, but equally quick to forgive.

Her dad was gone from the earth. She carried an ache in her heart for him she knew would be there for the rest of her life, and accepted it. Welcomed it even, the pain a reminder of the father she had lost but would never forget. It was through no fault of his own that he'd missed the significant events in her life and she knew if he could be watching down on her then he would be.

Her mum was alive and well and missing all those moments by choice.

But she'd been there for Anna's sixteenth birthday.

Except she hadn't come back.

'You've gone quiet,' Stefano mused, his accented voice breaking through her reminiscences.

She squeezed her fingers tighter to his. 'Sorry.'

'Don't be. What are you thinking?'

'Nothing exciting,' she said, telling him the first untruth since she'd known him.

'I don't believe that what goes on in your brain is ever boring,' he teased.

'It's full of mundane trivia.'

'What is mundane?'

'Like boring.'

Without warning he dropped her hand and grabbed her shoulders, pulled her to him and kissed her fully and passionately.

And then just as quickly he broke away and took hold of her hand again. 'I bet your thoughts are not mundane now.'

He had that right.

By the time they returned to the beach house the only thing on her mind was making love to him.

When they stepped over the threshold, he gave her a long lingering kiss and said, 'Wait for me in the sunroom while I get us a drink.'

The lights of the sunroom were off, the only illumination coming from the night lights surrounding the swimming pool and bouncing through the wall of glass. It lent the room a romantic quality that perfectly suited her mood and her desire for one last perfect night here.

She looked out of the window and gazed at the dark ocean, only the distant flashes of foaming surf and the twinkling stars in the night sky differentiating one from the other.

Stefano came back into the room carrying two glasses of white wine. He joined her at the window, his arm brushing against her as he handed hers to her. 'Are your feet hurting yet?'

Startled at his question, Anna looked down at the fabulous shoes that, now she thought about it, were crippling her feet.

She must have been mad to wear such high heels on an evening that required walking. If she hadn't been so dazzled by their brilliance she would have worn flats and now her feet wouldn't ache so much.

'They're killing me.'

He tutted. 'I thought so. You always wear silly shoes.'

'They're not silly,' she said in mock outrage. 'I just happen to like nice shoes.'

'You have nice shoes that don't require you to cripple yourself wearing them.'

'If I wear heels it stops people tripping over me,' she said, deadpan.

He wiggled his left eyebrow in the way that always made her laugh, then took a large drink of his wine and put his glass on the low round table in the centre of the room. He took her hand and guided her to the rounded sofa that looked so much like a bed.

'Sit down,' he ordered.

'Bossy boots,' she said, deliberately taking a slow drink of her wine before obeying.

Stefano sat next to her, took hold of her ankles and put her feet on his lap.

'What are you doing?'

He unzipped the heel of her left shoe and gently tugged it off. 'Someone has to look after your feet if you won't,' he answered, a sparkle in his eyes. 'You are lucky you have married a man who gives fantastic foot massages.'

'And how do you know that?'

Her other shoe went the same way as the first. The relief to her poor feet was indescribable.

'*You* told me,' he said with a patient shake of his head, 'because you always insist on wearing silly shoes and then complain your feet hurt.'

The retort she had ready on her lips died away when he pressed his thumbs to the sole of her foot and slowly pushed up to her toes.

Stefano noted the way her eyes glazed as he began to massage her feet and experienced a thrill of satisfaction. Anna adored having her feet rubbed and right then he wanted to do nothing more than give her pleasure and wipe away the memories of her past he knew were suffusing her.

He would have given anything to stop her from talking earlier. He hadn't wanted to see her pain.

Dannazione, he shouldn't be aching to comfort her and wipe her demons away.

He could feel himself losing control of the situation and was determined to regain it.

'Put your head back and relax.'

A knowing smile playing on her lips, she placed her wine glass on the floor. Then she did as he'd suggested and lay with her head against the rounded softness of the sofa's back and her body in recline.

After massaging her left foot for a few minutes he switched to her right.

Anna sighed and finally closed her eyes. 'You really do give amazing foot massages.'

'I know.'

A snigger escaped her lips before she gave another deep sigh.

When he felt he'd worked enough on her foot, he moved his hand up to her ankle and then to her smooth calf, kneading the muscles with the pressure he knew she liked.

It occurred to him that he still knew far more about the responses of her body and what gave her pleasure than she did.

Up his hands went, over her knee, brushing the silk of her dress aside as he reached her thigh. This was where he had to be gentler, her inner thighs one of her most tender areas.

She kept perfectly still, only her deepening breaths indicating any response as his fingers inched ever upwards, his hand burrowing under her dress, deliberately keeping away from her most intimate area, teasing her, tormenting her.

Sliding his fingers back down her leg, he switched his attentions to her other leg and began the same sensuous trail.

Dio, but this was turning him on.

When he reached her thigh this time and kneaded his way to her hip, he hooked his finger into the side of her knickers.

Her breaths were now coming in ragged spurts, her cheeks flushed.

Taking hold of the elastic on her other hip, he gently

tugged her knickers down. When the soft dark hair between her legs was exposed, her eyes flew open.

There was such desire and trust in that stare. When she looked at him like that all he could think was that he wanted it to be like this between them always.

It was too late for thoughts like that. Too late to erase the past. Too much had gone on between them but he couldn't shake the thought that she'd said she trusted *him* unaware that, come tomorrow, he planned to destroy her.

This would be his last gift to her.

Stefano threw her knickers onto the floor then placed a hand on her ankle and gently pulled her legs apart. She writhed beneath him and he pressed a hand to her belly to steady her and placed a kiss on her inner thigh.

When he pressed his mouth into the heart of her she gasped and jolted as if she'd had a volt of electricity shot through her. A hand flailed out and touched his head.

He inhaled, breathing in her scent that he had never tired of, *could* never tire of.

Taking greater care than he had ever done in his life, checking his own ardour, which wanted nothing more than to rip both their clothes off and take her without ceremony, Stefano kissed and caressed the most intimate part of her to gradually open her up to him.

The fingertips on his head moved imperceptibly in tiny circular movements. Her breaths caught then deepened and tiny moans escaped her lips. The fingers on his scalp tightened and dug into him until finally, with the breathiest of gasps, her back arched and she shuddered.

Only when he was certain her climax was over did he haul himself up and put his hands either side of her head to stare down at her.

Anna had faced down everything life had thrown at

her before, never flinching or hiding away. Over the past few days they had made love countless times, done everything possible, but this… This felt different. *She* felt different and opening her eyes to meet Stefano's gaze was one of the hardest things she'd ever done. She was afraid of what she would find there.

As she forced them open she knew the thing she most feared was not finding what she suddenly realised she so desperately wanted to see. Love.

She swallowed and met his gaze.

Her breath came unstuck again. If not love, there was tenderness in the dark, swirling green depths and it filled her chest so completely that she hooked her arms around his neck and pulled him down for a long kiss.

'You've got too many clothes on,' he said gruffly into her mouth, his hands sliding down to her waist.

'So have you.'

He made deft work of the belt. As soon as it was unclasped, her dress unwrapped itself, only one small button holding the last of the material together, which he undid with no effort before sliding an arm behind her back to unclasp her bra.

Gathering her to him, he pulled her up so he could slide the sleeves of her dress and bra down her arms, leaving her naked before him.

'*Dio*, you're beautiful,' he muttered.

'Your turn,' she whispered, lying back down. She stretched her arms above her head, luxuriating in his dilated gaze.

He removed his shirt, then got off the improbably large sofa only long enough to shed his trousers and underwear.

And then he was back on top of her, his mouth covering hers, and with one long thrust he was inside her.

He took her with a feverish passion, raising her thighs to drive into her as deeply as he could, deeper and deeper, faster and faster, their bodies fusing together to become one pulsating being.

Anna's climax bubbled back into life and when he came with a groan she followed within moments, biting into his shoulder and pressing herself as tightly as she could to him as the pleasure exploded out of her.

For a long, long time, the only sound to be heard was their ragged breathing and the thundering of their hearts.

It was the most blissful state.

Eventually Stefano shifted his weight off her and she twisted onto her side to rest her head on his chest.

She kissed the taut skin beneath her. 'I'm so glad I married you. I would do it again in a moment.'

His response was to tighten his hold on her and kiss the top of her head.

CHAPTER NINE

ANNA CARRIED HER BOWL of cereal to Stefano's study, eating as she went. For once he'd woken before her, waking her to make love before saying he had a conference call to take and work to catch up on. When she'd asked if there was anything she needed to be getting on with herself, he'd kissed her and reminded her that she was technically still off sick.

She hadn't protested. Five days of sex, sand and sea had left work far removed from her life. She'd left school at eighteen and had worked constantly since. There had been no grand plan, just a determination to work hard and be self-sufficient. She hadn't known how wonderful it could be to kick back and relax and to let the cares of the world pass her by and here, in this bustling beach paradise, she'd been able to do just that. In a few hours they'd be heading up Route 17 to San Francisco and their mini holiday in Santa Cruz would be over.

She found Stefano rummaging through a filing cabinet and talking to himself. It took her a moment to realise he was in fact having a video call with someone on his laptop.

He raised a hand and winked to acknowledge her and carried on with his conversation in rapid Italian with a woman Anna couldn't see from the angle of his laptop but whose voice replied in equally rapid Italian.

Perching herself on his desk, Anna ate her breakfast while the two chatted. Although she couldn't understand a word of what they were saying, judging by Stefano's tone this was no business talk.

By the time he'd finished the conversation, she'd finished her breakfast and put her bowl on his desk. 'Who was that?' she asked.

'My sister.' He came over to her, took her face in his hands and gave her a kiss.

She looped her arms around his neck. 'Is she okay?'

'She doesn't like her neighbours. She has three male students living in the flat above hers and they make too much noise at night. They ignore her complaints.'

'Is she not scary like you?'

'I don't scare people.'

'You revel in it.'

He grinned and kissed her again. 'Only people who deserve it. And I have never scared you.'

'I've never scared easily. So what are you going to do about her neighbours? Kneecap them?' she joked, then pressed her lips to his.

'I think a threatening letter will do as a start,' he said into her mouth.

She nipped his bottom lip. 'Very wise.'

Laughing, Stefano unlooped her arms from round his neck. 'I have a conference call to make. Give me an hour and I'll come back to bed before we leave.'

'You don't need me here for it?' She had never missed a conference call in all the time she'd worked for him...

But then she remembered she had a new role, one she

only had patches of memories of. She would have to get a handle on it from scratch.

She wouldn't worry about that until they were back in London, she decided, sliding off the desk.

'No underwear?' he said with a lascivious gleam.

She turned, giving a hint of her bare bottom beneath her skirt. 'I can sit on your lap.'

'You can sit on my lap any time you like. Just not when I'm taking a conference call.' He pushed her playfully. 'Now go.'

'Okay, okay, I know when I'm not wanted.'

He gave her a stern look that only made her laugh harder.

She sashayed deliberately to the door, a thought striking her as she made to leave. 'How do I get on with Christina?'

His brow furrowed.

'I ask because…well, I'm ashamed to say this but when I saw her getting out of your car last week…it felt like a knife in my heart.'

'What do you mean?'

'I assumed she was your latest girlfriend.' She must have seen the darkening in his eyes he wasn't quick enough to hide for she hastened to add, 'Don't forget, I had no idea we were married. I was used to your rolling conveyor belt of girlfriends, it was an easy mistake for me to make. I couldn't understand why it hurt to see you with what I thought was another lover.'

Stefano made sure not to show any reaction. Lying to Anna had been easy when she'd first had the amnesia diagnosed. Now, every untruth felt rancid in his guts. She didn't yet have the memories to know that she'd only met his sister the one time, when she'd walked into their London flat early that morning and found Christina wearing her robe. Anna not being able to speak Italian and Christina not speaking English had given them a language barrier that had allowed Anna to assume the worst.

It came to him how Christina had later described the scene.

'She went white,' his sister had said. 'I thought she was going to be sick. I tried to speak to her but she couldn't understand me; she kept shaking her head as if she'd seen something horrifying, and then she walked out.'

Did that really sound like the actions of a woman calculating how to turn a situation to her advantage?

Now he allowed himself to think about it with some distance from the aftermath, did it not sound like the actions of a woman who'd received a terrible shock?

'You and Christina have a language barrier,' he said steadily. That wasn't a lie.

She eyed him with the look of someone who knew something was being held back. Then she shrugged her shoulders. 'Maybe that's my cue to start learning Italian.'

He was saved from further talk of his sister by the tone on his laptop ringing out to notify him his conference call was about to start.

Anna shrugged again, a wry smile playing on her lips. 'And that's my cue to leave. Have fun.'

After she'd closed the door behind her, Stefano took the seat at his desk and accepted the call. While waiting for the others joining to connect, he rubbed his forehead.

The game he'd been playing, the revenge he'd been savouring…it sat like a bad taste on his tongue.

He'd learned more about his wife in the last week than he had in their entire marriage. Before she'd stormed into his boardroom and humiliated him that day he would never have dreamt she could be a gold-digger or that his trust in her could be unfounded. Every instinct in his guts and in his head were shouting at him that somehow, in some way, everything was wrong.

This was *Anna*. The woman he'd desired and admired from their very first meeting. The woman he'd trusted enough to pledge his life to…

His head began to burn and his guts twisted with something worse than nausea. With his revenge only hours away, he came to the realisation that he couldn't go through with it.

When his conference call was over he would call Miranda, the journalist he'd entrusted into his confidence, and tell her the embargoed press statement he'd given to her a week ago was to be scrapped and buried.

He'd get tonight's awards over with and then he would sit down with Anna and tell her the truth about everything.

The moment Anna walked into Stefano's apartment in San Francisco, more memories returned. Throughout their days in Santa Cruz, more and more had appeared. Her memory was like a giant jigsaw puzzle and what had started as a mammoth hunt for the pieces was now coming together rapidly.

'When did we get a new sofa?' she asked, surprised to find the plump white one replaced with chocolate-brown leather.

'You remember it?'

'It was my favourite thing here.' This apartment was furnished along the same lines as the London one, with everything designed to show off wealth and great taste.

She already missed their Santa Cruz beach house. For all its opulence, it had felt like a home.

He strode to the kitchen. 'It got damaged a few weeks ago. Tea?'

She followed him in. 'Looks like the concierge service has been in,' she said, noting the freshly cleaned scent of the place.

'I called them to get everything ready for us. We're eating at the hotel tonight but there's plenty of snack food if you're hungry…' Suddenly he turned to face her. 'Do you remember the concierge service here?'

She nodded and grinned. 'Like the one in London but with extra "have a nice day."'

'Your memories are coming back quickly now,' he observed.

'There are still holes but they're filling.'

At that, judging by the gleam in his eyes, his mind had taken an entirely different route. She was glad. Tension had been etched on his face since his conference call that not even a long bout of lovemaking before they'd left had been able to erase. When she'd asked what was troubling him, he'd said only that it was to do with work and that he'd tell her about it after the awards. With work still feeling a lifetime away, she didn't bother to pursue it.

'You have a filthy mind, Stefano Moretti.'

He pulled her into his arms and nipped at her earlobe. 'And you love it.'

Yes, she thought, yes, she did. She loved him.

But hadn't she already known she loved him? That tight, painful feeling that had been in her chest since she'd seen Christina follow him out of his car; that had been a symptom of it. It was liberating to finally acknowledge the truth to herself.

She loved him.

With only flat shoes on, her face was flat against his chest. She inhaled his scent greedily and sighed into him before tugging at his shirt to loosen it and slip a hand up it and onto his back.

The words rolled on her tongue, so close to being spoken aloud, but she held them back.

The last time she remembered saying those words had been to her father in the minutes before they'd turned his life support off.

Stefano gathered her hair and gently tugged her head back. 'You don't want tea?'

'I'm not thirsty.' She moved her hands to the front of his shirt and began undoing the buttons. She might not yet be able to say the words to him but she could show him. 'But I *am* hungry.'

As was always the case, Stefano was showered, shaved and ready a good hour before Anna, who'd had a beautician provided by the apartment's concierge service in to help her.

He pressed Miranda's name on his phone again and tapped his foot while waiting for it to connect.

He hadn't been able to get hold of her. He'd left her three messages and sent two emails. Anna had disappeared for a couple of hours' 'retail therapy' that afternoon and he'd tried Miranda again, even calling her newsroom.

Miranda Appleton was editor-in-chief of the US's bestselling celebrity magazine that had an accompanying website with the highest daily click rate of any media in the world. Miranda had her finger on the pulse of all celebrity news and in today's instant world a billionaire such as himself was considered a celebrity.

He'd chosen Miranda for his scoop because, for all her unscrupulous dealings, she was a woman of her word and he'd known she wouldn't break the embargo.

And now she had gone off-grid. No one knew where she was. No one could reach her.

His call went yet again to her voicemail.

'It's Stefano,' he hissed quietly down the line. 'Miranda, I need you to kill that story. I retract my statement. You cannot publish it. Call me back as soon as you can.'

Feeling sick to his stomach, he waited for Anna in the living room, sitting on the new sofa that had been delivered to replace the one he'd ruined when he'd made his first trip to San Francisco after she'd left him. He'd remembered making love to her on it and the rage that had ripped through him, which had caused him to rip up the one item of furniture she'd loved, pulling chunks out of it as *she* had ripped chunks out of *him*.

He'd been as out of control as he'd been before prison had cured him of his temper.

Jail itself hadn't been too bad but the six months he'd served behind bars had dragged interminably. He'd grown to hate the confinement, the suffocation that came from spending all day every day in an enclosed space surrounded by people there wasn't a hell's chance of escaping from. He understood why prisoners might turn to drugs, just to relieve themselves of the brain-numbing boredom. As he'd already been hooked on nicotine at the time he'd known better than to take that route himself. But, still, the days had been so *long*.

His temper had been the reason he'd been incarcerated. He'd walked out of those prison gates with a determination to never let it get the better of him again and until Anna had left him, he never had.

He took a deep breath then got up to pour himself a large measure of bourbon. He downed it in one, then poured another.

The doubts that had been amassing in his head since their arrival in California had grown. Yet he always came back to the fact of that damned letter from Anna's solicitor demanding a massive slice of his fortune. Whatever had been going on in her head at the time, that demand had come from *her*. He should not allow fantastic sex and the old sparring easiness they'd shared to overturn the facts of the situation because in that respect nothing had changed.

His plan had worked perfectly. He'd seduced her. She'd even said she would marry him again. That should fill him with satisfaction, not make him feel as if he'd been punched a dozen times in the gut.

Never in his life had he felt such indecision. Since his imprisonment he'd learned to keep a cool head, analyse the facts and then make up his mind. Once it was made up, nothing deterred him from his chosen path.

He shouldn't let the past week cloud his judgement or deter him from his path now.

But he'd learned more about his wife in the past week than he had in almost a year of marriage and all his instincts were telling him he couldn't go through with it.

Where on earth was Miranda? Had she got his messages?

They'd planned the timings down to the minute. His statement was due to go online halfway through the awards ceremony.

He heard soft footsteps approaching and composed himself.

Anna entered the living room serenely, like a goddess emerging from an oyster shell.

All the breath left his body.

She wore a floor-length fitted red lace dress that pooled at her feet like a mermaid's tail. The front plunged in a V showing the tiniest hint of creamy cleavage. Her bare arms glimmered. Her face was subtly made up except for the lips, which she'd painted the same shade as her dress, and her dark hair shone, blow-dried to fall thickly around her shoulders.

She spread her arms out and made a slow twirl. 'Well?'

He cleared his throat. 'I think I'm going to be the envy of every red-blooded male in attendance.'

Her eyes sparkled, joy resounding from them. 'I couldn't believe it when I found this dress in my dressing room. Did I buy it for tonight?'

'I assume so. I've only been on one shopping trip with you.'

She grinned. 'I remember that. Was it that bad for you?'

'I've had better times watching envelopes being stuffed.'

'I'd never been shopping with an unlimited credit card. Can you blame me for getting carried away?'

He shook his head, remembering the glee with which she'd attacked the shopping district he'd taken her to. He'd often given old girlfriends a credit card to buy themselves something for a night out and they'd always played a game; pretending to resist, pretending to want their independence and not wanting to take from him. Anna had made no such pretence. She'd snatched the card out of his hand—a card he'd given her to keep and not just for the one occasion—and raced to the shops like a roadrunner, virtually leaving a trail of dust in her wake. Her chutzpah had made him laugh.

And then he remembered a time before they'd married, when he'd caught her making calculations with a pen and paper. She'd been trying to work out her finances to see if she could afford to pay for her and her sister to go on a five-star spa weekend in Dublin for Melissa's birthday. He'd offered to pay and she'd dismissed it out of hand. She wouldn't even discuss it. He'd noticed in the weeks leading up to that particular spa break that she had brought her own lunch into the office rather than eating in the subsidised staff restaurant, and he'd admired that she was prepared to economise when necessary and forego little treats if it meant having a bigger treat at the end of it.

She'd often spent her money on her sister, he remembered, and for the first time wondered if it was her way of making up for Melissa giving up her freedom to raise her. For all Anna's current happiness, he knew Melissa wasn't far from her thoughts. He knew Melissa being in Australia with their mother had wounded her in ways he couldn't understand.

Anna had only been happy to spend his money *after* they'd married and that had only been to feed her addiction to clothes shopping. She'd cheekily described it as *the* perk of being his wife.

Miranda, check your damn messages.

'Where did you say the awards were being held?' Anna asked, rifling through her small red clutch bag.

'At the Grand Palace Hotel.'

Her hand stilled and she looked at him. 'The Grand Palace Hotel?'

'*Sì*. It's been held there for the past five years. What are you looking for?'

'Double-checking I've put my lipstick in,' she replied, but her eyes had glazed over, her words mechanical and said without any thought, her mind clearly somewhere else.

'What's wrong?'

After a moment she blinked and shook her head. Her mouth pulled into a smile but there was a brittleness to it. 'Nothing. Shall we go?'

Aware that to leave it much longer would make them late, he took her hand and together they left his apartment.

Only the cramping in his guts acted as a warning sign that something was very wrong.

CHAPTER TEN

ANNA'S NAILS, MANICURED FABULOUSLY by the beautician, dug into the palm of her hand. Stefano sat beside her in the back of the stretched Mercedes, filling the silence with talk of a new super-secure Cloud-based system his employees were developing. She made all the appropriate noises and asked all the obvious questions she would always ask but her thoughts were far away. A year ago away.

When he'd said they were going to the Grand Palace Hotel, she'd had an instant image flash in her head of being at that hotel with Stefano before, but just as the memory had crystallised another, equally vivid image had come to her of throwing a jug of water over him in his London boardroom, in front of the entire board of directors.

By the time they arrived at the hotel fifteen minutes after setting off, she wanted to tell the driver to turn round and take them back. She felt sick. Memories had come back to her—flooded back—and she wanted to sit somewhere on her own and make sense of them all.

Because none of it made sense. She'd already remembered arguments between them and had accepted them without dissection. She would have been more surprised if they hadn't argued. She remembered missing him when he went away on business without her and, shaming as it was, remembered the fears and insecurities that had crept up on her.

What she hadn't remembered until only a few minutes ago, and which Stefano hadn't bothered to mention, was that she'd left him. More than that, she'd confronted him in his boardroom and lost total control of herself in front of everyone. What she still couldn't remember was why or what the aftermath had been.

She had almost the entire picture there before her but the biggest, most significant pieces were still missing. Her painfully thudding heart told her that she didn't want to remember.

The car door was opened and before either of them had moved from their seats, lights flashed around them.

The Tech Industry Awards, if one was to go by its name, promised nothing more than a bunch of eggheads crowded together in a room congratulating each other on their supreme eggheadedness. The truth was that these awards were prestigious and glamorous enough to rival the ceremony for any national film or music award. These were the awards the big players wanted and paid a fortune to sponsor. It was estimated the collective worth of the attendees this evening would make up the largest concentration of money in the world, and the press was out in force to cover it.

Above them, thick dark clouds had gathered. Anna gave an involuntary shiver. A storm was on its way and her foreboding only grew.

She made sure to keep her face inscrutable as she climbed out and took Stefano's hand. Ignoring the shouts from reporters throwing inane questions at them—she distinguished at least three asking 'who' she was wearing—they went through the cordon opened for them. Waving at the thick crowd of spectators, they walked up the red carpet where only a select few journalists were allowed to stand.

As they passed one reporter doing a piece for camera, she caught some of what was being said.

'Rumours of the Moretti marriage being over have been scotched by the couple's first public appearance in six weeks.'

And then the reporter swung round and thrust the microphone in Stefano's face.

'If you could choose one award to win tonight, which would it be?'

'I couldn't choose just one,' Stefano answered with the easy smile that made millions of women around the world long to bed him. 'But whether we win anything tonight or not makes no matter. Moretti's is the leading software manufacturer and app developer in the world, and the technology my dedicated staff are developing will change the face of the world as we know it.'

'Fabulous!' The reporter gave the vacuous grin that meant she hadn't listened to a word of his answer and immediately turned her microphone to Anna. 'What do you have to say, Anna, about the reports on your marriage?'

Anna responded with an identical vacuous smile. 'What reports are you referring to?'

The reporter's composure wavered for only a second. 'The rumours that you had separated. Are we to believe that you two are still together?'

Stefano put his arm around her waist and opened his mouth to speak, but Anna couldn't bear to hear another of his lies.

She smiled and made sure to inject sweetness in her voice. 'I think my presence here with my husband can speak for itself. Enjoy your evening.'

And with a gracious nod and another wave to the crowd, Anna and Stefano were taken inside by a couple of burly bouncers.

His arm stayed around her waist in that protective fashion she'd always so adored. Outwardly he appeared completely unfazed by the reporter's remarks. He'd buttered her up well for it, she thought cynically. Hadn't he remarked when she'd been in the hospital that the press were always speculating on the state of their marriage?

If only she could remember those last pieces of the scene, she would know what had come after she'd drenched him in water.

Knowing Stefano as well as she did, she didn't think it was something he would have easily forgiven her for.

If only she knew what had compelled her to do it in the first place…

Now was not the time to try and work it all out, not in a reception hall filled with industry bigwigs all wanting to shake hands, exchange stories and assert individual dominance. There was a convivial atmosphere, however, as rivalries were set aside for the night, at least superficially.

The Moretti table was situated directly before the main stage and thus in the glare of the majority of the video cameras. Anna kept her head held high as they joined the executives and company nominees who'd been invited to join them on this prestigious night, pretending not to see the curious glances being flashed her way.

Only one member of the UK board was in attendance, the rest from Sweden, Japan and America. She knew with one look that they all knew exactly what had happened in that boardroom. And they knew she had received her P45 for gross misconduct the very next day and had had no contact with any member of staff or with her husband…

Until the morning she'd woken with a bang on her head and her memories wiped.

And now, she remembered…

It explained everything. All the stares she'd received, Chloe's appropriation of her desk, Stefano's anger…

She remembered everything.

Everything.

Oh, how she wished she hadn't. Ignorance had been more than bliss; it had been an escape from the unbearable agony that had become her life.

Stefano put his hand on hers. Her veins turned to ice and she fought not to snatch it away. He whispered something in her ear and she fought not to flinch.

She made sure to keep a smile on her face and play the role of the happy wife. It was the greatest role she'd ever had to play.

When Moretti's was given its third award of the night and Stefano took to the stage with the innovative hipster who'd been the brains behind it, she clapped as hard as everyone else.

Her pride would not allow her to show publicly that her heart had been irreversibly broken.

But she couldn't keep it together for ever.

Not long after the halfway point of the evening she rose from the table.

Stefano grabbed her wrist. 'Where are you going?'

'To the Ladies'.'

'Can't you wait?' His nostrils were flared, his jaw clenched.

'What?' She snatched her hand away. 'Don't be ridiculous.'

As she hurried her way through the tables she became aware that shocked faces were staring at her. Voices at every table she approached dropped to a hushed whisper and there was a furious tapping of phone screens accompanied by more shocked faces.

Fortunately the ladies' room was empty. She wished there were a window she could crawl out of but if all she could have was a few moments to compose herself then she would take that.

Sucking in some deep breaths, she pressed powder to her white cheeks and fixed her eyeliner and lipstick, then took some more deep breaths for luck and left her brief sanctuary.

The stares and whispers were even more pronounced now. There was still a handful of awards left to be given but Stefano had risen from their table and was taking great strides towards her.

'We need to go,' he said, grabbing her hand and practically dragging her to the exit.

'It's not finished yet.' As much as she longed to escape the stares, protocol dictated that everyone should stay to the bitter end.

He didn't answer or slow his pace. If anything he moved faster.

If he could get her out of the hotel and into his car before the press noticed them, Stefano knew he had a chance. A chance to explain himself before Anna learned of the bomb he'd detonated.

The weather had taken a turn for the worse since their arrival. Thick droplets of rain were falling and the breeze had picked up.

They almost made their escape. The press were too busy huddled together in little clusters, staring at their phones, chattering frenziedly among themselves, to notice the couple slipping out half an hour early or the gathering storm around them.

But then a driver got out of a yellow cab and called out loudly, 'Anna Moretti?' and with a violent curse, Stefano knew he was too late.

He'd forgotten his instruction that Miranda book a cab for Anna and to make sure the driver arrived early with a picture of the passenger he was to collect. Stefano had planned to put her in it as his final flourish, to shut the door for her and never see her again.

His plan had worked perfectly.

Success had never tasted so bitter.

At the mention of Anna's name the press sprang into action.

Pounding feet rushed towards them, a babble of shouted words pouring out so thick and fast they should be incomprehensible. But judging by the pallor of Anna's face and the tiny stumble she made, she had heard them clearly enough.

His own driver pulled up. Stefano opened the back door himself and bundled Anna's rigid body inside.

It was only as he slammed the door behind them that he caught a glimpse of Miranda Appleton standing like a vulture next to her magazine's photographer, a smirk on her ugly, rancid face.

Anna sat like a mannequin pressed against the far door. She didn't look at him. She hardly seemed to be breathing.

The rain had turned into a deluge and the driver slowed to a crawl. With the silence stretching between them and an air of darkness swirling, it was a relief when they eventually came to a stop at the front of the apartment building. A crackle of lightning rent the sky, illuminating everything for a few brief seconds that were still long enough for him to see the shock carved on her frozen face.

She didn't notice they'd come to a stop.

'Anna,' he said tentatively. 'We're home.'

Still she sat there, immobile.

Only when he leaned over to take her hand—*Dio*, it was icy to the touch—did she show any animation.

Slowly her head turned to face him. 'Don't touch me.'

Then, with no care for any passing cars, she opened her door and stepped out into the deluge.

Stefano jolted after her and breathed a tiny sigh of relief that the road was empty of traffic.

Maybe it was the lashing rain that forced her hand but she walked sharply into his apartment building. She bypassed the elevator to take the stairs, her heels clip-clopping without pause all the way to the eighteenth floor.

There was no sign of her exertion when she shrank away from him as he punched in the entry code to their apartment.

She headed straight to their bar, snatched up the nearest bottle and took a huge gulp from it. Then she took another gulp, wiped her mouth with the back of her hand and put the lid back on.

Only then did she meet his eye.

She stared at him for an age before her face contorted into something unrecognisable and she smashed the bottle down on the bar with all her strength.

'Bastard!' she screamed as the bottle exploded around her, then reached for a bottle of brandy and smashed that

too. The single malt went next, all accompanied by a hail of curses and profanities that seemed to be wrenched from her very soul.

The bourbon would have gone the same way had Stefano not sprung into motion—the destruction had happened within seconds—and wrapped his arms around her, trapping her back against his chest.

'Anna, stop,' he commanded loudly. 'You're going to hurt yourself.'

She thrashed wildly in his hold, kicking her legs backwards and forwards, catching his shin with the heel of her shoe, all the while screaming curses at him.

He winced at the lancing pain but didn't let her go.

In a way, the pain was welcome. He deserved it.

She caught his shin again and he gritted his teeth. 'Please, stop fighting me. I know you want to hurt me. I *know*. And I deserve it. Hit me, kick me, bite me, do whatever you want but please, *bellissima*, don't hurt yourself. There's glass everywhere.'

As if she could hurt herself after what he'd done to her. In the state she was in, he doubted she would feel any pain.

His words must have penetrated for gradually the fight went out of her and she went limp in his arms.

Cautiously he released his hold and braced himself for her to take him at his word and attack him.

Instead, she staggered to the centre of the living room and flopped to the floor. The mermaid tail of her dress made a perfect semi-circle around her. Her chest rose heavily and she lifted her head to stare at him. Misery and contempt pierced him.

Without saying a word, she removed each sparkling shoe in turn. There was a moment when he thought she was going to throw them at him but, after a small hesitation, she flung them to her side.

When she finally spoke there was a metallic edge to her tone that made his veins run cold.

'Did you enjoy your revenge?'

'I tried to stop it.' He knew it was a pathetic thing to say even before her face twisted.

He dragged a hand through his hair and took a deep breath before reaching carefully through the debris of glass for the saved bottle of bourbon.

'You couldn't have tried very hard.' She laughed, a robotic sound that made him flinch. 'I think your revenge worked. The ruthless Stefano Moretti shows the world that you mess with him at your peril, even if you're his wife. My humiliation will make front page news everywhere.'

He unscrewed the bottle and put it to his lips. The liquid burned his throat.

'It was too late to stop it. Miranda must have known I'd change my mind. She made it impossible for me to contact her.'

'Miranda Appleton? That witch?'

He nodded and drank some more.

'You're blaming *her*?'

'No. The only one to blame for tonight is me. I set it up.' After everything that had been said and done between them, the only thing they were left with was the truth. 'I called her last week, the day after I brought you home from hospital, and gave her a statement. I put an embargo on it that was to be lifted at nine thirty this evening.'

'And what did your statement say?' Though she was outwardly calmer, he could see she was clinging to her control by a whisker.

'That the rumours about our marriage were true and that I would be issuing you with divorce papers tomorrow morning.'

'Happy anniversary to me.'

'At the time I thought it fitting.'

'And all the times you made love to me? Treated me like a princess? Cared for me? Where did that all fit in? I suppose that was to humiliate me privately as well as publicly so that every time I thought of us together in Santa Cruz, the city I love, I would be reminded that I'd been a fool to think I could take you on and win?'

She knew him too well. Better than he knew himself.

Shame rolled through him like a dark cloud. He jerked a nod. There was nothing he could say to defend himself. He didn't want to even try.

'The cab? Where was that going to take me?' she asked.

'Out of my life.'

She laughed again. He had never heard such a pitiful sound.

'So, if I'm to believe you'd changed your mind—and in fairness I can see you got cold feet about the cab side of it, so let's give you the benefit of the doubt about that— what brought the change of heart about? You've played me like a violin all week to reach this point so why back out at the last minute?'

'I've been having doubts.'

She trembled but her voice remained steady. 'Doubts? That's a good one. Doubts about what?'

'About whether you really had set out to frame me for adultery and fleece me for as much money as you could get all along.'

Pain lashed her features. 'That's what you believed?'

He gripped the bottle tightly. He'd been so caught up with all that had just happened that he'd lost sight of what had driven him to these actions in the first place.

He'd done wrong—he knew that—but she had too.

'You're the one who found a strange woman in our apartment and immediately decided I was having an affair.'

She shook her head with incredulity. 'If you'd come back early from a trip abroad and found a strange semi-naked man in the apartment, what would you have thought?'

Stefano's heart was thumping violently against his ribs. 'I do not say I wouldn't have been a little suspicious but I wouldn't have made assumptions as you did.'

No, if he'd found a strange man in his apartment wearing his robe, his fist would probably have connected with the man's face before he'd had time to think.

'I would have asked you to explain,' he continued, pushing the thought away. 'I would have listened to your answer. You didn't ask for my side. *You* decided the facts to suit yourself. You swore at me and threw water over me in front of my most senior members of staff. You humiliated me.'

'You were ignoring me.'

'*When?*'

'That night. I called. It went to voicemail…'

'My sister who I didn't know existed had suddenly appeared in my life,' he interrupted. 'I had just been told the father I thought had died when I was a child had been alive all these years and had a new family but that there was no chance of me meeting him because he had died a few weeks before. Forgive me if I was too busy trying to make sense of my life to answer my phone.'

He hadn't even noticed it ring. Christina had sent a courier to his apartment with a letter and some photos—photos of *him* as a child—ending her note with a number for him to call.

She'd been waiting outside the apartment building.

'Too busy to answer the phone for your *wife*? Too busy to call when I left a message *and* texted you asking you to call me?'

'I didn't get the messages until four in the morning when it was too late to call you back, but I did text you. I told you I would call you later in the day, which I would have done after the meeting you interrupted, but you jumped to the conclusion that I was with another woman. You stormed into my boardroom and accused me of having an affair in front of my most senior members of staff. You threw water over me.' As the humiliation flooded back over him, his temper rose. 'You broke your word. You said you would trust me. You lied to me!'

Anna stared at him for the longest time, her lips parted but with no sound coming out. But then the colour rushed back across her cheeks and she got to her knees to thump the floor.

'You selfish, selfish *bastard*. Twisting this all round to hide what you've done. I've made mistakes and done things I'm ashamed of but you took advantage of my amnesia just so you could have your revenge. You let me think I still worked for you! No wonder you didn't want me calling Melissa—that wasn't for my sake, it was to protect your lie! You've been lying to me for over a week!'

'You hit me with a demand for a hundred million pounds!' he shot back. 'You knew I wouldn't take that lying down.'

'Of course I knew that! Why do you think I issued it?'

'You *wanted* me to react?'

'I wanted you to speak to me and I was crazy enough to think that demanding a hundred million and a load of your assets would force you to communicate. You'd cut me off. You fired me and blocked my number. You served me with formal separation papers. You changed the security number for the apartment so I couldn't get in. It was like I'd never existed for you. I wanted to hurt you as much as you were hurting me. I knew the only way I'd be able to get your attention was by hitting you where I knew it would hurt the most—your wallet.'

'You walked out on *me*,' he reminded her harshly. 'Did you think I would beg you to come back?'

'I came back the next day and couldn't get into the apartment. You didn't even give me twenty-four hours before locking me out.'

The cold mist in his head had thickened, nausea roiling in his guts as he thought of his own contribution to the mess that was the end of their marriage. He *had* cut her off. His pride and ego had been dented so greatly that he'd struck back before she could do any more damage.

'Why did you want to get my attention so badly?'

'Because I needed you and because, despite everything, I couldn't accept we were over.' She pinched the bridge of her nose and held out her other hand for the bottle. He took a nip himself before passing it to her.

She took a long slug.

'Don't you think you've had enough?'

Her hair swished as she shook her head. 'Nowhere near enough.'

The trembling anguish in her voice sent a fresh roll of dread through him.

Her hands were shaking so much the bottle slipped

from her hand and onto her lap, then rolled onto the floor.

In silence they watched the transparent fiery liquid spill onto the dark carpet.

'Anna,' he said quietly, 'why did you say you needed me?'

Her face rose to meet his gaze. Her eyes were stark, her bottom lip trembling.

All these weeks he'd been determined to think the worst. Anna had made assumptions but he had too. He could admit that.

She swallowed a number of times before saying in a voice so small he had to strain to hear, 'I lost our baby.'

'What...?' The question died on his lips as the cold mist in his head froze to ice.

The devastation on her face was so complete that he knew with gut-wrenching certainty that he hadn't misheard her.

He could no longer speak. His tongue felt alien in his mouth.

He gazed at his wife's white face and huge pain-filled eyes and the room began to spin around them. His heart roaring in his ears, he reached out blindly for her but then his knees buckled beneath him and he groped the arm of the nearest chair before they gave way completely.

Dio, what had he done?

CHAPTER ELEVEN

ANNA, HER STOMACH CHURNING, bile rising inside her, clenched her hand into a fist and shoved it against her mouth to stop herself from screaming.

How she'd prevented the screams from ripping out of her when it had all come back to her that evening she didn't know, could only guess it had been iron determination not to let the liar she'd married see her misery or the avid curious faces of their peers that had made her succeed. But now the words were out and there was no putting them back and it hit her like a tsunami that had been gathering into a peak and now came crashing down on her.

That last piece of her memory had come when she'd glanced at the menu in the hotel and read that their first course was smoked duck.

She'd been eating smoked duck in their Parisian hotel when she'd confessed to Melissa that her period was three days late.

She'd never seen Stefano lost for words before, never seen him be anything but arrogantly self-possessed. Seeing the colour drain from his horror-struck face sliced through the protective shield she'd been clinging to and her whole frame collapsed.

She fell onto her side and brought her knees up to her chin, wrapping her arms around them, and wept as she hadn't done since she was fourteen years old and she'd woken to the realisation that she would never see her father again.

The pain was unbearable, carving through her like a white-hot knife.

Through the sobs racking her body, she was aware of movement. Stefano had shifted to sit beside her on the floor.

It only made her sob harder. It was as if she were purging herself of all the pain in one huge tidal wave of grief. The loss of her father, her mother's desertion, her sister's betrayal and, fresher and more acute than all this, the loss of the man she loved and the child she'd so badly wanted.

That was something else her amnesia had anaesthetised her against: her increasingly desperate need for a child. Stefano's child. She'd sensed her marriage fragmenting around her and had tried to push the need aside, knowing theirs wasn't the stable marriage one should bring a child into. It hadn't stopped her craving one and when she'd discovered she was pregnant her joy had been so pure and true that for a few magical hours she'd allowed herself to believe that everything would work out between them and that Stefano would stop pushing her away and let her into his heart.

Now, with her memories acutely fresh, she had to accept what she'd been unable to accept in the month before she'd hit her head and slipped into blissful ignorance: that their relationship was over and all her dreams were dead.

It was a long time before the tears stopped flowing and her shuddering frame stilled enough for her to think clearly again. Her chest and throat sore, she dried her eyes with the hem of her dress and hauled herself into a sitting position with her legs crossed as she'd sat when she had been a child.

Stefano, who hadn't said a word, stretched his legs out beside her and gave a long sigh. 'You were pregnant?' he asked in a tone of voice she'd never heard before. He sounded…defeated.

She gulped for air, wishing with all her might that she could lapse back into ignorant bliss. 'Do you remember I switched the contraceptive injection I was using?'

He nodded jerkily.

'I forgot it was an eight-week course and not a twelve-week like the old one.' She sucked in more air, remembering how all over the place she'd been emotionally at that time, how her fears about her marriage had come to cloud everything. 'When I told Melissa I was three days late she couldn't believe I hadn't done a pregnancy test. She dragged me around Paris looking for a chemist so we could buy one.' She almost smiled at the memory. It was pretty much the first time in a long while that she had been happy and the last time she and Melissa had been comfortable with each other. 'I didn't think I was. I thought it was the kind of thing women knew instinctively.'

'But you were?'

She nodded and swallowed back the choking feeling in her throat. 'I was going to wait until the morning before I did the test but I couldn't resist doing it when we got back to the hotel. I was so distrustful of the result that I dragged Melissa back out to get another one and that came out positive too. That's why I called you. I was

so happy I couldn't wait to tell you.' She cast him a rue-
ful stare. 'And I was feeling a bit guilty for not taking
the test with you.'

He raised a weary shoulder. 'It doesn't matter. You do
everything with your sister. I'm used to it.'

'You think that but Melissa didn't see it that way,' she
whispered. 'We *used* to do everything together, until I
married you. I didn't realise how lonely she was without
me. After I left that message for you to call me back she
sat me down and told me she was going to Australia.'

Stefano whistled quietly.

'She'd been planning it for months. She'd been secretly
speaking to Mum and arranging it all. She'd booked her
flights, booked the time off work… All she'd been waiting for was the right time to tell me. She picked her moment perfectly, when I was on top of the world with news
of the pregnancy to dull the impact of it.'

'And did it?'

'Nope.' She wiped away a tear. 'We had a huge fight.
We said some *horrible* things to each other. She called
me a selfish bitch and she was right—I was. It was all
about *me* and how I felt. See? Selfish. I left her in the
hotel and went to the airport and stayed there until I
could get a flight back to London in the morning. I didn't
sleep at all. I kept hugging my phone waiting for you to
call me back. I was desperate to speak to you. I can't
describe how I felt—on the one hand thrilled and elated
that we were going to be parents, a little scared of how
you'd react, and devastated at what I perceived as Melissa's betrayal.'

'Why were you scared of my reaction?' he asked hol-
lowly.

She wiped away fresh tears, struggling to keep her

voice audible. 'You'd become so distant. I knew you were angry that I suspected there were other women but I *didn't* believe it. I *did* believe you but when you gave me that promotion and started travelling abroad without me…I thought you were bored of me.'

Stefano's voice cracked as he said, 'I promoted you because you were the best person for the job and I knew I could travel abroad leaving my company in the best hands.'

Promoting Anna had been a business decision. Anyone lucky enough to employ her would have done the same. And the time apart had done them good. Had done *him* good. Being together day and night hadn't been healthy. He'd expected their marriage to be eventful and fun. He hadn't expected to want to strip the skin from Anna's body to discover the secrets of her heart.

That had been dangerous. Unhealthy.

He'd thought some distance was necessary. He hadn't realised it would feed into her insecurities.

'I became paranoid. I couldn't sleep for thinking of all the women who would be flaunting themselves before you, lining themselves up to replace me.' Her red eyes were huge on his. 'I was terrified one of them would catch your eye and then the press published those pictures of you. I knew you were telling me the truth but by then I thought it was only a matter of when. I would wake every day wondering if it would be our last, always thinking, *Is this the day he meets someone else? Is this the day he tells me we're over?*'

'Anna, I made a promise to be faithful to you.'

'No, you promised to tell me if you met someone you wanted to sleep with so I could walk away with my dignity intact.'

'I kept that promise. I never cheated on you. I never wanted anyone else. I never gave you reason to doubt me.'

'Stefano, our marriage was based on two things. Sex and work. When you started pulling away from me and leaving me behind it was like you didn't need me any more. I knew you would never love me but I didn't think it mattered. I thought it was a good thing, better than having someone say they would love me for ever and then cheat and break my heart.' She shrugged and gave a choking laugh, then put her hand under her nose and closed her eyes. 'Oh, the lies we tell ourselves,' she whispered. 'I was already in love with you when we married but in total denial about it. What I really wanted was for you to tell me you didn't need to make that promise. I wanted you to say there would never be anyone else for you but me.'

The spinning in the room had turned into a whirlpool.

How could he have been so blind? So busy running from his own feelings that he'd dismissed Anna's fears thinking his word alone should be good enough for her.

He was feeling now. Feeling more than he had ever wanted, feelings he'd spent his life escaping from.

'And then you found Christina in the apartment,' he stated quietly.

She lifted her knees to wrap her arms around them and rocked forward. 'I lost my mind. Seeing a beautiful woman in our apartment dressed in my robe; it was my worst nightmare come to life. I wanted to hurt you. I was out of my mind. Truly, I wasn't thinking straight. What I did in your boardroom... I am so ashamed. I don't blame you for cutting me off as you did. I brought it on myself.'

Every word that Anna said plunged like a knife into Stefano's heart. How could she blame herself? This was all on him. If he hadn't been so full of outraged wounded pride he would have seen something had been seriously wrong with his wife.

But he hadn't thought of her. He'd thought of only himself.

Eventually he was able to drag out of his frozen throat the question he most feared hearing the answer to. 'What happened to the baby?'

'I lost it two days later.' A huge shudder ran through her and she buried her face in her knees, fresh sobs pouring out of her.

Feeling as if he'd been kicked in the stomach, Stefano pulled her to him. This time he allowed his instincts to take over, wrapping his arms tightly around her, pressing his mouth into her hair, wishing he knew the words that would make everything better and stop the cold agony he knew was consuming them both.

She clutched at his jacket, her tears soaking into his shirt. 'It was the only thing keeping me going. I know it must sound stupid but I'd pictured our baby. I'd planned its whole life out in my head...'

'It doesn't sound stupid at all,' he cut in. In his mind's eye he could picture their baby too...

Fresh bile rose swiftly inside him and grabbed at his throat, making his head spin.

'Where were you when you...?' He couldn't bring himself to say it.

'In my hotel room.' She took a gulp of air. 'I'd checked into a hotel because I couldn't face Melissa after our row and you wouldn't let me anywhere near you.'

'You were alone?'

She nodded into his chest. 'So, selfish creature that I am, I went back to my sister.'

'You are *not* selfish,' he stated fiercely.

Anna had had to go through that trauma on her own? The only selfish one here had been him.

'Aren't I? I hated the thought of her seeing our mum.'

'No,' he contradicted, 'you were scared you would lose her too. You lost both your parents when you were at an age when you needed them most. Your father, rest his soul, did not leave by choice but your mother did. Is no wonder you find it hard to trust people—the woman who should have been there for you left you behind.'

And if he'd ever allowed Anna to open up to him during their marriage instead of avoiding any kind of intimate talk he would have known how shattered her mother's emigration had left her. He would have known just how vulnerable she was and would have made that damned call to her instead of telling himself she would be fast asleep and wouldn't mind waiting.

You did know she'd mind but you were running scared. Anna got too close, didn't she? You were waiting for an excuse to push her away before she rejected you like everyone else you ever knew did.

She hadn't been asleep. She'd been in an airport waiting to return home to him with the best news of their lives and some shattering news of her own. She'd needed him.

He squeezed her even tighter to him. 'Melissa looked after you?'

'Melissa always looks after me.' Anna tilted her head to look at him. 'She's always been my lifeline, and you're right, I was scared I'd lose her. We muddled along as well as we could but it was hard. We'd both said things we couldn't take back. When she left for Australia it was without my blessing. She even left me a note asking for my forgiveness when it should have been me down on my knees begging for hers.'

'Anna…'

'No, please don't make excuses for me. I'm not fourteen any more. I've always known how much Melissa missed our mum but ignored it under my own self-righteousness.'

'Or did you ignore it because it meant you would have to confront how much you missed your mum too?'

'Don't say that,' she protested.

'You must have missed her. I always missed my mother and I never even knew her.'

'Did you?'

She sounded so surprised that he couldn't help but give a grimace of a smile. 'All my life. And I missed my father. I look now on all the years we missed out on when I could have known him and I think what a waste those years were.'

'But do you regret cutting the rest of your family out of your life?'

'Not at all. I will never have them in my life again but my situation with them is different from yours. I never loved them and they never loved me.'

Since his *nonno* had died, Anna was the only person who had loved him. Lots of women had claimed to love him but he'd always known their words to be a pack of lies. Anna was…

She was the only one.

'You still think I should see my mother?'

'You will never find peace until you do, that much I do know. Speak to her. Hear her side. Admit to yourself that you need her in your life. See if you can build a relationship.'

She fell silent.

'I can come with you.'

'Where?'

'To see your mother. I can come as support.'

Her laugh sounded genuine but as she disentangled herself from his hold he saw fresh tears were streaming down her face.

'I needed your support five weeks ago.' She shook her head and wiped the tears away then straightened.

'Let me give it to you now,' he urged. 'I wasn't there for you…'

'No, you weren't.' Her shining eyes bored into his. 'And I don't blame you. I understand what a shock it must have been for you having your sister turn up out of the blue and learning about your father.'

'I should never have cut you off.'

'No, you shouldn't, but I knew the type of man you were when I married you. I knew you didn't do forgiveness. One strike and the person's out—humiliating you was my strike and I accept that…'

'No, don't accept it. I was a *fool* to behave like that.' A fool and a cruel, selfish bastard. 'If I'd any idea what you were going through I would never have…'

'It doesn't matter!' She took a deep breath and got unsteadily to her feet. 'None of it matters any more, don't you see that? Our marriage is over and it's time I learned to stand on my own two feet.'

The freezing fog in his brain thickened, making his ears ring. 'It doesn't have to be over. We can start again.'

'It does.' She folded her arms across her chest. There was something in her stance that made her appear taller.

'We could forgive each other everything that happened, draw a line in the sand and start again, but I'll never forgive you for what you did to get your revenge.' She shrugged her shoulders but the whiteness of her face belied the nonchalance she was trying to portray. 'That was despicable and I hate you for it.'

On legs that were surprisingly weak, he got up to stand before her. Something was scratching at him, clawing at his chest, making it painful to breathe. 'You said that you loved me.'

'And I did love you. With all my heart. All through my amnesia I kept thinking you were holding back from telling me you loved me to keep the pressure off my recovery but the truth was you never loved me, did you?'

The pain in his chest increased. He couldn't form any words. Not one.

'You killed my love and all my trust in you,' she spat. 'If I ever marry again it will be to someone who wants more than just my body and my business brain.' Her voice caught but when she continued her tone didn't falter. 'It will be with someone who can love me too and trust me with their heart. I have to hope for that.'

And with that she turned her back on him, picked up her clutch bag from the table and headed for the front door.

'Where are you going?' Things were moving too quickly. She couldn't just *leave* like this. 'Look at the weather out there.'

The rain was lashing so hard it fell like hail against the windows.

She didn't turn around. 'I'm going to check into a hotel and in the morning I'm going to go home. *My* home. Mine and Melissa's flat. After that, all I know for certain is that I have to stop relying on other people to hold me up and learn to hold myself up. If Melissa stays in Australia then I will give her my blessing.' Then she did turn and gave the smallest, saddest of smiles. 'Maybe I will fly out there too. I don't know.'

There was nothing left to say. He could see it in her eyes. Anna was going to walk out of the door and this time it would be for good.

She didn't say goodbye.

She closed the door with the softest of clicks but the sound echoed like a ricocheting bullet.

Stefano stood on the same spot for an age, too numb and dazed about everything that had just happened to take it all in. A part of him expected—hoped—that the door would swing back open and she'd walk back in and tell him she'd changed her mind.

It didn't happen.

Her discarded shoes lay on their sides where she'd thrown them. Her feet were bare…

His legs suddenly propelled themselves to the window that overlooked the street below. He pushed it open and stuck his head out, uncaring that the storm soaked him in seconds and blinded his eyes.

Through the sheet of water running over his face he caught a glimpse of a red dress disappearing into a cab. Seconds later the cab pulled away from the kerb and soon he lost sight of it.

Anna had gone.

A week later Stefano strolled through the entrance foyer of his London apartment building. The two receptionists on duty greeted him warmly but with the same subtle

wariness he'd been receiving at work that had become
more marked since his return from San Francisco. He was
used to fear but this felt different. Now people treated
him as they would when confronted with a dangerous
dog they didn't want to provoke.

Anna had treated him like that before she'd collapsed
at his feet with her concussion.

He blinked her image from his mind.

It mattered nothing to him how his staff behaved towards him. He preferred everyone to keep their distance.
He didn't need their chatter. If someone wanted to speak
to him, he was all for getting to the point, cut the chit-
chat and get on. Small talk was discouraged.

Anna had taught him the term 'cut the chit-chat'. It
had made a sharp but smooth sound in his mouth that
amused him. *Had* amused him. It had been a long time
since he'd found anything funny.

He took the bundle of letters one of the receptionists
held out for him with a nod and was about to continue to
the elevator when he remembered Anna's not so subtle
way of pulling him up on his manners those two and a
half years ago.

With two short sarcastic words, *you're welcome*,
she'd reminded him that being Europe's top technology
magnate didn't stop you or the others around you being
human and that humans needed to feel appreciated.

He paused, looked the receptionist in the eyes and
said, 'Thank you,' then wished them both a good evening and carried on up to his apartment.

Only after he'd dumped his briefcase and poured himself a bourbon did he sit on the sofa and go through his
mail.

He put his thumb and middle finger to the bridge of

his nose and squeezed to keep himself alert but, *Dio*, he was ready for bed.

It was all rubbish. Rubbish, rubbish, rubbish… He should employ someone to take care of his personal life as he did his business life. Then he wouldn't have to deal with bills and the other necessary parts of life. Considering he'd abandoned running a household within weeks of having one, that thought would be funny if he hadn't lost his funny bone. Or would it be ironic? Anna had been a great one for finding irony funny. She'd found a lot of things funny. His life was a much less cheerful place without her. He hadn't noticed that when she'd left him the first time as he'd been too busy wallowing in his own sense of… What had she called it? Self-righteousness? She'd been describing herself when she'd said it but it applied to him too.

It had only been since his return from San Francisco when he'd refused himself the luxury of self-righteousness that he'd really noticed how the colour had gone from his life. Maybe it had been because she'd come back to him for that one week and they'd learned more about each other then than they had in the whole of the two and a half years they'd known each other.

Why couldn't he stop thinking of her?

He took a healthy slug of his bourbon and opened the last item of mail, a thick padded envelope with a San Francisco postmark.

This must be the gift the concierge in his apartment there had messaged him about. It had been delivered shortly after he'd left for London on the day that was his and Anna's first wedding anniversary. Not caring what was in it—not caring about anything—Stefano had told the man to forward it to his London address.

And now it was here.

Inside the packaging was a small square gift-wrapped box.

He twisted it in his hands, his heart racing as his mind drifted back to Anna's insistence on some solo 'retail therapy' that afternoon before the awards ceremony.

He'd thought it strange when she'd returned empty-handed.

He could not credit how much he missed her. It hadn't been this bad before.

No, it *had* been this bad before but he'd masked it from himself. And it had been more than self-righteousness that had masked it but a mad fury like nothing he'd ever known...

She'd made assumptions about Christina, but hadn't he made assumptions about Anna being a gold-digger? Hadn't he been as determined to see the worst in her as Anna had been to see the worst in him?

He sat bolt upright, his brain racing almost as madly as his heart.

Dio, he could see the truth.

Somewhere along the line he had fallen in love with her. The man who had spent his life avoiding serious relationships for terror of being hurt and rejected had fallen in love.

Because he *had* been terrified. For all his disdain at people who refused to let go of their childhood he could see he'd done the opposite and buried his under a 'don't care' bravado when all the time he'd been running, trying to stop it ever happening again.

He bent his head forward and dug his fingers into the back of his head as he strove to suck in air.

How could he have been so blind and stupid?

He'd blown it.

He loved his wife but the joke was on him because she didn't love him any more.

Breathing deeply, he looked again at the gift-wrapped box.

Feeling as if he were opening something that could bite him, he ripped the wrapping off and snapped the lid of the black square box open.

Nestled inside it were two gold wedding bands.

CHAPTER TWELVE

ANNA ACCEPTED THE bottle of water from Melissa with a grateful smile of thanks.

The sand on Bondi beach was fine and deliciously warm between her toes, the sun blazing down and baking her skin. As it was a work day and the schools were open, the beach was busy but not packed. While there wasn't the privacy she'd found at hers and Stefano's Santa Cruz beach house, there was an easy vibe that almost, *almost* gave her the peace she so longed for.

The rate she was going she would never find peace. Not in herself.

Melissa stretched out on the sun-lounger beside her and they sat there amiably, sunglasses on, soaking up the rays.

'What do you want to do later?' Melissa said after a while.

'I haven't got anything in mind. You?'

'Shall we borrow Mick's Jeep and go for a drive and explore the suburbs?'

'You'll have to drive. I haven't been behind a wheel in years.'

'All the more reason you should drive. Use it or lose it.'

Anna laughed but it was a muted sound compared to the way she used to laugh.

'Shall we invite Mum with us?' Melissa asked carefully.

'If you want.'

When Anna had flown out to Australia it hadn't been to make her peace with her mother but to make her peace with Melissa. She had been determined to do what Stefano had suggested though, and sit down and talk to her mother, if only just so she could move on.

Her mum hadn't quite seen it like that. Anna had arrived at the house to find the whole ground floor covered in balloons and banners to welcome her. All the neighbours and Mick's family had been invited round to meet her. Melissa had stood there, eyes pleading for Anna to go along with it—Anna could almost read her mind, realising her sister was begging her not to make a scene.

Making a scene was the last thing she'd wanted to do.

She'd looked at her mum, flanked by her husband and stepkids, and seen the desperate excitement in her eyes, and the fear.

Too much water had passed under the bridge for Anna to throw herself into her mother's arms as if nothing had happened but she'd returned her embrace coolly.

It had been almost a decade since she'd last seen her and she'd taken in the marked changes time had wrought. Her mother had done the same in return. They'd stared at each other for so long that Anna's eyes had blurred, her heart so full that it pushed up into her throat and then she really had fallen into her mother's arms.

As the evening had progressed and she couldn't make a move without tripping over her mother, Anna had come to understand exactly what it meant for her mum to have her youngest child under her roof and had cancelled her hotel reservation and agreed to stay there, sharing the guest room with Melissa.

That had been two weeks ago.

They had spent a long time talking. They'd been honest with each other. Many tears had been shed. A bucketful of them.

Her mother had apologised over and over for leaving her behind and for the cruel words she'd spoken the last time they'd been together. She hadn't made any excuses. She knew she'd been selfish and had effectively abandoned her daughters for the sake of a man. Her bone-deep guilt had been her punishment.

If Anna were being cynical she could say that if the guilt had been that bad, she could always have come home to them.

She didn't want to be cynical any more.

Things were still awkward at times but slowly they were forging a rapport. Perhaps they would never regain their old mother-daughter relationship but Anna was confident that when she returned to London they would retain some semblance of one. It was entirely in her hands. Whatever wrongs her mother had done, Stefano had been correct in his assessment that she had missed her. She needed her mother in her life.

She hadn't known how badly she'd needed her until she'd found her again and found the courage to let go of her anger and forgive.

She just wished the pain in her heart would ease. Not even the peace she'd made with her sister and the forgiveness she'd found for her mother had eased it. And it was getting worse, especially since Melissa had given her the pin code for her phone—it turned out she'd used Stefano's birthday—and she'd gone through all her photos and videos. There was one video where she'd sneakily filmed Stefano taking a shower. The footage showed his start of surprise when he'd spotted her, then his wolfish grin as he'd opened the glass shower door. The footage went dark when he grabbed her phone and threw it onto the floor.

He'd then grabbed *her*, she remembered, and dragged her fully clothed into the shower with him. Her clothes hadn't stayed on for much longer.

Her heart ached to think of him and when she closed her eyes all she could see was the despair on his face when she'd walked away.

She had never seen him like that before, not her strong, powerful husband. She'd seen him in passion and in anger but never in wretched defeat.

A fresh wave of pain hit her as she imagined him now and all he was having to cope with.

He'd been coping with it ever since she'd burst into his boardroom.

He was dealing with a father who'd been alive his whole life while he'd thought him dead. A father who *had* wanted him when no one else in his family had cared enough to even buy him shoes that fitted. He was dealing with a sister he hadn't known existed until a few months ago, his first true familial relationship since he'd been seven.

And now he was having to deal with the knowledge that he and Anna had conceived a child together but that its tiny life had died before he could even celebrate its conception.

She knew too that he carried guilt over his treatment of her.

It was a heavy burden for him to carry and he was having to carry it on his own.

But he probably wasn't alone, she scolded herself. This was Stefano she was thinking of; his bed was never empty for more than a week.

Immediately she castigated herself. He'd been faithful to her throughout their marriage and it was wrong of her to make assumptions now. She'd leapt to conclusions when she'd found Christina in their apartment and had been paying the price for it ever since. For all the horrendous wrongs he'd done, the only solid image in her mind was Stefano watching her leave his apartment, as haunted and haggard as she had ever seen him.

He'd asked her if they could start again…

But she'd dismissed him.

He hadn't wanted her to go.

She shook her head to clear it. She would have to see him in person soon. She needed to be strong, not let doubts creep in.

He'd had doubts. He'd tried to stop the revenge he'd plotted down to the smallest detail from being carried out.

He'd asked her if they could start again…

Discovering the truth that night in San Francisco had been the most soul-destroying thing she had ever lived through. Learning that he'd seduced her and made her fall in love with him for revenge… She'd understood all this at the same moment the awful memories of their parting and the miscarriage had come back to her. The two had become a singular issue in her mind and the pain it all had unleashed had been too much to bear.

Time apart had given her some perspective.

He'd told her he wanted to start their marriage afresh

and she'd dismissed it without properly listening to what he was saying. He'd told her he wanted to start their marriage again *after* she'd told him she loved him. This from the man who didn't do forgiveness or love.

Melissa's voice cut through her rambling thoughts. 'You okay, chook?'

'Sorry? *Chook?*'

'Mum says it's an Aussie term of endearment.'

Anna's lips twitched but that was the nearest thing to a smile she could muster.

'Anna? You okay?'

She blinked herself back into focus and shook her head. 'I don't think I am.'

'What? You're not okay?' Alarm spread across Melissa's face. 'Are you feeling unwell? Are you going to be sick again?'

'No, nothing like that. No. Mel…I think…'

'What?'

Her mind running this way and that, Anna got to her feet and started throwing her stuff into her beach bag. 'I need to go back.'

Melissa hastily slid off her sun-lounger. 'I'll come with you.'

In less than a minute they'd gathered all their stuff together and thrown their shorts and T-shirts back on and Anna was steaming along the beach, unwittingly spraying sand in sunbathers' faces, while Melissa struggled to keep up.

'Slow down,' she pleaded. 'The house isn't going anywhere.'

This time Anna did find a proper smile. 'I'm not going back to the house, I'm going to the airport.'

'*What?*'

'I'm going home.'

'You can't.'

'Watch me.'

'No, you idiot, I mean you can't go to the airport—your passport's at Mum's.'

'Oh. Yes. Right.' But it only slowed her for a moment and then she walked even faster, mentally calculating how quickly she could get to the airport. Her return flight was booked for a week from now. She was sure the airline had fixed flights so that would mean a plane would be leaving for London that evening. She needed to be on it.

'What do you want to go home for?'

'I need to see Stefano.'

'Anna, *no*...'

'Yes.'

'You were going to wait. Let things settle a bit more before telling him.'

'It's nothing to do with that.'

Melissa grabbed her arm and forced her to stop. 'Anna, will you listen to me? Please? Whatever you're thinking, don't do it.'

'Mel...I love him.' Totally. Utterly. Irreversibly.

'That man *destroyed* you.'

'No,' she contradicted. 'I think we've destroyed each other. And maybe we can fix each other.'

It was a fifteen-minute fast walk back to the house. Melissa was puffing behind her as Anna rushed through the front door, her adrenaline levels too high to need to catch a breath.

She hurried up the hallway to the stairs, about to go to her room and get her flight details so she could get straight on the phone to the airline...

'Anna, is that you?' came her mother's voice.

'Yes, sorry, give me a minute.'

Her mother appeared at the kitchen doorway, her face flushed. 'You've got a visitor.'

'Me?' Who would be visiting *her*? She didn't know anyone here apart from her mum's friends and family.

She stepped into the kitchen, turned her head to the large table and froze.

After several long, long moments she closed her eyes then slowly opened them again.

Stefano was sitting at the kitchen table. Her mum's golden retriever, George, had his head on his lap.

'What are you doing here?' she whispered, placing a hand to her chest to stop her heart from jumping out of it.

'Visiting you.' Slowly he rose to his feet.

She inched closer and drank in the face she hadn't seen in what felt like for ever until she was only a foot away.

A mere two weeks apart had left marked changes in him. He was paler than she remembered. His hair needed cutting. He looked as if he'd slept in his canvas shorts and crumpled shirt.

As if he could read her mind, one side of his mouth curved up and he said, 'It was a long flight.'

She couldn't think clearly. The joy bursting into life inside her was marred with caution.

He'd flown across the world to see her just as she'd been gearing up to fly across the world to see him and to find out if there was any chance of a future together for them.

But what if he was here for a different reason? What if he only wanted to discuss their divorce?

Every morning since she'd left San Francisco she'd promised herself that today would be the day she would call her lawyer in England and start proper divorce proceedings. After all, they'd been married for a full year. There was nothing to stop them.

And yet, for all her anger and misery, she hadn't been able to bring herself to do it.

Had the time apart that had been so painful to her only been a healer for him?

Until he told her his reasons for being there she would not allow the screaming excitement running through her to take control.

'Is there somewhere private we can talk?' he asked, breaking the silence that had formed while she stood there trying to catch a coherent thought.

Her mum and sister quickly shuffled out of sight but Anna didn't trust that they wouldn't listen in to what was going on.

'The garden?'

He nodded and, on legs that had gone from having bones supporting them to what felt like overcooked noodles, she led him outside. George slipped out with them before she could close the door.

Her mum's garden was a lovingly tended spot with a good-sized swimming pool. They sat carefully on the large swing chair with a canopy to shade them from the blazing sun, both making sure not to sit too close to the other. They were still close enough that Anna's body vibrated at his nearness and she had to fold her hands tightly together to stop them stretching out to touch him and feel for herself that she wasn't dreaming this.

George sat himself at Stefano's feet and he leaned down to rub the dog's head.

'I think you've made a friend,' Anna commented softly.

'I like dogs.'

She hadn't known that. 'You should get one.'

'One day. He's your mother's?'

'Yes.'

'How are things with her?'

'Better than I thought they'd be.'

'You've forgiven her?'

'Just about.' She would never be less than honest with him. 'It's so hard to let the past go but I have to. If I've learnt anything in recent months it's that holding onto anger destroys you as much as the other. She's made mistakes—massive ones—but I have too and I know she's genuinely sorry. I am too. I just want her back in my life.'

They lapsed into silence that stretched so unbearably tight that Anna couldn't endure it a moment longer. 'Why are you here?'

'Because I'm falling apart without you.' His shoulders rose and he turned his head to look at her. 'I want you to think about coming back. Not to me, I know you won't do that, but back to Moretti's. The staff are on the verge of mutiny because without you there I have lost my conscience. You can have your own office so you don't have to see me if you don't want to. You can boss me around just as well by email as in person. Name your terms and your price.'

Stefano didn't take his gaze off her. He sought every tiny flicker of reaction on her face.

Her forehead furrowed. 'You want me to come back to *work*?'

'I know I'm asking a lot of you.'

'You're not wrong.'

'Please. Hear me out. Anna, it's not just Moretti's that's falling apart, is me. *I'm* falling apart. I know you won't come back as my wife but I miss having you in my life. You keep me sane. You help me see things clearly. I need you.'

He'd never said that before to anyone. He'd learned at too young an age that people were too often faithless and cruel to each other to allow himself to ever need someone. The only person he'd ever needed was himself.

Much of the colour had left her face.

'If you come back then it will be on whatever terms you choose. Having you close by will be enough for me.' He ran his fingers through his hair to stop them from touching her. 'I know it's over for us. How I took advantage of your amnesia was unforgivable. I was furious about your assumptions that I was having an affair but I made assumptions of my own. I swore you had to be a gold-digger because I couldn't face the truth that you were in love with me and I was in love with you.'

She sucked in a breath and he grimaced. 'I know it's too late for you to hear that but, please, allow me to explain. I know I won't have your forgiveness but I would like your understanding.

'Your instincts about your promotion were right—I did give it to you so I could be rid of you—you *were* the best person for the job but that was secondary—but it wasn't because I was bored with you. You were scared I would leave you but I was already scared you would leave me. I've never been wanted for myself before, not since Nonno died. The rest of my family didn't want me and you know as well as I do that they treated me like dirt. When I left them to fend for myself, people didn't want *me*, they wanted to use me; bosses exploiting my age to try and underpay me, drunk women seeing me as nothing but a handsome face to have sex with. When I finally made my fortune people didn't want me for myself, they wanted my fame and money. You were the first person to see through the expensive suits and see the man inside. How could you like that man when no one else had ever liked or wanted him? I deliberately pushed you away because I was too much of a coward to acknowledge that I loved you. I pushed you away before you could push me.'

His soul laid bare, Stefano took a long breath and covered her hands. A glimmer of hope fluttered in him when she didn't resist, her eyes still on his face, wide and glistening.

'I can't be without you,' he said, willing for her to believe him. 'I can't even breathe normally. Days without you are an eternity. Please come back. If all you can offer is to take your place in Moretti's again then that's enough.'

Time itself seemed to morph into eternity while he waited for her to respond.

When she moved her hands out of his hold his heart sank so sharply it caused physical pain.

But then she placed one on his cheek and moved her face a little closer and his heart dared to rise back up.

'After all you've just said are you only offering me my job back?'

He trapped the hand palmed against his cheek. 'Anna, you have my heart. Whatever you can give I will accept. I need you and I will take whatever you can give.'

'But what do you *want*?'

Something in her expression sent warmth into blood that had been cold for weeks. 'I want you to ask me to make that promise I made to you again so that I can tell you I don't need to make it because there will never be anyone else but you for me.'

Slowly her face moved to his and then her eyes closed and her lips pressed gently against his.

He hardly dared to breathe. He'd flown out here knowing he needed to make that one last move and strip himself bare for her. He'd reconciled himself to them being over but had been unable to reconcile with Anna being out of his life for good. She was so much a part of him that her not being there had been like living with a piece of himself missing.

'I don't want to come back to London as your employee,' she whispered into his mouth. 'I want to come back as your wife.'

This was more than he had dared hope for. Far more. 'You do?'

Her nose brushed his as she nodded. 'I love you.'

A boulder settled in his throat and he swallowed it away. 'But can you forgive me?'

'We've both made mistakes. If we can't draw a line under them and make a fresh start then we'll both suffer for it.' She smiled, though her chin wobbled. 'It's been agony for me without you. I'd already decided to come home and see if there was any chance for us.'

'Really?'

She nodded. 'That's why I came back early from the beach. It had all suddenly become clear for me. I thought my love for you had died but that was my hurt and pride talking, not my heart.'

'I swear I will never do anything to hurt you again.'

'We're both stubborn and fiery. We'll probably spend the rest of our lives arguing with each other.'

'As long as we spend the rest of it making up then I can live with that.' And to prove his point he put a hand round the back of her head and pulled her in for another kiss, this one deep and full of all the love and desire he felt for this beautiful woman without whom he was nothing but a shell of himself.

She was everything to him, his lover, his confidante and his sparring partner. It would be easier to live without a limb than without her.

'How do you feel about us becoming parents?' she asked him between kisses.

He put his finger under her chin.

For all that they'd forgiven each other everything, Anna being alone when she miscarried their child was something he would never forgive himself for.

'When the time is right we can try for a child. I want us to have a football team of *bambinos* and a couple of dogs for them to play with but not until you're ready for it.'

He thought he would see sadness in her eyes but they were bright and…knowing.

'Anna?'

Suddenly the most enormous grin beamed from her face.

'You're not?'

'I am.' She snuggled into him, her head on his chest. 'I took the test last week.'

'With Melissa?' he asked drily. This was unbelievable. He'd left London feeling as if he were drowning, seeking Anna as a life raft, and now felt as if the sun were shining especially for them.

'Yes.'

'And one for luck?'

'Yes.' She pressed herself even tighter to him. 'Neither of us knew it at the time but I wasn't protected when we were in Santa Cruz—I never had another injection after

I lost…' The kiss on her head and the tightening of the arms around her showed that Stefano understood what she was struggling to vocalise. 'I'm sorry for not telling you sooner,' she whispered into his chest. 'I was trying to get my head around it and I knew it was something I had to tell you to your face. But I was going to tell you as soon as I got back to London. I swear.'

He ran his fingers through her hair. 'Don't apologise. I know you would have told me. How are you feeling?'

'A little sick at times but nothing to complain about.' Her face shone as she gazed up at him. 'And you?'

He kissed her. 'I feel that you've given me all my birthday and Christmas presents in one go.'

And speaking of presents…

He disentangled himself just enough to pull out the small black square box he'd carried on his person since he'd opened it a week ago.

She recognised it at once, her eyes widening and somehow brightening further. 'I was going to give you that…'

'On our wedding anniversary,' he finished for her.

She held out her left hand for him and he slid the smaller ring onto her wedding finger then kissed it. 'I love you.'

'I love you too,' she whispered before taking the larger ring and sliding it onto his finger and kissing it in turn.

It took a long time for Stefano to comprehend the magnitude of all that had happened, how his last throw of the dice had brought him rewards he'd not allowed himself to dream of.

He had his wife back and this time he would honour and cherish her until his dying breath.

EPILOGUE

ANNA SAT ON the side of the bath watching Stefano, who was leaning against the wall looking at his watch, light bouncing off his gold wedding band, a white oblong stick in his hand.

The bathroom door was shoved open and Cecily, their three-year-old daughter, came flying in followed in quick succession by her four-year-old brother and their slower, sappy King Charles spaniel, Alfie.

Cecily threw her arms around Anna's legs. 'Mario hit me,' she wailed.

'She threw my ice cream on the floor!' he hollered indignantly.

'Behave, the pair of you,' Stefano scolded, amusement lurking in his eyes. 'And no hitting.'

'But…!'

'If you can't play nicely together we won't go to the beach,' Anna cut in. With Mario due to start school in England that September, they'd decided to spend the summer in their Santa Cruz beach house, the unanimous family favourite of all their homes.

Two months before Mario had been born, they'd left their London apartment and moved into a rambling manor house in Oxfordshire surrounded by acres of land for their football team of children to play in. It was an idyllic existence. Picture perfect. Apart from having two children who liked nothing more than fighting furiously, of course.

'No fair!' they both shouted together. Still bickering, the pair of them toddled off to their playroom, no doubt leaving a trail of chaos and destruction in their wake. She found it remarkable that their mess didn't bother her at all.

'Are you sure you want another one?' Stefano asked, laughing.

She grinned. Their football team hadn't quite materialised. After having two children with a gap of less than a year between them, they'd decided to wait and enjoy them before having any more.

She'd come off the pill a month ago.

'I think we can cope.'

'That's a relief.' He passed the stick to her, his grin now as wide as his face. 'Because according to this, we're having another one.'

Anna read the blue plus sign, her own grin widening to match her husband's.

With a whoop of delight, Stefano picked her up and planted kisses all over her face.

Wrapping her legs around his waist and her arms around his neck, Anna returned the kisses. Even with two children and another on the way, their desire and love for each other remained undiminished. There wasn't a single aspect of her life she would change. Together they'd created a family filled with love and laughter, arguments and *lots* of making up.

'Daddy! What are you doing to my mummy?' Cecily was standing in the bathroom doorway, her arms folded and the same expression on her face that Stefano always used when he wasn't amused by something. 'Put her down at once!'

Stefano put Anna down, gave her one last kiss for luck, then scooped his daughter up and carried her, screaming with laughter, upside down to the playroom.

* * * * *

If you enjoyed ONCE A MORETTI WIFE,
why not explore these other
Michelle Smart stories?

MARRIED FOR THE GREEK'S CONVENIENCE
CLAIMING HIS CHRISTMAS CONSEQUENCE
WEDDED, BEDDED, BETRAYED
TALOS CLAIMS HIS VIRGIN
THESEUS DISCOVERS HIS HEIR

Available now!

A deep tremble overtook her as Emiliano closed the gap between them and slid strong fingers into her hair.

'You're mine now, Sienna Castillo,' he murmured against her lips, with a deep relish in his tone that escalated her trembling.

'As you are mine,' she replied, somehow noting the importance of establishing equal ownership.

'*Sí*, that is exactly so.'

His voice throbbed with possessive and binding forces, binding her even more strongly than the new ring on her finger.

One Night With Consequences

When one night...leads to pregnancy!

When succumbing to a night of unbridled desire
it's impossible to think past the morning after!

But, with the sheets barely settled, that little blue line
appears on the pregnancy test and it doesn't take long
to realise that one night of white-hot passion
has turned into a lifetime of consequences!

Only one question remains:

How do you tell a man you've just met
that you're about to share more than just his bed?

Find out in:

The Shock Cassano Baby by Andie Brock

An Heir to Make A Marriage by Abby Green

The Greek's Nine-Month Redemption by Maisey Yates

Crowned for the Prince's Heir by Sharon Kendrick

The Sheikh's Baby Scandal by Carol Marinelli

A Ring for Vincenzo's Heir by Jennie Lucas

Claiming His Christmas Consequence by Michelle Smart

The Guardian's Virgin Ward by Caitlin Crews

A Child Claimed by Gold by Rachael Thomas

The Consequence of His Vengeance by Jennie Lucas

Secrets of a Billionaire's Mistress by Sharon Kendrick

Look for more **One Night With Consequences** stories
coming soon!

THE BOSS'S
NINE-MONTH
NEGOTIATION

BY
MAYA BLAKE

MILLS
BOON

First Published in Great Britain 2017
By Mills & Boon, an imprint of HarperCollins*Publishers*
1 London Bridge Street, London, SE1 9GF

© 2017 Maya Blake

ISBN: 978-0-263-92516-6

Printed and bound in Spain
by CPI, Barcelona

Maya Blake's hopes of becoming a writer were born when she picked up her first romance at thirteen. Little did she know her dream would come true! Does she still pinch herself every now and then to make sure it's not a dream? Yes, she does! Feel free to pinch her, too, via Twitter, Facebook or Goodreads! Happy reading!

Books by Maya Blake

Mills & Boon Modern Romance

Signed Over to Santino
A Diamond Deal with the Greek
Married for the Prince's Convenience
Innocent in His Diamonds

Rival Brothers

A Deal with Alejandro
One Night with Gael

The Billionaire's Legacy

The Di Sione Secret Baby

Secret Heirs of Billionaires

Brunetti's Secret Son

Seven Sexy Sins

A Marriage Fit for a Sinner

The Untameable Greeks

What the Greek's Money Can't Buy
What the Greek Can't Resist
What the Greek Wants Most

Visit the Author Profile page
at millsandboon.co.uk for more titles.

To Carly, for making my stories shine!

PROLOGUE

NOTHING HAD CHANGED in six years.

Emiliano Castillo was mildly surprised at himself for entertaining the thought, even for a second, that things would be different. Wasn't 'the old way or no way' one of the endless tenets forming his family's foundations and beliefs?

Wasn't that rigid clinging to tradition one of *his* reasons for turning his back on his family?

He kept his gaze dead straight, refusing to turn his head to glance at the miles of rolling paddocks that usually held his family's prized thoroughbreds and foal training ground. Even then, he couldn't help but notice, as his chauffeur drove him towards his ancestral home, that the normally teeming landscape was now curiously empty, the dozen or so gauchos usually in each corral nowhere in sight.

He brought his wandering thoughts back under control. There would be no indulging in nostalgia on this visit. In fact, Emiliano intended the trip to the renowned Castillo Estate just outside Cordoba, Argentina, to be as brief as the summons that had brought him here.

He had only come out of respect for Matias, his older brother. Had Matias been in a position to speak, Emiliano would've made sure his brother relayed his refusal of the summons he'd received in London loud and clear to their parents.

Sadly, Matias wasn't in a position to do any such thing.

The reason for that tightened his jaw, even as a brief tinge of sadness assailed him. Thankfully, there was little time to dwell on it as the car drew up in front of the extensive luxury villa in which several generations of proud, intractable Castillos had lived.

Oak double doors opened as he stepped out of the car.

Emiliano tensed, for a moment forgetting that neither his father nor his mother had deigned to open doors of their own accord for as long as he could remember. Not when they had servants to do it for them.

Mounting the steps, he nodded curtly at the ageing butler's greeting. This particular member of staff wasn't one he remembered and for that he was marginally thankful. He wanted no more memories triggered, or to go down the lonely, dismal path he'd done his best to try to forget.

'If señor would like to come with me, Señor and Señora Castillo are waiting in the drawing room.'

Emiliano allowed himself the briefest of glances at the walls that surrounded the home he'd grown up in, the sturdy bannister he used to slide down as a child, the antique cabinet he'd crashed into and earned himself a long-since-healed fracture on his collarbone.

He'd had time to do all that because he hadn't been the firstborn son. His time had been his own to use or misuse as he pleased, because only one person had counted in this household: Matias. But it was only as he'd entered his teenage years that he'd grown to fathom exactly what that meant.

Securing the button on his single-breasted suit, he refocused his gaze and followed the butler into the wide, sunlit reception room.

His parents were seated in twin wing-backed chairs that wouldn't have been out of place in the throne room at the Palace of Versailles. But, even without the heavy accoutrements and almost-garish displays of wealth to punctuate their success, Benito and Valentina Castillo carried themselves with near-royal pride.

They both eyed him now with equal expressions of hauteur and indifference—both expressions he was used to. But Emiliano glimpsed something else beneath the brittle exteriors.

Nerves. Desperation.

He tucked that observation away, walked forward and kissed his mother on both cheeks.

'Mama, I hope you are well?'

Her expression twitched only for as long as it took for her to give him a once-over, before settling back into prideful superiority. 'Of course. But I would be better still if you'd bothered to answer us when we first reached out to you. But, as usual, you choose to do things in your own time, when it suits you best.'

Emiliano gritted his teeth and curbed the urge to remind them that it was the legacy of forgetful indifference they'd bestowed on him which had dictated his actions. Instead he nodded to his father, received a curt nod in return and selected an armchair to settle in.

'I am here now. Shall we get on with why you summoned me?' he said, then refused the offer of a drink from the butler.

His father's mouth twisted. '*Sí*, always in a rush. Always, you have somewhere else to be, don't you?'

Emiliano slowly exhaled. 'As a matter of fact, I do.' He was in the middle of a bidding war for a revolutionary social media programme back in London. The programme's creators were being courted by at least half a dozen other venture capitalists. Despite his company being the biggest and most powerful of them all, he reminded himself that he'd been the underdog once, before a daring move had set him on his way to stratospheric success. This wasn't a time to take his foot off the pedal.

He also had to approve the finishing touches for the birthday celebration his event planner had put together for Sienna Newman.

His vice-president of Acquisitions.

His lover.

Thoughts of the woman whose intellect kept him on his toes by day and whose body thrilled his by night fractionally allayed the bitter memories of his childhood. Unlike his past liaisons, she hadn't been an easy conquest, her reluctance even to give him the time of day beyond the boardroom was a challenge that had fired his blood in the months before she'd even agreed to have dinner with him.

In his quiet moments, Emiliano still silently reeled at the changes he'd made in his life in order to accommodate his lover. The few who presumed to know him would agree— rightly, in this instance—that this behaviour wasn't like him at all. His own disquiet in the face of the reservation he sometimes felt from Sienna made him question himself. But not enough to disrupt the status quo. Not yet, anyway. Although, like everything in life, it, too, had a finite shelf life. It was that ticking clock which made him even more impatient to be done with whatever this summons was all about and get out of this place.

He stared at his parents with a raised eyebrow, letting the silent censure bounce off him. He'd long ago learned that nothing he said or did would ever change their attitude towards him. He was the spare they'd sired but never needed. His place would be on a shelf, fed, clothed, but collecting dust and nothing else. So he'd left home and stopped trying.

'When was the last time you visited your brother?' his mother enquired, her fixed expression breaking momentarily to allow a touch of humanity to filter through at the mention of Matias.

The question brought to mind his brother's current state. Comatose in a hospital bed in Switzerland with worryingly low signs of brain activity.

Emiliano weathered the punch of sadness and brushed

a speck of lint off his cuff. 'Two weeks ago. And every two weeks before that since his accident four months ago,' he replied.

His parents exchanged surprised glances. He curbed the urge to laugh. 'If this is all you needed to know, you could've sent me an email.'

'It isn't. But we find it…reassuring that family still means something to you, seeing as you abandoned it without a backward glance,' Benito stated.

The fine hairs on Emiliano's nape lifted. 'Reassuring? I guess it should be celebrated that I've done something right at last, then? But, at the risk of straying into falsehoods and hyperbole, perhaps let's stick to the subject of why you asked me here.'

Benito picked up his glass and stared into the contents for a few seconds before he knocked it back and swallowed with a gulp. The action was so alien—his father's outward poise a thing so ingrained it seemed part of his genetic make-up—that Emiliano's jaw threatened to drop before he caught himself.

Setting the glass down with a brisk snap, another first, Benito eyed him with fresh censure. Nothing new there.

'We're broke. Completely destitute. Up the proverbial creek without a paddle.'

'Excuse me?' Emiliano wasn't sure whether it was the bald language that alarmed him or his father's continued acting out of character.

'You wish me to repeat myself? Why? So you can gloat?' his father snapped. 'Very well. The polo business, the horse breeding. Everything has failed. The estate has been sliding into the red for the past three years, ever since Rodrigo Cabrera started his competing outfit here in Cordoba. We approached Cabrera and he bought the debt. Now he's calling in the loans. If we don't pay up by the end of next month, we will be thrown out of our home.'

Emiliano realised his jaw was clenched so tight he had to force it apart to speak. 'How can that be? Cabrera doesn't know the first thing about horse breeding. The last I heard he was dabbling in real estate. Besides, Castillo is the foremost polo-training and horse-breeding establishment in South America. How can you be on the brink of bankruptcy?' he demanded.

His mother's colour receded and her fingers twisted the white lace handkerchief in her hand. 'Watch your tone, young man.'

Emiliano inhaled sharply, stopped the sharper words that threatened to spill and chose his words carefully. 'Explain to me how these circumstances have occurred.'

His father shrugged. 'You are a man of business…you know how these things go. A few bad investments here and there…'

Emiliano shook his head. 'Matias was…*is*…a shrewd businessman. He would never have let things slide to the point of bankruptcy without mitigating the losses or finding a way to reverse the business's fortunes. At the very least, he would've told me…' He stopped when his parents exchanged another glance. 'I think you should tell me what's really going on. I'm assuming you asked me here because you need my help?'

Pride flared in his father's eyes for a blinding moment before he glanced away and nodded. *'Sí.'* The word was one Emiliano was sure he didn't want to utter.

'Then let's have it.'

They remained stoically silent for several heartbeats before his father rose. He strode to a cabinet on the far side of the room, poured himself another drink and returned to his chair. Setting the glass down, he picked up a tablet Emiliano hadn't spotted before and activated it.

'Your brother left a message for you. Perhaps it would explain things better.'

He frowned. 'A message? How? Matias is in a coma.'

Valentina's lips compressed, distress marring her features for a brief second. 'You don't need to remind us. He recorded it before his brain operation, once the doctors gave him the possible prognosis.'

Emiliano couldn't fault the pain in her voice or the sadness in her eyes. And, not for the first time in his life, he wondered why that depth of feeling for his brother had never spilt over for him.

Pushing the fruitless thought aside, he focused on the present. On what he could control.

'That was two months ago. Why are you only telling me about this message now?'

'We didn't think it would be needed before now.'

'And by *it*, you mean me?'

His mother shrugged. Knowing the iron control he'd locked down on his feelings where his parents were concerned was in danger of breaking free and exploding, he jerked to his feet. Crossing the room to his father, he held out his hand for the tablet.

Benito handed it over.

Seeing his brother's face frozen on the screen, the bandage around his head and the stark hospital furniture and machines around him, Emiliano felt his breath strangle in his chest. Matias was the one person who hadn't dismissed him for being born second. His brother's support was the primary reason Emiliano had broken away from the glaringly apathetic environment into which he'd been born. He knew deep down that he would've made it, no matter what, but Matias's unwavering encouragement had bolstered him in the early, daunting years when he'd been floundering alone on the other side of the world.

He stemmed the tremor moving through him as his gaze moved over his brother's pale, gaunt face. Returning to his seat, he pressed the play button.

The message was ten minutes long.

With each second of footage that passed, with each word his brother uttered, Emiliano sank further into shock and disbelief. When it was over, he lifted his gaze and met equal stares that were now less indifferent and more… concerned.

'Are you… Is this for real?' he demanded.

'You're hearing the words from your brother's lips and still you doubt it?' his father asked, a trace of shame lacing his stiff demeanour.

'I don't doubt what Matias is saying. I'm questioning whether you truly gambled away millions that you knew the company couldn't afford!'

His father slammed his hand on the table. 'Castillo is my company!'

'It's also Matias's birthright! At least, that's what you drummed into him from the day he was born, was it not? Wasn't that the reason he all but broke his back to make it a success? Because you pressured him to succeed at all costs?'

'I am no tyrant. What he did for Castillo, he did willingly.'

Emiliano barely managed to bite back the swear word that hovered on his tongue. 'And for that you repay him by frittering away the profits behind his back?'

'The deal we made with Cabrera was supposed to be a sure thing.'

'A sure thing? You were duped by a man who spotted an easy score a mile away.' He stared down at the screen, still unable to believe the tale Matias had told. Bankruptcy. Destitution for his parents. Absurd promises made. Regret that the burden now fell on Emiliano's shoulders.

The naked plea in his brother's eyes and solemn tone not to let the family down.

That last entreaty, more than anything else, was what

kept Emiliano from walking out the door in that moment. Even though what Matias was asking of him—the request to honour the deal his parents had struck with Rodrigo Cabrera—was so ludicrous, he wondered why he wasn't laughing his head off.

Because every single word was true. He could tell just from looking into his parents' eyes.

'You really are serious, aren't you? You struck this bargain that Matias would marry Cabrera's daughter if the deal went south and the loans became due?' he rasped with renewed disbelief. 'Isn't she still a child?'

A brief memory of a little girl in pigtails chasing around the ranch during family visits flitted through his mind. Matias, as usual, had been patient and caring with Graciela Cabrera, but Emiliano, fully immersed in dreams of escape, could barely remember her, save for a few exchanges at the dinner table.

'She's twenty-three years old,' his mother supplied. 'She may have had a few wild escapades that have left her parents with more grey hairs than they wish, but she is more mature now. Matias was her favourite, of course, but she remembers you fondly—'

'I don't care how she remembers me. What I care about is that none of this set-up rang any alarm bells for you!' He seethed, unwilling to rise to the subtle dig. 'From a supposed family friend!'

For the first time, his father had the grace to look embarrassed. But the expression didn't last long. He regrouped, as was the Castillo way. 'We are where we are, Emiliano. The burden of our family's fortunes now rests with you. And don't bother taking out your chequebook. Cabrera has made it clear he wants only one thing. You either marry Graciela Cabrera or you can sit back and watch your mother and me lose everything.'

CHAPTER ONE

SIENNA NEWMAN STEPPED out of the shower, finished drying off and eased her black hair from the tight bun it'd been in all day. Swiping her hand across the steamed-up vanity mirror, she couldn't resist smiling at herself.

Sister Margaret from the orphanage where Sienna had spent most of her childhood had often told her to count her blessings. Of course, counting those blessings while smiling goofily at herself in the mirror would've been met with a frown. The orphanage matriarch certainly wouldn't have approved of the illicitly carnal thrill that went through her as she smoothed expensive and luxurious lotion over her skin, her senses revving up in anticipation of what the evening ahead held for her. It was a good thing therefore that Sister M, as the children had referred to her, wasn't here to see this tiny fall from grace. Because, even with the old biddy's beady eyes on her, Sienna didn't think she could've stopped smiling.

Today, her twenty-eighth birthday had started in spectacular style. Four giant bouquets of calla lilies and white roses, her favourite flowers, had been delivered to her desk on the hour between nine o'clock and midday, each time with a jaw-dropping present wrapped in white silk paper and black velvet bows. The stunning beauty of the diamond tennis bracelet delivered at eleven o'clock had only been topped by the magnificent sapphire teardrop necklace with matching earrings at midday. But even more special than all the presents had been the handwritten notes from Emiliano accompanying each gift. The scrawls had been as bold and domineering as the man, nowhere near flowery, but the intimate words of desire and felicitation had touched her deeply.

The afternoon had taken a different but nevertheless incredible turn, with culinary delights from edible-gold-dusted chocolate to caviar to a single pink-and-silver frosted cupcake with a lit candle for her to wish on and blow out.

She'd made a wish all right. One that had stealthily sprung into her heart and taken root about three months ago, around the time it had dawned on her that she'd been in a relationship with a hitherto unattainable man for almost a year.

Extreme self-preservation born of painful past experiences had fuelled her need to ignore the growing wish, but with each day that passed she'd began to hope rejection wasn't on the cards for her this time, as it had so often been.

As Sienna re-entered the bedroom, her smile dimmed a touch.

The only slight downside to her fantastic day had been the need to once more be evasive in the face of interest from colleagues about her love life and the knowledge that, although his extravagant birthday surprises had been thrilling to experience, Emiliano had once again run roughshod over her need to keep their relationship private.

The last time she'd touched on the subject, they'd rowed, Emiliano's Latin temper erupting in a torrent that had included his adamant refusal to 'skulk around in shadows' or 'pretend I'm not into you when we're in public.'

After a heated back-and-forth on the subject they'd retreated to the not-so-neutral zone of their bedroom, where he'd expressed his extreme displeasure passionately.

Sienna blushed in recollection, but her smile remained elusive, her heart skidding again as a different issue interrupted her happiness.

Another thing that would've made her birthday perfect was Emiliano's presence. Or, barring that, a simple phone call.

All she'd received was an email wishing her happy birthday and a single line to say he was aboard his plane, flying back home from Argentina. Although she'd been relieved that the unexpected extension of his overseas trip by four more days was finally over, she'd yearned to hear his voice. So much so, she'd called him straight back the moment she'd got home, only to have her call go to voicemail. Same as most of her calls the last three days. The one time he'd picked up, he'd been brusque to the point of monosyllabic.

She curbed the tiny spurt of anxiety and pulled on her underwear before sliding on the dress she'd shopped for for hours before discovering it in a tiny shop in Soho. The blood-red sleeveless gown showed off the slight tan she'd gained from their recent weekend away in St Tropez. Fastening her new necklace and earrings, she brushed out her shoulder-length black hair and stepped into black stilettos. The added height would be nowhere near Emiliano's six-foot-three-inch frame, but the confidence boost was nevertheless welcome.

Exhaling, she pushed away the insidious voice that wouldn't remain silent, reminding her that everything in her life—bar her career—thus far, had been ripped from her. That what she had with Emiliano would follow suit. After adding the finishing touches of perfume, clutch and wrap, she headed for the door.

She didn't want to, but Sienna couldn't stop the nerves that assailed her, or the equal amounts of excitement and dread that fluttered through her stomach at the notion of going out in public with Emiliano tonight. Even though they'd never resolved their argument, he'd grown increasingly possessive of her in public recently, his bold caresses almost baiting her to protest. Unwilling to provoke another disagreement, she hadn't, and in her quiet moments even admitted to enjoying those displays. Nevertheless, the butterflies in her stomach grew, their wings beating so loud she almost missed her phone buzzing with a text message.

Her heart skipped a beat when she saw Emiliano's name on her screen.

Slight change of plan. We'll dine at home. Restaurant delivery is taken care of. Let me know if that suits? E.

Her smile burst forth anew, her heart squeezing with happiness as she quickly answered.

That more than suits. Can't wait to see you! XXX

Hitting Send, she stared at the little faint bubble that said her message was being read. Then waited. He didn't answer.

Swallowing, she returned her phone to the clutch and left the bedroom.

The restaurant they were supposed to dine at was a mere two miles away from the Knightsbridge penthouse she shared with Emiliano. And, if Emiliano had already contacted her favourite chef, then the meal was most likely already on its way.

She walked down the stunningly decorated hallway and through the vast sitting room to find Alfie, their young live-in butler, setting the table in the dining room.

He looked up and smiled when he saw her. 'Good evening, miss.'

She returned his smile and nodded at the table. 'Looks like Emiliano has given you the heads-up on the change of plan?'

'Indeed. He's also given me the night off,' he replied

with a grin. 'I'll just wait for the delivery to arrive then I'll leave you two alone to enjoy your birthday.'

She fought the blush that threatened, recalling the butler's wry comment months ago about how he'd become the grateful recipient of many sudden nights off since she'd moved in with Emiliano. 'Thanks.'

Alfie nodded and went back to laying the table. Not wishing to intrude, she drifted back into the living room. Decorated with luxury and deep comfort in mind, the slate-coloured sofas, matching tables and the white walls were interspersed with dark-gold throw pillows and rugs that added welcoming warmth to the large room. A dominating fireplace was aglow to complement the November autumnal weather.

Sienna strolled to the mantel, picked up the single picture adorning it and stared down at the selfie she'd taken of herself and Emiliano three months ago. It had been a rare moment of throwing caution to the wind and all the more special for it. On a late-afternoon stroll in the park across from the penthouse, after a morning and afternoon spent making love, she'd confessed to sadness at not having photographic mementos of a childhood spent in foster care, no matter how wretched. Emiliano had insisted she seize the moment to make a memory. And, even though he'd refused to look into the camera, his years of avoiding the glare of the paparazzi's lens deeply ingrained, he'd posed for the picture. The end result was Emiliano staring at her while she looked into the camera, flushed and self-conscious from his brazenly hungry scrutiny.

He'd taken a look at the photo, pronounced himself satisfied and promptly printed and framed it for the mantel.

Sienna stared at the profile of the man who commanded her days and nights, the boss who'd changed his own company's rules, despite her many blithely ignored protests, in order to date her. Her heart skipped another beat, and with it the secret wish lurking in her heart.

Emiliano Castillo had done more than amend his company's rules. He'd gone on to trigger a few more firsts, as she'd found out in the months following the start of their relationship. For a start, he hadn't been one for *relationships*. Certainly not one with a vice-president of his venture capitalist firm. Most of his liaisons only lasted a couple of months. He'd also never lived with a lover. And he'd certainly never lived with one for going on six months!

Which was why Sienna was daring to believe that theirs was more than a supercharged physical affair. It was why she'd found herself hoping for more. They had never talked about a family, largely because the subject had been strictly off-limits for both of them, save for unavoidable instances that filtered through their lives.

As far as she knew, his relationship with his parents was strained at best, but she'd seen his devastation when his brother had been seriously injured in a car accident four months ago. And, with each trip she'd accompanied him on to the state-of-the-art medical facility in Switzerland where Matias was being cared for after his brain surgery had left him in a coma, she'd witnessed Emiliano's distress and sadness.

Hers was a different story. She had no past to discuss, so she never did.

The desolation she'd learned to live with overpowered her for a single moment before she pushed it back into its designated box. Today was her birthday. She was lucky she had a date to celebrate. But she'd also worked hard to make a life for herself, and she was determined it wouldn't fall victim to rejection and heartache.

So celebrate she *would*.

She returned the picture to the mantel in time to hear the penthouse door's electronic lock disengage.

Expecting it to be Alfie, taking delivery of their food, her heart leapt into her throat when Emiliano walked in.

He was supposed to have been gone for two days. He'd been gone for six. She hadn't comprehended just how much she'd missed him until he handed over the food boxes to Alfie and walked tall and proud into the living room. A rush of longing and happiness overtook her as her gaze met his.

At six foot three, with a powerful but streamlined physique, Emiliano Castillo gave the term 'tall, dark and handsome' full, visceral meaning. But he also carried an extra edge that ensured that heads, and hearts, turned whenever he graced humanity with his presence. His wasn't a flawless face, to start with. A scar sustained along his right jawline from a horse-riding accident as a teenager evoked a sense of illicit danger, if you just looked at him. Bold slants of jet eyebrows over brooding, dark, coppery eyes and a full and sensual mouth sculpted for long, steamy lovemaking nights made him very difficult to look away from.

So she stared, transfixed, heart slamming against her ribs, as he walked slowly towards her. He stopped several feet from where she stood. Electricity crackled through the air as they stared at one another. Then slowly, his eyes traced her body from head to toe, lingering, *possessing*, and back again.

Expecting him to stride forward and sweep her into his arms in that overwhelmingly possessive and blatantly male way he employed, she braced herself, her every sense leaping with excitement.

But he remained where he stood.

'Happy birthday, *querida*. You look exquisite.' His voice was deep, laced with the Spanish intonation he carried proudly. But the words, despite being felicitous and complimentary, were a touch grave. As were the hands he shoved deep into his pockets instead of using them to reach for her as he normally did when they'd been apart this long.

Her heart skittered, but Sienna pushed away the fizzle of anxiety. 'Thank you. It's great to have you back,' she replied, with her tongue lightly slicking lips gone nervous and dry.

His eyelids descended for a moment, then his head tilted slightly, dark eyes resting on her, seeming to absorb her every expression. 'Have you had a good day?' he asked.

The reminder of how her day had gone brought a smile. His breath seemed to catch as her smile widened. 'It was wonderful, Emiliano. I'm not sure how you planned everything without my knowledge but I loved every second of it. Thank you so much for these…' She caressed her necklace and earrings. 'I should be angry with you for forcing me to field questions, though.' She deliberately infused lightness into her tone, but her reluctance to incite another row didn't mean she was damping down what was important to her.

'No doubt you found your usual diplomatic way to deny my existence despite it being an open secret,' he returned with a distinct edge to his tone.

Sienna's breath snagged in her lungs. Yes, the subject was definitely still a sore one. But one she intended to tackle soon. Maybe tonight…

'I've never denied your existence. Merely not fuelled workplace gossip. There's a difference.'

His upper lip curled slightly, his jaw flexing a touch. 'If you say so.'

She floundered for a moment, the ground beneath her feet shaking a little. Was her continued denial of their relationship outside the privacy of their penthouse causing more damage than she realised?

Inhaling deeply, she widened her smile.

'I do say so. And it would've been perfect if you'd been

here, regardless of who knows about us.' Sienna knew she was offering a tentative olive branch, while subtly digging for answers to questions she wasn't completely certain were wise to pursue, but the worry that had taken root between her ribs was growing by the second.

'I'm sorry. The situation couldn't be helped.'

She wasn't surprised at the slightly cryptic answer. The enigma that was Emiliano Castillo operated at optimum capacity, always. She'd learned the hard way that to gain his attention she had to meet her lover and boss toe to toe. It was what had brought her to his attention in the boardroom. It was why their chemistry remained sizzling hot in the bedroom. A chemistry that had stunned and bewildered her in the beginning and continued to overawe her even now. It was the reason she checked herself now from leaving the safety of the mantel to close the seemingly yawning distance between them, even though every muscle strained to be in his arms.

Denying herself the pleasure, she remained where she was, sensing the deep, puzzling tension within him as a muscle jumped in his shadowed cheek. But even from a distance she experienced the jolt of electricity that lanced through her when his eyes remained fixed on hers. 'You didn't elaborate on what was going on. Is it Matias?' she asked.

A shadow drifted over his face. 'In a way, yes.'

'Is he okay? Has there been any improve—'

'His condition remains unchanged,' he interrupted.

Her gaze dropped, drifting over his lower lip. He inhaled sharply, gratifying her with his reaction. But his hands remained in his pockets.

'So you spent all six days with your parents?'

Another clench of his jaw. *'Sí.'* The word was chillingly grave.

Her heart dropped. 'Emiliano…I… Is everything okay?'

He finally breached the gap between them and grasped her hand in his. Lowering their linked hands, he stared at her upturned palm for several seconds before he released her. 'No, everything is not okay, but it's nothing that won't resolve itself eventually.'

She opened her mouth and started to demand more information. But he'd turned away.

'Come, the food will be getting cold.'

She followed him into the dining room and pinned the smile on her face as he held her chair and saw her seated. Again she anticipated his touch on her bare shoulders, a drift of his sensual mouth across her temple. She received neither.

She watched him take his own seat, the neutrality of his expression underlined with a grimness that lodged a cold stone in her stomach.

'Emiliano…'

'I belayed ordering oysters. I didn't want them to be ruined in transit. We'll have your second favourite.'

She waved him away as he opened the first of the specially packed gourmet dishes. 'It's fine. I don't care about the food. We can have oysters some other time.' Her blush at the mention of oysters and the special significance they held for them was suppressed beneath the blooming disquiet. Even then she couldn't help but be disturbed that he'd made the order without speaking to her first. 'Tell me what's going on.'

His firm mouth thinned for a split second and the eyes that met hers were closed off, bordering on cold. '*Querida*, I don't wish to upset your birthday celebration.'

She frowned. 'Why would telling me how your trip went ruin my birthday? What happened?' she pressed.

His gaze swept away from hers, back to the dish in his hand. Shutting her out. 'My parents happened.' He looked up, tawny-gold eyes piercing her. 'And since they come under the numerous subjects we don't discuss, perhaps we can drop it?' he drawled.

The statement hurt a little, but Sienna couldn't deny that it was accurate. There were swathes of their private lives they avoided, their common threads of familiarity were business and the bedroom. Again she experienced the ominous sense of shifting sands, prompting her to go against her better judgment.

'Maybe…this one time we can make an exception? And, before you bite my head off, I only request it because I can see that whatever happened is affecting you, Emiliano.'

'You are kind, *querida*, but I would also caution you against making those sorts of statements. There are some things you can't take back. Besides, I believe you're exaggerating things a little.' He dished the seafood salad starter onto her plate, served himself and poured them both glasses of chilled white wine.

'You think I'm exaggerating things?' She hated herself for the tiny catch in her voice and the needy words that spilled in the bid to make her point. 'Then why haven't you kissed me since you walked in the door? Usually, you can't keep your hands off me, yet you haven't so much as touched me. And, if you clench your jaw any tighter, it'll snap.'

'I've told you, you look breathtaking. I've wished you happy birthday. I showered you with presents all day, even in my absence. Perhaps I'm saving the rest for later. I know how much you love the anticipation,' he drawled before he raised his glass to her and took a large gulp.

Sienna caught a glimpse of the banked desire in his eyes. Her heart resumed its erratic thumping, but she couldn't dismiss the other, more terrifying feeling residing beneath her breast. Because there was something else lurking in his eyes. Something cold, bracing and soul threatening.

'Six days of anticipation is more than enough. "One day

is too long." Isn't that what you said last month when you returned from that two-day business summit in Athens?' That she had to remind him of that was even more shocking, the unusual recounting of gestures received but never spoken about making her reel.

'Careful, Sienna, or you'll have me thinking these declarations you've previously led me to believe are over the top are in fact secretly yearned for.'

A flush crept up her neck to stain her cheeks but she didn't drop her gaze. 'As I said, perhaps I wish to make an exception.'

His shrug was almost…bored. 'There is no need. I've had a long and turbulent flight, *amante*. Right now, I want to relax and see you sated with food. Is that too much to ask?' His voice held a definite bite. A warning to leave well enough alone.

She shook her head, convinced more than ever that something was seriously wrong. 'Whatever it is that's bothering you, I…I want to help.' Throwing caution to the wind, she abandoned her glass and, in a first move that made her insides quake, she initiated touch by placing her hand over his.

He tensed, his nostrils flaring as he gazed down at her hand.

Then he removed his hand from under hers.

Her heart stopped as another thought sliced through her mind.

'Emiliano? Is it me?'

The eyes that held hers were completely devoid of emotion. 'Sienna, leave this alone…'

'Oh, God, are you annoyed with me for finalising the Younger deal without you?'

'What?'

'You gave me carte blanche, remember? You said I should go ahead and offer whatever we needed to land the deal. And that's what I did. I know it was another five million more than we initially agreed, but I did the figures and judged that it was worth it.'

His brow clamped in a frown as he yanked his tie loose with his free hand. '*Santo cielo*, not everything is about business—' He ruthlessly checked himself and drew in a breath. 'Rest assured, I'm not annoyed with you about the deal. Without your quick thinking and acting, we'd have lost it. I believe I had Denise send you an email commending you for it today.'

She'd seen the email from his executive assistant, and again wondered why Emiliano hadn't contacted her himself. 'Okay, but—'

'You want further commendations from me? More flowers? More accolades on top of the presents you've already received? Is that what this show of neediness is about?'

Shock and anger scythed equal swathes of pain through her. 'Excuse me?' Despite having called herself the same only minutes ago, the label stung badly.

He drained his glass and set it down with more force than necessary. Charging to his feet, he rounded the table. His impressive height and bristling demeanour would've made a lesser woman cower. Hell, she'd seen grown men wither beneath the look displayed on his face now.

But she'd never been one of them.

Surging to her feet, she faced him, their untouched food abandoned. 'Did you just call me *needy*?'

'Am I wrong? Now that we're behind closed doors, where your precious reputation isn't at risk, do you not *need* something from me? Have you not been full of *needful* words since I walked in the door?' he accused.

'Don't twist my words. I just want to talk to you, find out what's—'

'I don't want to *talk*, *querida*. You're usually adept at

picking up simple cues like that. Has my absence affected you that much, or is there another agenda going on here?' he taunted.

The tightly furled subject she'd tentatively intended to broach with him tonight knotted harder, congealing into stone that chafed against her heart. Incisive eyes dragged over her face, probing her expression and then widening upon witnessing the evidence she couldn't quite disguise.

'*Sì*, another agenda,' he bit out. 'Do I get three guesses or shall I strike for gold and deduce that you're breaking your *unique* mould to broach the predictable "where do we go from here?" conversation women feel the *need* to have at the most inappropriate times?'

Sienna wasn't sure whether it was his uncanny acuity or the abrasive tone that alarmed her more. 'You're turning this around on me, Emiliano. We were talking about you.'

'A subject I've clearly expressed my abhorrence for. Now, are we to go around in circles, or are we going to eat?'

She lifted her chin, the distress and foreboding she'd staunched so fiercely blooming into life within her chest. 'I've lost my appetite.'

He took another dangerous step closer, swallowing the gap between them, extinguishing the very air that sustained them until only pure, sizzling electricity remained. Soot-coloured lashes swept down and paused, the heat in his eyes branding her mouth for endless seconds before his gaze rose again.

'For food? Or for everything else?' His voice was thicker. Deeper. His nostrils flared in blatant, carnal hunger.

'Why are you so angry with me?' she whispered, unable to stem the dread crawling over her skin.

An enigmatic expression blanketed his face for a blind second, his eyes blazing with a light she couldn't fathom. 'Perhaps I'm tired of being compartmentalised in your life, of being put on a shelf and taken down and dusted off only when your needs get the better of you.'

She gasped. 'What? I've never—'

The firm finger that drifted over her lower lip stemmed her answer. 'I wish to get off this merry-go-round. So I ask you again, what have you lost your appetite for?'

Lust, need, anger and hurt strangled her in equal measures. With a few pithy words, he'd reduced her to a needy female eager to sink her talons into a man she wanted to possess. With one label, he'd reminded her of the one thing she'd vowed never to be again.

Dependent.

They'd had disagreements before, but nothing like this. Sienna couldn't catch her breath, couldn't stem the hurt that flowed like a bloodied wound. But with each second that passed, with each intake of his breath and exhalation of hers, a different emotion surged forth. Familiar. Overwhelming. Devastating.

A deep tremble seized her, shaking her from head to toe. He saw her reaction and triumph coated his features, his eyes darkening as he watched. Waited.

'Emiliano…'

'*Sí*, Sienna?' he whispered against her mouth, but holding himself a breath away, taunting her with his proximity.

Her breath shook out. 'Something's going on. Don't make me think I'm crazy or that I'm overreacting. Please, just tell me—'

'Stop. You know better than to push a closed subject. You're an expert on closed subjects, after all. So do not let tonight be the moment you change your tune, *querida*, hmm?'

Another bolt of shock went through her. Her gaze collided with his. The hunger was still there, but everything else was just…wrong. 'Who *are* you? Why are you speaking to me this way?'

'You're the one who insists on incessant discourse,' he bit out at her.

'You don't want me to talk? Fine!' She grabbed his tie and pulled it free. One vicious twist of her wrist sent it flying across the polished table. Then she attacked his shirt. Buttons turned into tiny missiles launched across the room, the depth of unbelievable hurt and lust tearing through her and making her irrational.

Her actions felt surreal, an out-of-body experience that sent shockwaves through her other self, the one observing what she was doing from a safe distance.

The live, breathing one initiating hot-headed moves swallowed hard at the first sight of Emiliano's tanned, chiselled chest and gave a helpless groan, her body weakening and surging with desire at the same time.

Emiliano's breath hissed out when she reached for his belt buckle. *'Querida—'*

'No! If I don't get to talk, neither do you,' she insisted, probably because she was terrified that talking now would force her to think about what she was doing, and the possible reason behind Emiliano's behaviour. Which was wrong, but she couldn't help it. Not in this instance. Not when a mere hour ago she'd felt on top of the world.

Her fingers gained renewed power. Tugging the belt free, she jerked it away and heard it whistle through the loops on its way across the floor. Her fingers brushed the powerful erection behind his fly and a powerful shudder rocked him.

'Dios mio, Sienna…' His voice was thick, his arousal present and potent.

'Unless, of course, you're going to tell me I'm crazy to think you want me?' She kicked away her shoes and reached for the zipper of her dress. Lowered it. Watched the tops of his sculptured cheekbones flush with raw need.

His lips parted, his breath emerging in shallow pants

as he watched her dress loosen and drape, secured only by her heaving breasts.

But, as quickly as the alien bravado had risen, it died, leaving her once again flailing, distraught.

What on earth was she doing?

Dropping her hands, she hiked up the skirt of the gown and took one step back, then another. He followed, tracking her with the calculated steps of a ravenous predator.

They moved like that, locked in their erotic dance, out of the dining room. Somewhere along the way, the top part of her dress dropped, exposing her.

Emiliano stumbled. Then cursed under his breath. At any other time, Sienna would've smiled a wicked, teasing smile. Not now. Now each breath was weighted with desire, yes, but also with a fearful heaviness that left little room for hilarity.

'Am I crazy, Emiliano?' she pressed, even though part of her desperately urged herself to remain silent.

Long seconds ticked by as he prowled after her. Her back touched the bedroom door, swinging it open. Momentarily, his gaze flicked past her to the king-sized bed they'd shared insanely passionate moments in for six months. The eyes that returned to meet hers were heavy with need and regret. Whether it was for their argument or for something else, she didn't know. Although, with the ache in her chest she couldn't quite shift, she suspected the latter.

CHAPTER TWO

'NO, YOU'RE NOT CRAZY.'

The strained admission restored a little of her hurt. As did the slightly desperate aura about him as he nudged her backwards into the bedroom. Whatever else was going on, Emiliano still wanted her. It was by no means anywhere near what she ultimately wanted from him, but the knowledge soothed and settled the wild alarm racing through her veins. A little restored feminine power would sustain her. For now.

Tomorrow. She'd revisit the subject again tomorrow. Once they'd slaked far more immediate and urgent needs. Even though it went against her nature to leave a problem untackled, she would refrain from pushing for answers tonight.

With that thought, she let go of her dress. It pooled to the floor a mere second before Emiliano pounced, lifting her out of it to stand her naked except for her thong and his jewels. His arms dropped back to his sides, and she watched his hands clench with electric tension for a ragged second, then jerk towards her, beckoning her forward, his eyes burning gold. 'Come here, Sienna.'

Invitation of the most sinful nature. Invitation she grasped with both hands, stumbling forward into his arms.

Hard hands plastered her against his body and tangled in her hair, holding her still before she could satisfy the urgent need to kiss him.

He stared down at her, eyes endless pools of shadows, secrets and passion. But between one second and the next, she once again caught a glimpse of something that made her heart clench.

'Emiliano...'

He nudged her even closer, heat from his body chopping off her words, the disturbing look in his eyes resolutely erased. 'Take what you need, my little wildcat,' he breathed against her mouth.

With a moan, she rose on tiptoe, her hands sliding around his neck as her mouth pressed gloriously, ravenously, against his. Her eyes slid shut, the better to savour what she'd missed, what she'd craved so desperately, these past six days. Her senses sang when his hands wrapped tighter, mercilessly, around her, his deep groan relaying his mutual feelings.

Tongues meshing, relishing, devouring, the kiss deepened, their ragged breathing the only sound in the room as he walked her backwards on plush carpet, his aim the wide bed which was their personal haven.

Sienna gripped him tighter as he swept her off her feet and placed her on the bed. When he attempted to move, to shed the rest of his clothes, she stopped him, the idea of letting him go bringing a fresh wave of alarm.

If her unusually possessive hold on him registered, he didn't give an indication. Instead, he rolled them sideways, still delivering hot, pleasurable kisses as he impatiently shucked off shoes and trousers. His briefs followed and her breath caught all over again at the heat of his girth against her thigh.

Greedy hands closed over his steely hardness. They both groaned. Oh, how she'd longed for this.

'I missed you. So much!' she gasped between kisses, once again letting go of the tight hold she usually held on her emotions.

His body grew tauter, the carnal tension whipped through him, making muscles and sinew rock-hard beneath her touch. She expected him to reply with something wickedly decadent. His clever tongue would usually by now be whispering erotically charged words in her ear.

He remained silent even as his hands moved feverishly over her body.

Her often vocal, always possessive lover was choosing mute seduction, delivering his pleasure through his hands and mouth, ruthlessly dragging double bliss with harder kisses and rougher caresses. Sienna thrilled to the exchange even as she pushed back the million *whys* that demanded answering.

His tongue slid over her skin, tasting her nipples, sucking, teasing, melting her thoughts, to leave only pure sensation. A firm tug at her hips ripped free her panties, then he was there, at the centre of her need, delivering even more potent bliss. She sank her fingers into his hair, her cries growing louder as pleasure piled upon pleasure. Until it culminated in endless waves of ecstasy.

Sienna was still floating when he parted her thighs wider, filling her senses with his presence. Prying her eyes open, she stared at the god whose intellect and charisma left her in awe, whose touch lifted her from ordinary to extraordinary.

Who was staring at her with narrowed eyes even more shadowed than they had been minutes ago. Before she could attempt to voice her quaking thoughts, he slanted his mouth over hers and penetrated her in one smooth, urgent thrust.

Flung straight back to nirvana, Sienna could only hold on as she was completely, utterly possessed. Nails bit into flesh, cries turned into screams. Emiliano pushed her to the brink over and over, slowing down just before she reached her peak. As if he wanted their lovemaking to go on for ever. As if he wanted to be imprinted on her very soul.

As if he wanted the experience to be unforgettable.

Why?

The word blazed across her mind again, larger, louder. Her hands shook as she framed his face, searching his eyes.

'Emiliano...please...' she whispered.

His jaw turned to stone beneath her fingers. With a thick grunt, he pulled out of her body, flipped her onto her stomach and surged back into her. Brushing her hair out of the way, he sank his teeth into her nape, roughly tasting her, branding her. Raw pleasure ploughed through her, leaving her clawing at the sheets as another orgasm surged high.

Behind her, she heard his rough breathing, his own impending climax bearing down on him. She wanted to hold him in her arms, look into his eyes and be reassured that everything was all right between them. Or as near enough as possible.

Because, although it had hurt to have him point it out, she knew their relationship had a few inescapable flaws. Flaws that seemed to gape wider with each passing second. Flaws she needed to address.

But he had her pinned, six feet three inches of superior masculinity spread all over her delivering sensation she never wanted to end. So, closing her eyes, Sienna gave in, diving headlong into pure heaven as stars exploded across her vision.

Endless minutes later, when their bodies had cooled and their breathing calmed, he slid off her and gathered her in his arms.

Strong fingers slid into her hair, the movement unusually jerky. His gaze was hooded when it met hers, hiding his expression.

'Happy birthday,' he rasped.

'I...' She floundered for a second, wondering whether to go back on her resolution and tread the dangerous waters swirling beneath her feet.

'Emiliano...'

'These look exquisite on you.' He pulled her closer, his fingers slipping down to trace the skin beneath the diamond necklace even as the forbidding force of his stare punched holes in her resolve.

Tomorrow, she decided once again. 'Thank you,' she murmured.

Tilting her head up, he placed a hard, short kiss on her swollen lips. 'Sleep now,' he ordered.

In the aftermath of bliss and even with her mind churning, Sienna couldn't hold back the drugging effect of that command. So she gave in.

What felt like only minutes later, she jerked upright, her heart hammering. Beside her, Emiliano was lost in slumber, one muscled arm curved over his head. Heart twisting, she studied him, vainly trying to decipher what was wrong. In sleep, his breathtakingly handsome face was less forbidding, his jaw slightly slack and his forehead smooth. She didn't deem him any less intimidating but at least she could stare at him now without the bracing force field that usually surrounded him. She even dared to lift a hand to his full lower lip, tracing the velvet-smooth skin. He exhaled harshly in his sleep and she froze. Withdrawing her fingers, she lay back, knowing sleep was out of the question with her mind once again in churn mode.

Half an hour later, she gave up and rose from the bed. At 5:30 a.m. in early November, it was still dark outside. Going for a run outside in the dark without Emiliano would incur his displeasure, as she'd found out on the one occasion she'd attempted to do so. In fact, he'd completely banned her from running outside without him. But she needed physical exertion to prevent her from waking him up and demanding to know what was going on.

Quietly tugging on her running gear in the large dressing room adjoining the master suite, she silently let herself out and took the lift down to the basement, where the top-line gym reserved for the exclusive use of the penthouse owners was located. Plugging in her earbuds, she hit the treadmill, running at her top speed for a solid hour before her leaden legs forced her to slow down.

When she stepped off the machine, her resolution was firmly back in place, her mind no longer racing. Emiliano valued her professionally because she wasn't afraid to go after tough, seemingly unattainable deals. It was what had seen her rise from junior fund manager to junior vice-president in the three years she'd been with his venture capitalist firm.

While privately her lack of sexual experience placed her somewhat on a back foot, she'd never let Emiliano cow her. She was also brave enough to admit her new but secret emotions also factored in whatever situation was brewing between them. Which was why she would tackle it now.

Setting down the bottle of mineral water she'd rehydrated from, she left the basement via the stairs. She would pick up the newspapers and magazines they had delivered to the penthouse to prevent their talk from being interrupted by the concierge.

She reached the ground floor and crossed the polished marble foyer to the concierge desk. Exchanging a greeting with the manager, she accepted the stack and crossed to the lift. The other tiny secret she'd been harbouring for several weeks lightened her heart a little as she entered the carriage and pressed the button.

Having witnessed the pleased light in Emiliano's eyes whenever she'd responded in Spanish to a simple question, she'd embraced the idea to take it further.

She hadn't divulged her attempt to learn Spanish to Emiliano because she'd wanted to approach the outskirts of proficiency before she told him. Privately, she'd devoured Spanish newspapers and magazines in her spare time in the hope of quickly learning her lover's mother tongue, and even admitted that it had become a guilty pleasure to gorge on all things Argentinian.

Unfortunately, it was the reason the headline screaming from the front page of the glossy celebrity magazine made perfect sense to her once she fished it out of the pile.

Stumbling out of her lift, she froze to a halt, her heart dropping to her toes. Unable to catch her breath, she stared, first at the photo, then back at the headline.

A Castillo-Cabrera Union!

The rest of the papers fell out of her hand, her useless limbs unable to hang on to anything but the evidence of all her *whys* spelled out in bold white letters. Her shocked eyes dropped to the smaller print.

The Polo Match Made in Heaven!

Emiliano Castillo to Wed Graciela Cabrera.

There were other words, such as *wedding of the year... Dynastic union... Valentine's Day wedding...*

But her vision was blurring, her heart refusing to pump properly. She was going to pass out. She was sure of it. She wasn't sure whether to view her present state as a blessing. What she did know was that she wanted to block out the sight of Emiliano and the drop-dead gorgeous caramel blonde sitting at the intimate candlelit table, her hand on top of his, her smile holding a thousand delicious secrets as she stared at him.

And he stared back at her.

He wasn't smiling—Emiliano *never* smiled in the presence of a camera, especially one wielded by a paparazzo. Most of the time he glared at the intrusion. He wasn't glaring this time. The expression on his face was even...accommodating. Fond.

Lungs burning, Sienna forced herself to take a breath. Turn the pages. Her world turning to ash, she stared at glossy page after glossy page of Emiliano and his new *amor*. On the fifth page, she stared, tears surging into her eyes, at the ring on the finger which announced Graciela Cabrera as the brand new fiancée of Emiliano Castillo.

To add insult to injury, her heart tripped to a stop when she saw what Emiliano was wearing. If there was even a shadow of a doubt that this picture was a terrible, cruel hoax, it was wiped clean when she saw the tie. She'd gifted that tie to him on his birthday two months ago— had packed it in his suitcase herself exactly one week ago, when she'd sent him off with a kiss on his lips and hope in her heart. She was world-wise enough to know sometimes the tabloid media regurgitated old photos and manipulated images to suit their headline. The evidence of the tie confirmed these pictures weren't fakes.

Finally, *everything* about last night…about the past few days' silence…made sense.

She stumbled forward, the scattered papers forgotten as she made her way back inside, absently wondering how she was able to put one foot in front of the other when she felt so numb.

Time and space ceased to make sense until she was standing before the bedroom doors. Her hand shook as she raised it to the handle. She clenched her fist tight in a desperate bid to retain some control. She had to confront this, in spite of what the outcome would be.

Had to.

She jerked at the forceful wrench of the door from the inside, stealing away the control she'd barely summoned. Emiliano stopped short before her, his face in a deep frown.

'Sienna, what are you doing standing…?'

She stared at him. He was right there in front of her. Powerful. Magnetically charismatic. Drop-dead gorgeous.

Bastard.

She didn't want to look at him. Dear God, it hurt just

to lift her gaze to meet his. Because even now she wanted desperately to cling to the hope that she'd got it wrong. That the pictures in the magazine clutched in her fist, his lack of emails, his coldly forbidding expression upon his return, even his silent lovemaking, had all been in her imagination.

But she met his gaze. And knew she was clinging to false hope.

'Is it true?' she tried asking anyway. One last time.

Tawny gold eyes hardened a touch, the coldness returning. 'Is what true?'

A bolt of anger freed her frozen limbs. 'Don't play games with me, Emiliano. It's beneath—'

She'd been about to say *us*. Except there was no *us* any more. Had there ever been? Her frantic brain raced, desperately sifting, analysing every gesture, every word, wondering if everything she'd lived, revelled in and hoped for during their relationship had been based on a colossal lie.

'This!' She shoved the magazine into the bare steel torso draped with the navy blue shirt he'd been about to button. *'Is it true you're engaged?'*

Ripping off her MP4 player and earphones, she dropped them onto a nearby dresser and turned, watching him flip through the pages before tossing the magazine aside.

The eyes that met hers were arrogantly unapologetic. 'Yes.'

The last minute's anger had fooled her into thinking she was strong, that she could withstand whatever was coming her way.

She was wrong.

The punch to her solar plexus from his words robbed her of breath and weakened her knees. Shaking her head, she stared at him. Waited for him to continue. He didn't. He just stared back at her, his expression icily neutral.

'"Yes"? That's all you're going to say?'

He braced strong hands on lean hips, his stance cold and withdrawn. 'You're in no condition to hear any more right now—'

'Are you serious? So what, you expect me to just…go through my day until you *deem* me ready?' Incredulity rendered her voice hoarse and shaky.

'I would prefer to have this conversation with you when you're not emotionally high-strung, *sí*,' he rasped before raising his hands to begin buttoning his shirt.

Inhaling long and slow, Sienna fought for the control she was so good at attaining in the workplace. Except this wasn't work. This was so much more. 'You owe me an explanation. Right now. Or are you too much of a coward to grant me one?'

He froze, hard eyes lancing into her with the brutal force of a scalpel. 'Watch your tone with me, *querida*,' he warned.

'Do not call me that! You just told me you're engaged to another woman. Engaged! And you dare to call me your *darling*?'

A puzzled expression flicked like lightning over his face, as if he didn't understand her objection. Then it was gone and he was back to the stranger who'd walked into their penthouse twelve hours ago.

Her green eyes flashed. 'Were you seeing her behind my back?'

A black frown clamped his forehead as he secured the last button. 'I do not cheat.'

'No? You've never cheated? What was last night, then? Weren't you cheating on *her* with *me*?'

'You're my lover. She knows of our association. She understands that it needs to be taken care of.'

'Oh, how very accommodating of her. And is that what you were doing last night? *Taking care of me* before you dumped me?'

He jerked back, as if she'd struck him. 'Sienna, you need to calm—'

'You couldn't resist one last tumble between the sheets before you handed me my marching orders?'

He had the grace to look uncomfortable. 'It was your birthday...'

Hot pins stabbed her until she was a whisper away from howling. It was too much to take standing still. So she paced. 'How decent of you. I was the poor, pathetic soon-to-be ex-lover you couldn't stand to disappoint on her birthday, so you waited for me to find out what you'd been up to from the press?'

He slammed the cufflinks he'd picked up back onto the dresser. '*Basta!* This wasn't how I intended to break the news.'

'How very inconvenient for you!'

He pinched the bridge of his nose and inhaled deeply. 'I'm heading to the office now—I have a conference call scheduled with Norway which has been postponed twice. But let's catch up later. Maybe this evening? I don't mind if you take the day off to absorb the news. Then, tonight, we can talk about this rationally.'

'About the fact that you were going on a trip to see your parents but went and got engaged instead?'

His jaws gritted together for a second. 'Amongst other things, yes.'

She forced herself to stop. To face him. 'Fine, let's have it. Surely I'm worth five minutes of your time right now?'

'I don't think—'

'I do!'

Taking a deep breath, he stared at her. 'Sienna, it wasn't supposed to happen this way.'

'What wasn't? Please spell it out fully so I understand.'

One sleek eyebrow rose as if he was seeing her in a new

light. In that moment, Sienna wasn't sure she wanted to find out what he saw as he stared at her.

'The way you're reacting right now, I'm almost tempted to believe your career *isn't* more important to you than this thing between us, whereas I know for a fact that, if I asked you to choose, you wouldn't even blink before choosing the former.'

She inhaled sharply. 'First of all, if we ever found ourselves in the position of you asking me to choose, then we'd be in serious trouble, especially when I know how many female, family-orientated executives you employ. Which makes me think this would most probably be some sort of test. Why would you need to do that, Emiliano?'

He shrugged, but the gleam she'd witnessed in his eyes last night burned even brighter this morning. 'Perhaps the idea of coming second best doesn't sit well with me. Perhaps I'm thoroughly bored of it.'

Shocked laughter spilled from her lips. '*Second best?* How… When…have you ever allowed yourself to come second best? You win at absolutely everything!'

His lids swept down, his mouth twisting. 'That is where you're wrong.'

'Fine. Maybe we don't know each other as well as we should, but I guess you not even bothering to give me any option speaks volumes!'

He slashed a hand through his hair. 'I was going to give you… *Dios*, this wasn't how…I have to do this.'

She stilled, the combination of Emiliano struggling for words and the choice of those words unsettling her. 'You *have* to?'

'*Si*, I gave my word.'

'Your word? To *who*?'

He huffed, a breath filled with icy frustration. 'It's a family thing. I don't know enough about your own family circumstances, since you've never felt quite like sharing, so I will forgive you if you don't understand.'

That cut her off at the knees. 'How dare you?' She gasped, raw pain hammering her from heart to soul. 'You've equally withheld your own background from me. Don't punish me for thinking I was respecting your wishes. And, whatever my circumstances, you can't assume that I don't understand the concept of family.' Being an orphan had triggered a yearning for a family of her own, a wish she held dear in her heart, the fulfilment of that dream a hope she refused to give up.

Emiliano's mouth thinned. 'You mistook my meaning.'

'Looks like I've mistaken a lot of things. Things like you neglecting to tell me you've been *promised* to somebody else all along.'

'I'm not. I wasn't.'

'Then what is this?' She indicated the paper. 'Don't insult my intelligence. You know her. There's a familiarity there, so something must have been going on.'

'Our families are…connected. I've known her since she was a child.'

'And they needed a marriage, so you agreed to step in?' she mocked with a pained laugh.

Laughter that dried up when he nodded.

'Yes, something like that.'

She gasped. 'You're serious.'

He didn't blink. 'I'm serious.'

Her mouth dropped open, but no words emerged. Shaking her head, she tried to clear the buzzing growing louder.

'I'm going to go out on a limb and mention that there is another scenario I was thinking about for us in light of this news.'

He stared at her, a touch of something she absurdly wanted to label uncertainty flashing across his face before it disappeared. When her vocal cords refused to work, he continued, 'If you want our…liaison to continue, I'm willing to discuss how we—'

A punch of rage freed up her vocal cords. 'I sincerely hope you're not about to suggest I be your bit on the side while you're married to someone else!'

His face hardened into a rigid mask of fury. 'Please refrain from putting words in my mouth.'

She folded her arms. 'Okay, I'm listening.'

He started to speak, then clenched his jaw again and shook his head. 'Perhaps discretion is the better part of valour here. I'll be speaking to my lawyers this morning. You can keep the penthouse and everything in it. I'll have the requisite deeds drawn up. Also one of the cars. Pick whichever one you please. If you want anything else, let me know. I'll try and accommodate—'

'Are you discussing *possessions* with me, Emiliano? I want to know why you're engaged to another woman when you're supposed to be mine!' She was shouting, her pain raw and unfettered, her dignity in shreds. But she couldn't help it.

And with each word she flung at him he grew colder, withdrawing into a block of marble. Retrieving his cufflinks, he slotted them into place with calm, precise movements. 'I thought there could be a…negotiation…but it's clear I was wrong.'

Her hands splayed out in a bracing gesture, appealing for understanding in a world gone crazy. 'A *negotiation*? What on earth are you talking about?'

'It doesn't matter now. I didn't take this decision lightly, but it's done, Sienna. For the immediate future there'll be no changing it. It's clear that dissecting it wouldn't be productive to you. Not in this moment, anyway. Perhaps not ever,' he stated with a finality that chilled her to the bone.

'So that's it? I'm dumped with no proper explanation?'

He stared at her for endless seconds. 'Whether we want

to admit it or not, we were both aware this thing between us was bound to run its course sooner or later. Maybe it's better that it's sooner.'

Then he picked up his jacket and walked out the door.

CHAPTER THREE

THE NEXT FEW hours were spent in a semifugue state. Sadly, Sienna wasn't numb enough to remain painfully unaware of what was happening.

Her voice was hoarse as she called out to Emiliano. His stone-cold silence as he left the penthouse. Her cracking voice as she instructed her secretary to push her appointments to later in the day.

The deep concern on Alfie's face when she refused breakfast and asked him to procure packing boxes, and the endless waves of bewildered agony as she stuffed her belongings into boxes and suitcases, organised storage facilities and booked herself into a hotel.

Tears. So many heart-shredding, despised tears as she stood in the shower in a soulless hotel room, hating herself for not being stronger, excruciatingly aware she'd let herself slide into the danger zone of false hope based on useless foundations. But, as she dried off and dressed, she also recognised the slow build of anger. Of determination.

She'd put every safeguard in place to protect herself, yet she'd let herself hope, just as she had as a child staring yearningly out of the orphanage window for something *better*, when she'd known better should first and foremost come from herself. From *within*. She'd allowed herself to forget her history, to be lulled into disabling the locked-in belief that abandonment by those she let close was a thing of the past. She'd let herself indulge in fantasies built around a man who'd made it clear from his previous relationships that he would never settle down.

But he had settled.

What was an engagement, if not a precursor to the ultimate commitment?

But he didn't choose you, remember? Like your own mother chose a different life without you.

She tried to fortify herself against the savage pain the reminder brought. But she felt it like a raw wound exposed to salt, and couldn't stem the harrowing memories of growing up in an orphanage, the heartbreak each time a hoped-for foster family rejected her or, even worse, gave her the initial promise of a family only to yank it away weeks or months later.

She should have been used to rejection by now. Should've kept her steel-plated armour securely fastened in place. Instead, she'd let Emiliano in.

The ramifications of her stupidity held her hostage as she left the hotel and hailed a cab to what had once been a place of pride for her achievements and was now the secondary scene of her downfall.

As she walked through the grand, breathtaking marble-and-glass lobby of the Castillo Tower in the city, Sienna couldn't help but feel that, despite her staunchest effort to keep her private life under wraps, every gaze directed her way held a degree of mocking judgement of the poor choices she'd made.

Her secretary's furtive gaze and normally exuberant but now-hushed tone told Sienna her disguise had failed.

Or was it because news of Emiliano's engagement had already filtered through? Of course. Castillo Ventures, no matter how progressive a work place, was still a hotbed of interoffice gossip. She didn't doubt that every single member of the five-hundred-strong workforce would know the truth by now, although her stellar but straitlaced reputation would mean no one would say anything to her face.

Fresh pain battered her as she walked into her office and shut the door. On shaky legs, she approached her desk and sank behind it. Fingers trembling, she pulled up the requisite programme, typed a brief, succinct letter and sent it.

Ignoring the loud pings of emails that dropped into her inbox, she calmly set a notepad and pen on the desk before her and got on with planning for her future. For as long as she could remember, having a plan in place had helped keep her focus true. She'd only abandoned that plan when a dynamic, drop-dead gorgeous Argentinian had set her in his sights and piled on relentless pressure, leading her to imagine mistakenly that he was her future.

It was time to relocate her compass.

Ignoring the phone when it began to ring, she meticulously set out her to-do list, starting with finding a place to live.

Ten minutes later, she heard the soft rap on her door, followed by her secretary's entrance. When she didn't immediately speak, Sienna forced her heavy head up, frowning when she saw Laura's visible distress.

'Yes, what is it?'

'Um… Mr Castillo wants to see you.'

Her heart stuttered, then dropped to her stomach. Somehow, she managed a tight smile. 'Please let him know I'm busy. I have work to do.'

'I… He said you're to drop whatever you're doing and report to his office right away.'

'Tell him—'

'I'm sorry, Sienna,' her secretary interrupted, naked apprehension on her usually cheery face. 'I know you said you don't want to be disturbed, but he's been calling you for the last five minutes. He made it clear he wants you in his office. He said to let him know when you're on your way. And that he will hold me responsible if you don't come right away.'

Rage boiling in her gut, she surged to her feet just as her phone rang again. She didn't need to look down to confirm the caller's identity. 'It's okay, Laura. I'll deal with it.'

Her secretary was barely out of the door when she snatched up the phone. 'I'd thank you not to threaten my secretary.'

'She's my employee. If you didn't want her put in this position then you should have picked up your phone when I called.'

'What do you want, Mr Castillo?' She strove for a calm, poised tone and shut her eyes briefly in relief when she achieved it.

At the end of the line, Emiliano didn't respond for a few terse seconds. 'What I wanted when I called ten minutes ago. You, in my office. Now.'

'I'm—'

'Not as busy as you say. You forget I have access to your diary. Come now, Sienna. Or I'll come down there. My office affords us more privacy than yours, but either way you and I will be doing this face-to-face. The location is your choice. You have three minutes.' The line went dead.

Her hands shook as she hung up. Anger still rumbled in her belly, but the thought of seeing him again so soon meant a different kind of emotion—pain and loss for what she'd never really had superseded that anger, holding her immobile in her chair for a long moment before she forced herself to move.

Hushed whispers and quickly muted conversations trailed her as she made her way to the lift. For a wild, absurd second she wished she'd relocated her office from the twentieth to the thirtieth floor at Emiliano's bidding two months ago. But she swiftly conceded it would've been ten times worse to be in her situation now.

Either way was no consolation. So she put one foot in front of the other until she stood before a set of misted glass double doors. Emiliano's trusted PA was nowhere in sight. Whether by coincidence or by design, she didn't give herself time to dwell on it as she turned the handle and pushed the door open.

He sat at his smoked-glass desk, the iconic vista of the financial heart of London sprawled out behind him. He'd shed the jacket to his bespoke suit. Or perhaps he'd never worn it. His pinstriped tie was loosened, the top button of his shirt undone and his hair sexily dishevelled, as if he'd run his hand through it several times.

Not quite his usual impeccable, well put-together self. But the package was no less impactful. A direct hit to her severely flailing senses, especially when he raised his arrogant head, locked those gold eyes on her and tracked her approach.

She stopped a good distance from his desk, stepping deeper into his orbit, breathing him in… No. Better she stay where she was for her self-preservation, which was way past overdue for reinforcement.

'You wanted to see me. Here I am.'

Narrowed eyes tracked her from head to toe. 'Why are you wearing black? You know how much I hate it when you do.'

She refused to allow memories surrounding discussions of her clothes to intrude. Most of them had taken place in their once-shared dressing room when they'd been naked. 'You didn't summon me to discuss my work gear. That would be a colossal waste of both our time.'

'I asked you here to discuss this.' He waved a large, expressive hand at his computer screen, his jaw as tight as the pellet-hard words falling from his lips. 'What is the meaning of it?'

'If you're referring to my resignation letter, I would've thought it was self-explanatory.'

'Considering your dedication to your career, this is a

trigger response you *will* regret in the very near future,' he snapped. 'I'm willing to overlook it if you are.'

'No, thank you.'

He looked askance, genuinely puzzled. 'Excuse me?'

Sienna took a moment to breathe. 'I'm not going to debate the matter with you. Thankfully, my employment, like my attire, is no longer a subject you have a say on. The copy I sent you by email was unsigned. I believe this makes it official.' She took the requisite steps forward to place the signed resignation letter on his desk before retreating to her position in the middle of the room.

He took his time to scrutinise her face, probing long and deep with penetrating eyes, before he deigned to pick up the piece of paper. After a cursory glance, he flung it back on his desk.

'I do not accept this.'

'You have very little choice in the matter, Mr Castillo,' she replied, her voice less than warm.

His jaw flexed and his nostrils flared. 'You forget that I have to approve this ridiculous "with immediate effect" resignation. And give whatever future employer you choose a worthy reference.'

'If you're under the misconceived notion that I intend to bow and scrape to remain in your good books for the sake of a so-called *worthy reference*, consider this a heads-up that it's not going to happen. I've had assurances of my pick of the top five hedge funds for the last six months should I ever choose to leave Castillo Ventures.'

His head snapped back, his mouth thinning into a line of displeasure. 'You've been courting other companies behind my back?'

Unexpected laughter scraped her throat raw. 'Please let's refrain from flinging accusations of what's happened behind whose back.'

His face tightened. 'I can still make things difficult for you. You know this.'

She deliberately relaxed her limbs, returning his gaze with contrived boredom. 'To what end, though? Besides the rank display of sour grapes on your part, I know one or two CEOs who will hire me simply to get back at you for deals you snatched from right under their noses.'

His eyelids swept down and his fingers formed a steeple on his desk, both signs that his clever brain was ticking over, finding another angle of attack. Sienna braced herself.

'The requisite notice period for someone in your position is six weeks, or have you forgotten that clause in your contract? I can compel you to stay by law.'

Her insides hollowed. 'You would have me stay, be the subject of pitied whispers and lunchtime gossip?'

Indomitable eyes locked on her. 'It only affects you if you allow it. I still maintain that what goes on between us is nobody's business,' he hissed.

Words she'd heard before, the last time whispered against her mouth in this very office, right before a kiss that had made her whole being sing. Words that now made her insides bleed. 'You're wrong, first, to imply there's an *us*. There isn't. I'm beginning to think there never was. Second, you made it everyone's business by taking out a front-page spread about your engagement to another woman!'

He jerked to his feet and rounded his desk, striding towards her. 'I didn't take out a spread. These things just happen!'

She backed away several steps, already fearing her hastily stitched-into-place façade was crumbling. 'I'm sure they do in your world. I want no part of it. I'm leaving. Let me know who you decide to pick as my successor. I'll stay for the rest of the week to bring them up to speed on my projects. I have two months' accrued vacation. If you insist on me working my notice, take that.'

'That's not how it works.'

'Too bad. Sue me if you have to, but on this subject, and on everything else not directly pertaining to Castillo Ventures business, you and I don't have anything more to say to each other, Mr Castillo.'

'Damn it, stop calling me that!' The sharp words were accompanied by a savage shove of his fingers through his hair as he eyed her from the charged space between them.

The unexpected score of needling him should've soothed the torrent of despair inside her. Instead, rough anguish only dug its talons deeper. 'I will *never* call you by your first name again,' she replied in a ragged whisper. 'If you insist on prolonging this farce, I *will* find other names for you, though.'

He shoved his fists in his pockets, his unwavering stare drilling holes into her. 'You really insist on doing this? On throwing your precious career away?'

'How arrogant of you to believe I'll only be a success with you,' she returned with a scornful glare. 'How insufferable of you to imagine I won't thrive with anyone else but you.'

He sauntered towards her with slow, measured, predatory steps. 'You think anyone else can offer you what I have, *querida*? Fire up your intellect or stimulate you the way I do?'

She stared at him, a part of her still reeling and running for cover from the events of the past twelve hours. The other traitorous part wanted to unfurl itself at the warmth of the memories he was callously evoking, to bask shamelessly in bygones.

Brutally, she superimposed her to-do list onto the memories, reminding herself that she had a purpose far away from this man and this place. That she was worth more than this humiliation.

'You are far from the unique gem you imagine yourself to be, Mr Castillo. Don't worry about me. I'll be fine. I'm looking forward to the challenge, actually. Now, if we're done here, I think I'll take you up on that offer of a day off. I need to go apartment hunting.'

Emotion akin to shock flashed briefly through his eyes. 'You're moving out of the penthouse?'

'Moved. Past tense.'

'Why? The papers are drawn up, Sienna. It's yours, free and clear.'

'No, thanks. I don't want *anything* from you.'

Not entirely true. What she'd wanted, he'd cruelly made clear would never be hers.

His eyes darkened to hard stone. A muscle ticked in his cheek as he closed the gap between them.

'Are you quite sure, *querida*? You will not have a chance to change your mind.'

'One hundred per cent,' she replied through clenched teeth.

For endless seconds he stared at her while her heart hammered a wild tattoo against her ribs. Then he jerked his square chin at the door behind her.

'Go, then. Forget me…if you can,' he taunted.

She turned on her heel, forcing herself not to take that one last, desperate fill of him. Her hand grasping the door handle, she paused. Because she needed to say this, as much for herself as for him.

'I *will* forget you. With pleasure.'

There weren't many parts of the world she could go without memories of Emiliano dogging her. But she tried, rewarding herself the moment she left Castillo Ventures a week later with a plane ticket to South America.

The Inca Trail to Machu Picchu served a dual purpose of being an Emiliano-free zone and a physically taxing enough trek to aid her to dreamless slumber in her tent each night.

But any numbness she'd managed to wrap herself in fled the moment she landed at Heathrow four weeks later and turned her phone back on to floods of texts and emails. Sienna forced herself to ignore them as she settled into the back of her taxi and recited her to-do list.

Unpack and settle into her new flat.

Find a job.

Find a way to stop desperately missing the man who'd cruelly rejected her.

She clenched her fist when her heart lurched in that irritatingly dramatic way it did whenever she thought of him.

She had the rest of her life to get on with. Thankfully, the taxi journey to her new address in Chelsea was short. Sienna wasn't ashamed to admit she'd chosen to live on the opposite side of the city to where Emiliano's penthouse was located in East London. She had even contemplated moving out of London altogether. Except that would mean he'd won. She still had some pride left.

Pride that wobbled when she walked into her two-bedroom flat and saw the seven meagre boxes and three suitcases that formed the sum total of her existence. She'd never felt the lack of belonging as acutely as she felt it in that moment.

Angrily, she swiped at the tears that spiked her eyes and got to work. Two hours later, new furniture ordered and boxes unpacked, she tackled her emails.

The only communication from Emiliano was via his HR department. Her severance package was exactly what she was owed and not a penny more. Sienna had insisted on it. So, subject to a few final forms to sign and return, she was officially free of Emiliano Castillo.

Ignoring another squeeze of her heart, she scrutinised the job offers the headhunter had sent. She was about to respond to the one that looked halfway appealing when her mobile phone rang.

A quick check of the screen and she was berating herself for the jolt of disappointment. Pulling herself together, she answered.

'You're back. Thank the Lord! My phone has been ringing off the hook with offers. I have… Wait for it… *Six* hedge funders dying to talk to you.'

David Hunter, the aptly named headhunter who'd made it his business to call her at least once a month for the last year in an attempt to steal her from Castillo Ventures, was as relentless as he was charming. She'd met with him briefly twice before leaving for South America. At their second meeting she hadn't failed to detect the personal interest in his eyes. The warmth in his voice now was a welcome balm to a loneliness she didn't want to admit to feeling, even though she had no intention of entertaining that interest.

'Wow,' she murmured half-heartedly.

He laughed. 'Um, maybe try that again, with feeling?'

Sienna chose to view the small smile that curved her lips as progress. 'Sorry. Jet lag.' It wasn't completely a false statement. Her twelve-hour journey and her frenzied attempt to make her flat habitable had sapped the last of her energy reserves. Her head felt heavy and she wanted to sleep for a week.

'I'll let you go if you agree to have dinner with me tomorrow to discuss the offers,' he pressed.

'I'm not sure, David. Can I let you know?'

He paused for a beat before replying, 'Okay, here's my mini pitch. You're in a unique position to choose your next job, Sienna. Everyone wants you. Castillo is a market leader, sure, but there are other equally exciting opportunities out there for you. They won't stay on the table for ever. I don't want you to miss out on them.'

The vice around her heart squeezed painfully at the mention of Castillo. And as with every time it happened, it also brought a tiny spark of anger. She couldn't mope for ever.

'Okay, dinner tomorrow.'

'Wonderful. Do you have a cuisine preference?'

She thought for a single second before she named her favourite restaurant. As with every corner of her life, it was time to root Emiliano out of this one, too.

'Great, shall I pick you up at seven?'

Because that smacked too much of a date, Sienna shook her head. 'No, it's fine. I'll meet you there.'

His response remained enthusiastic, even if his tone held a touch of disappointment. Finishing the conversation, she made herself a cup of tea and slice of toast. Half-heartedly eating her meal, she took her first shower in her new apartment, then fell into bed.

Twelve hours later, she woke, refreshed if a little listless. Finding herself with next to nothing to do in the middle of a work week was a strange sensation. On a whim, she dressed, snatched up her handbag and caught the Tube to King's Road. After buying a few practical items she needed for her flat, she splurged on a bright bouquet of flowers and a new dress.

She hated that everything in her wardrobe had an Emiliano-sized reminder tag on it, but throwing it all out and starting anew was one step too far. The new emerald silk dress was chic enough for a dinner while projecting a professional air. And, when the time came to get ready, she teamed it with black slingback shoes, black pearls and a matching bracelet. After sliding on her favourite red lipstick, she picked up her clutch and made her way outside to the waiting taxi.

Zarcosta was a Michelin-starred restaurant, which specialised in European dishes with a distinct Mediterranean flavour. The owner, Marco Zarcosta, was effusive and temperamental, a short, bespectacled character who either loved or hated clients on sight. Sienna had been lucky enough to be enfolded in the former group and she was met with a hug and a kiss on both cheeks when she entered the intimately lit restaurant in Fitzrovia.

'A shame about this relationship business, *cara*,' the Italian murmured in her ear. 'Such a shame. But Marco is here for you, eh?'

Pulling back from the embrace, she nodded and plastered on a smile, while wondering if coming here had been a wise choice. But David, having spotted her, was rising from the table and making his way towards her.

With his gelled blond hair, sparkling silver-grey eyes and a flashing smile, it wasn't a stretch to picture David Hunter as a surfer, the only thing differentiating him from that carefree lifestyle being his three-piece suit and the look of determination in his eyes. Determination that morphed to intimate interest when his eyes met hers. A quick once-over of her body and his smile widened.

'Glad you made it. You look fantastic.'

'Um, thanks.'

Although she was a little taken aback when he cupped her elbows and repeated Marco's version of kissing her hello, she wasn't altogether surprised.

What did surprise her, though, and what sent a tectonic jolt of electricity through her as she cast a gaze across the full room on her way to their table, was the sight of Emiliano Castillo staring at her with chilling eyes.

CHAPTER FOUR

SHE STUMBLED. She *actually* stumbled.

Cringing and hating herself for the telling action, she plastered an even wider smile on her face as David caught and steadied her.

'Hey, you okay?'

'Of course, why shouldn't I be?' The question emerged a touch more aggressively than she'd intended.

His eyes widened a little before he offered her a sympathetic smile. 'Sorry if I came on a little strong yesterday,' he said as he pulled out her chair and saw her seated. 'Landing you will do wonders for my account,' he said shamelessly. 'Not to mention my street cred.'

Her laugh was a little forced, her nerves screeching with horror to find that her every sense was attuned to the man across the room. The one whose piercing gaze she could feel boring into her skin.

'Well, I do need a job, so let's hear what's on the table.'

'Excellent. First, I'll order us some wine. Or would you like champagne? We might have something to celebrate at the end of the evening, I expect. You don't think I'm jumping the gun, do you?'

She gave a carefree wave of her hand. 'Not at all. Go for it,' she replied with enthusiasm that echoed patently false inside.

His smile brightened. Thankfully, he was not picking up on her act. Their waiter arrived. David ordered their drinks and she ordered her favourite meal. Simply because she wasn't about to give in to the voice mocking her about her situation.

The moment they were alone, David started raving about the offers.

She listened. She nodded. She even managed one or two pertinent questions.

But they all sounded boring. Nothing as intellectually stimulating as the work she'd done at Castillo.

You think anyone else can offer you what I have, querida?

His voice was as clear as a bell in her head. So much so, her head snapped towards the man in question. His stare was direct and unapologetic. Cold and arrogant. His dinner companions, a male and female she didn't recognise, were making conversation. He nodded and said something back. All without taking his gaze off her.

Sienna grew hot. Then cold. Hot again. As if her body didn't know what to make of the circumstances.

Warm fingers drifted over the back of her hand. 'Hey, I'm not losing you, am I?'

She started, looked down at David's hand on hers. Then absurdly, because a part of her remained a glutton for punishment, she glanced back at Emiliano.

His already-hardened face had grown tauter, his jaw clenched in steel as his gaze dropped to take in the caress. The look in his eyes when their gazes reconnected was no longer Arctic cold. It was furnace hot with censure.

She wanted to laugh but she was sure the action would strangle her. So she turned away, focused her gaze on her dinner companion and smiled.

'No, you're not losing me. In fact, I want to hear more about Chrysallis. They sound like they could be a great fit.'

Their starters arrived. She ate without tasting a morsel while David dove into his role with even more gusto, pausing only when their plates were cleared away.

Needing a breather because the weight of Emiliano's regard was unsettling her more by the minute, she placed her napkin on the table and picked up her clutch.

'Would you excuse me for a minute? I need to visit the ladies' room.'

'Of course.' He rose immediately and solicitously came round to pull back her chair. Before she could step away, he leaned down towards her. 'And I know it's a little awkward having your old boss in the same room while discussing your next job. Sorry about that.'

Startled, she turned to look at him. Sympathetic grey eyes met hers and, for some absurd reason, a lump rose in her throat. 'It's not your fault, but thank you for understanding.'

He nodded, then stood back to her let pass.

The much-needed composure gathering took five long minutes of pacing the empty ladies' room, water splashed on her hot wrists and reapplication of her lipstick. Reminding herself that she'd been through worse adversity—because what was worse than being rejected by four different foster families within the space of a year when you're eleven years old?—she squared her shoulders and pulled open the ladies' room door.

To find Emiliano leaning against the wall, feet planted in patent aggression.

The look in his eyes hadn't changed. In fact, he looked even angrier, his every breath evocative of the dark rumbling of a volcano before it erupted and destroyed everything in its path.

Sienna reminded herself that they were done. She didn't need to engage him, even though every fibre of her being insisted on straining towards him.

Forcing her gaze from his tall, sleek body, she took a step away from him.

One hand shot out to grip her waist, long fingers imprisoning her.

'You really want to play it like this? You want to pretend I don't exist?' he snarled at her.

What his deep voice did to her insides, she didn't like. Not one little bit. 'You don't exist, not to me. You challenged me to forget you, remember? This is me forgetting you.'

'By bringing another man *here*, on your first date?'

'Why, did you think this place would stop being special to me because you dumped me? Why should I stop coming here? The food is great, the ambience is excellent and the company sublime. And what makes you think it's a first date?' she threw in with a raised eyebrow.

Leonine eyes glinted pure danger. 'How many times have you seen him?'

She sighed. 'Why do you care? It really is none of your business.'

He opened his mouth then clamped it shut again when a trio of women came down the hall. His hold moved lightning quick from her waist to her wrist, taking it in an implacable hold and using it to compel her through another door. Between one moment and the next, they were outside in a quiet alley, the sound of dining guests and cutlery cut off abruptly.

'How many?' he growled again.

A dart of apprehension lanced her that had nothing to do with the cold temperature and light falling rain. But with it came a dose of something else: excitement.

She hated herself for it. He'd left her. Rejected her in the worst possible way in favour of something better. *Someone* better. Just as her mother had done. Just as all the potential foster families had done. She didn't owe him the time of day, never mind this conversation. But she would answer him. If nothing else, there was the matter of her pride. The silent treatment never worked with him. She'd learned very early in their relationship—their *ex*-relationship—that Emiliano was arrogant enough to think he'd won an argument whenever she chose silence instead of answering.

'This is our third date.' She proffered the lie coolly, keeping her gaze squarely on his. She knew what her answer would mean to him. Was morbidly curious to see the effect it had on him.

Because Emiliano never forgot.

He went marble-still, his chest barely rising and falling. Sienna knew what it meant. She'd struck a very raw nerve. Part of her rejoiced. Even as a greater part of her curled up and died for that rejoicing. Because what did that say about her? That she was so hung up on him, she wanted to get a rise out of him for delivering information that was sure to remind him of them? That would remind him that they'd made love for the first time after their third date?

'Your *third* date?' he repeated ominously.

She raised her chin, shivering despite the volcanic atmosphere between them.

He spotted her reaction and started to shrug off his jacket, the way he'd done numerous times in the past when she'd needed an extra layer of warmth.

She stepped back quickly, unable to bear the thought. 'What do you think you're doing?'

He paused. 'You need to ask?'

She shook her head emphatically. 'No, thank you.'

Jaw clenched, he shouldered the jacket back on, his frown turning blacker. 'Answer me, Sienna.'

'Yes, *third* date. And it's going very well, even if I say so myself. I've just ordered the oysters. If you haven't had your main yet, I suggest you try them. Marco's outdoing himself tonight.'

He took a single, predatory step towards her, his face a mask of frozen fury. 'Who is he, Sienna, hmm? This guy you're eating oysters for?'

She affected what she hoped was a half-decent indifferent shrug. 'He's the guy who may or may not know what the significance of a third date with me means. He's witty, charming and intelligent, and we have oodles in common, so I'd say his prospects are—'

The single, filthy curse was her only warning before Emiliano grabbed her by the arms and slammed her against the wall. To anyone witnessing the action, it might have seemed violent, but it was a practised move perfected in their time together that ensured her no harm. The reminder sent everything inside Sienna screaming with mingled horror and sheer delight as electricity rushed through her. It was the most natural response in the world to start raising one leg in preparation to have him hitching her up. But the assist never came. And in the dark alley, the cold wind reminded her that it was over between Emiliano and her.

That this conversation should not be happening.

'You will *not* sleep with him,' he pronounced darkly, his thinned lips white with restrained fury.

She laughed. It was either that or succumb to something else—such as tears. 'Do you need a reminder of how I react to orders, Mr Castillo?'

His face tightened further at her deliberate formality. 'Unless you were seeing him behind my back, you barely know the guy. For all you know he could be—'

'What? Someone else who leads me along for over a year then dumps me for his fiancée?'

He had the grace to drop his gaze, to blink, but it was the only give in an otherwise rigidly unforgiving but breathtakingly striking face.

'Sienna, things aren't what they seem. I told you why I'm doing this—'

'Let me go. Go finish your meeting. Then go home to your fiancée. I'm not sure exactly what you intended by cornering me this way. But if somewhere in your twisted imagination you thought you were looking out for me, then don't. We both know I've never been the feeble, cuddly type. You hurt me, but as you can see I didn't curl up and die. I don't intend to. I've moved on.'

She placed her hands on his chest and pushed. For a moment, he didn't budge. Then he stepped back. Sienna wished he'd stayed a moment longer. And cursed herself to hell and back.

She moved from the wall and ran damp hands over her dress. When she raised her head, he was regarding her with icy mockery.

'I thought you many things, but I never thought the day would come when I'd think you a petty fool.'

Her mouth dropped open. 'Excuse me?'

He shrugged. 'Deny it if you will, that all of this was staged for my benefit. You didn't hope I would see you with another man and immediately come running back?'

She forced her mouth closed and raised a hand casually to flick her long hair over her shoulder. A sliver of satisfaction came with witnessing the trace of hunger on his face as he followed the movement.

'You have a particular word in Argentina for a donkey's behind, don't you, Mr Castillo? I'm sure I heard you use it once or twice, usually when things weren't going your way. Well, guess what? You're being a giant one right now.' She stepped close, even though her every instinct screamed at her to flee in the other direction, and she continued, 'The only thing I want you thinking about me tonight, when you get home and are enjoying your favourite cognac, is how much I appreciate everything you taught me in bed during our time together. And how much I'm going to be enjoying sharing all that gorgeous, decadent knowledge with David. And then I want you to raise that glass to yourself, because you truly deserve the kudos—'

'Cállate!' Grasping her arms, he pinned her back against the wall, a feverish light glinting dangerously in his eyes. 'Shut the hell up!' he repeated in English. With each snarled word, he moved her higher up the wall until he was eye level with her. 'You want a reaction from me, *enamorada*? Well, your wish is about to be granted.'

The kiss was hell. And heaven. And everything in between. The edgy hunger and fury with which Emiliano kissed her, devoured her, robbed her of thought in a single second. All she could feel, breathe, hear, was the riotous, ecstatic thundering of her senses.

With a helpless groan, she opened her mouth and welcomed a kiss that should not have been happening. Whether it was the illicit nature of it or, because contrary to what she'd been telling herself he continued to be vital to her very being, Sienna was too afraid to find out. All she could stand to entertain in that moment was that he was here for a brief moment in her arms. The man who had taught her the finest art of passion was in her arms. And she didn't want to let him go.

His moan echoed hers as the kiss deepened, their strained panting echoing in the dark alley as the rain intensified, hands roving, touch reacquainted. Her hands slid over his shoulders, locked into the vibrant hair at his nape and scraped over his scalp.

He jerked against her, the imprint of his powerful arousal a primal force at the cradle of her thighs. She couldn't help it, she moved against him, her tongue sliding sensuously against his in blatant, desperate need as her body melted. He shifted, placing a little distance between them.

Sienna whimpered and started to close the gap. Felt the mist of rain on her face. Then it all came rushing back.

Emiliano stepped away, eyes blazing but face frozen once more.

'Go now, *querida*. Return to your *date* with my touch all over your body. Go to him and tell him I was the one who made you wet, who caused that glazed look in your eyes and your swollen lips. Tell him how I could've had you right here, right now, against this wall if I wished. And if he wants you after that—' he shrugged '—try telling yourself he's still the charming and intelligent man you want.'

Anger swiftly followed shock and shame. 'You…you're disgusting. I hate you!'

'Be truthful. You don't hate me. You hate yourself because your little game has been turned back on you.'

Thick, gulping tears threatened. Sienna battled them back through sheer grit. But even after she got herself under a modicum of control she couldn't speak. She stared at him, the man she'd allowed to mean more to her in their time together than had been even remotely wise. She'd paid heavily for that gross misjudgement. Was still paying. As she gazed into his powerfully gorgeous face, she shook her head.

'You're right. I don't hate you. What I feel is sadness for you—that you feel the need to do this just to prove a point. But I don't hate myself for trying to move on. You can do your best to belittle my efforts—it's not going to stop me. You can either move on, too, or waste your time trying to corner me in dark alleys. No matter what you do or say or try to prove, all you'll get is me, walking away from you every time.'

A cryptic expression washed over his face, followed by another, before his mask slipped back into place. 'Great speech, *querida*, but perhaps if you'd stop for a minute you can hear what I have to say.'

'I don't want to hear it. You and I had nothing to talk about when I left you last month. We have even less to talk about now.'

He lifted a lazy hand and passed a finger over her tingling lower lip. 'Our kiss said otherwise.'

She jerked away. 'The kiss I'm already incredibly ashamed of, you mean?'

His face darkened and his hand dropped. 'Excuse me?'

'You're not deaf. You're engaged to another woman, and yet here you are, kissing me. Don't you have even a shred of decency?'

He shook his head. 'Sienna, it's not going to be like that—'

'No! Enough. And stop saying my name,' she snapped. Prying herself off the wall, she started walking away.

'Come back here,' he bit out. 'We're not finished.'

She hurried her steps, almost fearful her feet would disobey her and rush back to him, to hear him out if it meant hearing his voice, seeing his face for a few more precious minutes. She heard him behind her and quickened her steps.

'*Dios mío*, stop!'

She broke into a run, catching a sob before it slipped free.

'Sienna, slow down!'

She saw a mound of snow swept to one side of the pavement, she heard voices from pedestrians at the entrance to the alley and ran faster. The urgency to get back to civility, away from Emiliano's captivating presence, rushed through her. What had she been thinking? He belonged to another woman. He was no longer hers to kiss, to touch, to make love with…

The sob broke, horrible and pain-filled. Tears surged into her eyes, blinding her. She rounded the corner at full speed. She never knew whether it was a body or an object she bumped into. But she felt her heel slide over the icy sidewalk. Felt her body wrenched sideways as she lost her balance. Saw the ground rush up to meet her. Heard Emiliano's guttural shout from behind. Then felt excruciating pain as her head cracked on the side of the kerb, her braced arms doing nothing to halt her fall.

She moaned as stars exploded across her vision. Hands turned her, cradled her. Her vision cleared for a second and she saw golden eyes filled with concern blazing down at her. Then another rip of pain.

Then the blissful succumbing to nothing.

CHAPTER FIVE

'Miss Newman? Sienna?'

She turned her head a fraction towards the sound but kept her eyes closed. The effort it took to move even her eyeballs was too much.

'Hmm...?'

'Don't try and speak, Miss Newman. Take it easy. Open your eyes when you're ready.'

Miss Newman? Was there someone else in the room with her? Was the voice speaking to someone else besides her? She would much prefer it because having someone engage with her would mean she had to respond. She would have to speak. She turned away from the voice. She didn't want to speak. She wanted to sink back into the harmless abyss where there was no pain, only oblivion. Where there were no voices murmuring, drawing closer to where she lay.

'We need to take your vitals, find out how you're doing. You've been out for a while.'

Out? Where?

She tried to turn her head again, felt the restriction across her forehead and paused. She was wearing some sort of a cap. Tentatively, she lifted her hand to her head.

'That's your bandage. It needs to stay on for a while, I'm afraid,' a kind female voice supplied. 'Can you open your eyes for me, dear? The doctor needs to examine you properly.'

Doctor. She was in a hospital. But... Why?

Dropping her hand back onto her stomach, she carefully cracked her eyes open, then winced at the bright lights overhead.

'Nurse, turn down the lights, please?'

The lights dimmed. She opened her eyes a little wider.

Two faces stared at her. The male doctor wore glasses behind which dark eyes gleamed with serious intelligence. The nurse's face was kinder, more maternal.

She smiled broadly now, almost as if her patient opening her eyes was a personal triumph for her.

'I'm Dr Stephens, this is Nurse Abby. Can you tell me the last thing you remember, Miss Newman?'

She brought her attention back to the doctor. She blinked tired eyes again, casting a look around the room to make sure he was talking to someone else and not her.

He couldn't be addressing her.

Because she wasn't Miss Newman. Or Sienna.

Her name was…

It was…

She shook her head, trying to clear her brain of the thick fog.

'I…' she croaked. Her throat was raw and painful. Her voice felt disused. Raising her hand to her throat, she massaged her skin, then froze when she saw the needle inserted into her vein. Examining the back of her hand closely, she saw several puncture marks. For some reason, the sight of the tiny bruises struck fear into her heart. Her eyes sought the health professionals staring down at her. 'I… How long…?'

Dr Stephens scribbled on a sheet before he pulled out a pen light. 'You've been unconscious for a little over two weeks. The bandage on your head is because we had to perform a minor surgery to reduce the swelling on your brain.'

'Brain…*surgery*?'

'Yes.' He stepped up to the bed and held up the light, the question clear in his eyes. When she gave a small nod, he shone it in one eye, then the other. Then he stepped back. 'Can you tell me the last thing you remember?' he asked again.

A series of fragmented images flashed through her brain, like strobe lights in a dark room, on and off, before she could form a proper picture. Shaking her head again, she tried to concentrate, to capture one solid image. Her mind remained a dark, blank space.

She saw the doctor and nurse exchange glances.

'Please…' She stopped when her throat protested. The nurse stepped forward with a glass of water and straw. Gratefully, she sipped, relief pouring through her when the pain eased. 'What's… What happened?' she managed. 'Where am I?'

'You're at North Haven,' Dr Stephens replied. 'We're a private medical facility just outside London. As for what happened, you slipped on ice outside a restaurant and hit your head hard enough to cause a little brain bleed. You don't remember?'

She shook her head. 'No.'

'Do you remember going to the restaurant?' He stopped and checked his notes. 'I believe it's called Zarcosta?'

Again she shook her head, fighting the surge of panic. 'I don't…remember.'

The doctor fell silent for almost a minute, his professional mask slipping briefly to exhibit his concern. 'Miss Newman, can you tell me your date of birth?' he pressed gently.

She probed her mind desperately, and found only black space. Her throat clogged. She swallowed, refusing to succumb to tears. 'No,' she whispered. 'Is that my name—Newman? Sienna Newman?'

Dr Stephens nodded solemnly. 'Yes, it is. Do you know what you do for a living? Or where you live?'

'I don't know!' This time she couldn't stop the rise of

tears or the twisting of her hand into the sheet for something, anything, to hang on to. 'Why can't I remember?'

'I can't give you an answer yet. Not until we run a few tests.' He put away his pen light and attempted a smile. 'Try not to worry. We'll know what's going on very shortly.'

He turned and spoke to the nurse in medical jargon she couldn't decipher.

She looked down. Her hands were trembling. In fact, her whole body was trembling as confusion and panic rose in steady waves.

Sensing her emotions, Nurse Abby patted her hand. 'The technicians and I will run the tests the doctor needs, then we'll take it from there, okay?'

She couldn't do much else but nod and watch with climbing despair as they left the room. Then, forcing herself to calm down, she probed her mind again, searching every corner until tears spilled down her cheeks and exhaustion weighed her down.

She could barely summon the energy to take interest in what was happening when the nurse returned with two other medical staff. Blood was taken and her vitals recorded before she was wheeled away and placed in an MRI machine.

Time passed. Then she was returned to her room, by which time oblivion was a welcome relief. So she gave in. The sunlight outside her window had turned to night when she woke up. Her room was bathed in soft light and a breathtaking bouquet of flowers—calla lilies and white roses—stood on the dresser across the room.

The pain in her head still throbbed but she was getting used to it, enough to be able to recall the conversation with the medical team.

Even though a practical voice prompted her that panicking would bring no answers, she couldn't stop the fear squeezing her heart.

She'd had brain surgery. And now she couldn't remember her own name.

She was still grappling with the million questions teeming in her mind when Nurse Abby walked back in.

'Have I… Have there been any visitors? My family?' she blurted, the question seeming to come from nowhere.

The nurse cast a furtive glance at her before busying herself with checking the intravenous drip. 'We weren't given details of any family members to contact, but we called your…' She paused, unnecessarily straightening the sheets. 'Your friend. He's on his way.'

'My friend?' she repeated, hope momentarily robbing her of breath.

'Yes. He says he was with you that night. You're very lucky to have him. He's been here every day since your accident. He's had a bunch of those lovely flowers delivered every day, too,' she said, with a trace of envy in her voice.

Sienna—the name was still so alien to her—returned her gaze to the flowers. They were her favourite. She didn't understand how she knew, but the knowledge wasn't one that needed probing. That tiny revelation of self eased the panic threatening again. Not enough to keep her from going on a desperate hunt for her memory once again, though, and experiencing the hollowness in her stomach expand when she found nothing. Retreating from her mental flailing, she latched on to the only real thing available.

'My friend… What's his name?' she asked.

'It's… Oh, here he is now! We have our share of celebrities using this facility, but none of them arrive by helicopter,' she divulged in an excited whisper as she peered out of the window.

Although Sienna couldn't see the spectacle capturing the nurse's attention, she heard the distinct beating of rotor blades, the sound growing louder as the aircraft flew overhead.

As she absorbed the news that she had a friend who owned a helicopter, a buzzer sounded in the room. Nurse Abby dragged her attention from the window, reached into her pocket and withdrew a miniature tablet.

'Perfect timing. Your test results are ready. Dr Stephens will want to see them before he talks to you both.'

'Both?'

Nurse Abby paused by the door. 'I'm not one to gossip, but your man isn't the kind to take no for an answer. He's demanded to know every detail of your progress. And, with us not being able to contact any family members, we've had to rely on him to give medical approval. Which is a good thing, because his consent saved your life. It's clear he cares a great deal about you.' Again, Sienna caught wistfulness in her tone that told her Nurse Abby was a romantic at heart.

'So he knows I have a…um…memory issue?'

The older woman's face softened in sympathy. 'Don't worry about that, my dear. Everything will be all right. I just know it.'

Her tablet buzzed again. She was gone before Sienna could voice any of the questions burning on her tongue. And for the next twenty minutes they grew until she heard voices approaching.

Dr Stephens entered, a file in his hand. Paralysed with fear as to what that file contained and what her diagnosis was, she didn't immediately acknowledge the other presence in the room, not until she felt the tingle from the power of his stare. Not until her heart began to flutter wildly, from reasons that had nothing to do with the sorry state of her mind.

Her reaction to the man partly obscured by Dr Stephens's advancing form was so visceral, so primitively electrifying, her fingers locked on to the sheets and her breath strangled in her throat.

'Miss Newman, I have the results of your tests. Before we continue, Nurse Abby informs me she's told you of Mr Castillo's involvement in your medical care.' He rounded to the side of the bed, stepping out of the line of sight of the man behind him. The man who stood tall, imposing. Frozen at the sight of her. 'You won't remember him, most likely, but this is…'

The buzzing in her ears stopped her from hearing the rest of Dr Stephen's words.

From the tiny pieces of useless, broken memory, a single one began to form. Not a whole picture, but enough fractions coalesced to make her heart skip several beats. To make her whole body tremble into wakeful, joyful awareness when the piece held.

Enough to make her stare at the man whose face, like a blazing comet through the night sky, was beautifully real and infinitely magical to her.

'Emiliano…' Her voice emerged as a hopeful rasp. When he didn't disappear, when he remained a solid, towering reality before her, she struggled upright. 'Emiliano!'

He took a single step towards her then froze again, his face losing several shades of colour. 'You remember?' he rasped, a peculiar note in his voice as he stared with watchful, almost-alarmed eyes.

'Yes! I remember you. Oh, God!' Her gaze darted excitedly to the doctor and back to Emiliano. 'I remember!'

He still hadn't moved. Why? Did she look that horrific? She knew from the brief and cringe-making self-examination she'd conducted earlier that she'd lost weight. There were hollows not just on the inside of her but also on the outside.

But Emiliano had nursed her through a horrific flu and chest infection recently without batting an eyelash. And she was sure she'd looked worse then.

Realising she'd just had another memory, she gasped. 'The flu! I had the flu around a month ago,' she said.

Dr Stephens glanced at Emiliano. His jaw flexed for a second before he shook his head and they both stared at her.

'What?' she demanded.

'Your flu wasn't a month ago. It was in late September.'

'And?'

'And it'll be New Year's Day in three days,' he said, his deep voice curiously flat.

Her heart lurched, then thudded anew with dread. Before it could take complete hold, Dr Stephens cleared his throat.

'Miss Newman, can you tell me what your relationship is with Mr Castillo?'

She glanced at Emiliano, her panic receding a little as his eyes met hers. 'We're lovers,' she said, blushing when his eyes began to darken. The word *lover* had always felt a little too intimate to share, but she couldn't think of a better term to describe the relationship between her and Emiliano. 'We've been together for nearly ten months.'

A rough sound emerged from his throat. He must be worried about her. He hadn't liked it when she'd got her chest infection. She couldn't imagine what the last two weeks had been like for him. In a reversed position, she would've been out of her mind.

Tentatively, she reached out her unencumbered hand to him. 'Emiliano, I'm okay. I'm sorry if I worried you.'

After a tense little moment, he moved towards her. The hand that enfolded hers was warm, strong. Stimulatingly electrifying. Her breath caught all over again when she raised her head and saw their touch was having the same effect on him.

They both turned when Dr Stephens cleared his throat again. 'Mr Castillo, can you corroborate that?'

'No. It's been longer than that. About a year, to be exact,' he said.

'A *year*?' She searched his eyes.

'*Si,*' he confirmed.

Thrown into confusion all over again, she struggled to breathe. 'What's wrong with me?'

'You're showing all the signs of retrograde amnesia,' Dr Stephens said. 'Your head trauma has caused you to lose chunks of your memory. Can you tell me your earliest memory of you and Mr Castillo?'

She frowned, sifted through the jagged pieces. 'I… We were in Vienna…at the summer opera…in June?' She glanced up at Emiliano. He nodded.

'And the last?' the doctor asked.

'Um… It must be October, then. A client meeting in Vancouver, followed by dinner. I was feeling much better by then.' She couldn't stop the flow of colour into her cheeks as other memories burst forth. The tightening of his hand on hers told her he was recalling the hastily made excuses after the deal had been struck, the abandoned meal, the frenzied kiss in the lift, Emiliano lapping vintage champagne from her naked body.

He'd murmured thick, charged words to her in Spanish as he'd made love to her. Words she was beginning to understand. Words that had sparked the belief that she wasn't just another transient body, warming his bed for a finite spell.

'So you remember what you do for a living now?'

She nodded. 'I'm his… I'm the vice-president of Acquisitions at Castillo Ventures.'

Dr Stephens's gaze flicked to Emiliano before it returned to her. 'Anything else? Your age? Family? Favourite soccer team?'

She held her breath and delved deep once more, her hand grasping Emiliano's tighter as she came up empty.

Swallowing, she shook her head. 'No, but I know Emiliano's birthday is in September.'

The doctor nodded. 'Okay. Let's move on to other things—'

'Wait. What… When will I get my memories back? Is there anything I can do?'

Beside her, Emiliano shifted, his free hand sliding over her nape to gently direct her gaze to him. 'Dr Stephens stresses the importance of not forcing your memories to return, *querida*. Isn't that right, doctor?'

There was something in his voice. The bone-deep authority stamped into each word and deed was nothing new to her refreshed memory, but there was underlying terseness in there.

Dr Stephens nodded. 'It's better to let the memories return on their own. Unfortunately, there isn't a time frame of when that'll be. Your brain is still healing itself after the trauma. My recommendation is for the complete absence of stress of any kind, especially considering your other condition.'

She felt Emiliano tense as her own anxiety spiked. A quick glance at him showed his darkly questioning stare levelled at the doctor. 'My other condition?' she asked.

'You said she was healing,' Emiliano accused icily.

'She is. I don't mean that.' His gaze returned to her. 'Since the time frame of your relationship is right, I'm going to assume it's okay to share this information with Mr Castillo, as well.'

'What information?' she demanded.

Dr Stephens consulted the file one last time, then closed it. 'The result of the blood test we took when you were first admitted two weeks ago revealed you are pregnant.'

Her heart somersaulted into her stomach. 'I'm… *What?*'

The hand on her nape had tightened almost to the point

of discomfort, but she didn't mind too much. It was the only thing keeping her grounded.

'Yes, doctor. Repeat that, *por favor*,' Emiliano commanded through clenched teeth.

'Obviously with the gap in her memory we won't be able to determine how far along she is, but the scan shows she can't be more than three-months pregnant.'

'How is that possible? She never missed taking her pill.'

'And you? Did you use protection?'

Emiliano replied without embarrassment. 'No. We preferred it that way. We both got blood tests to prove we were healthy.'

'She mentioned the flu and an infection. Did she take a course of antibiotics?'

Emiliano nodded tersely. 'Yes, but she got her period after that. She's as regular as clockwork.'

'But the effectiveness of the pill may have been compromised by the antibiotics. It only needed to be disrupted briefly for pregnancy to occur. And menstruating in the first month of pregnancy isn't uncommon.'

Dr Stephens carried on speaking. Emiliano fired more questions at him.

'Is the baby okay?' she asked when a lull came in the interrogation.

'Yes, we've been monitoring you closely and, besides the head injury, your body is thriving.'

Sienna exhaled in relief and turned her hand within Emiliano's, needing even more of his touch as her senses went into complete free fall. First came shock, then panic. Then…utter elation. Something in her heart, an emotion she didn't completely understand, cracked wide open, spewing endless joy through her at the thought of the baby growing inside her.

But all she could do was stare at her lover, her insides singing with happiness.

'Emiliano…' she murmured softly, a tiny part of her afraid that, like her absent memories, her new joy would disappear if she spoke too loudly.

He heard her and stopped speaking to stare down at her. His deep shock was clear in his eyes. As was a tumble of other unfathomable emotions. Emotions she was confident they would work through eventually.

'Yes, Sienna?'

'Emiliano…I'm… We're having a baby,' she whispered in wonder.

His eyes blazed with a fierce light that turned her insides molten. His gaze left hers to track down her body. It paused at her still-flat stomach and stayed, the stamp of possession unmistakeable.

His eyelids descended, temporarily veiling his expression. '*Sí, querida.* It seems we are to be unexpectedly blessed.'

Turning her head, she raised their joined hands and on impulse kissed the back of Emiliano's hand before resting her cheek against it. She heard his sharp inhalation but she refused to be embarrassed about the public display of affection.

Silence reigned for a handful of seconds before Emiliano eased away.

'Rest now. I need to speak to Dr Stephens about when you can be discharged.'

She settled back into bed, her mouth curving in a smile. 'Oh, yes, please. I can't wait to go home. Alfie must be bored out of his mind with just you for company,' she teased.

He didn't return her smile. But her instinct told her that wasn't new. 'He wouldn't dare admit it to me, but I have a feeling he will be pleased to have you back,' he offered dryly. Then he walked out.

Despite the huge obstacles she was sure awaited her

future, Sienna couldn't stop her smile stretching wide as her hand drifted down to rest on her stomach.

Some of her memories might have been temporarily taken away, but while she waited for time to heal her she would revel in what she knew in her heart was a true blessing.

CHAPTER SIX

'YOU'VE KNOWN SHE was pregnant for two weeks and you didn't tell me?' Emiliano demanded the moment the doctor shut the door behind them. He wasn't sure why his blood was boiling so high. Nor did he welcome it. The shock he'd just sustained needed to be treated with cold, calculated precision. Not this frantic pacing and hammering heartbeats.

Sienna was pregnant. The woman who he had very little doubt hated the very ground he walked on was carrying his child. The same woman who'd told him coldly two weeks ago that she'd moved on from him, and who'd blatantly flaunted another man in his face.

His gut clenched hard, the punch of that statement nowhere near dulled despite the passage of time.

The situation with the Cabreras was nowhere near resolved, despite his best efforts to find a solution. They were intent on the son paying for the sins of the parents. And they were wealthy enough not to be influenced by the offer of financial compensation.

Only Emiliano's agreement to wed Graciela Cabrera had sufficed. He'd gone along with it, thinking he would find a quick alternative solution while they were temporarily appeased.

Emiliano would've consigned the whole situation to hell by now had it not been for Matias's plea at the end of his video message and his own meeting with Graciela.

It was clear the young girl was desperate to find a way out from beneath her father's oppressive thumb, her wild behaviour and risqué media courting simply outbursts of a cornered, bewildered victim. Emiliano wasn't ashamed to admit empathy had forced him to stay at the dinner that had been photographed by the paparazzi.

Even then, he'd been all set to walk away. Despite his brother's entreaty, he'd known he needed to find another way to honour Matias's wishes. Until Graciela's blatant plea for help, for him to go along with the ruse for a short time just to buy her some time. His agreement in that moment had been to buy *himself* more time.

What he hadn't expected was for the whole situation to blow up in his face even before his feet had touched the ground properly. In light of Sienna's accident, a different powder keg had been activated, a situation that needed to be dealt with very carefully.

As for the news that he was to be a father...

He pushed that to the bottom of the list. He was pragmatic enough to accept that, whether he liked it or not, this was his new reality. Sifting through his feelings to find the correct descriptive right now would serve no useful purpose.

Neither would dwelling on the fact that this was the last thing he would've wished for, given the choice.

His question, however, needed answering. He focused on the doctor, who shrugged. 'You're not my patient. She is. I shared those details that were pertinent to her continued health with you because I needed your consent to treat her head trauma. Her pregnancy didn't fall into that purview.'

'It wasn't up to you to decide what to share and what to withhold. I'm the father of her child!' The words felt alien and almost...alarming coming from his mouth. What did he know about parenting? His own experience had been beyond abysmal to the point of non-existent.

The thought triggered a deep unsettling inside him and he had to tighten his gut against letting it rule him.

'The history you gave me when she was admitted left

room for questions. I had to do whatever I could to treat her trauma, but I couldn't share confidential information with you, because you'd told me you two were no longer together. I had to consider the possibility that someone else was the father.'

A part of him understood the doctor's reasoning. A greater part of him raged maniacally at the thought of Sienna sleeping with another man, never mind taking his seed into her body and carrying his child. He'd seen her on a date with David Hunter and he hadn't reacted well. In fact, he'd go as far as to say he'd been ashamed of himself for the way he acted. That didn't diminish his rage. Or the guilt dogging him.

Telling himself his possessive instincts had spiked and remained fiercely active when she'd walked away from him was true enough. He hadn't been anywhere near ready to let Sienna go despite his growing misgivings about her. Having the decision taken out of his hands while he'd been in retreat and regroup mode had stung.

None of that changed the fact that he was the reason she was laid up in a hospital bed with gaps in her memory. Gaps he couldn't fill without causing further damage. To her or the child.

His child.

His responsibility.

Again he experienced a bolt of bewilderment and shook his head, everything that had happened recently making him ball his fists in silent fury.

'Give me the raw prognosis. And a way forward that enables me to come clean with her about our relationship.' He abhorred the thought of lying to her.

Dr Stephens shook his head. 'My recommendation still stands. Any further trauma, even emotionally, could have a severe adverse effect on her health. Remember, it's not just her in the picture now. If she's going ahead with the pregnancy—'

'*If?*' Icy waves of disbelief washed through him, followed closely by a total rejection of the very idea. 'Why would she not want the baby?'

The other man shrugged. 'She's an independent woman, who from all accounts seems to be blocking out the last few weeks of your relationship and the break-up. You need to prepare yourself for every possibility once her memories return.'

The stark words kicked him square in the solar plexus, rocking him back on his heels.

Normally, Emiliano prided himself on seeing every angle of a problem. Spotting an opponent's strategy, being half a dozen moves ahead, picking at the flaws and beating them at their own game had seen him walk away with life-changing deals before he'd turned thirty. At thirty-two, he'd made himself, and every single one of his elite clients, unimaginably rich in the process.

But it seemed, the moment he'd set foot back in Argentina, everything had gone wrong. He'd thought himself immune to anything to do with his parents. But, when it'd come down to it, he hadn't been able to walk away. Especially not when Matias had pleaded with him on their behalf. But hard on the heels of Matias's plea on behalf of Graciela had come words which had made it impossible for him to walk away.

You owe me. And I'm collecting.

Those six words had ultimately stopped him from walking out.

He'd lost his touch. He'd lost his woman.

Now, he was faced with the very real possibility that he might lose his child. Unbidden, the scene in the alleyway played through his mind. While he'd been grappling with the increasingly demanding Cabreras and his parents, Sienna had been busy moving on, *dating* another man.

Another man she might well go back to when her memory returned. Only now she would be walking away with something that was rightfully his.

Unlike the bewildering confusion surrounding his impending fatherhood a handful of minutes ago, his thoughts were crystal clear now.

His child would be going nowhere. He might not have the first clue about how to be a parent, but neither was he prepared to take a back seat in his child's life the way his own father had done with him.

Setting his jaw, he stared at the doctor. 'When can Sienna be safely discharged?'

'I'd like to monitor her for twenty-four hours, make sure there are no setbacks.'

'And after that? What does she need to ensure she and the baby remain healthy?'

'Complete rest for a few weeks, then she can resume normal activities as long as she doesn't overdo things. I'll make sure you have a detailed aftercare programme.'

The urge to pace once again attacked him. Glancing at his watch, he realised the late hour and forced himself to curb the rest of the questions firing through his brain. 'I'll be back to collect her tomorrow. In the meantime, if she so much as twitches in discomfort—'

'You'll be my first call,' Dr Stephen finished wryly.

His walk back to Sienna's private room was a little less agitated than when he'd made the last journey. Hell, he wasn't ashamed to say that, even with this unexpected news, the vice tightening his chest had eased.

Regardless of the unwelcome emotions she'd triggered in him by attempting to walk away, *again*, from him that night, watching her fall and injure herself had been an experience he never wanted to repeat.

Knowing now that she'd taken a fall while carrying his child…

Emiliano paused outside her door, clamped a hand that was less than steady and breathed deep.

Possessiveness of the things he valued was a trait he'd recognised and shamelessly embraced very early on in his life. He hadn't needed a psychologist to tell him it was a result of having been patently *valueless* to his parents that had driven him to surround himself with material things, even sycophants, in his early adulthood. It had brought him a modicum of satisfaction, hell even a sense of belonging after long years of having been placed on a shelf and consigned to second-best status. In later years, he'd grown very selective of the things he placed value on.

Loyalty and hard work from his employees.

The growing closeness between Matias and him.

A woman in his bed who knew the score and would quietly exit his life when her time was up.

Nowhere on that list of desirable possessions had there featured a child. Not for the foreseeable future, if ever. Simply because he didn't have the right tools to forge a father-son bond.

And yet it was all he could think about now as he raised his hand and pushed the door to Sienna's room open. In the space of an hour within which the news of his impending child had been placed before him, then immediately potentially threatened, all Emiliano could think about was how to protect it. *Possess* it.

The voice that warned him against making so bold and intractable a claim was ruthlessly suppressed.

His brain working a mile a minute, he entered and crossed to the bed.

She was asleep, her long lashes fanned out against her skin. Her complexion was paler than he was used to, but she was no less breathtaking now than she'd been the first time he'd seen her across the interview table at Castillo Ventures. Now, as then, the sight of her elicited a powerful response in him, the majority of which was sexual, he admitted. But there had always been something else, something *more*, to his relationship with Sienna.

He'd never liked puzzles. His area of expertise was strategizing. Somewhere along the line he'd satisfied himself with the sound rationalisation that he would've parted ways with Sienna once he'd solved the puzzle of why she triggered this unknown…*craving* within him.

That was before other factors had stepped in and brought things to an unsatisfactory conclusion.

They'd had unfinished business before her accident.

Now they had something…different altogether.

'Emiliano?'

His gut clenched at the sound of her voice. Mere weeks ago, she'd sworn never to say his name again. Hearing it brought a peculiar sensation he couldn't quite name. Whatever it was, it wasn't enough for him not to crave hearing it again.

'*Si*, I'm here.' And he intended to be here for the foreseeable future. For the sake of the child he hadn't known existed but now could not put out of his mind.

She raised her head a fraction off the bed, the silky black hair not restricted by the bandage sliding on the pillow. 'Are you… Is everything okay?'

He drew closer, reached out and caressed her cheek. The gesture soothed her, which was supposed to be his aim, helping her remain stress-free. But he couldn't deny that he really liked touching her. 'Everything's fine. Sleep now, *querida*.'

She smiled drowsily and turned into the caress. 'I love it when you call me that.'

He tensed. He needed to stop calling her that. The endearment had slipped out without thought. But it seemed breaking habits when it came to Sienna wasn't as easy as he'd imagined.

For one thing, he'd yet to fill the position she'd vacated at Castillo Ventures. In the weeks after she'd resigned, he'd sat in on interview after interview, discarding one application after another, until one of his subordinates had suggested that perhaps the void left by Sienna was immutable.

Emiliano had snarled his disagreement. Then cancelled all following interviews.

Now his brain ticked over. Perhaps he'd been wise to keep the position open. He would have to proceed very carefully because this game could only have one outcome.

But that didn't mean he couldn't arm himself with as much ammunition in his arsenal as possible.

Whether that included leaning down to brush his lips against the cheek of the woman who subconsciously hated him was a thought he wasn't content to dwell on.

At all.

What he did concentrate on was having Sienna's belongings relocated back to the penthouse as soon as possible. The moment that task had been achieved, he called North Haven. By early evening the next day, he was landing his helicopter on the extensive lawn of the private hospital.

Discharge papers were produced, which he signed, along with a very large, very gratefully received cheque. Emiliano knew he was buying expediency, which was gratifyingly supplied. Within half an hour of landing, Sienna was being wheeled out, her suitcase carried by a porter.

Her bandage had been removed, the two-inch patch of skin where her operation had been performed replaced with a plaster and half-disguised by her long, loose hair. The shapeless hospital gown had been replaced with a cashmere jumper dress, the navy blue colour highlighting her stunning green eyes.

Eyes that now smiled at the staff who'd lined up to say goodbye.

Emiliano watched, hiding his impatience as she took the time to thank the nurses on duty before handing Nurse Abby her calla lilies and promising to stay in touch.

When she requested yet another stop to thank yet another member of staff, he put his foot down and steered her to the lift.

'No more stops. We're leaving before you wear yourself out.'

'I'm being wheeled around in the Rolls Royce of wheelchairs. I'm fine,' she replied, a grin tugging at her mouth.

Emiliano dragged his gaze away from the appealing fullness of her curved lips and stabbed at the call button. 'You've been in a coma for two weeks. Save the meet-and-greet for when you're stronger.'

She gave a mock salute. A feeble one. 'Yes, boss. Anything you say,' she said, her voice turning smoky and husky as she cast him a glance from beneath her lashes.

His gut clenched hard as he fought his libido's eager response. The last time she'd used that term, he'd bent her over his desk and showed her in no uncertain terms who was boss.

The blush staining her cheeks suggested she recalled the incident, too. The lift arrived. He stooped low to mutter in her ear as he wheeled her in, 'Behave yourself, we have an audience.'

He caught her tiny shiver before her gaze slid to the porter trailing them. It would've been an easy job to take the suitcase and dismiss him but Emiliano welcomed the buffer. It would stop him from smoothing her hair back behind her ear or leaning in to inhale her perfume.

Somewhere in the middle of the night, when he'd been polishing the finer details of his plot, he'd concluded that physical distance was crucial in order to make this madness they were embroiled in bearable. He could provide what Sienna needed without further compromising himself. Or her.

She might be forming new memories now based on half-formed foundations, but even the half-truth didn't justify succumbing to their mutual desire for the sake of her peace of mind.

The tiny darts of regret that had stabbed him last night when he'd accepted his own decision returned, sharper this time. Sucking in a breath, he looked down to find her gaze on him, one shapely eyebrow curved. Before they'd met, he hadn't been one for public displays of affection. That had quickly changed with Sienna. The relentless need to touch her, to establish ownership, was an unquenchable fire that burned within him.

Finding that Sienna hadn't shared his new-found need to embrace his ownership had…unsettled him. Truth be told, it had been one of the many out-of-the-norm things that had disconcerted him about their relationship. That still did.

But he intended to handle it.

He saw the question in her eyes now triggered by his withdrawal. Before he could formulate an acceptable response, the lift doors parted on the ground-floor lobby. He wheeled the chair to the edge of the lawn then scooped her up in his arms.

Her breath caught lightly before her hands curled around his neck.

'Are you okay?' she breathed against his ear.

'I should be asking you that.'

'I told you, I'm fine. Whereas you seem…agitated.'

There was a little lingering teasing in her tone, but her face had turned serious.

'Look at the situation we find ourselves in. I think a little bit of agitation is warranted, don't you?'

'*Situation*... You mean the baby?'

He froze to a halt three feet from the chopper. 'The baby is one factor, of course, but I meant you, too.'

She made a half-comical face. 'Am I the first lover of yours to literally lose her mind?'

'Your attempt at hilarity is noted. And rejected.' He stepped into the aircraft and placed her on the back seat. Joining her there, he buckled her seat belt before nodding at his pilot.

When he went to secure his belt, her hand covered his. 'I wasn't trying to make light of the situation. I just…I may not have all my faculties intact, but I can tell you still brood over things. I don't want to be one of the things you brood over. I'm not fragile.'

He couldn't stop the bitterness that twisted inside him. 'Trust me, I already know this.'

'Emiliano—'

'No more talking, Sienna. There will be plenty of time for that. For now, just enjoy the ride.'

At that time of the day there wasn't much to see, save moving headlights on the motorway and then a spiderweb of lights as they flew over London. But she complied, curling her body against his as they headed to the penthouse.

As they swung east, her gaze tracked the iconic landmarks of the Shard and the Gherkin.

'It'll be good to be home,' she murmured.

Even though a bracing gust of guilt blew through him, he concluded that he was doing the right thing. '*Sí*, it will,' he agreed.

Except it wasn't. Alfie, alerted to the situation, showed his concern without giving the game away.

Not so much the large bouquet of flowers that was delivered half an hour after they walked in.

Emiliano's hackles rose the moment he spotted the over-the-top floral display the concierge manager was handing to Alfie. Unfortunately, Sienna spotted them at the same time, too.

'Oh, how pretty,' she gushed to a wary-looking Alfie. 'Are they for me?'

The butler nodded slowly and opened his mouth. Emiliano's single shake of his head had him clamming up, depositing the vase on a nearby table and walking away.

She approached the flowers and began to dig around for a card. Emiliano, close on her heel, found it first. A brief glance confirmed what he suspected about the sender. A wave of anger rising in his chest, he crushed the card and shoved it in his pocket.

'Are you going to let me read the message or tell me who they're from?'

His jaw clenched. 'No.'

'Oh, come on. Somebody's gone to a bit of trouble. The least you can do is—'

'Nothing! He's a nobody. Forget him.'

His harsh condemnation echoed around the room.

Her eyes widened. Then she frowned.

'You're overreacting. You don't normally overreact. Don't ask me how I know. Unless it's a new habit? Or this is more than just flowers? It's the person, isn't it?'

Emiliano realised her probing was unravelling him, reminding him of everything about their relationship—*Dios mio*, when had that word even become normal for him to utter?—that needled him beneath the surface. He sliced his fingers through his hair, the vow he'd made not to hide the truth from her as far as he could suddenly seeming like the worst idea he'd ever had. Still, he toyed with not answering.

Not until she walked up to him and laid a hand on his cheek. 'Tell me,' she insisted with a quiet firmness.

His skin jumped beneath her touch, a hunger flaring in him he had no right to feel. And yet...

'If you insist on knowing, yes. The sender is a head-hunter. According to you, he's made it his mission to poach you from me many times.'

'He's *tried*? That means I haven't entertained him. He's probably just trying to get under your skin.'

He turned away, his lip curling. '*Dios mio*, he's succeeding.'

She gave a startled laugh.

'What?' He frowned, failing completely to see the funny side.

'I never thought I'd see the day you'd admit to being anything but totally invincible.'

He shrugged. 'We all have our faults, *querida*. Some of us are better at hiding them than others.'

A puzzled line appeared on her smooth forehead. 'I'm not sure that's a good thing to boast about.'

'Boast or not, it's the simple truth. If your vulnerability or circumstance is constantly exploited, you learn to hide them. And, with everything that comes from frequent practice, you wake up one day to find you excel at it.'

'And in your case it's basic survival?'

'*Was*. I'm invincible now. Remember?'

She laughed, then sobered after a minute. 'Did I know this about you before? You're not telling me something I've forgotten, are you? Because that would upset me.'

Emiliano was hit by a bolt of shock at her naked admission. 'Why would it upset you?'

'Because, if I don't know this about you after a year, then what have we been doing all this time?'

He had a ready answer for that, but to do that he would need to reach into a box he preferred to keep shut for the sake of sanity. 'Rest easy, *pequeña*. This is a revelation of sorts for us both.'

'Wow. And all from a simple bouquet of delphiniums and baby's breath,' she murmured, reaching out to touch the nearest petal.

He scooped the vase out of her reach, curbing the urge to throw it across the room. 'You hate delphiniums. Baby's breath, too.'

She dropped her hand. 'Now you're exaggerating.'

'No, I am not. You're very particular about the flowers you love. These aren't on your list.'

Her eyes widened. 'I have a list?'

Despite his black mood, his mouth twitched. 'You have a list for everything. These flowers didn't make the cut. Which is why they're going in the bin.'

He derived a certain childish satisfaction in trashing the flowers before tracking down his butler. A three-minute revelatory conversation worsened his mood.

David Hunter had been in touch with his concierge several times in the last day, seemingly after an extensive search for Sienna. He had to give the man credit for his investigative skills. But that was where Emiliano's tolerance started and ended. Hunter had balls, sending flowers to a woman at her lover's apartment.

Ex-lover.

Whatever.

Emiliano had been hustled into letting her go before he was ready, not that he doubted he would have done so eventually.

Whereas Hunter was overstepping. Unless he felt an entitlement towards Sienna that extended beyond just hopeful interest...

Emiliano's teeth clenched tight as the possible answers to that question reeled through his mind.

Questions he couldn't ask.

Exhaling to restore much-needed control, he issued a new set of instructions to his butler, one that included prohibiting David Hunter from coming anywhere near his building, and returned to the living room.

'I've decided,' he announced, his thoughts sifting through pros and cons and demolishing every obstacle in his way.

Sienna turned in a graceful movement, her slender body drawing and keeping his attention.

'What?'

'A change of scene will do you good. Tomorrow, we're going to take the jet, head to Paris for New Year, then we're going island hopping around the Caribbean until you get disgustingly homesick and beg me to bring you back.'

Her full lips parted in surprise, then a light frown marred her forehead. 'But… What about work? You can't just take off.'

'I'm the boss,' he said. 'I can do whatever I want, work from any continent I choose.'

'What about me? I can't just—'

'Yes, you can. I decree it, so you're signed off indefinitely. Besides, it's the holidays. And you love the islands at this time of year. It made the top of your list, I believe.'

Her smile was wide and blinding, tugging at him in places he didn't want tugged. But still, he stood in place as she swayed towards him and rose on her bare feet to slide her arms around his neck.

'Okay, then, if the boss decrees it…'

'He does.'

'Then I'm all yours.'

He tried to keep his face and voice neutral, despite the thick pounding in his veins. '*Sí*…you are.' The possessive punch in his tone was to do with the child nestling in her womb he told himself. Nothing more.

'But I bet you get homesick before I do.'

'Care to put your money where your mouth is?'

Her gaze dropped to his mouth and he fought to suppress a groan. The eyes that met his were a darker shade of green. And the voice that responded was a sultry one that dared. 'Bring it.'

CHAPTER SEVEN

'EMILIANO?'

'Hmm?' His voice was a deep, sexy rumble that drew a delicious shiver through her.

Before her, Paris was spread out in stunning electric light, the hour before the year ended and a brand new one began filling the cold night air with palpable excitement. From their bird's-eye view from the top of their magnificent five-star hotel, it truly felt as if the world itself was laid out at their feet.

She had no recollection of previous visits to Paris, although Emiliano had informed her there had been a few. It disturbed her not to remember, but the idea of falling in love all over again with the romantic city wasn't too bad, so she embraced it.

The discreet terrace heater nearby was designed to keep the worst of the chill out of the air, but Emiliano had draped a cashmere blanket over her shoulders a moment ago, then stayed close when she'd tucked his arms around her. On the low wall in front of them, her glass of sparkling water stood next to his flute of champagne and behind them, in the living room of their presidential suite, soft sounds of French Christmas carols lent even more magic to the night.

Her sense of contentment should've been complete, but she couldn't dismiss the disquiet blooming within her.

'What is it, Sienna?' he pressed after a minute had gone by.

She hesitated, unwilling to taint the night with unwelcome conversation, but she couldn't hold it in, so she blurted out the question that had been looming large in her potholed mind for the last twenty-four hours. 'Why weren't the hospital staff able to locate any of my family?'

She felt him tense and for a second she regretted voicing her question now instead of later.

His breath stirred the top of her head and he pulled the cashmere blanket tighter around her. 'Don't worry about that right now.'

She shook her head, turning in his arms to look up into his face. 'Tell me, please. Otherwise I'll imagine the worst...' Her words drifted off when she caught sight of the regret in his eyes. 'It *is* bad, isn't it?'

'Sienna...'

'Are we estranged? Was it my fault? I can't imagine falling out with every member of my family, though. Unless my family is small. Even so, it's New Year's. Why would they not want to see me at—'

'Stop.' His voice was firm. 'No, there is no estrangement. There is no abandonment because...' He stopped, his jaw flexing for a moment. 'Because there is no family. Not one I could find, anyway.'

Pain and shock robbed her of breath for a moment. 'What? Why? Did...something happen?' She almost dreaded asking as much as she dreaded the answer.

His arms tightened convulsively around her. 'This is not the type of conversation I envisioned to usher in the New Year.'

She braced her hands on his chest, shamelessly taking strength from the steady beats of his heart. 'Then let's finish it quickly.' She saw the obstinate look in his eyes and pressed harder. 'Please, Emiliano.'

'I had my investigators look into your past these last couple of weeks.'

She frowned, her disquiet growing. 'You mean, I never told you?'

His face tightened, a neutral expression sliding over his features.

'You might as well tell me everything, Emiliano. My life is one giant question mark right now. I can't help that, but I don't want to bring this one into the New Year, either.'

He remained silent for so long she thought she'd lost the argument. His chest rose and fell beneath her hands. 'We never shared our pasts with each other. We preferred it that way. So, no, I don't know enough about your history to tell you why I couldn't find any family for you.'

The words, although stated evenly, still landed with cold brutality, probably because, contrary to what she'd imagined, she was nowhere near ready for them. 'I... Oh, God... What if I don't have any?' She didn't realise she'd swayed and slumped against him until he swore under his breath and gathered her even closer.

'This was a bad idea,' he stated grimly. That peculiar note was back in his voice again, but when she stared up at him his expression remained unreadable.

She shook her head. For several minutes she couldn't speak, the sheer starkness of her existence almost too much to bear. 'I, well, I'm glad you told me...'

A rough sound rumbled from his throat. 'Are you?'

She nodded despite the abject news. 'I don't want secrets between us.'

His jaw clenched for a taut second before his arms tightened around her. 'And I don't wish anything to stand in the way of your recovery, so I reserve the right to veto any questions or demands. *Sí?*' The demand was domineering.

She wanted to say yes, but a knot inside her refused to unravel. 'I can't help but think, if you hadn't been there for me when I was in hospital, I would've been alone...'

His grip tightened a fraction. 'But you are *not* alone. You are here. With me.'

She heard the words, wanted to bask in their possessive warmth, but she couldn't shake the confusion as to why she would keep secrets from this man who made her heart beat with wild desire every time he looked at her. She couldn't imagine he would let her keep something so important from him.

Unless he wasn't interested?

The question came from nowhere, slammed with force into her and left her floundering. She watched his nostrils flare, felt a new restlessness tinge the atmosphere. 'Why didn't I tell you about my past?'

He shrugged. 'Family isn't a subject either of us likes to dwell on. I left you to your reasons. Mine were…inconsequential.'

'Inconsequential?'

'*Sí*, and enough about this matter, too. I've answered your questions. Just bear in mind that, whether you do have family or not, it isn't uncommon to feel completely alone even in the largest of so-called families. It might look rosy and whole from the outside looking in, but appearances are often deceptive.' His tone held a trace of bitterness that brought her up short and bruised her heart.

She'd been firing questions at him with no regard for his own circumstances.

'Emiliano…'

She stopped when a muted roar rose from street level. Turning her head, she saw the countdown clock superimposed on the Eiffel Tower.

Thirty seconds until the old year was put to bed and a new one ushered in.

Firm hands touched her cheek, redirecting her focus to the powerful man in front of her. 'You're carrying my child. A child whose needs should come first. This is what should be at the forefront of our minds. Are you prepared to do that?'

'Of course. I want this baby. More than anything.'

'Then no more dwelling on the past, *si*? From this moment forward, we look to the future. Agreed?'

'Dix, neuf, huit, sept, six...'

Sienna held her breath as the clock counted out the last seconds. Exhaling in a muted rush, she nodded. 'Agreed.'

Fireworks burst into the night sky, drenching the heavens with colour as a loud cheer cannoned across the city. Eyes of dark gold held her captive, bore into hers, before drifting over her face to rest on her mouth.

'Happy New Year, *querida*,' he murmured huskily.

Her heart lurched wildly then banged hard against her ribs. 'Happy New Year, Emiliano,' she replied, her voice equally hoarse, draped with unvoiced hopes and desires. Catching one of the hands binding her, she linked it with hers and pressed them gently against her belly. 'Happy New Year, Baby Castillo.'

Emiliano inhaled sharply. After a moment, his hand freed hers to splay over her belly in a display so potently possessive, she would've protested had she not completely revelled in it. In the tumult of the past couple of days, many questions had plagued her. One she hadn't been brave enough to confront was how Emiliano felt about this unplanned pregnancy. With his words, his touch, a part of her settled. They needed to have a more in-depth conversation at some point down the line, but she was prepared to rest her mind on that score for now.

Caught in the maelstrom of emotions she couldn't name, she raised her gaze to his. One desire in particular rose to the fore, the need pounding through her as forcefully as the pyrotechnic display thundering overhead. Locking her fingers at his nape, she pressed herself against him. 'Kiss me,' she begged.

A strangled sound emitted from his throat a second before he shook his head. 'No, Sienna.' His voice held pained reluctance.

Had she not felt the evidence of his formidable need against her belly, or the blazing hunger in his eyes, she would've thought he didn't want her. She could only conclude that his reluctance stemmed from somewhere else.

'It's okay. I'm not fragile. I passed all the tests the doctor put me through this evening.' Despite her protests, Emiliano had refused to leave London without a doctor and nurse accompanying them on his private jet to monitor her every twinge. After much negotiation, they'd agreed on a check-up every twelve hours.

A grimace tautened his face. 'Nevertheless, I don't think you should—'

'A kiss isn't going to harm me, Emiliano. Not when it'll make me…happy.'

A deep shudder shook his frame. *'Dios mío. Esto es el infierno.'*

This is hell.

She didn't stop to ponder how she understood his words. Or why a simple kiss was so hard for him. It probably had something to do with the fact that nothing between them felt simple. All she knew was that he was still denying her a kiss. And she was being consumed by the desire for it.

'Please. Isn't it tradition to kiss the one you're with at the stroke of the New Year? I won't break, I promise.'

A short bark of self-deprecating laughter rolled out before he inhaled deeply. 'You don't know what you're asking.'

'Yes, I do. And I'm not taking no for an answer.'

She'd barely finished speaking when he gave a pained groan, spiked his hands into her hair and slanted his mouth over hers. Hot, potent and more exhilarating than the fireworks still echoing around them, Emiliano's kiss was intensely thrilling and completely addictive. With a deep, thankful moan, she opened her mouth beneath his, granting him the possessive entry he sought without hesitation.

He kissed her with an expertise that resonated all the way to her toes and back up again. When his tongue danced with hers, the flames—already stoked high with anticipation—rose higher, threatening to consume her.

Breasts aching, sensitive nipples peaked with shameless arousal, it was all she could do to whimper and hold on as sensation soared. Sienna wondered if it was the hormones raging through her that made this kiss more special than any she'd shared with Emiliano before, but by the time the need for oxygen drove them apart she was trembling from head to toe. Trembling and on the point of tears.

'Sienna?' A thick vein of alarm threaded his voice as he stared down at her.

Chagrined, she brushed away a tear. 'It's…I'm okay. Hell, I don't even know why I'm crying.'

'Maldición,' he swore thickly before he swung her up in his arms.

Striding through the opulent suite fit for a king, he entered the master bedroom.

Tugging the blanket from around her shoulders, he crouched before her and slid off her stone-coloured platform shoes. Her cream wrap-around dress, secured by a simple tie, came loose with a single pull. Sliding it off her, he tossed it onto a nearby chaise before striding into the dressing room and returning with a silk nightie.

In the bathroom, he stood next to the vanity, watching with eagle eyes as she brushed her teeth.

By the time they re-entered the bedroom, irritation was beginning to take hold.

'I can put myself to bed, Emiliano. And you can stop beating yourself up about the kiss, too. This…' she indicated her drying tears '…is just pregnancy hormones.'

He paused a second before he carried on his self-imposed task of disrobing her. 'It wouldn't have been triggered if I'd kept my hands off you,' he stated grimly.

'You've had your hands on me in one form or another since we left the hospital. You take my hand and walk me to a chair when I enter a room. You tuck my hair behind my ear when I'm talking to you and you can't see my face properly. And who dressed me tonight, despite me saying I was quite capable of putting my own dress on?'

A wave of shock washed over his features before his brows clamped in a dark frown and his features shuttered. 'You have my apologies. I'll be more careful in the future.'

She let out an exasperated breath. 'I don't want you to be careful!' Pulling back the sheets with a little more force than necessary, she slid into bed. 'I'm fine with all of it, Emiliano. I just don't want you treating me like I'm made of delicate glass because we kissed.'

'Calm down.'

'I am calm,' she said, then took another steadying breath, the corner of the luxurious bedspread twisting between her fingers. 'The way you treat me…I feel as if I'm missing something vital, which is ironic, considering I only have a fraction of my mind working correctly.'

'Your mind is fine,' he stated in a tone that said he wouldn't welcome challenge on that declaration.

She sighed, a thread of weariness weaving into her limbs despite her protest. 'We'll agree to disagree. For now. But I reserve the right to resume—and *win*—this point.'

One corner of his mouth twitched even though the forbidding expression remained. 'I don't doubt it. Your superb cognitive skills were the reason you were my vice-president of Acquisitions.'

She frowned. *'Were?'*

He froze for an infinitesimal second. *'Sí,* before your accident.'

'Oh. Right. I suppose I can't return to work now with my mind the way it is.'

His jaw clenched. 'You can't return to work because

you've been through a trauma. From which you're recovering while carrying a baby. You won't be gracing the inside of a boardroom with your presence anytime soon.'

'Is this my boss or my lover talking?' Her challenge was half-hearted, the warm sheets seducing her into sliding deeper, pulling the duvet to her chin.

'It's the man who has a vested interest in your wellbeing. The man who also intends to win his argument, and a few more besides, when the time comes.'

She didn't want to start another argument, or delve beneath the somewhat cryptic remarks, simply because her eyelids were growing heavier by the minute. And also because she'd become painfully aware that Emiliano was making no move to undress and join her in bed. He'd taken to sleeping in the adjoining bedroom, while Alfie and the medical staff slept in the suite next door.

It was a situation she'd hoped would be altered come New Year. But it seemed her hopes were to be dashed when he stared down at her for a long moment before he stepped back with a resolute expression.

'Sleep well, Sienna.'

He was gone before she could respond in kind. As, she discovered an hour later, was the sleep she'd thought would be quick in coming.

Changing positions for the umpteenth time, she replayed the evening in her mind, including the kiss, memory of which still glowed like embers inside her. Sienna wished the heat of that kiss could erase the cold reality of the past Emiliano had divulged.

There was no record of a family out there.

For all intents and purposes, and until her memory supplied her with the information, she only had Emiliano, the man she would be connected to for ever through their baby.

The man who consciously didn't want to touch her. Telling herself her condition was very much a factor and that it was early days didn't soothe the tiny prickles of anxiety within her.

Something was wrong. And, if she couldn't rely on her memory to supply her with the *whys*, she'd just have to find another way.

Emiliano threw back the cognac he'd poured for himself before settling in his study chair to place the call. He didn't dread it—he was too much of a pragmatist for that—but he wasn't relishing it, either. All he knew was that it needed to be done. The twinge of guilt that lanced him for letting Matias down was ruthlessly suppressed. He would find another way to help Graciela and make it up to his brother if...*when*... Matias emerged from his coma.

He entered the number from memory, surprised he still retained it. It was answered on the third ring.

'It's about time you called,' his father said by way of greeting.

Emiliano barely managed to stop his lip from curling. 'You forget that I am the one coming to your rescue. A little appreciation wouldn't go amiss.'

His father hesitated a moment before he spoke, and Emiliano was gratified to hear the less belligerent tone. 'We haven't heard a word from you, save a call from your assistant to say you'd be in touch. That was a week ago. We were...concerned.'

'My life doesn't stop simply because yours is in free fall.' He didn't see the need to mention his own life had been in free fall, too, from the moment he'd returned from Argentina.

He heard his father clear his throat and refocused. 'Rodrigo Cabrera has been expecting your call. He feels insulted to be kept waiting. He's being hounded by the press for an official announcement.'

'He should've thought of that before he planted his tabloid hacks to create a relationship that doesn't exist.'

'A relationship you agreed to.' He heard the definite note of panic in his father's voice.

'My only agreement was to have dinner with his daughter in the hope of convincing her to talk some sense into her father and get him to drop this whole ridiculous situation before it went any further. What I should've done was walk away then.' If he had, he wouldn't be in this situation.

'But you didn't.' The panic was much more pronounced. 'You made promises, which Cabrera wants you to honour now.'

Emiliano's hand tightened on the handset, the knowledge that he wasn't as immune to his father's distress as he'd like to be making his jaw clench. 'That is not going to happen. We need to find another way to deal with the matter of your debt.'

'Impossible. I have an agreement with Cabrera.'

'An agreement that had neither my knowledge nor consent. An agreement you forced on Matias. Did you stop to think how your selfishness would impact on him, or did you blithely sign away his life the way you're attempting to sign away mine?'

'What are you talking about?'

'Do you even know where Matias was going when he crashed?'

'Of course I know. He was on his way to conduct Castillo business—'

'No, he was on his way to the airport after ending things with his girlfriend. He destroyed his relationship with her in order to save your skin.'

The irony of the full circle his family seemed to have come would've been laughable if it wasn't so eerily spine-chilling. Except, this time, he wasn't the one who'd fallen into a coma. It was the mother of his child. The woman whose presence in his life hinged on the absence of her memories. The knot that had resided in his gut for far longer than he cared to contemplate threatened to unravel. Ruthlessly, he grappled it into place.

'Your brother understood the true meaning of family and sacrifice, whereas you don't seem to have second thoughts about breaking your—'

'Save it, old man. You lost your right to guilt me into submission a very long time ago. And don't speak of Matias in the past tense. You may have written him off, but I haven't.'

'Have some respect, boy,' his father bristled. 'You wouldn't exist without me.'

He wouldn't exist. The words struck a deep chord within him, causing his fingers to fist on his desk.

Yes, his father was responsible for bringing him into the world. Just as he himself was now responsible for another. Only, Emiliano didn't intend to be little more than a biological footnote in his child's life.

He would be more.

He didn't know how, but would be *better*. He wouldn't fail or ignore his child as he had been failed and ignored.

'Are you listening to me?'

His attention refocused, sharpened until his intent was as clear as the finest crystal. 'I'm listening and I'm hearing you, but I don't think *you* are hearing me. The deal with Cabrera as it stands doesn't work for me. He can accept my financial terms, or I'm prepared to hear him out if he has an alternative that suits me. But marrying his daughter is irrevocably off the table.'

'Why?' his father demanded.

'Because I'm getting married to someone else.'

CHAPTER EIGHT

'*BUENOS DÍAS, CARIÑO.*'

   '*Buenos días, guapo. Has dormido bien?*'

Emiliano froze in surprise and stared at the woman bathed in sunlight on the terrace of his villa.

'You speak Spanish?' he asked.

A light flush tinged her cheeks before she responded hesitantly, '*Un poco, pero estoy tratando.*'

He carried on walking towards her, his senses reeling a little as he pulled out the chair and joined her at the breakfast table. In the typical style of the woman who'd managed his acquisitions with exemplary intelligence, she'd perfected the nuance and intonation of his mother tongue, and even found a way to thread sensuality through the words. 'You're more than trying,' he responded, noting the gruffness in his voice. 'You excel at it.'

She grinned before a plump segment of mango found its way into her mouth. Watching her tongue dart out to lick a drop of juice from the corner of her mouth lit an instant fire in his groin. Combined with the white bikini set clinging to her body, its existence poorly disguised by the see-through mesh sarong, he knew the next half hour would be a true test of his control.

They'd been on his private island off the coast of the Bahamas a little over a week. Each day had brought the challenge of seeing her in a different swimsuit and wrestling with the increasingly uncontrollable urge to touch her. It also hadn't gone past his notice that her costumes were getting skimpier with each passing day.

It was the reason he'd banished the villa's employees to the staff bungalow yesterday. Only Alfie was allowed into the main residence without express permission, the fact that he was gay barely giving him a pass.

'How long have you been keeping this from me?' he asked, concentrating all his efforts on pouring steaming black coffee…slowly…to take his mind off the satin-soft skin on display.

Her smile widened, still blindingly beautiful, her green eyes lighting up. 'I woke up this morning and the memory just appeared. I remembered I'd been listening to tapes, although I can't remember where I got them from or how long I've been learning. I'm guessing from your reaction that you didn't know, so… Surprise!'

The rigid tension charging through his body made him wonder how he was managing to set the coffee pot down without breaking it. 'No, I didn't know. And, yes, it's a wonderful surprise.' He paused a beat, then asked off-handedly, 'Did you remember anything else?'

Her smile dimmed then switched off completely. A vice tightened viciously around his chest. He wanted to pre-empt the words that she was about to utter with…something. But none were forthcoming. So he sat and awaited the falling axe.

'I…I know now why no one came to see me at the hospital. Besides you.'

His gaze probed her face, noted her distress. 'Tell me,' he encouraged, the need to know overcoming whatever consequences lay in his future.

Her gaze dropped. He fought the urge to nudge her delicate chin up and watched her.

'I remember my childhood. I'm an orphan, Emiliano. I was left with nuns at a children's mission in Surrey when I was a baby. My first name was folded into my baby blanket. The nuns gave me a last name.'

She gave a laugh that sounded surprisingly similar to the one that coughed up whenever he thought of his own childhood. 'I was abandoned by a mother who only stopped long enough to scribble a name she thought was appropriate for the child she didn't want to raise before disappearing.'

Her hand dropped to her stomach and her face twisted in anguish for a brief second. 'So that's my history. And now you know.'

Despite her words, the eyes that met his held a touch of vulnerability that had him going against his better judgement and capturing her chin in his hand.

'And it changes nothing. You are who you are, regardless of the mystery of your birth. Even armed with full knowledge of one's birth, there are never any guarantees of affection or acceptance.'

She blinked, her full mouth trembling for a few moments before her head rose and the strength and determination he'd glimpsed many times across his boardroom table powered her spine straight.

Nodding, she said, 'I remembered something else.'

Emiliano swallowed hard. And again. *'Qué?'* The question was a rough croak.

'Switzerland.'

'What about Switzerland?'

Troubled eyes rested on him. 'I remembered that your brother is in a coma. We went to visit him on the way back from Prague. In July…?'

It was a disgrace to feel the enormous relief that punched through him. But he'd never professed to be perfect. Relief tingling through his extremities, he picked up his cup and took a gulp of coffee. *'Sí,* that's correct.'

'Is he… Has there been any change?'

Recalling the last time she'd asked him the same question, Emiliano schooled his features before he shook his head. 'I visited him two weeks ago. There's been no change. The doctors are debating whether to try an experimental procedure to wake him.'

Her breath caught. 'Is it risky?'

'Every procedure carries an element of risk, but they think he can withstand it. His brain activity is promising. The doctors believe he should be awake by now.'

'So are they going to do it?'

He took another sip of coffee before he answered. All he tasted was bitterness. 'If I had my way, they would do it tomorrow. Matias needs to wake up and live his life. Unfortunately, my parents have to provide consent. They're... debating the matter.' The raw anger eating through him that Matias's life was wasting away because of his parents' indecision mounted.

'What? Why? I would've thought any parent would jump at the chance to see their child well.' Her genuine puzzlement and response settled something inside him he hadn't even been aware needed tending.

Or perhaps he had. His own silent floundering about his ability to be a father had also thrown up questions about the mother of his child. He didn't doubt Sienna would rise to the challenge of motherhood with the same vigour she'd brought to his company...should she choose to, once her memory returned.

And there was the other conundrum. Sienna might be excited about the pregnancy now, but what would happen in the future, when perhaps she would conclude that he fell short of the task of being a father?

Emiliano knew first-hand that love for one child didn't necessarily transmit to another. For the longest time, he'd tried to unravel that particular puzzle in his own circumstances, until he'd realised he was wasting his time.

Warm fingers touched the back of his hand, bringing him back to the present and her questions.

'Because keeping Matias the way he is now keeps him alive and safe, which is an appropriate action any parent would consider on behalf of their child. But their indecision also serves the dual purpose of elevating me to the position of temporary firstborn, which means his responsibilities become mine.'

Her eyes had been growing rounder with consternation with each utterance. 'Are you saying they're using him as a *pawn*?'

A few weeks ago, he would've given an unequivocal affirmation. 'Perhaps not deliberately, but I can't hide from the evidence that their indecision plays to their advantage while keeping him in a glass box,' he ground out through the tide of fury blanketing him. He'd yet to find a way to circumvent the current impasse with his parents. But he would. His brother deserved better than the hand his parents were dealing him.

'Has it always been like this between you and them? The distance and the...bitterness?'

'Until Matias's accident, I hadn't seen or spoken to them for over ten years. I left home the day I turned eighteen.'

'Why?' she asked softly, passing him a peeled orange before reaching for a warm croissant.

He took his time to chew and swallow, certain the dull ache in his chest was residual anger from the situation with Matias. His history with his parents was dead and buried. 'I realised very early on in life that Matias was the chosen son. That I was merely the spare, brought and paraded as and when I was needed, but otherwise there was very little use for me.'

There was no trace of a smile on her face now, only naked anguish. For him. 'Oh, Emiliano. I'm sorry,' she murmured.

Her voice soothed him. *She* soothed him. So he found himself continuing. 'I don't think they even noticed the day I left.'

Her green eyes turned stormy dark. 'That's not true. I'm sure they did.'

A long-forgotten conversation with his brother unspooled in his mind. 'Perhaps. Matias told me once they asked about me. But they didn't care enough to pick up the phone. Not once.' He shrugged, but the gesture didn't quite flow.

'Did Matias ever try to talk you out of leaving?'

He nodded, the recollection opening a new vein of pain he'd thought healed. 'Many times in the weeks before, when I told him of my plans. I think it hurt him more to admit he was our parents' favourite. When he realised my bags were packed, and that I would leave with or without his help, he gave up.'

Her face pinched in deeper sympathy and for several moments Emiliano wondered why he hadn't told her this before, why he was choosing now to tell a story that he'd buried so deep.

It wasn't as simple as not having other things such as work or sex in the way. No, sex was very much on his mind. *Dios mío*, he only had to catch a glimpse of her chest rising and falling to feel his temperature soaring. And ever since he'd walked onto the terrace his fingers had been itching to sink into her thick, luxurious hair and kiss her the way he'd done at New Year.

But he admitted there was an openness to this version of Sienna that appealed to him. It made talking to her easier. Made him want to reach out to her... Hell, maybe be a better version of himself, too?

He mentally shrugged, took the buttered croissant she'd set in front of him and took a large bite. For a few minutes they fell into easy silence as they mulled over his revelations.

She picked up another pastry and buttered it for herself but didn't eat it. Instead, she glanced back up at him through long lashes. 'So, where did you go? What did you do after you left?'

'I'd planned on staying in Buenos Aires, finding whatever job I could. But Matias had other ideas.'

'Oh?'

'He drove me to the airport and handed me a ticket to London. He'd enrolled me in night school so I could continue my education and got me a paid internship at a financial institution.'

'Oh, my God, that's amazing.'

His throat clogged for a brief moment. '*Sí*, he was...*is*... amazing. The only thing he wanted in return was that I wouldn't forget our family, and that I would offer my help should he need it. He didn't ask for over ten years.'

'So we were both abandoned, in our own way, by those who should've cared for us,' she mused quietly, her croissant now in shredded pieces on her plate.

He hadn't taken the time to make that connection, but now he nodded, a swell of feeling widening inside him as he stared into her eyes. 'But we have risen above it, *sí*?' Her nod wasn't altogether convincing. And, when her green eyes clouded over again, he leaned towards her. 'What is it?'

'I can't help but wonder if our scars will affect our child somehow.'

He was shaking his head before she'd finished speaking, everything inside him rejecting the possibility of that notion. 'We will do better for our child, *querida*. On this you have my full promise.'

He cursed under his breath as her mouth gave the faintest tremble before tears filled her eyes. 'You're crying again.' God, he was becoming a master at stating the obvious. In his defence, he'd never been faced with a tearful Sienna in the year they'd been together. He grimly admitted that this was yet another thing that pushed him right out of his comfort zone.

She waved him away before swiping at her cheeks. 'I'm

fine. I told you, my emotions are a little heightened, that's all. And, yes, this time it's definitely your fault.'

'For throwing my unsavoury skeletons at your feet?'

She rolled her eyes, rose from her chair and slid sinuously into his lap. Emiliano stifled a desperate groan as her arms wound themselves around his neck. She smelled of lemongrass sunscreen and pure, intoxicating woman. And he was drowning in the hunger that shook through him. 'For easing my fear that this baby isn't going to regret having me as a mother one day.'

Another knot unravelled. 'Your concern means you care, so he will be lucky to call you Mama,' he replied gruffly, the hands he'd ordered to stay at his sides somehow finding their way up her thighs and over her hips.

She bent forward until their noses were almost touching. '*She* will be equally blessed to have you as her father,' she whispered, another well of tears filling her eyes.

He gently brushed them away with his thumb. 'Enough with these tears, *querida*. I don't like them.'

'Okay, Emiliano, I'll do my best not to bother you with my unsightly tears,' she said, her breath washing over his lips. The plump curves of her mouth were a lesson in raw temptation. As were the nipples peaking beneath her flimsy bikini top.

'There's nothing unsightly about you, *guapa*.'

'The scars on my skull tell a different story, but I'm prepared to let you win this argument. *Gracias, hermoso.*'

Emiliano decide there and then that, with her soft voice echoing in his head, he would encourage her learning so she would only speak to him in Spanish. He also decided for the second time since he sat down that he was fine with not being perfect. Because *not* kissing her right then, denying himself the pleasure of her soft lips, was one ask too far.

So he lowered his head and tasted the sweetest nectar

known to man. Her response was unfettered and immediate. As if, like him, she'd been caught in the talons of
hunger for far too long. He took her mouth the way other,
more ravenous parts of him wanted to take her body.

She whimpered, moaned and pressed closer until a red
haze of arousal overtook his entire world.

He needed to stop before things went too far. He'd come
out here to discuss their future with her. A discussion that
required delicate handling. Following the words he'd spoken to his father—words he hadn't realised had been on the
tip of his tongue before he'd spoken them, but had known
immediately that he would act upon—he'd been biding his
time until Sienna was stronger. The week on his island had
worked wonders for her, a brief bout of morning sickness
lasting a few short days before abating.

He'd thought long and hard about waiting for her memory to return before going ahead with his plans, but the
doctor had reiterated that they were dealing with a piece of
string of indeterminate length where that was concerned.

And, with each day that passed, Emiliano was losing
the conviction that waiting was the better option. Whatever the future held, they were having this baby. And, before the issue with his fake engagement had broken them
apart, they'd been content together. He wasn't willing to
accept that that was gone for ever.

So he kissed her, infusing his need into the act until she
was breathless and pliant against him. Only then did he
pull away to look into her desire-drugged eyes.

Yes, he was doing the right thing.

'I have to touch base on a few things this morning, but
come out on the boat with me this evening,' he invited,
after taking another all-too-brief kiss.

A smile lit up every dark place inside him. 'Where are
we sailing to this time?'

His hands moved from her hair to her shoulders, down

her warm, silky skin, and it was all he could do not to pick
her up and find the nearest bed.

All in good time.

'It's a surprise.'

The package he'd requested had arrived from Turks and
Caicos late last night. The rest of the preparation would
be underway soon enough. Before then, he needed to step
up his investigations on Cabrera, find a weak spot to use
to his advantage.

He rose with Sienna still in his arms. It disturbed him
that she still weighed much less than he was used to, but
the staff were under strict instructions to reverse that situation. And so far she wasn't objecting to being fattened up.

'Where are you taking me?'

He didn't miss the slightly breathless anticipation in her
voice. He nearly altered his course, only the stern voice
warning him to do this right keeping his compass true.

'To your second-favourite spot on the island.'

Although she made a tiny face when he rounded the terrace and made a beeline for the pool, she laughed. 'And
my first is?'

'A certain king-sized bed, of course. Your happy snores
shake the whole house at night.'

She thumped his shoulder playfully as he set her down
at the lounger next to the table which had been set up with
a cooler of drinks and several snacks. He knew Alfie would
be out like clockwork every hour to make sure she didn't
want for anything.

Taking a step from him, she untied the knot and dropped
her sarong.

'Madre de Dios, tener compasión.'

Her very shameless, very feminine grin as she caught
her hair up to secure it in a loose bun atop her head told
him she relished her effect on him and wasn't interested
in the mercy he pleaded for. Her gaze dropped to the very

visible, very inconvenient evidence of his arousal before rising to his. He was gratified to see her quickening breath.

'*Hasta la vista, cariño.*'

She bit her lip as she turned away and spread her delicious body out on the lounger. He needed to leave, head back inside, but he stayed for one more look. And, as his gaze paused on the barest hint of roundness at her abdomen, that well of feeling in his chest expanded.

Yes, he was doing the right thing. All he had to do now was to secure her agreement.

At the stroke of six, Sienna heard a light knock on her bedroom door. She turned away from the mirror, loving the way the loose white sleeveless dress floated around her body before the hem dropped to her ankles. On her feet, she wore gold flip-flops, her deeper desire to go barefoot overridden by common sense. The path around the villa to the jetty where the launch would take them to Emiliano's yacht was a little gravelly. She couldn't risk twisting an ankle or falling on her behind.

Flipping her hair over her shoulders, she quickly secured the gold hoop earrings and answered the door.

Alfie stood on the threshold dressed in a smart white tunic and dark trousers.

'I've come to escort you to your date,' he said, offering his arm.

Although his smile was easy now, she'd caught a questioning look in his eyes in the past week which she'd shrugged off. She knew he and the rest of the staff had been given an abbreviated version of her illness and instructed to take special care of her. They weren't intrusive and every assistance offered to ensure she took care of her baby's health was welcome, so she didn't mind.

He conversed easily with her as they went down the long hallway to the grand staircase leading to the stunning hallway. Solid light oak floors polished to the high-est gleam beautifully complemented whitewashed walls decorated with nautical blues and greens that gave the ex-tensive luxury villa a fresh vibrancy. Every glass door and shuttered window was built to slide aside during the day to let in the salt-tinged breeze from the sea. According to Emiliano, the first time she'd set foot on Castillo Island, she'd remarked that the inside of the villa made her feel as though she were walking on sunshine and she couldn't help but smile now as she walked outside and inhaled the fresh, clean air.

Along the path that led past the garden to the beach, small flame lamps had been positioned to guide their way. Crickets chirped among the colourful plants, and palm trees swayed softly overhead. Although her gaze touched on and absorbed the heady paradise surround-ing her, her senses leaped eagerly, fast-forwarding to the evening ahead.

To Emiliano.

She'd spent most of the day outside but her thoughts had dwelt very much on the innermost secrets he'd revealed to her and the secret hope in her heart that she wasn't afraid to admit to herself any longer.

She wanted Emiliano. Wanted to be with him, to claim him in the most primal way possible. It had nothing to do with the baby and everything to do with the fact that she recognised and accepted her deeper feelings for him.

She didn't know whether she was ready to put a label on how she felt or even probe it past mere acceptance. For now, she was going to acknowledge its existence. Maybe nurture it with care and attention.

Emiliano stood waiting at the end of the twenty-foot-long jetty. He wore casual white trousers teamed with styl-ish loafers. The sleeves of his open-necked white linen shirt were folded back to reveal strong muscular arms bronzed by the sun. At some point the breeze had ruffled his hair, lending him a raffish air that threatened to blow her composure to smithereens.

Intense eyes tracked her progress from path to launch, his hand extending to her as she reached him.

He took both of her hands in his and kissed each cheek. Her heart tripped over itself as he shamelessly inhaled her scent before tucking her hair back to rasp in her ear, 'Buenas noches, Sienna. You look breathtaking.'

Suddenly tongue-tied, she smiled and murmured, 'Thank you,' as Alfie readied the launch.

They didn't have far to go, only a mile or so to where Emiliano's superyacht was anchored in deeper waters. The vessel was a stunning masterpiece, its sleek white-and-silver lines spotlighted by coloured lights that magnified its beauty in the early-evening sun. She'd been on board twice since they arrived and each time she hadn't failed to be awed by the craftsmanship.

She hadn't made a 'wow' list yet, but she was sure the yacht would make the top ten. Of course, the item that would top that particular list would be the man whose hand rested on her waist to guide her up a short flight of stairs to the middle deck. There at the open-air end a candlelit table had been set, complete with crystal goblets and sterling silverware.

A member of staff hovered nearby. At Emiliano's nod, he stepped forward with a tray holding two coconut drinks. Accepting the drink, she sipped, giving a pleased little moan as exotic flavours exploded on her tongue.

She was about to take another sip when she felt a slight jolt. They were moving. About to ask where they were headed, she remembered it was a surprise. So she followed Emiliano when he took her hand and walked her to the railing, enjoying her drink as they sailed towards the setting sun.

'It's so beautiful here,' she murmured in hushed awe.

'Yes, it is.'

She turned and looked at him. His gaze was on the horizon, but it met hers a second later, his lips curving in a smile that tugged wildly at her heart.

'I take it then that you're not homesick yet?'

The urge to blurt out that she would never be homesick as long as she was with him was caught back at the last moment. Her feelings were still new and untried. She didn't want to risk exposing them to scrutiny yet.

'No, not yet. But I have been wondering about having a scan, though.'

His gaze sharpened. 'Is something wrong?'

She shook her head quickly. 'No, but according to the pregnancy books I'm due for one about now.' Since learning that, she'd been quietly excited about hearing her child's heartbeat for the first time.

Emiliano's fierce expression eased a touch. 'If that's what you want, we don't have to leave. I can have that organised for you here.'

She grinned. 'Careful, or you'll have me thinking you want to keep me barefoot and pregnant here for ever.'

Tawny eyes raked her from head to foot before he shrugged. 'The idea isn't unappealing.'

She laughed. Although he joined her, she caught a serious look in his eyes that twanged a brain cell. Unbidden, she was thrown back to their night in Paris, when she'd sensed an undercurrent in his mood. After searching his expression and seeing nothing but heated interest, she shrugged off the feeling.

As they finished their drinks, they settled into easy conversation, which continued when they sat down to dinner. Chilli-and-lemon-flavoured grilled calamari sharpened her appetite for the chicken and rice dish that followed.

She looked up in surprise when Emiliano stood after their plates were cleared away.

'Don't look so disappointed, *belleza*. We're having dessert over there.'

She followed his pointing finger to a deserted beach where a wide picnic blanket was illuminated by two tall, flaming lamps. Below them, Alfie was readying the launch. She held on to Emiliano's hand as he guided her back downstairs and into it. A few minutes later, he was swinging her into his arms and treading shallow water towards the beach. Alfie deposited the cooler he'd carried ashore before returning to the yacht.

Sienna turned in a circle, looking for other signs of humanity.

'Why do I get the feeling we're all alone?' she asked Emiliano.

One corner of his mouth tilted upward. 'Because we are.'

'Who owns this place?'

'I do.'

'You own two islands in the Bahamas?'

He shrugged. 'I own five, but who's counting?' Reaching into the cooler, he extracted a single item.

She lost interest in the subject of islands and rushed to the blanket. 'Oh, my God.'

He gave a low, sexy laugh. 'I thought the ice cream would capture your interest.'

She grabbed a spoon, impatiently waiting as he tore off the top of the ice-cream tub. 'I don't know how I'm going to live without these when we go back.'

Again she caught a hint of something in his eyes before it disappeared again. 'You won't have to. Everything you crave, you only have to ask for and it'll be yours.' He held out the mango-and-caramel concoction to her and she dove in.

They ate in silence until she couldn't manage another mouthful. After setting the cooler to one side, Emiliano pulled her close.

All evening, she'd been secretly terrified that he would reintroduce his no-touching policy. Relief had her melting into his arms.

'Thank you for tonight. It's been wonderful.'

'De nada, querida.'

Sensing the quiet tension in him, she raised her head to meet his eyes. 'But there's something else, isn't there?'

He nodded. 'Yes.'

A vein of apprehension threatened her bliss. 'What is it?'

'We agreed today that we both wanted the best for this child, *si*?'

She nodded a touch warily. 'Of course.'

'In that case, I think we should make the ultimate commitment.'

Her heart swan-dived from dizzying heights before taking up extreme drumming lessons against her ribs. Telling herself to keep breathing, she pulled away to look deeper into his eyes, make sure her ears weren't deceiving her.

'The ultimate commitment?'

His eyes darkened as he nodded, the flames from the lamps leaping in the gold depths as he reached into his pocket. The black velvet box bore a distinct, portentous logo. But she was more interested in the words falling from his lip. Words that made her jaw drop.

'Yes, Sienna. I'm asking you to marry me.'

CHAPTER NINE

'MARRY YOU?' SHE didn't need clarification. Not really. She just wanted to make sure she wasn't dreaming.

'Yes. Unless the idea is unsavoury to you?' The tension hadn't left his body. In fact, he was even edgier.

Sienna frowned. 'Of course not. At least, I don't think so. God, I really hate that I can't remember...'

He stared at her for a handful of seconds before he gave a decisive nod. 'Ask me what you want to know and I'll tell you.'

She rose onto her knees on the blanket and faced him. 'Have we ever discussed marriage before, even in passing?'

His jaw flexed for a second. 'No.'

Her gaze fell to the box clutched in his fist. 'So this... is really for the baby?' The drumming in her chest slowed to a dull thudding.

Emiliano's expression shuttered. 'It's for us. A united front going forward.'

'That sounds more militaristic than...'

'Than?'

She affected a careless shrug that was purely for show. 'Than I don't know... A romantic union?'

His hand dropped and his eyes narrowed. 'You've found this lacking in some way?'

Thinking about the whole evening up till now, she answered truthfully. 'No, it hasn't been lacking.' But something didn't sit right. With her memory still on vacation she didn't know how well to trust her gut. The Emiliano she could remember wasn't an openly affectionate guy, although this last week he'd shown her a different side to himself. A side she liked even more than the previous version. And, as proposals went, she was sure very little could top the magical production he'd put on for her this evening. And yet...

'You require more flowery words, perhaps?' His tone had a tight clip to it that sent a tiny shiver through her.

'Not unless they are meant, no.'

He expelled a rough breath. 'I thought we were on the same page this morning.'

'We were. We *are*. But this...'

'Your future doesn't accommodate such a commitment to me?'

'Don't put words in my mouth, Emiliano.'

He shoved his free hand through his hair. 'We are compatible in and out of the bedroom. We're dedicated to doing the best for our child. Every other obstacle can be overcome.'

Put like that, Sienna had no counterargument. Except the reality of the feelings locked within her heart. But they, like this new facet of her relationship with Emiliano, were new and untested. Didn't she owe it to herself to nurture them and see if they blossomed into something worth treasuring? Especially if her child stood to benefit, too?

Her gaze fell to the jewellery box, her heart resuming its wild hammering. Slowly, she licked her dry lips, the step she was about to take thrilling and terrifying all at once.

'Sienna?' he asked, mirroring her stance and rising onto his knees.

'What if I regain my memories and remember that you snore louder than I do?'

She expected him to laugh or shrug off her joke. But his eyes remained dark and intense. Cupping her elbows, he stared down at her for a long moment, before sliding his hands up her bare arms.

'When your memories return I hope you will give me

a chance to offer up my better qualities and plead my case on any faults you find.'

She opened her mouth, ready with an answer, because she couldn't think of any further reasons not to take the next step that promised more of everything she found enthralling about him. 'Okay.'

He seemed to stop breathing, his hands gripping her tighter as he drew closer. 'Say the words, Sienna. I need to hear you say the words.'

Swallowing, she rested her hands on his solid chest, taking strength from the heart thundering beneath her touch. 'Yes, Emiliano. I'll marry you.'

She should've known Emiliano would move with lightning speed once he had his answer. She should've known the kiss he'd delivered after she'd said yes would rock her to the foundations of her soul. She should've known the ring nestling in the box would be one of the most beautiful things she'd ever seen.

The impact of all three had her still reeling two days later as she stood in the master suite, a simple, sleeveless white gown draping her body, and two attendants who'd been ferried in from Miami fussing over how to put up her hair.

In the gardens below her bedroom, a beautiful wedding arch had been set up and a celebrant waited to perform her wedding.

Her wedding.

Emiliano's answer to her half-hearted request to wait had been, 'What for? There's no one besides Matias I wish to have at my wedding. And I am all *you* need.' The arrogant but true statement had knocked the wind out of any argument. The knowledge that he stood as a solid buffer between her and abject loneliness warmed her heart.

Enough for her to give her agreement when he'd pressed for an immediate wedding.

Now, she stared at the stunning engagement ring adorning her finger. Contrary to his denunciation of flowery words, the ring spoke volumes with its huge heart-shaped diamond and similarly shaped gems set in cascading layers on either side of the platinum band. She hadn't been able to stop staring at it since Emiliano placed it on her finger. And, within the hour, an even deeper symbol of commitment would be joining it.

She dragged her gaze from the sparkling gem and huffed beneath her breath. 'Leave it loose.'

The attendants stared at her. 'What?' the older one finally asked.

'Emiliano likes my hair loose so let's just brush it out and be done with it.' She tagged on a smile to hide her impatience.

The women exchanged glances, then they both dove into their bottomless bag of tricks and emerged clutching a delicate filigree diamond tiara.

At her nod, a hairbrush was produced and her long, black hair coaxed into a gleaming waterfall before the tiara was set into place. A touch of eye make-up and lip gloss and she was ready.

Butterflies sprouted motorised wings and beat wildly in her stomach as she descended the stairs, two long-stemmed calla lilies bound together with white velvet rope clutched in her hand. Their familiar scent calmed her a little as she walked through the living room and stepped onto the terrace, but nothing could suppress her see-sawing emotions for very long.

She was joining her life with a powerful, formidable man primarily for her baby. But she couldn't deny that she was emotionally invested, as well. And that investment seemed to be growing with each passing day. It was that knowledge that rattled her the most as she stepped onto the lawn.

One look at him and everything fell away. No, not fell away. It was more like a complete overtaking of her senses. Even from across the wide expanse of green grass, his eyes hooked on to her, holding her captive, claiming her with an implacable will that reduced all her feeble fears to nonsense.

Predatory eyes gleamed, mesmerised and pulled her close as if compelling her to the altar by his sheer will alone. Seemingly between one breath and the next she was by his side, relieved of her bouquet, ready to say the words that would join them for ever.

For ever with Emiliano Castillo.

Dressed in a dove-grey suit and a white shirt, his feet planted firmly apart, he looked larger than life... An alpha in total control of his kingdom.

Her breath shuddered out. He sent her a narrow-eyed glance then caught her hand in his. Whether his touch was meant to be reassuring or to stop her from fleeing, she wasn't sure. And she wasn't given time to dwell on it.

The celebrant was clearing his throat, his Bahamian lilt marking the start of her life-changing journey. Traditional vows were exchanged, rings slid onto fingers and blessings offered.

A deep tremble overtook her as Emiliano closed the gap between them and slid strong fingers into her hair. 'You're mine now, Sienna Castillo,' he murmured against her lips, a deep relish in his tone that escalated her trembling.

'As you are mine,' she replied, somehow noting the importance of establishing equal ownership.

'*Si*, that is exactly so.' His voice throbbed with possessive satisfaction, binding her even more strongly than the new ring on her finger.

His mouth closed over hers, hot and demanding, uncaring that they had an audience. Over the pounding in her ears, she heard applause from the gaggle of staff and attendants. Her hands found Emiliano's waist, to hold on to and to touch him.

A mere second and an eternity later, he freed her, the feral hunger in his eyes promising the main course to the starter he'd just delivered.

Champagne was poured, a glass of sparkling mineral water handed to her, congratulations offered and received. Then she was strolling beside Emiliano along their private beach, another spectacular sunset robbing her of the breath not already captured by the man whose hand imprisoned hers.

Her husband.

His jacket had been discarded a while ago and his shirtsleeves rolled up. Despite his casual attire, he remained a powerful, magnetically handsome force, commanding her attention with no effort at all. The sense of bewilderment snapping at her heels finally caught up with her in the form of a tiny hysterical giggle.

Emiliano stopped, his bare feet digging into the soft white sand next to hers. 'You find something amusing?'

She shook her head in wonder. 'I can't believe I'm married,' she said in a reverential whisper.

He circled round to face her, lifting her chin with a firm finger. 'Believe it. You're married. To me. And tonight I will make you mine again.'

This time her shiver was pure decadence coupled with anticipation of the highest kind. Desire flamed through her, setting the secret place between her legs alight.

She couldn't help the moan that broke free. He heard it. One corner of his mouth lifted in an arrogant smile. 'Are you ready, Sienna?'

'Sí, mi esposo,' she replied.

He jerked as if a powerful charge had jolted him. Catching her hand in his, he stalked up the beach. He stopped at the edge of the lawn and instructed her to lift her gown. Then, sinking low before her, he grabbed the water hose and washed the sand off her feet. Sienna didn't know if Emiliano's touch on her feet had ever felt this electrifying or whether the new dimension to their relationship was lending this night an extra enchantment. Whatever the reason, the urge to touch him grew too strong to contain. She slid her hand over one broad shoulder to his nape, then she snaked her fingers through his silky hair. He paused in his task, his head snapping up. Their gazes met. Meshed. Need pounded between them.

The hose was cast aside. Then he was on his feet again, tugging her after him once more.

White rose petals greeted their path when they stepped onto the terrace, and were crushed beneath their feet as they hurried down the hallway. At the foot of the stairs, Emiliano swept her into his arms. Effortlessly, he carried her into her suite. *Their* suite.

He stopped in the middle of the large, opulently decorated room. The French doors leading out to their private terrace had been pulled shut, but the last rays of sunshine streamed in, basking them in an orange-gold glow.

Letting go of her fingers, he stepped behind her. She felt a slight tug in her hair as he removed the tiara and set it aside. Moving her hair out of the way, he placed a single kiss at her nape, the breath feathering her skin and sending a delicious shiver coursing through her.

Hands drifted over her shoulders and down her arms to circle her wrists. Slowly, he lifted her arms above her head.

'Stay,' he commanded, tracing his fingers back down.

She stayed, her heartbeat frenzied, her every sense poised in wild anticipation.

He found and slid down the side zipper securing her

dress. The satin sheath pooled at her feet, leaving her in a silk strapless bra and matching lace panties.

Behind her, his breathing altered and turned choppy.

'*Madre de Dios*, you're so beautiful.'

'I feel beautiful. Right here. With you.'

'You're beautiful, always,' he insisted. He recaptured her hands, kissing the back of one, then the other, before he let them fall to her sides. A single tug and her bra was undone and at her feet. In the next breath, Emiliano resumed his position before her, his eyes ablaze with feral hunger as his gaze moved over her.

Sliding his fingers into her hair, he planted kisses on her forehead, her eyelids, cheeks. Everywhere but where she needed him most.

Fastening her arms around his waist, she strained towards him. 'Kiss me. Please.'

He teased the corner of her mouth. 'Ask me again. In Spanish,' he ordered in a guttural voice.

'*Bésame, por favor,*' she begged.

He granted her wish and more, strong arms wrapping her in heated muscle and hot desire as he tasted, devoured and mercilessly fanned the flames of her need.

The sun had dipped beneath the horizon by the time he lifted her off her feet and placed her on the bed. Retreating, he turned on bedside lamps. Eyes never leaving hers, he deftly undid his buttons, baring his toned, bronzed chest to her everlasting delight.

Suddenly nerves overtook her. Her recollections of making love with him were a little fragmented, the memory of how *he* made her feel more sharp than the reverse. What if he found her a disappointment? Hands twisting in the sheets, she swallowed as he kicked his trousers and boxers away and prowled onto the bed.

He became absorbed in the hand he drifted down her

body, following each caress with a kiss that almost defused the troubled questions in her mind.

Almost.

Licking her lips, she cleared her throat. 'Emiliano?'

His mouth brushed against her collarbone as he answered. '*Sí, querida?*'

A moment of silence passed when words failed her.

He raised his head and frowned. 'You look troubled. Why?'

'I'm not… Show—show me…how to please you,' she stammered.

His nostrils flared with his sharp inhalation. 'You already know how. Here—' he touched his lips to her temple '—and maybe even here…' His mouth drifted down to kiss the space over her heart. 'But rest assured in the knowledge that, if you do this to me—' catching her hand, he kissed her palm then lowered it to settle over his groin, shuddering deep when she gripped his thick, impressive length '—then you're halfway there.'

He renewed his caresses, his kiss even more passionate, his strokes a touch more rough, taut cheeks flushed with arousal as he raised himself over her body. Mouth drifting over her skin, he kissed every inch, lingering over the rosy flush of her ultrasensitive nipples.

She cried out, one hand tangling in his hair to hold him there for a little while longer. Need crested high. Higher. Just when she believed she'd lose her mind if he tugged on her one more time, he freed her to continue his erotic exploration.

His hands stroked reverently over her womb, his eyes taking on a glaze of wonder as he lowered his head to place a kiss on her abdomen.

Tears she'd sworn not to shed filled her eyes. Quickly, she blinked them away, unwilling to spoil the moment. Impatient hands drew off her panties, then she was bare before his heated eyes. Parting her wider, he stroked her, growling in blatant hunger, before lowering his head to deliver the most intimate of kisses.

With his skilled tongue and deft fingers, Emiliano brought her to completion. She was still basking in delicious aftershocks when he kissed his way back up her body. She read the naked intent in his eyes, but she didn't want this to be one-sided. Raising herself onto her elbows, she nipped his firm lower lip, then used his momentary surprise to reverse their positions. His raised eyebrows nearly eroded her nerves.

But his potent scent drew her, tempted her to lower her head to his washboard torso, to attempt to deliver a fraction of the pleasure he'd just bestowed on her.

She dropped an open-mouthed kiss on his pecs. Warm and faintly salty from the sea breeze, he tasted like vitality itself. Next, she flicked her tongue over one flat nipple.

He bucked wildly against her. *'Dios mio,'* he cursed thickly.

She froze, her breath stilling with alarm. 'Did I do something wrong?'

He gave a rough groan. 'You did something right, *belleza,'* he rasped. 'So very right.'

Flush with feminine power, she repeated the caress, again and again, until not-so-steady hands bore her back onto the bed.

The eyes that met hers were the stormiest she'd ever seen. They held hers captive. Parting her thighs, he guided himself to her heated entrance.

Slowly, inch by delicious inch, absorbing her every gasp and shiver, he entered her. Fully seated inside her, he held himself there, their breaths mingling.

'Amante, you feel sublime.'

She wanted to answer. To say more. So much more. But

the indescribable feelings cascading through her robbed her of breath. That was even before he started to move.

He possessed her completely, each thrust stamping his ownership of her. Sienna could only hold on, senses and heart soaring as pleasure mounted.

She crested the wave first, but Emiliano was hard on her heels. A series of rough groans preceded hot Latin words that touched her soul and prolonged her bliss.

He was still murmuring low, deep words to her when her body cooled and she drifted off to sleep, curled up against his warmth.

Sienna wasn't sure what prompted her awake. Perhaps it was the tension vibrating off Emiliano's frame even from across the room. Or maybe it was the disturbing dreams where she'd tried repeatedly, futilely, to cling to his hand as they weathered a storm.

Whatever it was, her heart was hammering with a very different sensation from the one she'd gone to bed with when she sat up suddenly.

'What's wrong?'

He jerked around, the fingers he'd been spiking through his hair dropping to his side.

He didn't answer immediately. She got the feeling he was trying to find the right, precise words.

'Is it Matias?'

He shook his head. 'No. There's a situation in Argentina. One that I need to deal with personally.'

His parents. 'When will you return?'

Dark brows furrowed. 'Return?'

'I'm assuming you want to go on your own?'

The statement seemed to take him aback. Slowly, he walked back to bed, shedding his briefs along the way. Sliding into bed, he pulled her into his arms, tunnelling his fingers into her hair. 'On the contrary, I think it's time we faced the world. Together.'

CHAPTER TEN

THEY LEFT THE island three days later, Emiliano taking the
time to make sure the information he'd received regarding Rodrigo Cabrera and his business practices was accurate. He wasn't ashamed to admit he'd deliberately delayed
triple-checking his facts because, having finally allowed
himself the ultimate indulgence of making love to his wife,
he hadn't been in a hurry to abandon his marriage bed.

But the debt he owed his brother needed to be fulfilled.
And he was done with his parents and Rodrigo Cabrera
imagining they could call the shots on his and Matias's
lives. They needed to be dealt with, quickly and decisively.

He ended the conference call on his private jet and re-
entered the main lounge.

Sienna was curled up on the large sofa with a cashmere
throw tucked around her. The book she'd been reading was
propped on her chest, her delicate lashes resting against
her cheeks as she slept. Disposing of the book, he took the
seat next to her, his hand reaching out almost of its own
accord to tuck a swathe of hair behind her ear.

For a moment, he wondered whether he'd worn her out
with his lustful demands since their wedding night. Then
he recalled with satisfaction her equally fervent responses.

If anyone had told him three months ago that they were
capable of achieving another level of carnal intimacy, he
would've dismissed it out of hand. The past three days had
proved conclusively otherwise. But, while he was more
than pleased with their activities in the bedroom, Emiliano was becoming aware that intimacy was creeping in
elsewhere. He felt unsettled when she was out of his sight;

her laughter made his heart race in ways he couldn't quite describe.

Last night, when a nightmare had disturbed her sleep, he'd lain awake with her, talking long into the night about their hopes for their child. In the past, his conversation with Sienna had mostly circled around work and broad outside interests.

Those quiet hours together had brought a certain…contentment. One he wasn't used to. One he wasn't sure he could trust not to get in the way of logical thinking in future.

Because there was still the matter of the weeks they'd been apart to deal with when her memories returned. He might prefer this softer, more open version of Sienna, but there were no guarantees she would remain the same woman. No guarantees that her feelings would remain mutual. His child's legitimacy was safeguarded—not really necessary in this modern world, he knew, but still a firm foundation on which to build a life. And Emiliano was certain that a little foundation was better than none. Without Matias's support underpinning his own attempt at a new start in life, Emiliano wouldn't have been the man he was today.

Which meant that while he could lose himself in his wife's arms every now and then, getting used to it—or, worse, imagining he could rely on any unknown feelings she might have—was dangerous.

'You're thinking far too hard, *cariño*,' her sleep-soft voice murmured.

Despite the severe caution he'd just placed on his floundering emotions, Emiliano experienced a buzz at the effortless endearment and an even deeper thrill when sultry green eyes connected with his.

'I'm strategizing,' he replied. 'Go back to sleep.'

She made a face and sat up. 'Your game face just scared

away any notion of sleep. Tell me what you're strategizing about. Maybe I can help.'

He forced his body not to tense, and again momentarily wished he hadn't been so hasty to let her leave the insulated safety of his island. Looking away from her face, he chose his words carefully.

'My parents got themselves involved with the clichéd unsavoury businessman who was supposed to be a friend. They entered a deal with him hoping to make maximum profit with minimum output. Elite polo outfits are difficult to break into in Argentina. Rodrigo used his family friendship with my parents to gain a foothold, then cut them out, giving them the option to buy in again at a steep price. They embezzled from their own company to save themselves from bankruptcy.'

She made a disgusted sound. 'That's the definition of a recipe for disaster.'

'Exactly. My father would deny it to his last breath, of course, but he doesn't have the first clue about business. His strategy for dealing with this problem has been wrong from the very start.'

Intelligent eyes rested on him. 'But you have a way?'

'Of course. There is always a way, if you take the time to look.'

Her laugh was low, sexy, incendiary to his senses. 'I'm glad I'm not facing you across the boardroom table.'

He rose from his seat, crossed to the sofa and slid in next to her. 'It would be a delight to have you facing me. I could savour the thought of what I would do to you once I won.'

One sleek eyebrow curved upward. 'Really? By the time I *let* you win, you'd probably be too worn out to follow through.'

Something swelled in his chest, the way it did lately whenever they were immersed like this in conversation. 'Is that a challenge to my manhood?'

Faint colour tinged her cheeks as her gaze dropped to his thighs, but she tried to project an air of nonchalance. 'I'm just stating a fact. I don't need my memories to tell me I'm no slouch in the boardroom.'

He wisely conceded the argument. 'You're no slouch anywhere.'

A wide smile transformed her face. 'Thank you.'

From then, it seemed the most natural thing in the world to lean in and kiss the full, tempting mouth. And carry on kissing her until a throat cleared nearby.

He turned to find Alfie, hovering with a tray.

Sienna groaned half-heartedly. 'Between Alfie and all the cooks you have stationed at your residences, I'm going to get hopelessly fat.'

'It's a privilege to care for you while you care for our child.'

Had he not been totally absorbed by the sunlight slanting through the window onto her face, he would've missed the bruised hurt that momentarily clouded her eyes.

He frowned inwardly, wondering where he'd made a misstep. But then her gaze swept up and she was smiling at Alfie as he set out her meal.

Excusing himself, because he wanted every single cog in place before he landed in Buenos Aires, he returned to the conference area. The last time he'd flown to his homeland, he'd been woefully unprepared, and that had cost him. He didn't intend it to happen a second time.

For the next four hours, he worked. But, although his business brain sifted meticulously through facts and figures, his subconscious couldn't dismiss the look he'd seen in Sienna's eyes. His mention of the baby—had that been wrong? He didn't think so. They'd talked openly about their child. They'd talked about him. About Matias. But not about much else… Not about her.

The pen he'd been bouncing in his hand froze. Did she

feel neglected? In a bid to follow the doctor's orders—and, yes, perhaps selfishly to keep the problem-free status quo—was he in danger of making her feel the loneliness she thought was behind her?

Frowning, he rose from his desk and stood at the entrance of the short galley that led to the living area. She was still seated on the sofa, legs curled underneath her, her book back in her hand. Beauty and sharp intelligence shone from her face and that peculiar sensation in his chest grew as he stared at her.

Sensing his gaze, she raised her head. Smiled.

Although the smile transformed her face, Emiliano caught the shadows in her eyes. He wanted to tell himself it was nothing, but the fine hairs prickling his nape told him it was something. *Something* that needed to be dealt with.

But first, he needed to come clean. Ensure their marriage held no secrets.

Sienna was strong. Had been growing stronger still with each passing day. They would talk things through, he would admit his faulty choices and they would move on.

'Emiliano?' Her head was tilted and she was staring at him with questions in her eyes.

He started towards her, then cursed under his breath when his co-pilot emerged from the cockpit to announce they would be landing in fifteen minutes.

Taking his seat next to her, he ensured they were both buckled in. 'Later, *querida*. We'll talk later, when this is all over, yes?'

Her nod was wary, the shadows under her eyes a little more pronounced. The nightmares she'd experienced in the last two days had clearly taken their toll. Or could it be something else?

Yes, it was most definitely time to clear the air once and for all. But first, he had to deal with Cabrera.

What he'd planned might take a little time, depending on how obstinate his opponent chose to be.

He planned to be quick and merciless, but he didn't intend to be in Argentina one minute longer than necessary. He had a life to live and a wife to plan it with.

The mansion in Cordoba—rarely used, according to Emiliano—had its own lake and man-made waterfall that dropped dramatically onto rocks in enthralling fashion. The orange-roofed, whitewashed residence was large enough to house several families, two additional wings having been added when he'd purchased it.

The whole property seemed to go on for acres and acres, even from the bird's-eye view of the helicopter circling to land on the manicured lawn.

'Why did you want to make it bigger?' she asked him.

To her surprise he seemed a touch embarrassed, but the look was quickly replaced by his customary self-assured shrug. 'I was newly successful and a little cocky and, yes, I wanted the world to know it. Contrary to popular belief, size does matter.'

She searched his face and saw the emotion he was trying to hide. 'You wanted your parents to finally see you, witness your success and acknowledge their shortcomings,' she offered softly, having discovered that talking with him about his past helped ease the bitterness she sometimes glimpsed in his eyes.

She also selfishly used their talks to work through her own emotions about her mother's motivation for abandoning her. She would never know the true reason, but she was beginning to accept that not everyone was cut out to accept the huge responsibility of caring for another life, even one they'd brought into the world. Emiliano's parents hadn't abandoned him, but they might as well have. That new kinship between them strengthened her even more than before. Where she'd been brave enough to face the world on her own, and thrive, it warmed her to know she didn't have to face every single obstacle on her own.

But it didn't stop her heart aching for Emiliano, for what he'd been through, every cell in her body wishing she could take his pain away.

His jaw flexed for a second before she got another shrug. 'Like I said, I was cocky. And misguided.'

'You were reaching out, the best way you knew how. Don't regret that you tried.'

His gaze searched hers for several heartbeats, before he exhaled and nodded. 'Enough about that. Come, I'll show you around.'

There was much to show. Swimming pool, stables, an internal courtyard with meticulously tended potted plants, an extensive wine cellar, countless bedrooms, a tennis court and even a tiny stone bridge over the narrowest part of the swan-inhabited lake.

To one side of the large outer patio, there was a *quincho* complete with double barbecues and roasting pits. Vintage saddles hung on the walls along with old black-and-white photos of gauchos. The wear on the saddles indicated they'd been well used at one point. Everywhere she looked, she saw evidence of past care and present attention. Emiliano hadn't bought a property to flaunt in his parents' faces, he'd invested in a potential home bursting with history.

It broke her heart that a place clearly intended to be lived in and loved had been left maintained but essentially abandoned. 'When was the last time you came here?'

'It's been two years. But Matias used it when he visited the city.'

She smiled. 'I'm glad. It feels wrong somehow for this place not to be lived in.'

He sent her a puzzled glance before leading her back

inside. Ochre tiled floors perfectly balanced white walls and arched windows.

Their suite repeated the same theme with a massive four-poster bed made of dark oak and laid with a rich, multihued spread.

Tugging her to where he stood, he began to undo the buttons of her yellow sundress. She thought about protesting that she could take care of her own undressing, but the wide yawn that overtook her put paid to that.

Once his own clothes were taken care of, she followed him into the bathroom, keeping her ogling to a few dozen stares. In the shower, she braced her hands on the wall and let him wash her, wrap her in a warm towel and lead her to bed. Her eyelids were drooping by the time he stepped back. 'Dinner will be served after you've had your rest. I'm not sure when I'll be back. Don't wait up for me.'

She nodded drowsily, the sleep that had eluded her for the past few nights determined to drag her under now. 'Go slay 'em.'

Cool arrogance glittered in his tawny eyes. 'I fully intend to,' he replied, his voice attaining an edge of steel. Bending, he touched his lips to her temple. 'Sleep well.'

She didn't.

In fact the pattern continued for nearly a week. With Emiliano fully immersed in the situation with his parents, she was left pretty much to her own devices. She would swim, visit the horses in the stables and potter around the herb garden that the housekeeper, Blanca, tended with meticulous care. All activities designed to provide the exercise she needed and, hopefully, grant her a good night's rest.

But barely an hour after going to bed she would jerk awake, sharp, dark images piercing through her subconscious and transforming into physical pain. On the seventh night in a row, she lay in the dark, her heart hammering as she tried to breathe through the ache in her head. After endless minutes, the pain began to subside.

Rising, she shrugged on a dressing gown and made her way to the kitchen. Emiliano was out at yet another meeting and the staff had retired.

Fetching a glass of water, she sipped as she wandered through the house, gratefully noting her headache had retreated to a dull throb. She eventually ended up in the inner courtyard, taking a seat before the low firepit that warmed the cool night air. When Alfie found her a few minutes later and offered to bring her a snack, she shook her head.

She had no appetite. And she was finding it increasingly difficult to shake off the sense of déjà vu crawling over her. Realising these past few days was the first time she'd been on her own without Emiliano nearby sent a jolt of alarm through her.

She'd already acknowledged that her feelings were getting troublingly intense when it came to her husband. The idea that craving him was manifesting in other ways made her heart lurch before she pursed her lips.

No. She wasn't a feeble, wilting flower unable to function without her man by her side. She didn't need to be told she'd risen to the position of a vice-president at Castillo Ventures through anything other than sheer grit and determination.

All this...anxiety bubbling beneath her skin was just a natural reaction to readjusting to the real world. Castillo Island had been a perfect, heady paradise. But not a place she could realistically stay for ever.

With that thought in mind, she rose and followed the sounds of crockery to the kitchen. Alfie turned at her entrance.

'Did you need something?' he asked.

'A pen and pad, please, if you have any handy.'

His smile widened as he opened a nearby drawer and took out the items. 'Is it time for a new list?' he asked, then he visibly checked himself. 'I'm sorry.'

She shook her head. 'Don't be. Emiliano has already told me about my list-making habits.'

She noted the relief on his face as she pulled out a stool at the kitchen island and sat down. Her first list consisted of baby names divided into male and female columns. It didn't escape her notice that the top ones were Spanish.

Next she made a list of things a baby would need.

At some point, Alfie slipped a plate of food in front of her. The grilled chicken cutlets and herb potato salad was half finished by the time she'd finished her third list.

Somewhere in the house, a clock chimed eleven o'clock. Her mind started to drift to Emiliano. Resolutely, she pulled it back.

But her husband was intent on making his presence felt despite his absence. Because on the pad in front of her, his name was written in bold letters and circled beneath it she'd written 'don't fall in love.'

She was back in bed but wide awake when she heard the crunch of tyres on gravel. Pretending she was asleep was childish and beneath her, although she did contemplate it for an absurd second.

The truth was she'd been craving elusive oblivion since her subconscious had blurted what her heart feared—that falling in love with Emiliano would be her undoing. Her panic that it may already be too late, that she was in all probability more than halfway there, was what had kept her body poised on the brink of full-blown panic.

Footsteps approached. She sat up, an intrinsic vein of courage stopping her from cowering away from her fears.

Emiliano entered and froze at the sight of her. For a few charged seconds, he stared at her, then a slow smile curved his mouth, the palpable tension blanketing him easing a touch.

'I meant it when I said don't wait up. But I do like the idea of you waiting up in bed for me.'

Despite his easy words, grim lines bracketed his mouth. Gleefully pushing aside her own disturbing emotions, she focused on his.

'Did everything go according to plan?'

The muscles in his neck bunched as he tossed his head in a purely Latin motion of vexation. 'Cards were laid on the table. A few threats tossed in. I expect compliance to be forthcoming in the next twelve hours.'

'How did you do it?' she asked. She'd been probing him on the subject since they arrived, but he'd remained tight-lipped about his dealings.

He hesitated for a moment then he prowled forward, shrugging off his jacket and discarding it on a scrolled seat. The innate sexiness of his every movement dried her mouth and spiked her heartbeat. It was all she could do not to lunge for him when he dropped onto the bed and slid one hand over her thigh.

'Men like Cabrera operate on greed and tend to spread themselves thin in the hope of making multiple paydays at any one time. I targeted his most lucrative companies and convinced a few key shareholders to part with their shares for a considerable markup. Then it was just a matter of making it clear that I would take pleasure in making his life hell if he didn't leave Castillo Estate alone.'

'Wow.'

He rubbed his free hand over his growing stubble. '*Sí.* Wow.'

She frowned. 'You don't wear victory well,' she commented.

'I'm dealing with a slippery bastard. I won't celebrate until the ink is dry on our new agreement.' His hand reached her hip and circled sensuously before continuing its path of destruction. The unique scent of sandalwood and alpha male invaded her senses.

She forced herself not to lean in, not to abandon cheerfully all her caution for this man. But the sensation of being on a slippery slope escalated. So she covered deep disquiet with more conversation. 'Nevertheless, you should allow yourself a moment of satisfaction for progressing this far, this quickly.'

His mouth pursed. 'The prospect of spending time with my parents kills my celebratory spirit.'

'Spending time...?'

'I went to deliver the news of their...impending freedom...and to discuss Matias. They refused to talk about it tonight.'

'Have you considered that they're scared?'

'Being scared is acceptable. Burying their heads in the sand and refusing to even discuss it is not,' he stated. 'They wish to sleep on it before making their decision. They will give me an answer when they come to dinner tomorrow.'

Her eyes widened. 'They're coming here?'

He nodded grimly.

'If you're this unhappy about it, why did you agree to it?'

The corners of his mouth turned down. 'My happiness doesn't matter in this. I agreed for Matias.'

'Why a meal, though?'

He eyed her for a long second. 'Matias isn't the only reason for their request. They also want to meet you.'

Her mouth dropped open. 'Me? Why?' she blurted.

His gaze swept down for a handful of seconds. 'To satisfy whatever curiosity keeps them from facing reality, I guess.'

'Do they...do they know about the baby and my accident?'

His lip pursed. 'They know you're recovering from a trauma, but I didn't see the need to tell them about the baby. They were never interested in their son. I don't wish for them to have any interest in a grandchild.'

His tone was firm. Bitter. Punctuated with definitive finality as he dragged her lower and climbed on top of her.

Lowering his head, he brushed his mouth over hers in a whisper-thin caress. 'Since you seem rested and were considerate enough to wait up for me, *belleza*, I think we shouldn't let this opportunity go to waste, hmm?'

Every single pre-emptive she'd mentally erected crumbled to dust the moment he slid his tongue across her lower lip. As her hands found their way to his shoulders, she told herself she would take up arms to safeguard her feelings again tomorrow.

Tonight, she needed to experience her husband's lovemaking one more time.

CHAPTER ELEVEN

'You're making a list?'

She heard the trace of amusement in Emiliano's voice a second before he dropped a kiss on her head.

'If you were given less than a day's notice to host your first ever in-laws' dinner, you would make a list, too. Don't scoff.'

His amusement disappeared. 'They are not your in-laws, except in name only. And don't fret about it. Alfie and Blanca will take care of everything.'

She looked out through the open doors of the kitchen to the courtyard where Alfie was hosing down the tiles. 'He has his hands full. Besides, keeping *my* hands full will stop me fretting.'

Emiliano's eyes glittered with the beginning of displeasure. 'Sienna…'

'It's done, Emiliano. The driver's taking Blanca and me into town in half an hour. She does the grocery shopping and I get to practise my Spanish. It's a win-win.'

'I disagree. You can stay at home instead, go for a swim, practise your Spanish on me. Win-win-win.'

She'd woken up this morning with a sense of dread hanging over her. She couldn't deny that a large part of it stemmed from last night and how fast she'd succumbed to the magic of being in Emiliano's arms. And, whichever way she tried to dress it up, she wasn't looking forward to meeting Emiliano's parents, knowing they had deliberately rejected one son while being cavalier with the other's health. Before she'd sat down to start a fresh list, she knew she needed some distance. And she was going to take it, regardless of the fumes of ire vibrating off the sleekly built man standing before her.

'It's a tempting offer, but I'm still going, Emiliano,' she stated firmly.

His jaw flexed with irritation. 'I'm beginning to think I should've booked a restaurant for tonight and been done with it.'

She hopped from the island counter, quickly dancing out of his reach when his hands started to move towards her.

Yes. Distance. Definitely.

Steady footsteps approached the kitchen and she looked up, relief spiking through her as the housekeeper entered. 'Well, it's too late now.' She started to walk out.

'Wait.' The bite in his tone was definitely growing.

She stopped, her nerves jangling as he strolled towards her. He hadn't yet shaved his stubble from last night and, with the predatory gleam in his eyes, he resembled a dark overlord intent on one thing only: establishing claim.

'Bésame adiós,' he ordered in a near growl.

There was no getting away from the demand. Not if she wanted to escape. Inhaling deeply, she rose on tiptoe and pressed her mouth against his. Hard. Quick.

She started to turn away.

One hand captured her nape, the other cupping her jaw, totally halting her retreat. Incisive eyes narrowed, he bared his teeth. 'Once again, with feeling.'

Sienna was at once elated and terrified by how high her senses leaped. So much so, she stood immobile as he slanted his mouth over hers and kissed her in a way that left little room for doubt that she was well and truly owned, her heart unmistakably on the line.

When he raised his head, she was panting. And his eyes gleamed with arrogant satisfaction. She stared dumbly when he held a granite-black credit card in front of her face between two fingers, before reaching behind her to tuck it into the pocket of her white capri trousers.

'Enjoy your shopping,' he rasped. 'And Alfie comes with you. Non-negotiable.'

Sienna stumbled away, barely noting the drive out of the villa or the expansive *pampas* that whizzed by her window.

Time passed. She wasn't sure how long. Alfie, in the passenger seat, glanced back at her, his gaze concerned. 'Everything all right, Sienna?'

She attempted a reassuring smile that failed completely. Because she wasn't all right. With one kiss, one final blow against her poorly erected defences, the truth had been laid bare.

She was in love with Emiliano. Irrevocably. Completely.

Her senses flared wide, utterly vulnerable at that silent, devastating admission.

Had it been heading there since that first admission of her deeper feelings on that forgotten trip to Hong Kong? Had it grown even more during the months now buried in the darkness of her memories?

Did he know how she felt?

Recalling the look she'd caught on his face on the plane yesterday, her heart dropped in further alarm. Was that why he wanted to talk?

'Sienna?'

Pushing the tsunami of questions away to be dealt with later, she summoned a smile. 'I'm fine.'

You hope.

Refusing to grant victory to the inner voice that mocked, she raised her chin. Yes. She hoped. When she'd bravely stepped up to the altar and said her vows, it'd been because she wanted this union to work. For her baby and for herself.

If the father of her child didn't want the love that blossomed in her heart for him, then…then…

Her breath shortened, actual physical pain lancing

through her head, as if the thought was dead against being formed. She gasped.

Over the buzzing in her ears she heard Alfie instructing the driver to pull over. 'No, it's okay. I'm okay.'

She would be. For her baby's sake, she had to be.

Letting that vow strengthen her, she resolutely shut off her thoughts, focusing on her first glimpse of the more urban parts of Cordoba. Like every other cosmopolitan metropolis, it contained flashy new buildings. But it was the more traditional architecture that she watched out for. Beside her, Blanca proudly pointed out pale gold stone churches, piazzas teeming with tourists splashing through fountains and Manzana Jesuitica, a UNESCO World Heritage site.

She smiled and nodded, aware of Alfie's frequent sidelong glances. It was almost a relief to arrive at the bustling square that was Cordoba's main produce market and lose herself in the sights and smells of Argentina.

Cured meats and Wagyu beef were chosen and expertly sliced… Wild pink salmon was carefully packaged and added to the ever-growing pile. Plump fruit and fresh vegetables were placed in cool boxes to protect them from the growing heat and, all too soon, they were piling back into the SUV.

But they only went a few streets before the driver was pulling to a stop once more.

'Why are stopping? Did we forget something?' she asked.

Alfie grinned. 'Yes, proper retail therapy for you. Boss's orders.'

She took a closer look at the street and shops in front of which they were parked: expensive cars and chic boutiques which reeked of exclusivity. Alfie got out and held her door open. Blanca smiled and waved her out with expressive hands.

A little relieved at the reprieve she'd been given before facing Emiliano again with the new knowledge burning in her heart, Sienna alighted and entered the nearest shop.

The staff was busy bustling around two women holding court at one end of the shop. One harried server offered her champagne, a look of relief crossing her face when Sienna refused. A second later, she darted off.

Not minding the peace, she took her time to browse. Her pregnancy wasn't overly visible yet, but she'd noticed a definite thickening of her waistline and a general tightness in her clothes. The chance to outfit herself with a confidence-boosting dress was suddenly welcome.

The drop-sleeve gown she found was a floaty, gossamer-light affair. In dark, layered purple, it was elegant enough to wear to dinner and loose enough to disguise her slight bump. The price tag however was staggering enough to give her pause.

'The dressing room is that way,' Alfie said. 'Here, I'll help you.' He took the dress from her and firmly led the way, as if he could sense her hesitation.

The harassed server approached them again and showed them to the large changing room before hurrying off once more. Alfie rolled his eyes, but grinned as he nudged her towards the wide cubicle.

The dress fitted like a dream, but she was still biting her lip about the price as she changed into her clothes and emerged from the changing room to hear raised voices.

'*Sí*, Señora Castillo. *Immediatamente!*'

Sienna frowned. She didn't know how common the Castillo name was in this part of Argentina but what were the chances of coming across another one in Cordoba?

The older woman was still on a diva tirade. Alfie rolled his eyes when his gaze met hers. Deciding to buy the dress and leave as quickly as possible, she took the credit card out of her back pocket.

About to dismiss the scene, she froze when a younger voice joined in the haranguing.

'*Lo siento*, Señorita Cabrera,' one of the assistants offered.

The rest of the rapid-fire words were lost to Sienna as the fine hairs on her nape jerked upright. It would be a coincidence that the two names behind the reason for her being in Argentina belonged to random strangers.

Slowly, she emerged from the changing area, her attention on the two women seated behind the roped-off VIP area, each clutching a chilled glance of champagne in one hand and gesticulating to distraught assistants with the other.

The younger woman spotted Sienna first. Her dark brown gaze drifted over. Paused. Returned. Widened.

She turned, nudged the older woman and muttered under her breath. Then both glanced her way, eyes filled with curiosity.

The older woman rose first. Tall and willowy, she only needed to take a couple of steps towards her before Sienna became certain that she was looking at Emiliano's mother. They had the same eyes. The same curve of her lip. But, where Emiliano's regal posture and innate grace of movement was absorbingly effortless, everything about Señora Castillo seemed affected, right down to the tips of her manicured fake nails.

'Your name?'

Sienna blinked. 'Excuse me?'

She gave an uppity sniff as her gaze raked over Sienna. 'I am Valentina Castillo. My friend seems to think we might have a person of interest in common. I merely wish to ascertain if this is correct.' Her tone was clipped, the bites of heavily accented English supposed to give an impression of class. Sienna could only concentrate on the words that had just come out of her mouth.

Her friend? *'Person of interest?'*

The younger woman joined them, the swing in her shorter, voluptuous hips more natural. Up close, Sienna couldn't help but notice her stunning beauty. And the fact that something about her made her senses tweak in alarm even though, at closer scrutiny, her expression was more welcoming than Valentina's.

'You are Sienna Newman, *si?*' she asked in a soft, husky voice, her eyes now transmitting friendliness.

Sienna smiled. 'Sienna Castillo,' she corrected.

The women exchanged glances then stared back at her. From the corner of her eye, Sienna noted Alfie's concerned frown but she concentrated on Emiliano's mother, desperately probing for a sign of warmth or humanity. Coming up empty, she took a breath and attempted a smile regardless. 'If by *person of interest* you mean Emiliano, then, yes, we do. It's lovely to make your acquaintance, Señora Castillo.'

'That remains to be seen, my dear.' Her gaze dropped to the dress in Sienna's hand, then to the credit card. She couldn't have failed to see Emiliano's name embossed in gold letters. A look lanced through her eyes, even as one carefully plucked eyebrow rose.

Sienna wanted to shove the card back in her pocket, but she forced herself to remain still. She had nothing to be ashamed of. All the same, she made a mental note to find out where her own bank cards were when she got back.

Valentina dismissed her but, just before she turned away, Sienna also spotted something in the woman's gaze.

Fear.

'We will see you this evening. I hope you don't feel too out of your depth catering for our particular tastes.'

'Your son prides himself in having the best of everything. Don't worry, we have you covered.'

Sienna witnessed the tiniest grimace tweak her mother-in-law's features before a stiff smile slid into place. 'In that case, we look forward to making your better acquaintance, as you say. *Vamanos*, Graciela.' Her gentle tone as she addressed the younger woman spoke of a fondness.

Graciela Cabrera trailed behind the older woman, then at the last moment before they reached the door she darted back.

'I hope we meet again, but if we don't you should know that Emiliano is a wonderful man. One you should treasure.'

Sienna's mouth dropped open. 'I… Thank you.'

Graciela nodded, her eyes staying on Sienna's a moment longer before she turned and quickly walked out.

'Um… What was that all about?' Alfie enquired.

'I have no idea,' she murmured a split second before she experienced that twinge again, sharper this time. But the pain of her burgeoning headache was nowhere near the ache she felt in her heart for Emiliano. She hadn't wanted to believe that a mother could be so unfeeling. Having met Valentina Castillo, Sienna was willing to bet the woman's demeanour was a front. She might have taken a wrong path in the past where her second child was concerned, but the need she'd glimpsed ever so briefly in her eyes gave Sienna a little hope for her husband.

As for Graciela…

She frowned, touching a hand to her temple when the jumbled thoughts made her head pound harder.

'What do you say we get out of here?' Alfie suggested.

'Yes, good idea,' she replied.

The assistants, chattering quietly and looking relieved now that the drama queens had exited, came forward and rang up the dress.

Sienna got back into the SUV, feeling as if her life had changed but unable to put her finger on how.

Like the outbound journey, the return trip went by in a blur. The first thing she knew about being back at the estate was Emiliano bearing down on her, his face a mask of displeasure.

'I understand you met my mother,' he growled, taking her hands in his and peering down at her with dark, searching eyes.

'I had the pleasure, yes. Graciela Cabrera was there, too.'

He stiffened, his body taking on a grim alertness that twanged her already jangled nerves. 'What did she say?' he bit out.

'Graciela? She was nice. Your mother…' She paused, unwilling to pass negative judgement on the woman, especially when her beliefs about Valentina had grown stronger. Somewhere deep in her heart, she still harboured hope that his parents would wake up to the incredible, arrogant man who so easily held the world in his hand. The stunningly charismatic man she'd fallen in love with.

The reality of her ever-growing feelings rammed home just then. So powerfully that she couldn't stare into his eyes for fear he would decipher her emotions. Drawing her hands from his, she waved the question away. 'It's fine. She was probably as surprised as I was to meet me this way.'

He huffed with annoyance. 'I am one hundred per cent certain it is not fine, and you do not need to make excuses for her, but in the spirit of peace I will leave the subject alone.'

'Thank you,' she murmured. Then, eager to escape, because the temptation to stay was mounting by the second, she turned towards the kitchen. 'Blanca probably needs help—'

'No.' Emiliano's mouth thinned, despite the proffered peace. 'Blanca has assistants who have minions. You're officially barred from the kitchen until further notice.'

'But—'

'Let's not argue a pointless issue, *querida*. Come.' Without waiting for her consent, he caught her elbow, steered her into the living room and pressed her onto the wide sofa. Encouraging her to lie back, he eased her shoes off and propped her feet in his lap.

Sienna gave up attempting to find fortitude in the storm of domineering attitude. Just as she couldn't help greedily drinking him in, or stop the heat dredging through her pelvis at his dark, devastating looks. When his thumbs dug into her soles with pinpoint accuracy, she closed her eyes and moaned, surrendering to his touch.

'Cancelling tonight seems like a better prospect by the second,' he rasped.

Her eyes popped open. 'No, don't cancel. Your mother will think it's my fault.'

'I don't care what she thinks. Neither should you.'

She shook her head, hope still burning in her chest. 'But you do care how it might affect Matias. Once they satisfy their curiosity, they won't have a leg to stand on.'

He sighed, his jaw flexing for a second before he jerked out a nod. They stayed like that, Emiliano massaging her feet, Sienna desperately biting her tongue to stop the thick, emotive words that surged forth.

Because, really, what was the worst that could happen? *He could reject you. Reject your love.*

Chains tightened around her heart, which in turn robbed her of breath and silenced the words.

When he rose an hour later and held out his hand to her, she went with him upstairs to their bedroom. The impending dinner ominously had taken up room in their minds, which left very little room for banter as they undressed and got into the shower. Emiliano made no move to make love to her, much to her soul's mournful surprise. Telling herself it was for the best, and hearing the silent words ring hollow, she busied herself with getting ready.

Still in silence, they came downstairs and walked

through the house with the sound of last-minute preparations signalling his parents' imminent arrival.

He stood tall and proud next to her but she nevertheless felt him tense when headlights travelled slowly up the long drive. Even after the Mercedes stopped, his parents didn't alight for a full minute. Anger slowly building inside her on his behalf, Sienna linked her fingers with Emiliano's. His jaw tightened, but he didn't look at her, his focus unmoving on the idling vehicle.

When it opened and a man stepped out, her eyes widened.

She'd imagined she would be meeting a male version of Valentina. But the man who slowly walked up the steps and shook her hand appeared less…rigid. She even dared to consider that there was a malleable side to Benito Castillo as his eyes lingered on his son during their handshake.

Nevertheless, as he stepped back formally to introduce his wife, it was clear the two presented a united front.

It was also clear Valentina hadn't shared the fact that she and Sienna had already met with her husband. The knowledge wasn't worth puzzling over. The objective tonight was to wine, dine and somehow persuade Valentina and Benito Castillo to do the right thing by their older son sooner rather than later.

So she followed Emiliano into the living room where Alfie was waiting to prepare drinks.

While the men opted for scotch and Valentina a glass of white wine, she chose a lemon spritzer. They indulged in stilted conversation for interminable minutes before her mother-in-law's gaze settled on her. 'That dress suits you. You look…radiant.'

Beside her, she felt Emiliano's tension mount but she kept the smile pinned on her face. 'Thank you. Allow me to return the compliment.'

Valentina looked startled for a moment at being called

radiant, then her gaze skittered to her son. And, just like her husband's had, it lingered.

Sienna breathed easier, not sure how they would navigate themselves out of the quagmire but choosing to believe they would.

After a minute, Benito cleared his throat. 'About this business with Cabrera...'

'It's been taken care of. As of this afternoon, he will no longer be a problem. Castillo Estate is back under full Castillo care.'

A wave of relief washed over his parents' faces, although Valentina's mouth pursed. 'You have our undying gratitude, of course, but I can't help but think all this... unpleasantness could've been avoided if you'd honoured your word at the start.'

Emiliano inhaled sharply, his eyes darting to Sienna's before narrowing with vicious intent on his mother. 'I understand that gratitude is an alien concept to you, but we will *not* discuss subjects that are in the past.'

Valentina drank more wine and waved a compliant hand. 'Of course, I understand. Now that you're married, it would be distasteful of me to bring it up.'

Sienna's heart lurched. The glass in her hand shook wildly, spilling several drops of liquid on her dress. Thin-lipped and a little paler than he'd been a moment ago, Emiliano reached into his pocket and passed her a handkerchief.

She took it, but she was nowhere near interested in the stains on her dress. 'What...what does that mean?' she asked, the dread that had been haunting her growing exponentially.

'It means that whatever insane ideas they entertained to extricate themselves from their situation is no longer worth discussing, since Cabrera is no long an issue. *Está claro?*' The warning in his tone was deadly.

Enough to convince her there was more going on beneath the surface. Enough to tell her he'd just given her a non-answer.

Eyes a shade darker than her son's snapped. 'We are your parents, Emiliano. Show some respect!'

Emiliano surged to his feet. 'I will not be dictated to under my own roof. Perhaps you misunderstood what I meant when I said Castillo Estate was back in Castillo care. What I meant is it's back in *my* care. Part of my agreement with Cabrera was that he sells me all his shares. As of this afternoon, I own seventy-five per cent of the business. I will oversee the business from now until Matias is back at the helm. Then I will transfer control to him.'

Both Benito and Valentina wore equal expressions of astonishment. Valentina recovered first, a touch of anguish mingled with her shock. 'You would do that to us?'

'It's already done.' His merciless gaze flitted to the door leading to the dining room, where Alfie hovered. 'I believe dinner is served. While we eat, you will tell me when you will be instructing the doctors in Switzerland to bring my brother out of his coma,' he spat at his mother. 'But, make no mistake, by the time dessert is served I will have your agreement. Or you can kiss your precious estate goodbye.'

Dinner was a disaster. Fraught silence was followed by sniping between Valentina and Benito, followed by an increasingly circumspect Benito. Every now and then, his gaze landed on his son, his expression slowly changing from brooding to acceptance and eventually to grudging respect.

Emiliano finally laid down his fork. 'Is there something on your mind?'

Benito shrugged and picked up his replenished glass of red wine. '*Si*. We wouldn't be in this mess if it weren't for your mother's obsession with the Cabreras. A habit I indulged unfortunately. We're lucky enough to have salvaged our family name. So we will do everything you want. And when Matias is back he will manage the Castillo business, with no interference from us.'

Valentina's gasp was followed by hot Spanish words exchanged with her husband, who shrugged some more and drank even harder. When she realised her tirade had lost its legs, she shifted her gaze to her son. 'I… We will do as your father says. And, for what it's worth, you should know we talked to Matias's doctors this morning. They are…hopeful.'

'Good, then everything is resolved.'

Valentina's expression dropped, her eyes displaying a greater depth of anguish than before.

Sienna glanced at Emiliano, curious as to how he was taking this turn of events. He wasn't looking at his parents. His eyes rested on her, their expression intently watchful. Almost dreading.

A shiver went over her as terror crept closer to her heart.

Throwing down her napkin, she stood. 'I'll go and see about dessert.' The ungracious voice that said she was up for anything that hurried this overwrought meal to its conclusion was ruthlessly silenced as she entered the kitchen.

Blanca had everything under control, of course.

Feeling superfluous and unwilling to return to the warped atmosphere of the dining room, Sienna carried on walking through the kitchen, stepping out into the outer courtyard. Inhaling the fresh, clean air did nothing for her raging thoughts and the almost fatalistic, dreadful premonition haunting her.

Footsteps sounded behind her, a click of heels bringing certain doom.

Sienna turned.

Valentina stood six feet away, her gaze resting on Sienna's stomach. 'Is that how you got him to go back on his word? By getting yourself pregnant? And don't bother denying it. Your abstention from drink and Emiliano watching you like a hawk tells me what I need to know.'

'I don't know what you mean. Go back on his word on what?' she asked through lips turning numb with fear.

'Ah, of course, you don't remember.'

'Don't remember what?' she probed again.

Valentina turned, as if she was about to walk away. 'It doesn't matter now that he's married, I suspect.'

'You do care for him. So why do you treat him like that? Why are you so afraid to show it?' Sienna blurted before she thought better of it.

Valentina's eyes widened. 'You don't know what you're talking about. I don't treat Emiliano in any particular way.'

'When was the last time you told him you loved him, or that you were proud of him?'

'He doesn't need that from me. The bond we share is enough.'

'Really? Well, I wouldn't know about that. I grew up without a mother, you see.'

'Is that supposed to make me feel sorry for you?'

Sienna stared at the older woman for a moment before she shook her head. 'No, but take it from me—your son needs to hear it from you.'

'Don't presume to think you know me enough to lecture me.'

'Very well. Please tell me what you meant by what you said before. "Now that he's married"?'

She spread her hands in a gesture so reminiscent of Emiliano's it was unsettling. 'I've been forbidden from talking about it.'

Her fists balled. 'Not by me.'

Her eyebrows rose. 'You have a backbone. You will need it to deal with my son. But are you sure it's strong enough to handle the truth?'

'What truth? Tell me,' she insisted, her voice rising with a touch of hysteria.

'Very well. A couple of months ago Emiliano was engaged to Graciela Cabrera. Their wedding had been planned for next month, on Valentine's Day. Benito thinks I'm obsessed but I only want what's best for both my sons. Graciela would've made him a good wife.'

'That's…that's a lie.' Her voice was bled of all substance.

Valentina's eyes, so similar to those of the man Sienna loved, narrowed. 'If you don't believe me, *ask him.*'

She didn't need to. Because she knew. Even before Graciela's words to her in the shop that had spoken of something else… Even before Emiliano's proposal that hadn't quite sat right… Deep in her heart, she *knew.*

Sienna opened her mouth to speak. Then quickly shut it, her hands flying to her head as every single twinge, tweak, dread and fear coalesced at the same time into a bolt of lightning that forked through her brain.

She stumbled forward, her hand flailing out in search of something, anything, to hold on to. Another arrow of pain cracked through her head. She cried out as the edges of her vision blurred.

Her baby. *Oh, God, her baby!*

Powerful feet thundered towards her, hands catching her as she lost feeling in her legs.

'*Madre de Dios*, what did you do to her?' was the last thing she heard.

She woke on the sofa to find Emiliano on his knees beside her, his face a grey mask as he gripped her hand. His breathing was hopelessly ragged, his eyes black, haunted pools.

'Sienna.' His voice was a hoarse, desperate plea.

She couldn't look at him. It simply hurt too much. So she directed her gaze over his shoulder to the heated argument going on between Valentina and Benito.

'*Basta!*' Emiliano snarled. 'My wife is like this because of you. Alfie will show you out. You're no longer welcome here.'

The bubble of pain bloomed as she shook her head.

'You're wrong. They had nothing to do with it. I remember, Emiliano. I remember everything. And this… *this was all because of you.*'

CHAPTER TWELVE

'WE NEED TO talk about this, Sienna.'

Three days had passed since her memory had returned. Since the sheer depths of Emiliano's cunning betrayal had shredded her heart to a million pieces.

Concern for her baby had made her agree to see the doctor Emiliano had summoned, the same concern keeping her confined to rest for three days when every screaming atom of her being wished she was elsewhere. Far away from here. From Emiliano.

God, just thinking about him hurt more than she would ever have thought possible. And having him here in her bedroom, speaking to her...

She took a deep breath and turned from the window to face him. Better to get this over with then she could go back to staring at the devastation that was her life.

Her face must have reflected the true depths of her wretchedness because he inhaled sharply. 'You need to be in bed.'

'I need to be several thousand miles from here. Away from you.'

His jaw clenched hard, as did the hands by his side. But he didn't leave as she wanted him to. He stayed put. Immovable. She found it overwhelmingly brutal just taking every breath.

'This isn't productive.'

'Productive? I'm sorry that regaining my memories to discover the man who dumped me for another woman has lied and manipulated me into marriage because he got me pregnant isn't *productive* for you.'

The doctor from Haven North with whom they'd videoconferenced had mentioned that more of her memories would return with each passing day. Sienna desperately prayed they didn't. With each new memory revealed, her heart broke all over again.

'I didn't lie to you. I just couldn't tell you the whole truth because it might have caused irreparable damage.'

'You twisted the situation to suit your own needs!'

'What needs? The need to ensure my brother didn't remain on a breathing tube for the rest of his life? Or the need to provide for my child's future?'

Her hand flew to her stomach, the thought that she would want less for her child ramping up her anger and misery. 'This child will want for nothing and I resent your implication otherwise. As for Matias, I get that you made a promise to him that you had to keep. What I can't live with is that you didn't see fit to tell me about it. You went ahead and made plans *for your life* that didn't take our relationship into account. Plans that involved another woman. Plans that were splashed all over the tabloids for the world to see and salivate over.'

'I never intended to marry her. But she asked for my help in dealing with her father—'

'I don't care! You knowingly put yourself in a position that would hurt me. And, when I tried to talk to you about it, you walked away.'

'Because you weren't in a state to listen to what I had to say.'

'Which was what? That, when it came right down to it, I featured very low on your list of priorities?'

His hand slashed through the air. 'I don't want to hear about lists!'

'I'm sorry if what's important to me doesn't coincide with what matters to you!' she snapped.

'*Dios mío*, I was hit with an unexpected situation on

what was supposed to be a turnaround visit. I had very little time to act.'

'You've made tougher decisions in a boardroom full of intransigent negotiators in a matter of hours. You were in Argentina for *six days*. And not once during that time did you call to tell me what was going on.'

'How would you have reacted if I'd called and told you that my brother had left me a message on what he thought was his possible deathbed to tell me to honour a ludicrous promise he'd made to get my parents out of their mess? That I was expected to hand myself over like a prized stud in some deal I wasn't aware of until I walked into my parents' house?'

She floundered for a second before she firmed her spine. 'I guess we'll never know, because you didn't.'

'I didn't because it was an absurd situation. One that I couldn't find an immediate solution to that didn't involve letting Matias down.'

'So you chose to let *me* down instead?'

'No. I chose to wait until we were together to tell you but…'

'But what?'

'I put myself in your shoes, considered how I would feel if you informed me you were engaged to another man.'

She stared at him, perverse curiosity eating at her. 'And?'

The feral growl that erupted from his throat startled her. She watched him spike a hand through his hair and pace for a minute before facing her. 'It was your birthday. I wanted you to enjoy your evening so I decided to wait till the next day to explain the situation. But the tabloid spread put a wrench in that.'

'So you thought the best solution then was to break up with me?'

'I thought I'd give us both a little space to regroup and for me to find an alternative solution.'

'And that involved trying to buy me with the penthouse and a car?'

He shrugged and she noted absently that his face was creased in lines that resembled anxiety. 'It was wrong, perhaps, but I wanted to keep you sweet while dealing with Rodrigo Cabrera. And I knew you loved the penthouse.'

'Not enough to live in it after it was clear we were over.'

'We weren't over. We're not over,' he denied through clenched teeth. 'We will *never* be over.'

She shook her head. 'You know what all of this tells me? That you were more concerned with everyone else's feelings than mine. And right now you're only here out of guilt and because I'm carrying your baby.'

'*Dios mío*, be reasonable.'

'No! You had weeks to fight for me. You didn't bother. I've seen you go after deals with more aggression simply because you were bored. How do you think it makes me feel to know I didn't even warrant a *bored* chase?'

His teeth bared. 'Because a large part of that time, you'd disappeared off the face of the earth. Then you had the audacity to turn up with another man whose presence in your life you rubbed in my face.'

She flushed, then felt a snap of irritation for feeling guilty. 'Don't turn this back on me. We are where we are today because of you. I don't hate you for trying to do right by your brother, but you didn't need to cast me aside to do so. Rejection like that isn't easy for me to forgive, Emiliano.' She stopped then regrouped when her voice broke. 'You know what it feels like to come second, to be discarded like an unwanted object. I may be strong enough to withstand it, but that doesn't mean I wish it to happen to me. I…I just can't come second in anyone's life. Ever again.'

He froze, the only movement in his whole formidable frame the eyes that narrowed with laser-like intent on her. 'What are you saying?' he asked in a clipped tone.

'I'm saying that I can never be sure that you're not here in this marriage just because of our child.'

'I'm here for you both!'

'But would you have asked me to marry you if I wasn't pregnant? Or was this whole thing staged to protect your position in your child's life?'

His mouth thinned and his nostrils flared. 'Nothing was staged. We're having a baby together. It's the most natural thing in the world for couples to take the next step.'

'Even when one of the couple has previously made it perfectly clear that marriage doesn't feature anywhere on his life's to-do list?'

He stalked in a tight circle before facing her again. 'I'm trying to do right by you, Sienna. Will you condemn me for that?'

Her heart lurched then broke. 'No, but I won't let you sacrifice yourself for me.'

'*Por el amor de Dios!* It is *not* a sacrifice.'

She took one step back. Then another. To stay here was to weaken and she would hate herself for it one day. The thought of what that would do to her child firmed her resolve.

'Call it what you will. But I don't want it.'

He stared at her with something akin to shock. Which turned to disbelief then cold determination. 'You don't want it. Explain to me in clear terms what you *do* want, then,' he demanded hoarsely.

Before she gave birth to the words, they burned like acid in her chest. But she had to speak them. Continuing to perpetuate a lie would kill what remained of her heart. Staying, knowing Emiliano wasn't in it for love, for *her*, would annihilate her soul. 'It means I want a divorce.'

Tawny eyes turned an eerie dark gold, the lines around his mouth deepening as his face hardened into a terrifying mask. 'I'm not prepared to dissolve our marriage over a simple disagreement.'

'It's not simple to me. I married you without the benefit of remembering that you hurt me deeply, Emiliano. And I can't trust that you won't do it again.' Not with what was most important to her besides her baby. Not with the feelings that were screaming under the weight of her hurt.

His face had lost a healthy dose of colour but the eyes that were locked onto her were dark pools of grim purpose. 'Be that as it may, my responsibility is to our child. We will not break up because you feel aggrieved. We once were in agreement that we would give this child the best of ourselves. That hasn't changed.'

'How can we do that when we're locked in battle?'

He spread his hands out in a gesture she would've been foolish to believe was harmless. 'You're the only one armed to the teeth here, *querida*. I'm just telling you where my hard boundaries are. We can work together to find common ground or you can attempt to take shots at me. Before you do, I should warn you that you will lose.'

'You can't force me to stay. Just as you can't keep what you never truly had.'

He looked stricken, as though he'd been gut-punched. His nostrils flared as he took rough, deep breaths.

Then, without another word, he walked out.

She'd come full circle. Her hand crept over her stomach. Fuller circle.

Sienna stared despondently around the flat she'd rented and tried to decorate but felt alien. Despite being back for almost two weeks and barely having left the flat, it still felt as if she was living in a stranger's property. A stranger who moved listlessly through the three rooms, eating for her child's sake and doing very little else.

In a way it was good that she hadn't grown attached to this flat. Having a baby who would quickly grow into an active toddler meant she would need a house with a garden. Somewhere more child-friendly where she could establish roots.

Her bump was definitely more rounded. Time was marching on whether she chose to acknowledge it or not. She only wished she could breathe, eat and sleep without the raw pain that dogged her whenever she thought of Emiliano.

Which was constantly.

How could she fall in love with the same man twice in one lifetime—and both times have her heart torn to pieces?

After their row in the bedroom, Emiliano had given her a wide berth for the rest of the day. When she'd requested dinner in her room, Alfie had delivered it.

The next morning, deciding it was a good time to start reclaiming her life, she'd come down to breakfast and been confronted with a grim-faced Emiliano. He'd stated with point-blank finality that he wouldn't discuss a divorce.

They'd compromised on a separation. And once again he'd walked away from her, but this time with a look that closely resembled fierce anguish.

That look had crossed her mind more times than she cared to recall.

As did the riddle of why he was so against regaining his freedom.

He hadn't needed to marry her. This wasn't the Middle Ages, where marriage was paramount in ensuring one's child's legitimacy. He didn't love her, granted. But he hadn't had to marry her. *But he had.*

The Emiliano she knew wasn't that selfless when it came to his freedom. Hadn't she, in the months before their relationship had started, predicted when his liaisons would end with almost clockwork precision? And hadn't that end been triggered by the first signs of clinginess?

'I'm here for you both,' he'd said. At the time, pain had been the dominant force riding her. Now, with time and distance, she thought, might she have dismissed those words too hastily? When they'd *both* agreed that their marriage primarily benefitted their child?

On the day she'd left Argentina, she'd breached the cold silence between them to let him know she wouldn't stand in the way of maintaining equal custody of their child. He'd coldly replied that they wouldn't need to discuss custody if they stayed married.

She shook her head now, feeling a little pathetic for desperately trying to find a salve for the constant wildfire that was her pain. A fire she feared she would never be able to put out.

Grabbing her laptop, she settled on the sofa and brought up the list of properties she'd put together for a possible viewing. Having made a shortlist, she was about to make an appointment when her phone rang.

David Hunter.

She'd sent him an email thanking him for his concern after having come home to dozens of messages from him. She'd declined his further calls about finding her a job. She was financially sound enough for now not to need a job right away. Although that would soon need to change.

She eyed the ringing phone then picked it up at the last moment.

'David, hello.'

'Sienna! Good to hear your voice,' he responded eagerly then checked himself. 'Um, I mean, I thought I would be talking to your voicemail again,' he semijoked.

'What can I do for you?' Her gaze landed on the sidebar of the property website and took note of the giddy advertisement for love and happiness, and her heart lurched.

Today was Valentine's Day. Hopelessly commercialised, but a day for lovers the world over nonetheless.

The day Emiliano would've married someone else…

But he hadn't.

Because he married you!

She pushed the insistent voice away as David cleared his throat. 'Uh, I know you aren't looking for anything right now, but I think I have something that might interest you.'

'Why?'

'It's a start-up, but the CEO thinks you might be able to put your own stamp on the job. And it's completely flexible. Hell, you can work from home if you want.'

She frowned. 'It sounds a little too good to be true. No start-up hedge fund can offer terms like that unless they're prepared to make a huge initial loss.'

'Well, this guy is pretty confident he can make things work. But he insists he wants you. And the meeting has to be today. He's flying out of the country tomorrow.'

Sienna looked down at herself and grimaced. She'd taken a shower this morning but she'd slipped back into her comfy onesie, preparing for a day of mindless TV to drown her pain.

She opened her mouth to say no then reconsidered. Her funds wouldn't last for ever, and if this offer was real she owed it to herself to consider it.

'Okay, where do I need to go?'

'It's just out of the city. He'll send a car for you. In, say, half an hour?'

'Uh…okay.'

'Great. Good luck, Sienna.' The wish was deep and heartfelt.

Frowning a little, she said goodbye and hung up.

Rising, she went to her small bedroom and critically

examined her wardrobe. She hadn't been in the mood for clothes shopping since her return, and with her expanding waistline most of her clothes no longer fit. Her gaze lit on a cashmere batwing-style jumper dress Emiliano had bought for her on a visit to Milan. The memories they evoked threatened to clog her throat but she had no time for painful trips down memory lane.

Briskly she tugged it off the hanger and slipped it on. The grey-and-black colourblock design was professional enough to pass muster. Adding tights and a pair of soft grey heeled boots, she caught her hair up in a loose but stylish bun. She was shrugging into her coat when her doorbell sounded.

Grabbing her handbag, she shut her front door. The February wind threatened to chill her to the bone as she hurried. The sight of the idling limo gave her momentary pause, but she wasn't unaccustomed to CEOs in her field of work wooing fund managers this way. Nodding to the driver, she settled into the back seat. An hour later, they turned into a long driveway.

The country house in Surrey was a stunning Georgian masterpiece. Sienna fell in love with it long before the limo pulled up to the imposing double front doors.

Stepping out, she walked up the shallow steps and pressed the bell.

For a moment, when he opened the door, she couldn't believe her eyes. Didn't want to. And then she didn't want to blink in case he was a figment of her imagination.

When he exhaled and swung the door wider, she took a short, desperate breath.

'Is this some sort of joke, Emiliano?'

'No, *amante*. This is far from a joke.' His voice was deep. Solemn. His eyes pleading.

She swung her head towards the limo. The *departing* limo.

'Come in, Sienna. *Por favor.*'

It was either stand out in the freezing cold or step into the warmth. Her feet moved forward before she'd given them complete control.

When the door shut behind her, she turned. For a moment, she couldn't find her voice. Emiliano dressed all in black had always had that power over her. This time wasn't any different. She didn't want to acknowledge the way the black sweater moulded his muscular chest or the tailored trousers clung to his powerful thighs.

So she dragged her gaze up to his.

'What is the meaning of this?'

'Give me ten minutes of your time. After that, if you want to leave I will send for the driver.'

Ten minutes. Not much time, considering the wasteland of pain that stretched before her. And this unexpected chance to be in his electrifying presence again, breathe him in, felt too hard to refuse.

Again her body reacted without total consent from her mind, her nod triggering a similar nod from him.

He led the way down a light oak-panelled hallway into a study. To one side, floor-to-ceiling bookshelves held hundreds of books. On the other side, a teak desk held pride of place. It was there that Emiliano headed. But he didn't take a seat. Instead, he reached across the desk and picked up a single sheet of paper.

'My next venture is one I intend to pour my heart and soul into, so I have taken a leaf out of your book and made a list.'

She gasped, her breath clogging in her chest. 'Emiliano...'

Turbulent eyes stopped her. 'Hear me out, Sienna. Please.'

She gestured for him to continue.

'For this venture, I need a partner who will steer me true. Who will forgive me when I misstep—and I will occasionally, because I'm not perfect. I need a partner whose trust I hope to gain and who knows she can rely on me day or night. I need a queen who will bear my children, love them and me without reserve, even when we mess up. I need a partner who will hold my heart in her hands the way I hope she will let me hold hers. I need a partner who will believe me when I say I will *always*, without exception, put her first.'

He lowered his hand, holding her captive with his mesmerising gaze.

'*Por favor, querida*, I need *you*.'

'Oh... Emiliano.'

He shuddered hard, emotion exploding from his eyes as the paper dropped from his fingers and floated to the floor, forgotten. In one desperate lunge, he arrived in front of her. 'I need you, Sienna. I *love* you. You think I married you because of our child. I married you because I couldn't see a day in my future that you weren't a part of. And, yes, I was terrified that if you knew *how* your accident happened you would leave me. If I hadn't dragged you out into that alley that night, you wouldn't have fallen. But, believe me, I would've come for you, fought tooth and nail for you. I only found out the day before you returned from South America where you'd gone. My pilots were on standby to fly out to Peru the next morning.' He shook his head. 'Seeing you in that restaurant with Hunter made me lose my mind.'

'Seeing you on that magazine cover with Graciela made me lose mine,' she confessed huskily.

'*Lo siento.* If it's any consolation, know that I've never messed up anything in my life the way I messed up then. And I will move mountains to make sure I don't cause you pain like that ever again.'

The solid promise in his words made her heart stutter, then beat wildly against her ribs. 'I love you. I was going to tell you that night…on my birthday. I was going to be brave and put my feelings out there,' she confessed brokenly. 'Tell you about my past, tell you I didn't care who knew about us, ask if you would be mine the way I was yours.'

He squeezed his eyes shut and his chest heaved in an audible inhale. '*Dios mío*. Forgive me, *mi corazón*. I beg you.'

'Tell me you love me again. Please. I would feel so much better.'

'I love you. *Te amo*. I love your bravery, your spirit, your kind heart. I love your body. I love your soul.' His hand dropped to her gently swollen belly. 'I love that our baby is nestled warm and safe inside your body. I love—'

She flung herself at him, shameless, happy tears spilling from her eyes as she pressed her mouth against his.

With a helpless groan, he caught her up against him, deepening the kiss almost immediately. Claiming her.

An eternity later, he lifted his head, brushed away her tears. 'The past few weeks have been hell, *querida*,' he muttered. 'Enough for me to confess I don't even mind these tears this time, because seeing them means you're here in front of me, not a figment of my desperate imagination.'

She laughed. Kissed him again just because she could. Of course that led to heat being generated at an alarming rate. Which led to her being scooped up in strong arms, carried to the living room, undressed and laid on a sheepskin rug before the roaring fire.

It led to exquisite lovemaking that had her crying out in ecstasy and wonder. And, afterwards, softly murmured admissions of love in dual tongues.

'I can't believe you used David,' she mused many hours later.

Her husband shrugged arrogantly. Oh, how she'd missed that shrug.

'He needed to be made aware that you were off limits

to him in this lifetime and the next. I merely utilised his expertise, and he earned a fat commission in the bargain. Win-win.'

She laughed. He joined in. Then they both sobered and stared deep into each other's eyes, letting their feelings speak for a moment.

'I asked myself how I could fall in love with you twice in one lifetime,' she whispered, her thumb tracing his full lower lip.

His fingers traced reverentially along her jaw. 'And?' he demanded gruffly.

'It was because my heart knew you were the one. My heart will always know you and love you, *mi amor.*'

'As will mine.'

EPILOGUE

'OKAY, *MI ÁNGEL*. Time for our big moment in the spotlight. I'll try and keep it together if you will. Deal?'

Emiliano smiled as he entered the nursery to the sight of his brother cradling his eight-week-old daughter. The size disparity was ridiculous, as was the extracautious way Matias was cradling Angelina, but his heart flipped over all the same.

He was getting used to that feeling. Getting used to it knocking him for six several dozen times a day. It started from the moment he woke up next to the woman of his heart, the woman who made him glad to be alive every day. Then it went on, a relentless insanity he never wanted to be cured of.

'You know she can't high-five you just yet, right, *mi hermano*? Or even understand a word you're saying?'

Matias spun carefully on his heel, his gaze touching briefly on Emiliano before returning to the treasure in his arms. 'Of course she can. I'm her godfather, which means we share a special bond. She smiled and pumped her fist just before you interrupted us.'

Shaking his head, Emiliano strolled closer, the magic of his daughter impossible to resist. He caressed her soft cheek with the back of his finger, his heart expanding when she leaned into him.

Angelina's eyes, a soft turquoise at birth, were slowly changing, taking on her mother's green eyes. Her hair was also soot-black like Sienna's, and Emiliano secretly hoped his daughter would take every single one of her mother's attributes, both inside and out. Every element of his wife's character and spirit deserved celebration.

'You look like a sap, you know that?' Matias mocked. But Emiliano noted the gruffness in his voice.

'What can I say? I'm a lucky man and I'm not ashamed to show it.'

'*Sí*, you are indeed lucky. As I am, after what you did.' The gaze that met his was solemn and fiercely sincere. It also held a brotherhood that Emiliano had severely missed and almost lost. 'I know what you risked for me. You have my undying gratitude.'

'You would've done the same for me.' He knew that in his soul and was only beginning to appreciate what that truly meant. He clasped his brother on the shoulder and deep understanding passed between them.

His daughter gurgled and his attention was immediately absorbed by her once more. Leaning down, he inhaled her sweet baby scent before kissing her gently on the forehead.

'Yeah, I still think you need to dial down the mush, though. It's unbecoming in a grown man,' Matias chided.

'Says the man who wept when I asked him to be godfather.'

Matias snorted. 'You shouted the question at me when I was in the middle of training a temperamental filly and I got kicked for my troubles. I invite you to experience that and tell me whether you wouldn't shed a tear, too.'

Emiliano laughed. After a few seconds Matias joined in. They were still laughing when his wife, the reason for his heartbeat, walked in.

'There you are. I was beginning to think you three had hopped on a plane and hightailed it for Tahiti.'

Sienna tried not stumble as two sets of tawny eyes looked up from her daughter and met hers across the nursery. One set held an everlasting love she still pinched herself over each time she felt that visceral connection. The other held warmth, acceptance and love.

Matias had made a full recovery since waking up from

his coma eight months ago. After having been released from the private Swiss hospital, he'd moved into the Cordoba mansion with them, Emiliano having decided to split his work life between Argentina and London.

Once Matias had completely recovered, he'd resumed the reins of Castillo Estate on the proviso that Benito and Valentina retired and relinquished all say in the running of the estate to him. They'd agreed and had since embarked on a world cruise, courtesy of Emiliano's yacht. Emiliano had deemed it a small price to pay to be rid of them for a while.

The relationship between Benito and Emiliano had altered for the better since the night Sienna had regained her memory. She held out hope for a further thawing in Valentina's character, as well. But, for now, she had all the family she needed.

A family she worshipped with every fibre of her being.

Emiliano held out his arm and she swayed to his side, accepting his kiss before smiling down at her precious daughter.

'The guests are waiting. This little angel needs to make her christening debut.'

The christening attendees included new friends they'd made here in Argentina and old acquaintances turned friends from London. The intimate affair was just what they'd both wanted.

'Let them wait a while longer. She is a female and it's her day. I believe it's her divine right to be fashionably late,' Emiliano said.

When Angelina gurgled her agreement, they all laughed. While Matias smiled with complete infatuation at his niece, Sienna's eyes met her husband's.

'*Te amo, mi corazón,*' he whispered against her lips. '*Para siempre.*'

* * * * *

If you enjoyed
THE BOSS'S NINE-MONTH NEGOTIATION,
take a look at these other
ONE NIGHT WITH CONSEQUENCES
themed stories!

CLAIMING HIS CHRISTMAS CONSEQUENCE
by Michelle Smart
THE GUARDIAN'S VIRGIN WARD
by Caitlin Crews
A CHILD CLAIMED BY GOLD
by Rachael Thomas
THE CONSEQUENCE OF HIS VENGEANCE
by Jennie Lucas
SECRETS OF A BILLIONAIRE'S MISTRESS
by Sharon Kendrick

Available now!

MILLS & BOON®

EXCLUSIVE EXTRACT

Persuading plain Jane to marry him was easy
enough – but Shiekh Zayed Al Zawba hadn't
bargained on the irresistible curves hidden under
her clothes, or that she is deliciously untouched.
When Jane begins to tempt him beyond his
wildest dreams, leaving their marriage
unconsummated becomes impossible…

Read on for a sneak preview of
THE SHEIKH'S BOUGHT WIFE

It was difficult to be *distant* when your body seemed to
have developed a stubborn will of its own. When she found
herself wanting to push her aching breasts against Zayed's
powerful chest as he caught her in his arms for the traditional first dance between bride and groom. As it was, she
could barely think straight and wasn't it the most infuriating
thing in the world that he immediately seemed to pick up
on that?

'You seem to be having trouble breathing, dear wife,'
he murmured as he moved her to the center of the marble
dance floor.

'The dress is very tight.'

'I'd noticed.' He twirled her around, holding her back
a little. 'It looks very well on you.'

She forced a tight smile but she didn't relax. 'Thank you.'

'Or maybe it is the excitement of having me this close
to you which is making you pant like a little kitten?'

'You're *annoying* me, rather than exciting me. And I do
wish you'd stop trying to get underneath my skin.'

'Don't you like people getting underneath your skin, Jane?'

'No,' she said honestly. 'I don't.'

'Why not?'

She met the blaze of his ebony eyes and suppressed a shiver. 'Does everything have to have a reason?'

'In my experience, yes.' There was a pause. 'Has a man hurt you in the past?'

This was her chance to tell him yes—even though the very idea that someone had got that close to her was laughable.

Zayed had already guessed she might be a virgin, but that didn't even come close to her shameful lack of experience.

Trying to ignore the way his groin was brushing against her as he edged her closer, she glanced up at him, her cheeks burning. 'I refuse to answer that on the grounds that I might incriminate myself. Tell me instead, do you always insist on interrogating women when you're dancing with them?'

'No. I don't,' he said simply. 'But then I've never had a bride before and I've never danced with a woman who was so determined not to give anything of herself away.'

'And that's the only reason you want to know,' she said quietly. 'Because you like a challenge.'

'All men like a challenge, Jane.' His black eyes gleamed. 'Haven't you learned that by now?'

She didn't answer—because how was she qualified to answer any questions about what men did or didn't like?

Don't miss
THE SHEIKH'S BOUGHT WIFE
By Sharon Kendrick

Available May 2017
www.millsandboon.co.uk